MYSTIC FEAR

a Nikki O'Connor novel

by
Jan Evan Whitford

Jan Evan Whitford

MYSTIC FEAR
All rights reserved.

Copyright © 2012 Jan Evan Whitford.
Original cover art painted by Barbara H. Whitford © 2012

All rights reserved. Jan Evan Whitford has asserted his right under the Copyright, Designs and Patents Act 1988 to be identified as the author of this work. No part of this book may be used, reproduced, or transmitted in any form in whole or in part by any means, including graphic, electronic or mechanical, including photocopying, recording, or by any information storage and retrieval system, without written permission of the author, except for brief quotations embodied in critical articles or reviews.

This is a work of fiction. Names, characters, places, and incidents either are the product of the author's imagination or are used fictitiously and are not intended to refer to specific places or living persons. The opinions expressed in this manuscript are solely the opinions of the author. The author has represented and warranted full ownership and/or legal right to publish all the materials in this book. Any resemblance to actual persons, living or dead, events, or locales is entirely coincidental
www.janwhitford.com

MYSTIC FEAR

Trade paperback ISBN: 978-1-84961-156-5
E-book ISBN: 978-1-84961-154-1
Published by: RealTime Publishing
Limerick, Ireland

Also by Jan Evan Whitford:
Mystic Island

WHAT PEOPLE ARE SAYING

ABOUT JAN EVAN WHITFORD'S BOOKS

"Like his first novel, *Mystic Island*, Whitford sucked me into *Mystic Fear* with the characters, setting, and story with the first line. His characters are off-the-wall and he introduces them in such a vivid way, they literally jump off the pages at the reader. Whitford's writing is fresh, witty, and vivid. He invites us to join him on an adventure and it's impossible to say no."
—**Jan Campbell, author of *Champagne on Naked Sunday***

"Whitford cleverly combines mystery, romance, action, and adventure, with an old-fashioned dollop of sex and violence. *Mystic Island* is filled with characters so real they leap off the page, a corker of a plot involving long buried secrets, murderous cover-ups and one helluva hurricane. Put this on your must-read list."
—**J.A. Konrath, author of *Whiskey Sour, Bloody Mary, and Rusty Nail***

"After thoroughly enjoying Whitford's *Mystic Island*, it is another pleasure to be entertained by the dexterity of this author. In *Mystic Fear*, he once again gives his characters the freedom to be exactly who they want to be and we are captured and then seduced by their ways. Fast and provocative, *Mystic Fear* holds all the keys to another great mystery, as well as a fun read."
—**J. DiBello, "Beach House Bookie"**

"… a marvelous mystery-romance in the Nora Roberts tradition."
—**Tom Walker, NY Times best-selling author of Fort Apache, The Bronx**

"Mr. Whitford hooked me fast and kept me on the line for one wild ride; his sense of scene and place is impeccable, his characters all distinct and believable. He nailed it."
—**Joanna Enderlin,** *Hampton Roads Magazine*

"Get ready for *Mystic Island* to make you laugh, cry and bite your nails. Whitford's novel is full of ordinary people just like you and me. How will they all deal with the lies, deceit, betrayal, murder and a category five hurricane?
—**Romance Junkies, Blue Ribbon Rating: 4**

"*Mystic Island* is the debut novel of Jan Evan Whitford. Get ready for to laugh, cry and bite your nails. A tautly exciting thriller . . ."
—James A. Cox, Midwest Book Review

"*Mystic Fear*, by Jan Evan Whitford, is a real page-turner, leaving the reader in suspense from beginning to end. He uses wit and wisdom to address the issues of his protagonist, Nikki, as she wends her way through problem situations common to many people, including eating disorders, grief, and guilt—finally tying the threads together in a dramatic ending that will leave you breathless. Whitford's quirky characters alone will keep you entertained as they fumble their way through one dilemma after another."
—Portia, Little, author of *Bread Pudding Bliss*

". . . there's a 'fatass Jesus freak', a 'fudge-packing' ex-con, a half-Chinese man who speaks 'in the language of fortune cookie sayings', an imbecilic 'pothead burnout', and a 'cadaverous, tattooed Hispanic" who speaks in pidgin. The heroine, on the other hand, is a perky, happily- married woman with 'cinnamon hair', a 'generous smile' and 'sexy eyes that promise bliss'."
—*Publisher's Weekly*

"I was really intrigued by the premise of *Mystic Fear* and sure wasn't disappointed as I started reading. The first sentence caught my attention and made me laugh. The author's writing style was very easy to read and did not seem to be a chore at all. I would recommend this book and look forward to seeing it in print."
—**Amazon Top Reviewer**

"The character of Nikki O'Connor is a mix of Janet Evanovich's Stephanie Plum written with a slightly more "testosteroned" point of view. This mix makes for a great female lead that has the potential to keep readers interested in her odd life, much like the Stephanie Plum series, far beyond the island of Mystic. Look for her again in Whitford's upcoming novel, *Mystic Fear.*
—**Jackie Bell, North Kingstown Standard-Times**

Jan Evan Whitford

Dedicated to my five sons, from whom I've learned so much.

Mystic Fear

Acknowledgements

First of all, I'm indebted to my Higher Power for giving me ideas and the compulsion to get them down on paper. Next, of course, comes my wife, Barbara, for the first line of editing and for keeping me on track. Thanks to Janet Cooper for further close editing and to first readers Dave Stec, Kevin Exley and Annie McIntyre. I also got great input from the Emerald Coast Writers critique group, in particular: writer Mary Brown, mystery author Vincent H. O'Neil and the best yet-to-be-published writer I've ever read: Jan Campbell. Many thanks also to Kevin Hebert, Olga McMaster, and John Fenton for their early technical advice and expertise. And finally, no way this novel could've ever happened without all the high-spirited campers at Ft. Getty. Virtually everybody kept bugging me until I finally got 'er done.

J.W.

Jan Evan Whitford

PROLOGUE

Spring, 1976

HIGH SCHOOL CHEERLEADERS: Giggling over their cokes and fries while they chatter and coo about how much their classmate, Marion Hess, looks like that dreamy, sexy Billy Jack guy, Tom Laughlin. Only with an even better bod. *Bubbilicious!*

"Marion. Can you believe that name?" says Nikki O'Connor, the head cheerleader. "Parents must've wanted a girl."

"Well, he certainly isn't even *close* to a girl," says Robin Leigh, the sassy one.

All the girls burst into a fit of laughter, then try to stifle their giggling with their palms.

"And you know what?" continues Robin. "I know where he lives. I think we should sneak up and spy on him, check out his home life. Maybe we'll see why he's so weird. Who knows? We might even see more of that hunky bod of his. Surely that humungous bulge in his Levis isn't real . . . is it?

Cheri Winkler, the shy one, turns scarlet but looks at Robin and smiles, then both girls turn inquisitively to Nikki.

"What," Nikki says, while nibbling at a solitary french-fry with her front teeth.

Robin narrows her eyes, winks. "Nikki's got a crush on him, don't you Nikki? C'mon girl, you can tell us . . ."

Nikki sighs, does a dramatic eye roll. "Marion Hess is definitely cute, but you know I'm going out with Bill."

Robin rolls her own eyes, saying, "Pul-eeze. Bill's studley, for sure. But you can tell us the truth. Aren't you just the least bit interested in Weirdo Marion's Levis? I mean, does he have a scrumptious looking package or what?"

"Ever hear curiosity killed the cat?"

"Whatever. Let's make a plan."

"Yeah," pipes Cheri. "Okay, my Sosh teacher? He's always going on about political this, political that, Watergate fact-finding commissions, blah, blah, blah, right? So let's call this something like: 'The Marion Hess Fact-finding Commission'."

THE GIRLS SLURP the last of their cokes. Once it's dark, they clamor into Cheri's grungy Camry and head for the Hess house. On the radio, The Bee Gee's are oo-oo-oo-oo, staying alive, staying alive.

Robin plucks the remains of a joint from her purse, saying, "Ta-da!" She clamps it with a cute little alligator clip she got from the head shop, lights up, inhales deeply, and holds the smoke in. The familiar, sweet and pungent aroma drifts toward the other girls' eager nostrils. Bug-eyed, and holding her breath, Robin presents the roach to Cheri's lips.

Cheri takes a deep toke, her own eyes going wide.

"Hey," shouts Robin, exhaling in a gush. "You're Bogarting!"

By the time Nikki gets it, there's hardly any left. Sparks burn her hand as she finagles a hit, trying not to scorch her lips. She manages a deep drag, holds her breath as long as possible. Once she can hold it no longer, she exhales and the girls all burst into laughter. They try to harmonize with the Bee-Gees but their enthusiastic effort sounds about as mellow as a rock in a blender.

Robin whips out a bag of M&M's. Heavenly! The girls gobble handful after handful: the munchie effect for sure. And before they realize it, they've arrived at their destination.

Cheri mutters something about hoping Hess's fruitcake mom isn't home.

"Fruitcake mom?" Nikki says, sucking on her last M&M, savoring it.

"Some sort of fanatical fundamentalist religious nut, so my mom said. Everyone avoids her," explains Robin.

"What about his dad?"

"Out of the picture. Mom said Old Lady Hess was raped. Hey wait a minute . . . I guess that makes our stud muffin a bastard, right?"

Everyone giggles. The three of them sneak closer and crouch behind a huge Rhododendron. They can't see much; the window shades hang down too far.

"Bummer," Cheri says.

"I got an idea," says Robin, turning to Nikki. "In history, we're studying the Plains Indians, you know?"

Nikki wonders what that has to do with anything. "So?"

"Well. According to Mr. Beaner, a warrior didn't necessarily have to kill the enemy. He could get great respect by just being brave enough to touch him. They called it 'counting coup'."

Nikki sighs. "I don't know why, but I'm not really interested in history right now."

"Yeah, but you're part Indian, right?"

"A little. So?"

"Well then dare, Pocahontas," Robin says, eyes sparkling. "Dare you to march right up there, knock on the door. Ask if his mom's there and if she's not, ask if you can see his bedroom."

"What? No way!"

"Maybe ask him to kiss you? Then sort of press against him and, um . . . *accidentally* . . . feel him up and then run. Count coup, right? We'll be waiting."

Jan Evan Whitford

PART I

SEABREEZE

What is past is prologue.

—William Shakespeare

Jan Evan Whitford

CHAPTER 1

Twenty-five years later…

JUNIOR FERGUSON should've known he was going to have a bad day when his mother caught him spanking his monkey before breakfast. At least, that's what he just told Nikki O'Connor, the new park ranger.

"More information than I need to know," said Nikki. She'd caught Junior in possession of undersized fish he'd poached from a restricted area and was waiting for an Environmental Police officer to come and cite him for it.

Junior scowled, whipped off his Red Sox cap, and threw it down. "You know what? Life sucks!"

Nikki looked around. Her job site—here at the Seabreeze RV Resort and Campground on Mystic Island in Narragansett Bay—was breathtaking. Snowy egrets tiptoed through thin tendrils of morning fog, making their way along the marshy wetlands. With stealth, they combed through eelgrass, spearing baitfish. The fragrance of sweet honeysuckle graced the air and a red-winged blackbird rasped out its distinctive cry. A cool breeze ruffled the sea oats and from all outward appearances, life did not, in fact, suck.

Junior continued his tirade: "Bad enough I always gotta get hassled by the local clam cops without you doggin' me."

Nikki sighed. "Just chill out, okay? They shouldn't be long."

He narrowed his eyes. "Fuckin' clam cops, anyway. Hey, wait a minute. You used to be one a them, right?"

"I did."

He sniggered. "How come you quit? Job too hard?"

"Private matter, Junior. No need to concern yourself."

"Yeah, well, 'Ms. O'Connor, Clam Cop' has got a nice ring to it. Gotta admit."

Newly wed to Steve Marshall, Nikki had kept her maiden surname of O'Connor for simplicity and to feel a little autonomic security. Steve had no problem with that. After getting married a scant three months previous, she'd resigned from her full-time environmental police job in favor of the low stress, part-time park ranger gig this summer. Sure, it paid less but had its perks, including a free seasonal camping spot at one of the prettiest oceanfront RV resorts on the east coast. And since she'd had such great qualifications, she'd gotten the position easily.

"Anyway, ever'one's always on my case," Junior growled. "Ma harpin' for me to get a job, makin' me go to summer school so I can graduate, and now this."

"Good for your mom," said Nikki. "But that doesn't change the facts."

Junior hung out in the campground area quite often, so she'd kind of gotten to know him. And, despite his many fishing violations, she found him to be basically likeable—even through his façade of bravado. Of course, his attitude didn't surprise her, probably par for an insecure, eighteen-year-old, death-camp-thin, pothead burnout.

He shot her a sour look, flipped back his filthy blond tresses, and snorted. "Anyway," he said, "Don't you got anythin' better to do than hassle me? Like, get a life and stuff?"

"Maybe you should take your own advice, Junior. I see you're still driving your mom's minivan."

He shuffled his feet and averted his eyes. Not only was his mom's minivan pastel pink, but it also had Mary Kay Cosmetics decals plastered on both side doors and the tailgate window. A sticker on the back bumper read:
I LOST MY SELF-RESPECT AT WES' RIB HOUSE.

By that time, the Environmental Police officer had arrived so Nikki said goodbye, climbed into her little Honda CR-V and headed back toward the gatehouse at the entrance to the campground. On the radio, a pompous talk show host pontificated about how he thought things ought to be, so she changed stations and found Al Green singing about how his woman made him feel brand-new. That suited Nikki better.

Her cell phone rang. She turned down the radio and picked up. "Hello?"

"Nikki?"

It was Frank Anderson, the chief of Police in nearby Benedict's Landing, the small village on the island, a couple of miles from the campground. Nikki and Frank had dated *once*, way back in high school. Despite the fact that they were both married, he continually finagled to get Nikki between the sheets.

"Hello, Frank. What's up? . . . As if I didn't know."

He chuckled. "You're reading me wrong. This isn't a social call. Listen, babe, you remember a guy named Marion Hess, Franklin High, our class of '78?"

"Sure, I remember Hess. Really good-looking kid, but weird."

"Yeah, huh? You know he ended up at a psych ward after his mother died, right? Then I heard they stuck him in that Socanosset Boys Training School—one scary, nasty-ass place."

Nikki seemed to recall that Hess'd had an intense mommy thing going on. After his mom's stroke, she'd heard that he'd just about glued himself to the woman's side in the hospital room. She also remembered a prank she and her cheerleader friends had once played on Hess, with pretty ugly results. Surprisingly, it still made her feel guilty even after all these years.

She shook her head, cleared it, saying, "I remember his mother was a little uh . . . bizarre."

Frank cackled. "Bizarre? Shit, Nikki, the woman was certifiable. Anyway, the night she croaked? A nurse found Hess, on the floor, curled in a ball. And get this, he had chewed *chunks* out of his dead mother's boo—uh, breasts. Bits of flesh and gore were all over his face, the bed sheets and the floor."

"C'mon Frank. Those're just ancient high school rumors. You don't know—"

"Rumors my furry ass," he said, interrupting. "Anyway, they say the goofball was babbling incoherently and chanting some religious bullshit. That's how come they sent his ass to a psych ward. And after that: Socanosset, the 'bad boys school'."

"More rumors."

"Nope, it's true shit, I swear. In my job? I know people. I ask around. Back in the day, your folks ever tell you scary stuff about Socanosset?"

"Not really. I heard that some of the boys' parents and teachers used to threaten to send them there if they didn't behave. For us girls, they used to threaten us with Oaklawn Girl's School, something like that. The girls' equivalent to Socanosset, I guess."

"Yeah, huh? Well, I heard Socky was real abusive to the kids, kinda like that Wilkinson Home for Boys there in that Brad Pitt movie. You know the one?"

"*Sleepers.*"

"Yeah, babe. That's it. When I saw that movie? I thought about Socky right away."

Nikki, frowning, thought about that for a minute. "We're getting sidetracked here," she said. "Let's get back to Hess, okay? You're telling me all this stuff about him because . . ."

"Why do you think?"

She had no idea. She remembered hearing that Hess had eventually moved out west was all. But hadn't he been featured on one of those *48-Hours* or *Dateline* true crime shows or whatever? Years ago? Wait a minute . . . he'd murdered a couple of young women out there! "Oh, Jesus, Frank. The murders? Anything to do with that?"

"Bingo."

Nikki felt a little short on breath. "If my memory serves me correctly, they only convicted him of one of those murders, right?"

"Yep. And second-degree, at that."

"Well, he's still in New Mexico, isn't he? Doing time in the State Penitentiary at Santa Fe?"

"Yeah, well, maybe not much longer. *That's* why I'm telling you all this. The bastard is up for parole."

"You're kidding."

Frank snorted. "Do I sound like I'm kidding? Horrific what he did to those women out there. Those sexual mutilations? I heard there was some damn problem with the evidence—shades of O.J. Anyway, deal is: he did his years as a model prisoner, I guess and now he can get out. Can you believe that?"

"It seems to be par for the course these days. Anyway, I still don't see how it concerns me."

"Well, it sure does, babe. Word is, Hess is *obsessed* with you."

"And you know this . . . how?"

"I told you, I got a million sources and I hear lotsa stuff. This came from an old army buddy of mine. The guy's an Albuquerque detective now. We talk now and then. He knows I'm from Rhode Island and it's a small state and stuff and everything."

Nikki picked at a cuticle, frowned. "Bull crap, Frank. You want to know what I think? I think this is some elaborate scheme of yours to scare me and get close to me, somehow get into my pants."

"Don't believe me? Call my detective buddy in Albuquerque there."

"I don't have time for this. I have to go."

"Hey, I'm serious here, Nikki. Serious as a goddam heart attack."

"Goodbye, Frank," she said, and hung up. Feeling a little unsettled, she continued on to the campground gatehouse, where she pulled over. Her mood lifted when she saw her husband, engaged in conversation with the gatehouse guy. Having sold his sailboat and no longer working for the campground, Steve was now trying his hand at lobstering. That, and small carpenter jobs on the side. Usually, he could only be found out to sea on *Bugs,* his new lobster boat, or else pounding nails somewhere. He ambled over as she pulled up.

"Well," he said. "If it isn't my favorite park ranger. And working on her birthday, yet."

"Don't remind me."

Handsome in an offhanded sort of way, Steve seemed to get better looking each time she saw him, even though they were almost joined at the hip. She noticed how his back was growing broader, stronger from the physical punishment of hauling lobster pots. In addition to being physically sexy, he was thoughtful and romantic. Plus, he always made her laugh. His Mel Gibson blue eyes never failed to make her a little more than weak in the knees, and he had this special talent for blowing away her self-doubts, excising her from occasional binges of self-pity. Okay, he wasn't perfect: besides being a recovering alcoholic, he sometimes smelled like baitfish, but that was easily taken care of in the shower. And he regularly attended AA.

Then again, Nikki had her own downside, occasionally falling prey to episodic or periodic attacks of bulimia. Hey, we all bring baggage to a relationship, right?

"How come you're not out on your boat?" she asked.

"Gotta meet a guy in Bristol. What's up with you?"

"Just park rangering. I nabbed Junior Ferguson, again." Steve grinned, a flash of white against rough, sea-weathered skin. "No surprise there," he said. "Illegal fishing, right?"

"You got it. Anyway, I'm going to make another round of the campground and then stop off at home, get a bite to eat."

By home, she was referring to their 34-foot Pace Arrow motorhome. They'd live in it during the summer so Steve could be close to his boat, which he kept at the campground dock. Of course, they held on to her old apartment in nearby Benedict's Landing to store things and to stay in once the camping season came to an end.

"I probably won't make it back until six or so," Steve said.

"Uh-huh. I see. This wouldn't have anything to do with my birthday, would it? I told you: no presents and no fanfare. You promised."

He shook his head. "This has *nothing* to do with your birthday. I swear."

"If you say so. See you later, then." She blew him a kiss, said her goodbyes, and headed back into the camping area.

Nikki's thoughts turned to her daughter. Erin was a product of an ill-fated and ill-advised previous marriage, many years ago. Nikki recalled how, way back, close to graduation from high school, she'd foolishly gotten pregnant. She'd married her high school boyfriend and they moved to St. Louis.

Once her daughter became old enough for daycare, Nikki had attended the St. Louis Police Academy and pursued a career in law enforcement. Eventually, her cheating loser of a husband ended up in prison in Potosi, Missouri, where another inmate shanked and killed him.

Years passed, until Erin graduated from St. Louis University and took a job in Boston. Nikki happily moved back to Rhode Island to be close by. But not feeling quite up to tackling the mean streets of Providence as a regular policewoman, she had taken a job as an Environmental Officer, where she'd excelled.

By the time Nikki finished ruminating, several campers were out and about. As she drove around, she could whiff the tantalizing aroma of bacon and coffee. Combined with the wood smoke and salt air, the atmosphere was euphoric. Most of the 140 RV sites had already been filled and a few people occupied the tent area. You'd never know that, less than a year ago, a Category-5 hurricane named *Dora* had leveled the campground. In fact, Nikki and Steve, after only a couple of months of going out together, had almost perished in it.

Arriving now at the campground dock, which jutted out into the bay, she marveled at the all-encompassing new construction. The wind had picked up. High tide slapped at the pilings.

She parked, hopped out, took a deep breath, and appreciated her surroundings. She strolled out on the dock to where small clusters of Asian Americans were fishing for scup. Nearby, a few of the locals from town cast plugs for striped bass. Feet shuffled and heads turned away as she passed.

She couldn't help but notice the overt body language as she headed for a guy she knew well: a redheaded, jug-eared little troll of a man named Petey Fottler. In contrast to his diminutive stature, Petey had enormous feet that looked to be about size thirteen. Encased in classic Chuck Taylor black hi-top Converse sneakers, Petey's feet always brought to mind Barnum and Bailey or Bugs Bunny. He worked the second shift at the campground gatehouse, a job he'd taken up since retiring from a career at a fortune cookie factory in Brockton, Mass. Being half-Chinese on his mother's side and in deference to that heritage, he preferred to speak in the language of fortune cookie sayings: Fortunese.

Nikki glanced into Petey's empty bucket. "No luck?"

"Luck finds those who seek it least."

She laughed. "You're a jewel, Petey."

His brow furrowed. "Riches and jewels are not always what they seem," he said, with exaggerated sincerity.

"Okay, whatever you say. By the way, love your shoes." Moving on down the line of fishermen, she checked their catches. One of them overturned his bucket and, with the help of his toe, a dozen or so undersized fluke slithered off the dock and into the water.

Grinning like a lotto winner, he tipped his cap to her, saying, "Whoopsy-daisy."

She felt her jaw tighten, heat infusing her face. After checking a few more buckets, she walked out to the end of the dock. Even though lead-colored, mackerel clouds were forming up in the west, sunlight winked in magical sparkles off dancing waves and a soulful buoy cling-clanged in the distance.

From all outward appearances and despite Junior Ferguson's opinion or Chief Anderson's gossip regarding Marion Hess—life did not, in fact, suck.

Of course, she'd been wrong before.

CHAPTER 2

TWENTY-FIVE HUNDRED miles west, behind the razor wire and bars at the Penitentiary of New Mexico, an underlying current of impending violence wormed its way through the usual stink of body odor, stale semen, and fear. Once, during a riot at this infamous penal hellhole, inmates had broken out of the main area into a new block construction site and slaughtered snitching inmates by ramming iron reinforcing rods up their rectums.

Inmate Marion Hess thought that was a *fine* legacy, but he didn't need to relish such thoughts or endure the stench much longer because today, he was getting paroled. On his bunk and in civilian clothes, he sat hunkered over with his elbows on his knees, waiting. Once he was outside, he knew the desert air would smell of cactus and baked alkali. And to him, that'd be just about as sweet as the smell of blood.

Snake Taggert, his cellmate, had propped himself against the opposite wall, thick arms crossed. Snake hadn't acquired his nickname because he was mean, even though that was true. No, Taggert had gotten his name because the other inmates figured he'd fuck anything— even a snake.

Hess glared at Snake, thinking about how the man's disgusting tattoos sickened him. He'd grown sick of the Aryan Brotherhood bullshit, weary of Snake's colossal bald and pimple-peppered head. And that copycat Charlie Manson swastika etched between his eyes.

Hess's glare softened and he tossed up a wry smile.
"What," said Snake.
"Nothing. I finally figured it out, is all. You look like some goddam reject from the World Wrestling Federation."
Snake snorted. "Blow me."
Snake had proven himself to be a man of protection and infinite connections. And as for Hess's fetishes? Well, let's just say his skill with a shiv had shown all badasses that he wasn't to be trifled with. No sir.
"Dickweed," Hess countered, continuing the banter.
"Asshole fuckwad."

"Recidivist."

"Whoa," said Snake. "Big fucking word."

"That's right, shitbird."

Snake held up an index finger. "Talk trash all you want but don't forget, man. I'm the tits. My boy Paco? He'll take care of you on my say-so. Anythin' you need."

Hess leaned back on his bunk, laced his hands behind his head, closed his eyes and smirked. The stupid parole board had bought his act. Soon, he'd be free to emancipate all the bitches of their stupidity, liberate their body parts—succulent parts that caused The Temptations in the first place. After all, hadn't Mother always said the First Sin was Intercourse, leading to Fiery Agonies in the Eternal Damnation Pit? Well, in the not-too-distant future, he'd start by seeking out and taking care of that Wanton Jezebel Whore Nikki and—

"What," said Snake, interrupting Hess's demented reverie. "What you thinking?"

Hess got up, crossed the cell. With care, he removed the woman's photograph that'd been taped to the wall since day one.

"Nothing," he said. "About Jezebel Nikki, is all." He studied the yellowed image, a head and shoulder shot clipped from his old high school yearbook. He never ceased to be captivated by her beauty: that lovely red hair, generous smile, and sexy eyes that promised bliss (but damnation). Why, she looked almost *exactly* like Mother, when Mother was young. In that old scrapbook Mother kept.

Hess's eyes glazed over . . .

. . . Mother is puffing cigarette after cigarette, the basement cloudy with smoke, stinking of nicotine and candle wax. She's brushing her long red hair: stroke, stroke, stroke. One hundred strokes a day she's always saying. To be offered up to the Lord. He's only nine, just wanting only to play football in the park, be one of the guys.

"Nooo," she keeps harping, her beautiful face pinched, mouth in a downturn, like she just whiffed a sulphur supreme fart or something. But her silky hair—all beautiful in the flickering

glow of the candle novena she's arranged is so shiny. The spooky Crucifix hangs on the basement wall, with impaled Jesus, slumping all bloody and stuff.

"But Mother..."

"Let us pray for your sinning soul," she snaps. From her bag, out come band-aids and antibiotic ointment.

He feels his eyes widen...

Now she's lighting yet another cigarette off the old one, inhaling deeply, scrunching her eyes shut. "Let us pray. O Lord, remove this boy's sinful thoughts."

"Mother, I won't ask again, I swear."

"Those boys say they want to play football but they really only want to touch you inappropriately. You are my precious little innocent, 'eer sin and demons abound. I have to protect you. I will relieve your Unholy Tensions and then administer The Purging. Now, boy, remove all your clothes. Make it snappy."

After he's standing in only his Batman undies, he says, "I don't understand this, Mother."

"Underwear off," she orders, yanking them down to pool at his feet. She straps him to a basement support pole, ties his hands behind him with an extension cord.

Shivering in his nakedness, he starts to cry. "M-mm–mother?"

She starts touching him... down there. She moans, starts talking in those 'tongues', the way she does.

He's feeling weird, kind of dizzy. His muscles are tensing, he's quivering... and then nothingness until he awakens, cozy in his bed in the morning. The sheets smell so fresh.

But his bottom hurts where—under a new band-aid and ointment—a brand new cigarette burn tries to heal.

... Snake coughed, bringing Hess out of his trance. Hess blinked rapidly, only to focus on his disgusting cellmate digging into his ear with his little finger, extracting a waxy glob.

Snake examined the morsel, flicked it away. "You know what?" he said. "I been listenin' to that 'Jezebel Nikki' shit for seven longass years. I think I get it."

Hess shot Snake a smoldering, baleful glare. "Yeah, well, I know where she is and I'm going to find her and split her like a chicken. Bitch killed my mother."

"So you said, 'bout a gazillion times and I'm—"

"Jezebel Whore cast some evil spell or something, got into Mother's head and caused her to have a stroke," interrupted Hess. "Mother told me so, before she passed."

Snake laughed. "Sheeeee-it. Evil spell? You believe that?"

"Go ahead, laugh. Anyway, I already googled the whore's particulars."

Snake's eyes flickered with excitement. He licked his lips. "*Googled* her particulars?"

Hess left Snake to his warped imagination. "Listen asshole," he said, "You can find out anything about anybody on the Internet these days. For instance, there's a campground right near my old hometown in Rhode Island and they have a website. And guess what? There was an article about a certain Nicole O'Connor in the online campground newsletter, with a picture. It's her, all right. Bitch is newly married, they said. Anyway, the article also told me she's the fucking park ranger at that campground. Fantastic, huh? Not only that, but she also lives there."

Snake was excavating in his ear again. "Married. Hunh. Yeah, well, you're married too, y'know. What about your new wifey?"

"What, that fatass Jesus freak? You know as well as I do that she's just my ticket out of here, that's all. Fuck her."

"You just might have to. How come you married her, anyway? Shit, with that pretty face of yours, you could have any cooze you wanted."

"Too true," agreed Hess. He offered up a malevolent smile

Snake cocked his head, wet his lips. "Uh . . . you're gonna fuck that Nikki chick before you waste her, right?"

"Sure."

Snake chuckled. "I was just wondering, cause you never liked to do the nasty in here, you know?"

"Shut the fuck up, " growled Hess, glowering.

"I'm just sayin'—"

"Anyway. Nikki isn't the only bitch on my dance card."
"Dance card? Fuck're you talkin' about, man?"
"I've hatched a second plan."
Snake licked his lips. "What kind a plan?"
"A good one. To get even with all the assholes."
"Assholes?"
"At good ol' Franklin High. They made my life miserable."
Snake grinned. "Revenge. I like that kind of talk. What're you gonna do?"
"Oh, you'll hear about it, don't worry."

A LOUD BUZZER and welcome clanking of bars announced the opening of the cell door. A guard sidled up, grinned. "Drop your cock and grab your socks, convict. You're about to be a free man."

A cardboard box sat next to Hess, filled with the sum total of his worldly possessions: a few paperbacks, some toiletries and first aid supplies, and the Bible he'd memorized in order to con his gullible new bride and the parole board.

He took great care inserting the old photo of Nikki between the pages of Mother's dog-eared Bible, eased the book back into the box, clutched it to his chest, and stood. Before leaving this fine correctional institution—with its legacy of death by iron re-rod up the ass—he glared, one last time, at his cellmate.

Snake turned away, saying, "Get the fuck outta here, man."

Outside, just as Hess had figured, the desert air smelled of cactus and baked alkali but also something else: freedom. He took a deep breath, looked around, and appreciated the *free* view. Fluffy, cumulus clouds embraced the *Sangre de Cristo* Mountains in the distance. Overhead, a red-tailed hawk soared. Like shimmering entities, brutal heat waves danced off the blacktop parking lot. Asphalt turning to licorice.

Patricia Deeb-Hess, his jailhouse bride, had already arrived. Grinning like a young girl at Christmas, Trish was sandwiched between the wheel and the captain's chair in a brand-new Winnebago Chieftain motorhome: beige with Hunter Green trim.

She squeezed her considerable self out the door. "At last," she cried, her voice a squeal. "We're together!"

Hess cringed, thinking, what a lard-ass. He adopted a plastic smile. "Yeah, finally."

Trish modeled her western-style skirt and peasant blouse. A multitude of bulky silver and turquoise bracelets jangled on each wrist and her sagging earlobes were festooned with dangling *Kokopele* earrings. "Lord, how I've longed for this moment," she said, holding her arms out.

Right away, Hess noticed three things: the rolls of blubber that jiggled under her triceps, her liberal application of electric-crimson lip gloss (with sparkles), and her tiny, tiny feet—feet that looked *way* too small to support such a load; teensy footies encased in penny loafers and bobby sox. With actual pennies in the loafers.

"Sweetheart," he said, mustering as much enthusiasm as he could. "You look ravishing."

She clutched him in a smothering hug, forcing him to inhale the cloying fragrance of what seemed like a quart of cheap perfume—perfume that reeked of a cross between roses and those raspberry scented urinal cakes they used in the prison. And if Hess hadn't been convinced that he had no desire to consummate his marriage before, he was now, thank you very much.

"Let's get out of here," he said. After stowing his things in one of the cargo compartments, he climbed up behind the wheel.

Trish scurried around to the passenger side, shoehorned herself into the seat and slammed the door. Inside the coach, so suffocating was her perfume, Hess was forced to breathe through his mouth.

She batted her Tammy Faye Bakker eyelashes, giggled, and blushed. "I can't believe we're actually going on our honeymoon! I saved myself for this, you know."

"You're a virgin?"

"I told you."

"You did? Oh, right, you did. Well, hallelujah and uh . . . praise Jesus."

"Yes, praise Jesus. Amen."

"Uh, listen, honey. Did you take care of everything?"

She blushed again. "Honey? Ooh, I like that. And yes, I did. No more ties with Albuquerque. We're free to go wherever we please, my love."

"Outstanding," he said. "You get cash?"

"Uh-huh. In my purse."

"You're a peach. Uh, with Jesus' help, we can start our lives anew. Far away from here."

"I can't wait. And He will guide us."

"Amen to that. What about the motorhome registration?"

"Not yet. The certificate of origin is in the glove box."

He smiled. "Good girl. We can register it wherever we decide to settle."

"Yes."

He thought a moment. "Wait a minute . . . don't you think we ought to get all that cash out of your purse and put it in a safer place?"

"Oh, don't worry, silly. I didn't get *all* of it."

"What do you mean?"

She sniffed. "I would *never* carry such a large amount of money around with me. I kept five thousand dollars, that's all. I put the balance in our safe deposit box at the Manzano Bank & Trust. My sister has a key. She can get the money wired to us, later, to wherever. After the honeymoon."

"Jesus H. Christ!"

"What?"

"Uh . . . in Jesus we trust."

She pursed her waxy lips. "You do believe in Jesus, Our Savior, don't you?"

"Let's just say Jesus and I sort of parted company years ago." *Mother is my Salvation now.*

She shook a finger at him. "Jesus is there for you, you just have to come back to him."

"Sure, I'll work on it." *In a pig's eye. Shake that goddam sausage of a finger at me again? I'll break the chubby motherfucker off and feed it to you.*

She beamed. "Good. Anyway, the safe deposit box? Of course your name is on it, too. Did you forget when I had you sign the card a couple of months ago?"

"Oh, yeah. That. Guess I did forget. And the key? Where is it?"

She thrust her pudgy fingers down into her ample cleavage and plucked it out, secured to a gold chain around her neck. "Right here," she said, fluttering her fake lashes and giggling. "Next time, you'll have to get it yourself."

"I'll look forward to that," he said. *When pigs fly.*

She beamed.

He took a deep breath, but when he did, he was once again reminded of raspberry-scented urinal cakes.

CHAPTER 3

ACROSS THE COUNTRY in Rhode Island, Nikki's mind raced. What had Chief Anderson been intimating? Could she somehow be in danger, if Hess got paroled? She didn't think so, hoped not anyway. Then again, there *was* that time when she and her cheerleader friends had sort of played that joke on him, the prank that'd gone bad. But surely he'd forgotten all about that, right? Wait a minute. That *had* been pretty close to the time his mother had had her stroke.

Oh my God.

Nikki thought back, remembering, envisioning three cheerleaders peering out from behind some bushes outside Marion Hess's house. She even recalled smelling the pungent new Bayberry growth . . .

It's chilly, but summer's just around the corner. They're sneaking closer, crouching behind a huge Rhododendron. They can't see much, the window shades are down too far.

"You're part Indian, right?" Robin asks Nikki.

"A little. So?"

"Dare, Pocahontas," Robin says, eyes sparkling. "Dare you to march right up there, knock on the door, and ask if you can see his bedroom. Maybe ask him to kiss you? Then sort of . . . accidentally . . . feel him up and run. Count coup, right? We'll be waiting .."

. . . A passing RV honked, jarring Nikki out of her little trip down memory lane. She moved over, giving the huge rig plenty of room to get by. Shaking her head, she admonished herself to pay attention to the road. Anyway, she didn't need to pollute her mind with any more ancient nonsense.

As she completed her rounds of the campground, she came across Junior Ferguson's pink minivan parked at the gatehouse so she drove over to see what shenanigans he was up to. She imagined him inside, bending the gatehouse guy's ear, probably bitching about how life sucks. As she parked and walked over, rain started to fall so she hurried to join them in the gatehouse hut.

The hut was tiny but it was Spartan. About eight feet square, it boasted a small desk, a board on the wall displaying the occupational array of campsites, a fan, and small black and white TV set. It reeked of dead mice and no-pest strips. Rain drummed on the roof but at least the hut stayed dry. Mostly.

When he saw Nikki, Junior rolled his eyes. "You again," he said. "Ever'where I go."

She smiled. "At your service."

"Well, hello," said the gatehouse guy. "Junior here was just mentioning something about getting busted for possession of undersized fish. Right, Junior?"

Ignoring that, Junior turned to Nikki, started singing a horrible rendition of "Happy Birthday".

She narrowed her eyes. "No secrets in this campground, are there?"

"None whatsoever," said the gatehouse guy. "Sorry."

"How old are you?" blurted Junior.

"Never ask a woman's age or weight," advised the gatehouse guy.

"He's right," Nikki said. "But I don't mind telling. I'm forty-four."

"Whoa," said Junior. "Forty-four? That's geezerville. You're older'n you look."

"I'll take that as a compliment," she said.

Junior cut his eyes away, shuffled his feet. As if to fill the pregnant silence that followed, the sound of mellow, gurgling mufflers preceded the approach of a classic car. Junior pointed, saying, "Hey! Check it out."

A '67 Camaro, bearing New York plates and black as Alice Cooper's wardrobe eased up. Smoky window tint hid the interior and the stereo thumped along with the wipers. The gatehouse windows even started to rattle. The three of them stepped outside.

"Christ!" cried the gatehouse guy. "My eardrums are throbbing. Even the fillings in my teeth are vibrating."

"Clam doggies!" said Junior. "Cool!"

The driver's window went down and he stared openly at the girl who sat slumped behind the wheel. Fashion-model thin and dressed in black, she was apparently heavy into Goth. She sported a startling shock of colorful hair and even a barbed-wire tattoo encircling her neck.

Nikki counted eight earrings in the girl's left ear and her lips were moving but Nikki couldn't make out the words over the megawatt bass thuds of the car's stereo.

The gatehouse guy moved an index finger across his throat, saying, "Kill it."

The girl cut the ignition. Silence flooded in.

Junior stepped forward, pumped his eyebrows up and down. "I think I know you," he said. He whipped his Red Sox cap around backwards and jutted his chin forward.

She cracked her gum: *Snap!* "Well, I don't know you. And, like, I don't want to either." Turning to the gatehouse guy, she asked, "Got any tent openings?"

"A few."

"Cool." She popped her gum a few more times. Midnight lip-gloss glistened on her pouty lips. "How much?"

"Twenty dollars a night."

"Well, that sucks." She studied her ebony fingernails, fluffed her wild hair, and picked up the gum chewing: *Snap! Snap-Snap!*

"I'm sure I know you," Junior insisted, moving his face a little closer.

Nikki watched Junior as he looked down, did a little foot shuffle thing, and cleared his throat. *This is first-rate entertainment here.*

"What's your name?" Junior asked the girl.

"Adrienne," she snapped. "Now back off." She turned her attention back to the gatehouse guy. "Okay, mister. I'll take it. I guess for a week right now? I might be here for, like, the rest of the summer, though. Until school starts."

"Oh, yeah?" he said. "Which school?"

"Brown."

"Well, aren't we something?" interjected Junior. He chortled, saying, "I thought it might be that famous Gyna College I heard about."

Nikki cringed, thinking: smooth talk, Casanova. Way to go.

"Oh, funny," snarled Adrienne. She gave him a sour look, rolled her eyes.

But when the gatehouse guy disappeared into the hut to write up the registration, Junior gave it another try. Executing a bold move, he leaned on the window of the Camaro and installed his face about six inches from the girl's.

"That's a mean crop a zits you got there," she observed. "And that scraggly beard? I'd say it's a little, um . . . *follicly* challenged."

Junior scowled. With hooded eyelids, he said, "I'm tellin' you: I know you. That's some awesome hair you got there. Uh, what color is it? Red? Purple?"

"Magenta."

"I knew that. By the way, I'm Junior Ferguson. You kin call me Junior."

"Figures."

"So, Adrienne. What's your last name?"

"LeDoux."

Junior grinned, cocked an eyebrow. "Adrienne Lee-doo? How cool is that?"

The gatehouse guy brought out the registration slip and took the girl's money. As she drove off into the campground, he turned to Junior, saying, "Magenta hair, huh? Pretty wild, eh kid? Maybe you two could have a wild hair contest."

Junior scowled. "Hey!" he said. "Eddy McGuirl's little sister tole me I got the coolest hair on the island. Said I look just like Kurt Cobain."

"Kurt who?"

"Cobain! You know, man. Nirvana? Where've you been, dude? Kurt was the lead guitar and vocalist for the most righteous group ever, man. They say suicide, but lots of us think he was murdered and—"

Mystic Fear

A rusty Toyota pickup rolled up and parked, interrupting Junior's spiel. The evening gatehouse shift had arrived in the form of Petey Fottler, elucidator of Fortunese.

"Glad you're finally here, man," said the gatehouse guy. "I'm more than ready to get out of here."

"Haste makes waste," quoted Petey. He hustled into the gatehouse, gargantuan sneakers spanking the floor. Like a dog, he shook off the rain.

"I have to go, too," Nikki said, and headed for her vehicle.

"Every person must be somewhere; everybody must be someplace," announced Petey.

"Hey, Fottler," said Junior. "What's the deal with all those goofyass sayin's?" He struck out for his mom's pink minivan with his baggyass pants—crotch down to his knees—sweeping the ground, wicking water from the puddles.

Nikki thought that he had a new, optimistic bounce to his gait though.

"I'm tellin' you," he shouted over to her, "I know that girl from somewhere. She's definitely a hottie."

"Give it a rest. It'll come to you."

"Yeah, huh? You know, maybe life ain't so sucky after all."

Nikki agreed. But lightning flashed with a quick crack of thunder and nasty thoughts of Marion Hess infiltrated her mind.

Again.

"We'll see," she said to herself. "We'll see."

LATER THAT NIGHT, wind gusts whipped Nikki and Steve's motorhome, causing it to sway. Sheets of rain pelted the roof. Fresh out of the shower, Nikki cocooned herself in a thick bathrobe, plopped on the couch and phoned her daughter. Erin now resided in Hingham, Massachusetts, just south of Boston, where she worked in the advertising business.

Nikki would love for her daughter to get married and have some kids someday, but wasn't ready to be a grandmother—not just yet. Anyway, since they talked almost every week, there wasn't a whole lot of catching up to do. Not wanting to burden

Erin with any of her irrational fears about a convict who was two thousand miles away, Nikki tried to keep it light.

" . . . Pretty much the same old, same old," she was saying.

"You sound kind of stressed, Mom. Is it because of your birthday?"

"Not really. Birthdays don't bother me but at this point I'd just as soon ignore them. No fanfare, you know?"

"I mailed your present. It'll be a little late."

"No problem. Thank you, sweetie."

"Anyway, maybe your stress is just hormones, right?"

"Sure. Maybe early menopause, brought on by another birthday."

Erin laughed. "Probably just PMS. Have some chocolate."

"I can do that. Godiva?"

"Whatever."

"Well," Nikki said. "Steve should be home pretty soon. I guess I'll let you go."

"And how're you newlyweds getting along?"

"Terrific."

"Glad to hear it. I said it before, but I'll say it again: good for you, Mom. It's about time you found a good man."

"You think?'

Erin laughed again. "I'm gonna go. Love you."

"Love you, too, sweetie. Bye." Nikki hung up, clicked on the TV, and started watching a rerun of *NYPD Blue*. She was applying turquoise polish to her toenails when Steve came back.

Sinbad, her recently acquired mammoth orange tabby cat, snoozed nearby in his favorite chair. Nikki had a thing for oversized cats, her previous one being named Moses Malone. She figured maybe the next one should be Wilfork.

Sinbad lifted his massive head, yawned, and meowed.

"I lied," said Steve, closing the door against the storm and toweling himself off with his jacket.

Nikki gave him her ho-hum look, picked up a magazine and started fanning her toes to dry the polish. "Really. How so?" Lying just wasn't in his makeup.

"I didn't really have to meet anyone in Bristol."

"Aha. You went birthday shopping, right?"

He shook his head. "Nope. You remember that antique store there? The one with all the antique jewelry?"

Abandoning her toenails, she sprung from the couch. "You went to Pementel's? You *do* listen to me when I tell you things." She sashayed over and threw her arms around his neck. "But I told you, no birthday presents. You promised."

"It's not a birthday present; it's an *anniversary* present."

"Anniversary? What—"

"—Three whole months," he said.

She kissed him on the nose. "Of course. How could I forget? Is that the silver anniversary? Gold?"

"Actually, this time it is. Silver."

"What? You lost me. Anyway, as you know, I just *love* that antique store."

"It's comforting in there, somehow. Smells just like my grandmother's house."

"Um-hum. So . . . something catch your eye?"

"Maybe. If you'll back off for a second, I'll check my pockets."

"Let me help," she offered. Slipping her hands deep into his front pockets, she felt around.

He laughed, cocked an eyebrow. "I'll give you about an hour to stop that."

Her fingers closed in on a small, velvet-like box. She pulled it out, held her breath, and opened it. Inside the box, lay an exquisite brooch. Thin as a membrane, delicate, intricate filigree silverwork surrounded the centerpiece, nesting a remarkable pearl—remarkable because it was *purple* and looked to be a perfect sphere, about the size of a marble. When she could exhale, she found that she was speechless.

"I've never heard of a purple pearl," he said. "Have you?"

She swallowed hard and shook her head, unable to take her eyes off it.

"Old man Pementel said they could come from quahogs."

"A pearl from a clam? No way."

"That's what I thought, but after I bought the brooch I went outside and got on my cell phone. I called my cousin who owns a jewelry store in Providence. He said quahog pearls are very rare, maybe one in a hundred thousand quahogs even contains one. He also said they can be worth a lot, so I ought to have it appraised. Not only that, but he said if the brooch is really old, the silver-smithing might be colonial. Holy shit, what if someone like Paul Revere made it? Anyway, that's why I'm claiming it's sort of is a *silver* anniversary present."

"Wow," she said. "Paul Revere? Well, I don't care if Petey Fottler made it, I've already fallen in love with it. I can feel that purple pearl drawing me in, like a magnet. Thank you so much, you are *so* thoughtful. I can't wait to wear this with that new black Traveler's diamond-V sleeveless dress I got on sale from Chico's. And you know what? I think I saw some Via Spiga shoes at Macy's, too. They're fifty percent off and would go perfect and … what?"

Steve was looking away, pursing his lips. "Nothing."

She tilted her head and smiled. "What, you got a problem with new shoes?"

"Not at all. I just don't need all the details. Anyway, I'm thinking. What if the pearl really *is* super valuable? Shouldn't you have it appraised before you start parading it around?"

She sighed. "You don't get it. I treasure it. I want to wear it, show it off. I don't care what it's worth in terms of dollars."

"But if it's worth big bucks, we shouldn't take any chances on it getting stolen, right? Just have it checked out, if only to put my mind at ease. Please?"

She bit down on the corner of her mouth, frowned. "Oh, I suppose you're right. I do know a woman over in Newport who's an expert on antique jewelry and gemstones. I could ask her."

He reached for the phone, picked it up and held it out to me. "Give her a call."

"Right now?"

"No time like the present. Just see what she says, okay?"

"I suppose." She looked the woman up in the phone book, dialed, and got an answering machine. Steve moved closer, encircled her waist with his arms, and nuzzled her neck.

She giggled and put her hand over the mouthpiece. "Do you mind?" Back to the phone, she said, "This is Nicole O'Connor, from across the bay in the Seabreeze campground, near Benedict's Landing. My husband bought me a very old brooch with a stunning, perfect pearl in it. The thing is, the pearl is purple and we think it might've come from a quahog. I'd appreciate it if you could take a look at it, at your convenience. Please give me a call." She left their number and hung up.

Steve continued nuzzling, kissing. "Care to celebrate in a more intimate manner?"

Nikki turned into him, pressed her body to his. Moments later, she pulled back a little, reached down, loosened his belt, and slipped her hand inside. "Celebrate? Something like this?"

He closed his eyes, groaned.

"Just looking for any more hidden presents here," she whispered huskily.

He groaned again, reached into the front of her robe with one hand and loosened the tie with the other. Moments later, her bathrobe and his clothes littered the floor.

"Nice toenails," he observed, eyeballing the turquoise polish.

She put her hands on her hips. "Here I am, seductively posed in the altogether and you're focusing on my toenails?"

He took her into his arms but before he could answer, a call shrieked across her scanner.

Despite the heavy rain, a fire raged—right there in the campground.

CHAPTER 4

ALBUQUERQUE: only an hour away from the New Mexico State Prison. In their new Winnebago motorhome with Trish, his Virgin Jailhouse Bride, Marion Hess exited off I-25 at San Mateo Boulevard. He drove a few blocks before pulling into a parking lot next to an adobe building.

"My P.O.'s office," he explained. "I have to check in."

"P.O.?"

"Parole officer," he said, getting out. "Won't be a minute."

"Okay, darling. In the meantime, I'll fix us some tuna sandwiches and—"

"I *despise* tuna!"

All along her mascara-clotted eyelashes, tears welled up, threatening to spill. "I'm sorry. Maybe I can . . . ."

Oh, for Christ's sake, get a goddam grip. "Look," he said, softer now. "I didn't mean to yell at you, okay?" He tried his best to look contrite. "My mother forced me to eat tuna and it always made me puke. I didn't mean to snap at you, darling. Besides, I'm craving some decent Mexican food. Or maybe one of those fantastic green chili-cheese burgers from the Owl Café."

She lowered her head, dabbed at her streaked eyes with a tissue, and mustered a wan smile. By the time she looked up, he'd disappeared into the building.

Less than half an hour later, he came back. "All set," he said, climbing back up behind the wheel and starting the engine. He leaned over, willed himself to plant a peck on Trish's pink cheek. A wave of tuna assailed him. He backed off.

She looked surprised. "What."

"Nothing. Uh, you have a glob of mayo on your chin."

She reached into her purse, plucked at a tissue, extracting it from the bristles of a hairbrush, along with enough stray strands to supply the Hair Club for Men for a year. She kleenexed her chin, wiping away the offending glob. "Did I get it?"

"Most of it. Listen, sweetheart, I'm starving. Where can we get some decent *chiles relleños?"*

"Head over to Central," she said. "There's a terrific place there. They've got excellent *sopapillas,* too."

"Sounds good. But first, I need to stop at a public library. I need to use a computer so I can send an e-mail. Uh, it's about a, uh, a . . . job."

"A job? But I thought we weren't settling anywhere just yet."

"Just a feeler, okay? For the future. That Mexican restaurant you were talking about? Do they serve margaritas?"

Her face fell. "Oh, darling. You know I don't drink alcohol and you shouldn't either. Jesus doesn't want us to violate the temples of our bodies."

He cut his eyes to her. "Right. How could I forget?"

After a visit to the library, and once they'd gorged themselves on *enchiladas* and *chiles rellenos,* they hefted themselves back up into the motorhome.

"If you're still hungry, they have great green chili cheese burgers at the Owl Café," she suggested.

"Oof. I don't *think* so," said Hess, around a gargantuan burp.

"No? Well, they got terrific taquitas over there at Mac's Steak in the Rough place," she said. "They're small, but tasty. And they have fresh-squeezed limeades, too. Yum."

Hess rolled his eyes, saying, "Are you kidding me? I'm stuffed. Let's gas up and get out of here."

After pulling in to the nearest gas station, he started pumping premium octane into the thirsty tank, thinking: Christ on a crutch, gas prices what they are, it'll take five fucking large just to fill this goddam thing. Once the nozzle clicked off, he opened the door and leaned into the coach.

"I need money," he said.

Trish reached into her purse, whipped out her pocketbook, carefully peeled off some bills, and handed them to him. "Will this do it?"

He counted them and nodded. "After we're done here, we should drive over to the bank. If we get the balance of our money, we won't have to come back to Albuquerque at all."

She clucked her tongue, sniffed. "I don't think so. It's not such a good idea to carry all that cash on the road. Why, it's not even in traveler's checks."

"But—"

"No buts, darling. I must insist on this. We have plenty of money, for now."

Grumbling, Hess paid the attendant. Back in the coach and on the road, he found himself grinding his teeth as he headed up an on-ramp and pointed the RV east on I-40, toward Tucumcari. In the RV's mirrors, the sun set in a multitude of hues as they started the climb into the *Sandia* Mountains. He flicked on the headlights.

"Okay, baby," he said evenly, with a smile. "Where would you like to spend your honeymoon?"

She giggled into her palm. "Gee, I don't care, as long as I'm with you. But I can't wait. Why don't we just turn around and go back to Albuquerque? I have a coupon for the Motel-6."

He laughed. "As exotic as that sounds, why don't we head for someplace a little more romantic? Someplace like, say, Niagara Falls?"

"Ooh. Niagara Falls! That *is* romantic!"

BY THE TIME they were out of the pass and back into the desert, Hess heard soft snoring and looked over. Trish's multiple chins had compressed, she was drooling onto her cleavage, and he detected a faint odor of tuna and *chiles relleños*.

He shook his head. "Too much food and excitement for one day?" he whispered, sneering with contempt. "Why, we're just plumb tuckered out." *Soon, I'll be free, Mother—free to go after that Jezebel Whore. Free to get sweet, sweet revenge for your suffering.*

Trish stirred. "Where are we?"

"A few miles out of Santa Rosa."

She started squirming in her seat.

"Something wrong?" he asked.

"Not really. Well, yes. Uh, darling? Can we make a pit stop? I kind of have to go potty."

"Correct me if I'm wrong, but don't we have a toilet onboard?"

She giggled. "This is *so* embarrassing! I have to, you know, go, uh . . . number twosies."

Jesus, there's an image I don't need. "So?"

"Well, you know, I didn't get any of that potty treatment stuff for the black tank. I don't want—"

"I get the picture," he snapped, interrupting. "Listen, I saw a sign for a scenic rest area coming up. They'll have a facility and we can stretch our legs." *And it might just serve my needs perfectly.*

She smiled. "I dreamed about Niagara Falls."

He tossed her a sideways glance, thinking: that's right, keep grinning you fat fucking cow because your blubber ass won't live to see Niagara Falls. And you know what else? . . . You won't even live to see the state-fucking-line.

"Are you hungry?" she asked. "Want a tuna sandwich or something?"

He did a mental cringe, found he was grinding his teeth again. "No. But thanks for asking."

CHAPTER 5

NIKKI SNUGGLED CLOSER to Steve.

"I hate that damn scanner," he growled, his face flushed.

"Yeah, wonderful timing," she said, reluctantly breaking their embrace. She picked up her robe and headed for the bedroom to get dressed.

"Ignore it," he pleaded, following close behind.

"I have to go. The fire's right here in the campground. I have to check it out. Sure, we're both all heated up but I'm still the park ranger. Come with me?"

It took only minutes to put themselves together and drive across the campground. The storm had passed and the volunteer fire department already had everything under control; with tight efficiency, they'd doused the burning tents where, luckily, nobody had been hurt. Nikki and Steve pulled up, hopped out. Overriding the sweet aroma of ozone, a wet, charred nylon stench hung in the air, irritating her nose.

A police cruiser from Benedict's Landing splashed through the puddles and pulled up just behind them, blue lights winking. A female officer Nikki didn't recognize got out. Right behind her, Chief Anderson arrived in his own prowler. Nikki wondered why he was here, figuring he'd never schedule himself on second shift.

As he got out, he winked at her.

She cringed. *Here we go again.*

"Hello, Nikki," he said, as he slid his baton into its belt loop. "You're looking gorgeous, as usual."

"Why, thanks, Chief," interjected Steve, coming between them. "Compliments are always welcome—no matter *what* the source."

The chief scowled but didn't respond; instead, he introduced Nikki to the female officer. When they all walked over to the scene of the fire, a gaggle of spaced-out teens eyeballed them.

"Uh-oh," mumbled one of the youths, backing away. "I'm outta here."

Following his lead, all the kids bolted for a clump of cedars at the edge of the woods. One of the kids, a short, Hispanic youth, tripped in his baggy cuffs and Nikki grabbed him. Steve started to chase the others.

"Let 'em go," said the chief. "You'll never catch 'em in those woods."

"What's going on here?" Nikki asked the kid.

The kid got to his feet, shrugged. "I din't do nothin', lady. The dude over there, leanin' against that tittie-pink minivan? Go ask him."

Nikki did a mental eye roll. *Junior? Cripes, doesn't the kid ever go home?* "Why him?" she asked the Hispanic boy but he squirmed, slipped her grasp, and bolted. He skidded on the wet grass, but regained his footing and sprinted away.

"Hey! Get back here," she yelled. But Frank was right: with no moon and the kid's familiarity with the woods, she knew he was gone.

Flashlights punctuated the darkness as inquisitive campers started to gather and gawk. Now that the rain had shrunk to a misty drizzle, fresh campfires winked in the distance and the pleasant aroma of wood smoke helped cut the pungency of the burnt nylon. A faint whiff of marijuana floated here and there.

While the female officer pulled out her notebook and started questioning other campers, Nikki decided to see what Junior had to say. When she approached, he schlepped forward, sopping wet pants slung low and dragging. She marveled once more at how they stayed up. The back pockets were aligned with the back of his knees for crying out loud.

"Well, hello again, Junior. What happened here?"

He stuck out his chin, tossed his hair, and looked away. "Beats me. I was just tryin' to get close to some chick. Any law against that?"

"Depends on how close she wants you, I suppose." Nikki looked past Junior to where the chief was prodding a melted boom box with the toe of his boot.

"Good riddance to ba-aad noise pollution," Frank said.

Once Frank moved on, she turned back to Junior. "Now tell me what—"

"Hey!" yelled Steve, getting everyone's attention. He was on the other side of the charred tents. "There's a *body* over here!"

They all rushed over. A girl lay sprawled in the wet grass, breasts bared, tube top riding high above them. Her hair stood up, a shock of reddish spikes.

"Yeah, it's that Adrienne chick," said Junior. "The one I was lookin' to get close to? Nice tits, huh? Small, but nice."

"Put a sock in it," Nikki said, frowning at him. She knelt down and readjusted the girl's tube top, restoring her modesty.

"Shit," muttered Junior.

Nikki checked the girl's pulse and breathing and pronounced her alive.

"Anyone know her?" asked the chief, looking around.

"Oh, I know her," volunteered Junior. He started doing a little rooster strut.

"She's one of the campers," Nikki said. "You can get her name and address off the registration slip at the gate."

"Her name's Adrienne Lee-doo," crowed Junior. "Cool name, huh?"

The female officer and Nikki helped Adrienne up. The girl looked to be coming around a little and managed to stand. Still, she had to hang on to them. She moaned, bent at the waist, and threw up. When Nikki stepped back to avoid the splash, the girl started to topple over again. The officer held firm until Nikki could grab Adrienne's other arm. A vomit slick greased Adrienne's chin and stained her tube top.

Chief Anderson turned to Nikki. "This girl here with anyone?"

Nikki shook her head. "I'm pretty sure she's alone; at least, she drove in by herself."

With her free hand, Nikki flashed her own light around and spotted a small purse. "Wait a minute," she said, snatching it up. "This is probably hers." She handed it to Frank.

He took out the billfold and examined the girl's I.D., saying, "Well, she's underage, plus she's blotto. We'll take her in and notify her parents to come get her."

Adrienne opened one eye, slurred, "Good fuckin' luck", and slumped back against Nikki.

She and the female officer walked the poor, wasted girl over to the officer's cruiser. Holding her lolling head so she wouldn't bump it, the officer helped her into the back seat. While supervising, Frank lit one of his putrid cigars.

Nikki fanned the air. *Ugh.*

The woman officer snicked the door shut. "Nice meeting you," she said to Nikki, then slid into the driver's seat and pulled away.

Once she was gone, Frank whipped out his notebook, and stared Junior down, saying, "Alright, Pothead. Want to tell me what the hell happened here?"

Junior shrugged. "Nothin'. It was like party time, right? Guess a campfire was too close to the tents an' one a them caught fire, is all. End of story."

"Well, I imagine we can question the girl in the morning," said Frank. He clomped around to the driver's side of his own cruiser, grunting while he got in. Before heading out, he leaned out his window and looked at Nikki. "Looks like the campground would be better served with you on second shift," he said.

"You're probably right," she admitted.

"By the way, babe, no news on Marion Hess or his parole or anythin'."

Jesus, she thought, why'd he have to remind me? She hadn't entertained thought one about Hess since Steve came home. She nibbled at a thumbnail, then said, "I'm sure you'll keep me posted."

As Frank pulled away, she turned back to Junior. "Okay, how about giving me some more details about the fire?"

"Details?" he cried. "Okay, Mz. Park Ranger. There's one detail you prolly dint notice. That hot Adrienne chick? . . . She's got an awesome nipple ring."

Nikki knew Junior thought he'd grossed her out with that last comment. Wrong. Hands on hips, she stared him down. It looked like he might be sobering up a little.

He blinked rapidly. His prominent Adam's apple bobbed a few times and he cleared his throat. "Well, um, er, ah," he stammered. "It was like the party got kinda, you know, outta control."

She smiled. "That's better. Drugs involved?"

He shrugged, started strutting his rooster strut again. "Yo, dawg," he said, positioning his arms and hands, gesturing like a homey. "I be comin' back to the campground is all, lookin' for that Adrienne girl, tryin' to get a little trim, know what I'm sayin'? Yo, be knowin' the beeotch from somewhere, right?"

"Junior," said Nikki. "If any of the brothers ever hear you talking like that, they'll turn you into a eunuch."

"You nick?"

"Cut your doodles off."

"Whoa."

"So talk white boy speak, okay?"

"Okay, okay. Look, she was kinda with some other dude so I just kinda hung out, you know? Anyway, that hottie's a *college* girl. Goes to Brown."

"I heard," said Nikki dryly. "And she likes to camp."

"Just 'til school starts. Or so she said."

"So tell me what all went on here."

"It was wild," cried Junior. "Some guys pulled up a bunch a campground signs and burned 'em. And tents were ever'where, man! Like I said, some a them were, like, too close to the fires, know what I'm sayin'? It started rainin' bigtime but nobody gave a shit. A boom box was boomin' an' Adrienne started gettin' wasted."

"Wasted."

"I mean, chickie was drinkin' straight Everclear. Whoa!"

Nikki kept nodding, urging him on. "Grain alcohol, huh? Heavy duty stuff."

Junior snorted. "Yeah, like you'd know."

"Oh," she said, "I might surprise you."

He snorted again. "Yeah, right. Anyway, Adrienne was head-bangin' to *Godsmack!,* you know? She danced over by the campfire, flung her drink into it. Shit, man, turned the fire into a freakin' inferno, know what I'm sayin'?"

"That when the tent caught on fire?"

"Yeah. Adrienne said the drink tasted like shit anyway. She was dancin' all crazy, all flappin' her elbows and shufflin' to the beat. Her purple, or, whaddyacallit, uh, *magenta* hair was whippin' around. An' she was way close to the fire, right?"

"Uh-huh."

"Somebody yelled, 'You go, girl', and that's when she pulled up her tube top and did a 'Girls Gone Wild'."

"Why didn't someone steer her away from the fire?"

Junior looked shocked. "What, you kidding? She had that nipple ring, for chrissakes!"

Nikki couldn't help but do an eye roll. "So you already said."

"Yeah, huh? I tole her the ring was, like, pretty cool. That's when she said that she'd given consideration to a ring down *south*, right there in the best part of the, uh . . . Promised Land. Her words, not mine."

"Okay," Nikki said, raising a hand. "Please stick to what happened."

Junior beamed, obviously pleased with himself. "But she also said a ring down there might be 'pushin' the envelope.'"

"A pun. Good one."

"Pun?"

"Never mind."

He crossed his arms, lifted his chin. "Myself?" he said, "I call a spade a spade. An 'envelope' down there wouldn't be a *pun.* It'd be a pussy."

"Junior, I've about had it with your foul mouth and attitude. Maybe I ought to call the chief back here. He'd be more than happy to haul you in."

The possibility of a night in jail seemed to cool his jets. "No need for that," he said.

"Alright, then. Can you tell me anything else?"

"Well, just that all that spinnin' around musta got her dizzy an' she sort of fell down, passed out, you know? I started to go over to her an' that's when the skunk showed up."

"I thought I smelled—"

"Uh-huh," he interrupted. "And while we were dodging the skunk? The wind blew the fire to where it caught hold a that tent flap."

"Ah."

He became animated: "One a the dudes panicked, you know? Started runnin' around yelling 'Fire! Fire!' It was wicked awesome! All the yelling musta woke Adrienne 'cause she crawled a dozen yards away an' passed out again. The rain had pretty much let up and wasn't puttin' out the fire so a couple of us tried peeing on it but it was no good. The skunk ran around, sprayed a couple a dudes. By that time the fire jumped to a couple more tents. That's when I drove on over to the gatehouse and got that Fottler dude to call 911."

"Good for you."

He shrugged. "Anyway, you guys showed up, right after the fire trucks."

"Still, that was quick thinking on your part."

He stared at Nikki for a second, probably trying to decide if she was just buttering him or playing him or something. Or not. He tossed his hair.

"Those other kids?" she said. "You know who they are?"

"Naw. They're just a buncha freaks from Franklin High, acrost the bay there."

"Okay. Anything else you can tell me?"

"Did I tell you that chickie's going to Brown?"

CHAPTER 6

NEAR SANTA ROSA, New Mexico, Hess wheeled the motorhome into a deserted rest area, parked, and looked around. "Uh-oh," he said. "Looks like there aren't any restrooms here."

Trish shrugged. "Oh, well. I'll just have to use ours. Tomorrow, we can stop at a Wal-Mart and get that tank treatment." With that, she heaved herself out of her captain's chair, made her way aft, and squeezed into the tiny bathroom.

Hess had no idea how she could stuff her bulk into such a small space, let alone get her massive ass down on the crapper. It gave him a new appreciation for the strength of RV toilets. Loud grunting and flatulence preceded a foul odor that seeped out from under the bathroom door, undoubtedly a direct result of the *chiles relleños*. And tuna.

He slipped into the motorhome galley, opened a drawer and discovered an eight-inch Henckels Professional "S" model chef's knife. "Outstanding cutlery," he whispered to himself. Noticing a honing steel, he picked it up and ran it over the blade a few times, just to make sure it was sharp enough.

He tested it on his thumb. It drew blood.

Satisfied, he slid it into the back of his belt and licked up the tiny blood trail on his thumb. He felt a stir in his groin, taut against his pants. Quickly, he peered out a window, found they were still the only vehicle in the lot. Excellent.

"This is for you, Mother," he said, aloud, unconsciously stroking the increasing bulge in his trousers.

"What?" Coming from behind the bathroom door, Trish's voice sounded muffled.

"Oh, nothing," he said. "Just waiting for you, sweetheart."

"How nice. I'm just finishing up."

He heard her flush, a rustle of clothes, and the water pump growling as she washed up. She opened the door, turned, and bumped into his chest.

"Oh! . . . You scared me," she said. "Why are you standing there?"

"Just waiting. In fact, I can't wait for Niagara Falls. I've got to have you now."

Her eyes widened. "Now? Here? But I need to take a bath."

"Never mind that," he cooed, taking her hand and squeezing.

She squeezed back weakly and he shuddered, thinking her hand felt like a microwaved lump of fish.

"Are you cold?" she asked.

He extricated his hand. "No, baby. Just excited."

She looked down, gently touched him through his trousers. Giggling into her palm, she said, "I can tell."

He slipped his fingers under the elastic of her peasant blouse and eased it off her shoulders. Her massive breasts, restricted and pushed up by her Plus-Size bra, loomed bigger than the *Sandia* Mountains.

He spotted the gold neck chain and his gaze followed it to where it disappeared down into her cleavage. The safe-deposit key was hiding at the end, buried somewhere in all that pink flesh. He started herding her aft, shuffling toward the queen-sized bed.

She moaned, reached behind her back, and unclasped her bra. She stripped it off, releasing melon-sized breasts. They tumbled free, jouncing about themselves.

He fondled the handle of the knife in the back of his belt. His phallus was painfully hard now, throbbing with The Temptations. "Are you ready?"

"*More* than ready," she said, her voice husky with desire.

"That's nice," he said. Reaching back, he drew out the knife and plunged the blade into her abdomen. Slowly, and to the hilt.

"*Ungh*," she said. Her eyes went owlish and her mouth formed an "O", exaggerated by her sparkly, electric-crimson lipstick. As her breath eased out in a measured, raspy flow, she whispered, "Why? *Why?*"

"Why? Well, for starters, you're a fatass cow."

She jerked, gurgled, flailed.

Once she went slack, he pushed her back on the bed. Wasting no time, he removed her clothes, and stood back. His eyes roamed over her pale, lifeless body and the moment they fixated on the fine cutlery protruding from her belly, he ejaculated into his trousers.

"Not yet!" he cried out in anguish, shuddering and watching the wet spot spread. In a frenzy of anger, he went about his sexual butchery: slicing her, gouging, hacking. Biting.

"Forgive me, Mother, " he cried out. "I was weak." He closed his eyes and his hands started to tremble.

In anticipation of The Purging.

Even though Hess was a non-smoker, he carried a package of cigarettes, a lighter, and a few votive candles in his kit bag. He placed the candles nearby, lit them, and the waxy, familiar stench he'd dreaded since as long as he could remember filled the confines on the motorhome. He fumbled in the cigarette pack, plucked one out and lit it from one of the candles. Once he'd puffed it to a fiery glow, he steeled himself by biting down on a nearby pillow.

I love you Mother. I'll make it right.

Tears streamed down his cheeks. Into the pillow, he muffled a howl not unlike the cry of the damned as he ground the glowing tip of the cigarette into his backside, adding yet one more scar to the many; yet another ugly testament to The Purging. The stench of burning flesh filled his nostrils, mingling with that of the candles and Patricia Deeb's death.

But he felt Absolved, Redeemed.

In the bathroom, he showered quickly and—ever aware of how easily burns got infected—applied antibiotic ointment to his fresh burn and carefully applied a band-aid. Then he ran his hands over both sides of his backside, feeling the cratered landscape and contours of former Purgings. With satisfaction.

He was, once again, free of The First Sin.

See, Mother? I fell under the spell of The Temptations.
But I did The Purging like you taught me.
Am I a good boy?

He wrapped Trish's ruined corpse in the bed covers and with great difficulty, hefted her onto his shoulder, more than glad that he'd taken the time to pump iron in prison. At the doorway, he sloughed his load off, opened the door, and peered out. He saw no approaching lights in either direction.

Satisfied, he finagled Trish's bulky corpse through the restrictive doorway and let it plop on the ground. The moon had risen high now, about three-quarters full, offering eerie light. The air smelled like mesquite.

Grunting and sweating with effort, he hoisted the body back onto his shoulder and toted it down a winding path, which lead into the desert. About fifty yards out, he came across an arroyo, choked with tumbleweeds and cacti.

"Outfuckingstanding," he said, tossing his burden into the arroyo where it partially disappeared beneath the tumbleweeds and settled onto a huge, flat, prickly pear cactus.

The cops would find her corpse and tie him to her murder but Hess didn't care because by that time, he'd be long gone and under another identity, thanks to his jailhouse connections. Besides, he thought, maybe the coyotes and other desert critters would take care of her, right?

He chuckled, did a little dance of self-congratulation, and scurried back to the motorhome where he showered again (taking care not to wet the fresh bandaging), changed clothes, and cleaned up as best he could, making sure there was no overt blood. Once that was done, he climbed behind the wheel, started up the coach, and was just about to leave but jammed on the brakes.

"Shit!" he cried. "I forgot the fucking key."

CHAPTER 7

IN THE CAMPGROUND, Nikki figured nothing more could be pried out of Junior, so she told him to go home and went looking for Steve. She found him in the parking lot.

"Ready?" he asked.

"All set."

"Thank God we can finally go home. Um, think you can get back into the mood?"

She sighed. "I've got the stink of skunk and burnt nylon up my nose, I feel kind of queasy, and I'm exhausted. Not exactly conducive to sex. Can I take a rain check? How does tomorrow morning sound?"

"Well . . . sure."

She grabbed his hand and squeezed, saying, "Glad you understand." They started walking back toward her little SUV. "Before we go home," she said, "let's stop by the gatehouse. I want to see what Petey Fottler has to say."

They surprised Petey, outside his hut and urinating in the shadows. Caught in the beam of her headlights, he looked like a lost dog on the interstate. He hustled back inside. They got out and followed him in.

"Yo, Petey," said Steve, throwing his arm over the little troll's rounded shoulder and taking him aside. "Your zipper's wide open, pal."

"There is no rose without a thorn," piped Petey, cryptically. He ignored Steve's tip.

"Listen," Nikki said. "Junior Ferguson told me he reported the fire from here tonight. Is that right?"

Petey looked puzzled, considered that. "Everything serves to further," he said.

"Pardon?"

He beamed, nodded with vigor. "Pardon is the choicest flower of victory!"

"Let's get out of here," said Steve.

Nikki got in Petey's face. "No more fortune cookie crap. Out with it."

"Okay, okay," he said, frowning. "Junior came in here, we called 911, and that's all I know."

He turned his attention toward the gatehouse TV where he alternated between watching a *Seinfeld* rerun and admiring his new aviator style glasses in the reflection of the gatehouse window. On the TV, Elaine pressed George Costanza's face into her bosom and mashed it around, yelling something about it being George's Christmas card.

"Okay, thanks," said Nikki. "That's all we wanted to know." She and Steve said goodbye and left.

"Never did zip his fly," said Steve.

"Never did," she agreed.

"And he peed on his Converse All-Stars."

"With feet that size? ... How could he help it?"

THE FOLLOWING MORNING found Steve and Nikki showering together, all lathered up. With the pulsing water cascading off them, she had full intentions of redeeming her rain check.

"I love the color of your skin," he said, soaping away. "It's like a very light, creamy caramel."

She laughed. "With ugly dots."

"I told you . . . I love your freckles."

"Well, then, my dad, one hundred percent pure Irish, can be thanked or cursed for the freckles, whatever. You can thank my great-grandmother for the caramel skin tint, I guess. She was a full-blooded Narragansett. Anyway, how come whenever we shower together, my breasts end up so clean?"

"Can't ever be too clean. I'd better suds 'em some more."

She laughed, started doing a little intimate soaping of her own and that's when the phone rang.

Steve groaned. "Let it ring."

"What if it's that antique expert in Newport calling about my purple pearl? You don't want me to miss her call, do you?"

He made a face. "She wouldn't call this early. Let the machine get it."

"Okay." Nikki resumed soaping and stroking. In earnest. With both hands.

The phone kept ringing; the answering machine must've been turned off. After about a dozen rings, her concentration started to falter and his state of arousal reacted accordingly.

"Go on," he mumbled. "Better get the goddam phone."

"Be right back," she promised. She hopped out of the shower, wrapped a towel around herself, padded over and picked up the phone. No one was on the other end. She hung up and started back toward the shower when the phone rang again. Irritated, she picked up.

"What," she snapped.

"Well, aren't we in a mood so early in the morning," chirped the voice. It was Chief Frank Anderson.

"Oh, you. What do you want?"

"My, my. So cordial. Well, I got more on Hess, babe. Can you come by the office?"

"Can't you just tell me over the phone? And when will you get that I'm not your babe?"

"Better if you come to my office."

Uh-oh, Nikki thought. *Why?* The little hairs on the back of her neck stood up. "Oh, all right," she said. "I'll be by later. Bye."

Click.

She went back into the steamy bathroom.

"Was it her?" called Steve, still in the shower.

Nikki dropped her towel and joined him. No way was this Hess thing going to mess with her sex life. "Huh? Oh, the lady in Newport? No, it wasn't her."

"Why are you frowning?"

She shook her head. "It's nothing, really, just Chief Anderson. He said he wanted to see me."

"What's that idiot want? He's—"

She cut the statement short by putting her hand behind Steve's neck, pulling his face to her, and kissing him. No perfunctory kiss, either; it was one of those deep and passionate kisses with a definite purpose in mind. Moments later, she broke the kiss and molded her body to his.

"Now," she said, her voice husky. "Forget Frank. Where were we?"

He nuzzled in her neck, saying, "Whoa. *That* got my motor going in a hurry." He nibbled just below her ear. His hands started moving, probing.

And that's when an insistent fist pounded at the front door.

"Jesus Christ," he growled.

"I know," she said. With great reluctance, she got out of the shower, wrapped her hair in a towel, and slipped into her robe. On the way to the door, she peeked through the side window and saw that it was Junior Ferguson, probably the first time he'd been up this early—ever. She tightened her robe and opened the door.

The sun was bright and there were no clouds. She could smell campfire smoke. Several gulls were gliding about, searching for breakfast, and complaining loudly.

"What can I do for you, Junior?"

"Uh, I just wanted to say I'm sorry I was an assh . . . uh, jerk last night, when you were questioning me. I was kinda wrecked, you know?"

"You got up this early to apologize? To me?"

"Uh-huh. I din't mean nothin'. Like I said, I was zonked."

"Zonked on what?" she asked.

"The usual. Beer and a little pot what a guy shared with me."

"Well, apology accepted. Now, go home, get some sleep. You look like you could use it."

"Uh, there's something else."

"I figured."

"I called the police station to check on that Adrienne chick. She's such a hottie!"

"What's that got to do with me?" Nikki asked.

"Well, they asked if I knew her parents, said they couldn't get ahold of 'em. I thought if you'd go get her, they'd turn her loose, you bein' tight with the cops and all."

"I don't have any pull there. Anyway, I'll bet they didn't charge her with anything. They'll let her go on her own recognizance."

Junior looked pitiful. "Please?" he whined. "Please, please, please?"

Nikki *really* wanted go back inside with Steve, finish what they'd started, and then call that antique expert in Newport again about the purple pearl. But she knew she'd never be able to relax and get her mind right until she found out what Frank was being so secretive about. Besides, Steve had contracted a job to fix someone's porch stairs this morning and she knew he had to get going.

"Oh, all right," she said, with a heavy sigh. "I have to go there anyway. Just let me get dressed and I'll take you."

"Awesome!"

Steve came out, dressed for work. With a sad look, he kissed Nikki on the cheek.

"Later," she whispered in his ear. "I hope."

He took off in his truck.

While Junior waited by the outdoor picnic table, she tucked her hair into a ponytail. She was thinking buttered bagel to go but when she had to suck in to button her uniform pants, she changed her mind. She went right out, locking the door behind her. She and Junior hopped into her Honda, headed for town.

Junior was fidgeting. "Uh . . . Ranger O'Connor?" he said.

"Ranger O'Connor?" she asked, incredulous. "Excuse me? What's with the formality?"

He shrugged. "Whatever."

"Well, why don't you just call me Nikki? We don't have to be enemies, you know."

He looked puzzled by that. "Okay, um . . . Nikki. Anyway, I remembered where I know that chick from. We used to live in the same neighborhood when we were kids."

"You're *still* kids," Nikki said.

"I mean like little kids. We used to play together and stuff and everything."

Benedict's Landing wasn't far. Nikki parked in front of the police station and they headed up the steps. Inside, they could hear Adrienne in the lockup, singing off-key—some oldie about shooting the sheriff but not the deput-ee.

The chief greeted them. "We never could get ahold of her parents," he said. "She wouldn't tell us a thing, except they're divorced and they don't give two shits for anything, including her."

"So she can go?" asked Junior, obviously filled with hope.

"Yeah, she can go. Hell, we kept her overnight just to keep an eye on her because she was so hammered."

"Well, alright!" cried Junior. He spun about in a joyful little celebratory circle until a glassed-in case of shotguns on the wall captured his attention. He sauntered over and studied them, saying, "Clam doggies!"

"So . . . you said you had some news for me?" Nikki asked Frank.

"Yeah, but later, babe. Alone."

She glared at him, put her hands on her hips. "What the hell is it?" She said evenly. She was starting to get alarmed. "Why all the secrecy?"

"Well, we need a little time to get into it. I've got stuff to do and you probably have some campground shenanigans to deal with, right? Could you meet me later for lunch? At the deli?"

"Oh, I suppose so. Just call me when you're ready."

Moments later, Junior, Adrienne, and Nikki were standing outside together. Adrienne—blinking like crazy in the harsh sunlight—eyeballed Nikki. Nikki could tell the girl was trying to focus but her eyes were bloodshot and watering.

"You, like, a cop or something?"

"Park Ranger is all," Nikki said. "Junior here wanted me to help get you out. You're out."

Junior cut in. " 'Member me?" he asked Adrienne, his eyes cast downward.

She frowned, chewed at an ebony-lacquered fingernail. "Sort of. Last night?"

He shuffled his feet. "Even before that."

"Huh?"

"Yeah, we used to play together when we were kids. Over on Ocean Avenue? I was the doctor and you were—"

"Whoa! Enough."

Junior continued to grin. "Can we give you a ride somewhere?"

"Thanks for making sure it was okay with me first," Nikki interjected.

"I just meant—"

Nikki waved dismissively.

"I could use a ride," said Adrienne. "To the campground?" She adjusted her stained tube top. The top button of her hip-hugger jeans was undone, so she buttoned it.

Junior missed none of it.

Nikki hopped behind the wheel while the girl and Junior slid into the back. In her mirror, Nikki saw the girl study Junior for a moment, and scoot to the other side. Junior dropped his eyes, rubbed his palms on his thighs. After a moment, he appeared to work up his nerve and moved closer to the girl.

She mashed herself against the door, saying, "Get back. You're not going to try and, like, molest me or anything, are you?"

His mouth fell open and he moved back. "Where'd that come from? Whadda you think I am?" He tossed his hair.

Adrienne tapped Nikki's shoulder. "Can we get going, please?"

"Sure."

The girl hipped Junior a safe distance away, scooted to the middle and leaned up over the front seat so she could check herself in the rear-view mirror. Nikki could see Junior's gaze crawl over the girl's backside, up close and personal.

"Awesome," he said.

Adrienne paid no attention, started reapplying her black lipstick. "Damage control," she explained. "Like, I'm a mess?"

"Hair looks good though," observed Junior. "Uh, what color did you say that was? Pink?"

"Magenta," she said, fluffing it up.

"Right."

Once they arrived at the campground, Nikki headed straight for the tent area. By that time, Junior had managed to get his arm around Adrienne. She didn't protest. Nikki noticed Junior just couldn't keep his eyes off the girl's bare midriff, probably enchanted by the ring in her navel. He licked his lips, moaned, and angled his body closer, pressing into her thigh.

"*Eew!*" she said, jerking away. "Get *off* me!" She scooted back against her door.

As if scalded, he jumped back to his own side, saying, "What. What?"

"We're here," Nikki said, pulling over. She turned toward Adrienne. "By the way, who were those kids you were with last night? Can you tell me what happened?"

The girl gnawed on her lower lip, frowned. "I kinda overdid the partyin'? Like, I don't remember too much. Sorry."

"Yeah," Nikki said. "I figured as much. Well, Junior? You want me to take you back to your minivan or are you getting out here?"

"Minivan?" asked Adrienne, turning to him. "You drive a *minivan*?"

"It's my ma's," he explained, shooting Nikki a sour look.

Adrienne hopped out. "Thanks for the ride." As she trotted off, she blew a black lipstick kiss over her shoulder. "See ya," she said and pranced away with an exaggerated waggle of her rear end.

Junior whistled his appreciation. "Well," he said, "her ten-watt boobs ain't much to write home about, but she's sure got a cute little ass."

"Great hair, too," Nikki said, shifting into gear and pulling away.

"And she goes to Brown," he added, pumping his eyebrows.

They drove away from the tent area, back toward her RV, where Junior had parked. Nikki let him off and started making her rounds.

As she drove, her mind drifted, settling in the past—back to that evening her high school cheerleader friends and she had gone out on their 'Marion Hess Fact-finding Commission' . . .

. . . All the shades pulled down too far, the girls can't see a thing.
"Bummer," Cheri says.

"Dare, Pocahontas," says Robin. "Dare you to march right up there, knock on the door, and ask if you can see his bedroom. Maybe ask him to kiss you? Then sort of accidentally *feel him up* and run. Count coup, right? We'll be waiting."

"No way," Nikki says. "Too risky. What if he attacks me or something?"

"Don't be a wuss."

"But that's what girls are, aren't we? Wusses? Where do you think the name came from?"

"Just do it, you know? Like the Nike *commercial?*"

What the hell, Nikki's thinking. It'll be fun, right? Okay, maybe not. But maybe curiosity didn't really kill the cat after all, right? And before she can think any more about it, she's running up to the door and knocking. Timidly, like a mouse.

There's shuffling sounds from inside. Someone's coming to the door.

It opens and Hess is right there in front of her. Omigod.

"I know you," he's saying, eyes wide. "You're Nikki O'Connor."

"You alone?" she hears herself asking.

"Yes . . . but Mother will be home from bible study in—"

"Never mind your mom," Nikki interrupts, unbelievably bold. She pushes his chest gently but with enough force to get inside. She eases the door shut behind them. She does a little pirouette thing, short skirt swirling. Leaning back against the wall, she smiles her most excellent and seductive smile.

"What do you want?" he asks, his throat sounding dry, raspy.

His eyes are just about bulging out of their sockets. But, Omigod, is he cute! Nikki moves forward, presses herself against his broad chest and looks up into his gorgeous eyes. She can't believe she's being such a flirt, she's tussling his hair. How crazy is this?

He's stammering. "I . . . I . . .I . . . your . . . hair . . ."

"What about it?"

"Lovely. Red. Silky. Like Mother's . . ."

Nikki sneaks a look down at the front of his Levis; his eyes follow hers.

"Fact-finding time," she announces. "Us girls want to know . . . is that for real?"

His Adam's apple starts bobbing up and down. Like a yo-yo.

"Would you like to kiss me?" she blurts out, thinking: girl, you have really lost it.

Clumsily, he grabs her, crushes his sensuous lips to hers, lips firmly pressed together and . . . eech! Worst kiss ever! Even worse, his breath stinks all like rotten cheese or something even more putrid. Eeuw. How is she ever going to get out of here?

She moves sideways but he's moving with her, sort of humping at her bare thigh like a dog, and trying for another kiss.

She starts to panic. Gotta get away!

A loud bang! His mom is suddenly there, bursting through the door, seeing them all smushed together and screeching like some sort of loony-tunes woman or something. She starts grabbing Nikki's hair, pulling, pulling, YANKING! Ow! Pulling a patch of it clear out!

"Jezebel Whore!" his mom keeps screaming. "Using your sinful feminine wiles to seduce my innocent boy."

Feminine wilds?

The crazed woman is holding her bible up to Nikki, like she would a vampire or something, then hitting her with it. Nikki falls to the floor, bumps her head. She sees little squiggly things dancing before her eyes.

"The First Sin, you Jezebel!" the witch screams. "Damnation! Damnation!" She is down on her knees now, right next to Nikki in an attitude of prayer. "O Lord . . ."

Nikki hears Hess crying, sobbing. He yanks his mom to her feet and starts shaking her, really hard, saying, "Stop it! Stop it! Stop it!" He's like a dog with a rag doll.

His mom's head is whipping with each shake, then lolls.

Her eyes go wide. She starts convulsing.

He releases her as if she was radioactive or something and starts backing away.

She crumples into a formless heap.

"Mother!" yells Hess. He drops to all fours, scuttles like a crab to her side, and cradles her head. With horror, Nikki sees him squeezing and kneading one of his mother's breasts, saying, "I didn't mean it."

His mom opens her eyes, blinks. Looks lovingly at him.

She's okay! Thinks Nikki. I gotta get outahere! But did she see what she thinks she saw? Gross! Did she imagine it? Yeah, probably, after that hit on the head. Anyway, grabbing the chance to boogie, she leaps up and blasts out the door like Jackie Joyner Kersee at the Olympics.

Nikki's friends are ready for her outside; the girls are all giggling hysterically as they make a run for Cheri's car. In no time, they clamor in and Cheri peels out. While the Bee-Gee's sing about how they should be dancing, yeah! on the radio at full volume, Cheri and Robin cackle and wave their arms. They're, like, having this conniption fit or something.

Saturday Night Fever!

Nikki just wants to forget they ever hatched this stupid 'Marion Hess Fact-finding Commission' plan . . .

. . . Blinking, and visibly shaken, she returned her attention to driving and continued on her rounds of the campground.

CHAPTER 8

IN HIS WINNEBAGO, at the rest area near Santa Rosa, New Mexico, Hess flipped off the ignition. *How the hell could I forget that fucking key?*

An anemic flush of light was just starting to infuse the eastern sky as he bolted from the coach, and sprinted back to the arroyo. Out of breath, gasping for air, and sweating like a marathon runner, he peered down through the tumbleweeds where he could barely make out the blanketed body. He scrambled down, pushing his way through and ignoring the cactus thorns until he reached Trish's body and pulled back enough bloody bed clothing for what he wanted.

Her disfigured body appeared milky blue in the dawn's early light—the blood, black. Her sightless eyes still looked surprised. At the vision of his carnage, Hess felt a sexual stirring again but pushed The Temptations to the back of his mind.

The key! Get that goddam key! . . . It's not here! Where the fuck is it?

Panicky, and with fingers pincushioned by cactus needles, he felt around in the folds of clammy flesh sagging off Trish's neck until he located the gold chain. During all the butchery, the key had somehow slipped around, over her shoulder, and was now hidden behind her massive back.

He grasped the key, tugged, and broke the chain. The prize was his.

In the distance, coyotes wailed, as if mourning for lost souls.

He eased away from the thorny entanglement, climbed back out of the arroyo and was just starting back up the path when he saw headlights in the distance, turning off the highway. A vehicle was slowing.

"Jesus H. Christ," he muttered. Once again, he had to sprint but by the time the car had pulled into the rest area, he was safely in his RV and had it started.

A state trooper! Shit!

Mystic Fear

The Statie executed a U-turn, pulled up alongside the motorhome, and gestured for Hess to roll down his window. Beads of cold sweat broke out on Hess's forehead as he complied. His hands were shaking.

"Yes, officer?"

"Everything all right, sir?"

"Fine. I was getting a little sleepy so I stopped for a quick nap. I'm okay now."

"I noticed that you have temporary tags, sir."

"That's right, officer. Just bought it."

"How do you like it?"

"Well, it's the, uh, maiden voyage, you might say. Been just fine, so far."

"Okay, sir. Have a safe trip."

"Thank you, officer."

Hess clicked on his turn signal before easing the lumbering motorhome onto the highway and heading east, toward Tucumcari, a small town that boasted one of his top-ten, favorite 24-hour cafés. A thin orange line heralded the upcoming sunrise.

JUST OVER AN hour later, emerging from the café and stuffed with *huevos rancheros,* bacon, sausage, hash browns, toast, OJ, and coffee, Hess hoisted himself back up into his RV. But this time, instead of heading east, he pulled a U-turn and headed back toward Albuquerque. On the way out of town, he looked over at the ancient Bluebird motel, a throwback to the fifties. It had been outside that motel, years ago, where he'd abducted that girl because she'd looked so much like Mother. Not as much as Jezebel Nikki, but still, the thought of it brought a smile to his face.

Were you proud of me Mother? Did I do good?

But then his smile faded and he clenched his teeth.

I'm sorry I was weak, succumbed to The Temptations. So sorry. But you know I did The Purging, cleansed myself. Don't you worry. I always do The Purging.

For you.

For us. And now?

I'm free.

On the ride back, as he passed by the Santa Rosa rest area, he stopped along the shoulder and idled in park. He looked across the highway.

"Poor, poor Trish Deeb," he said to himself. "Looks like those cactus needles are the only pricks you'll ever get, you fat, stupid cow. Never, ever, not one real prick, not even your basic maiden's delight on her honeymoon night . . . thank me."

He lowered the side window and let the dry wind refresh him. In his rear-view mirror, the sun was climbing, and the air felt much warmer. In the distance, a few coyotes continued to wail but they were tapering off. Hess wondered if maybe they found Trish and were having their own version of *huevos rancheros.* What a delicious thought . . .

As he moved the gearshift into drive, he took notice of several tumbleweeds rolling across the highway and recalled how he'd once stopped close to here where an old Navajo woman had set up on a blanket, selling her turquoise and silver jewelry to tourists who stopped at the rest area. He'd purchased a nice watchband and the woman told him a funny story about a particularly stupid tourist in a Cadillac with New Jersey plates who had just been there. Pointing to some wayward tumbleweeds stuck in the nearby fence, the tourist had asked how much the woman wanted for them. Thinking quickly, she told him the big ones went for one dollar, the smaller ones: fifty cents.

The tourist had bought one of each. Duh!

Ready to roll again, Hess raised his window and pulled out onto the highway. Inside the motorhome, he was pleased to notice the pleasant, lingering fragrance of this new vehicle.

And the coppery reek of his late wife's blood? . . . Barely noticeable anymore.

BACK IN ALBUQUERQUE, Hess parked his Winnebago at a Wal-Mart, purchased a gym bag, and beelined across the street to the Manzano Bank & Trust where he signed a card and was admitted to the safe deposit box. The cash was all in hundreds, filling the box. As he stuffed it into his bag, he did a quick count and estimated around maybe seven hundred large. *Holy Shit!*

After leaving the bank, he crossed back over to Wal-Mart, got in his rig and drove over to Central Avenue where he found an ancient motel, and parked in the back. The motel hailed back to the fifties or maybe even further: a cheap, cockroach-infested, cracked adobe jobbie that smelled like stale vomit and incense. Phony, Navajo-style logs poked out near the roof like so many fat penises and Hess wondered if there'd been any phallic intention. Nonetheless, the sleazebag motel offered anonymity, cable, HBO, and pay-per-view.

Before he hit the sack, he made a long-distance call to the Heartland of America. Once that was done, he started channel surfing.

No porn tonight, though.

The Purging wound was still sore, needed to heal.

.

CHAPTER 9

WHILE NIKKI TOOLED around the campground, she kept wondering what the hell Frank had to tell her. Realizing that speculation would get her nowhere, she forced her focus onto the lovely brooch Steve had given her. It was such a romantic gift and she was dying to wear it, show it off. And, she supposed she'd find out soon enough if that gorgeous pearl was valuable. She was dying to tell her daughter all about it but that could wait until she found out more.

Her cell phone rang. She figured it'd be Chief Anderson but it was Roger Starkweather, the campground manager.

"Hey," he said. "You needa check out the women's restrooms."

"Why?" said Nikki.

"Some gook gals're actually cookin' rice in there, with goddam Crock-Pots. Where folks go to the bathroom for chrissakes. B'lieve that shit?"

"I think they prefer to be called 'Asian-Americans', Roger. But they're . . . what? Cooking in there? That's definitely a health code violation. I'll get right on it."

"Okay," he said . . . and he must've thought he'd clicked off because then Nikki heard: "Yeah, right. Female park rangers? Useless as foam dildoes."

Her phone rang again. This time it *was* Chief Anderson.

"Ready for lunch?" he asked. "One hour?"

"I'll be there," she said. *Click.*

She was just about to leave when her next-door neighbor, a guy named Clyde Haywood, pulled alongside in his truck. Clyde's nickname was Tugboat and aptly so. At six-foot-seven and weighing in at close to three hundred, he'd once been a reserve offensive tackle for some NFL team. Being half Native-American, half African-American, and bearing a remarkable resemblance to Sidney Poitier, Tugboat was impressive to say the least.

Last spring, Tugboat and her husband Steve had became tight once they found out they were both ex-Marines. Both had

Mystic Fear

served in Desert Storm, although in separate units. Tug had gone on to serve two more tours in Force Recon, the baddest of the badasses, but Nikki soon found out that he was a gentle giant and she'd grown quite fond of him.

"Hey, Nikki," he said. "Got a minute?"

"For you? Always."

"Steve told me about that purple pearl he gave you. Think I could see it?"

"Well, I was just headed for town but, okay, I suppose I've got time. Besides, I just can't resist showing it off."

Tugboat followed her and pulled in next door, in front of his fifth wheel trailer. She invited him in, went to her jewelry box, produced the brooch, and handed it to him.

"It's incredible," he said, slack-jawed.

"I know. Would you believe it came from a quahog?"

"Sure. When I was a kid, my mom told me a legend about a quahog pearl like this and that's why I wanted to see it. By the way, the term 'quahog' comes from the Narragansett word, *poquauhock*."

"Ah. So your mom is where you got your Native-American heritage. I'm one-eighth Narragansett, you know."

"Really? That's great, kindred blood. You care to hear the legend?"

Nikki looked at her watch. "I'd love to but I don't know if I have the time."

"Won't take long. You'll love it. Promise."

"Oh, all right. I'll put on some coffee."

Once the coffee was ready, they sat at the dinette. In Tug's ham-like hand, the cup looked like it came from a child's tea party set.

"So tell me," she said, stirring in cream.

"Well, so the story goes, way back, in the late 1600's, a young brave discovered a purple pearl in a quahog shell. It was magnificent: about the size of a marble and an almost perfect sphere. Sound familiar?"

She sat up straight. "Definitely."

"Yeah, huh? Anyway, the young brave had his eye on the *sâchim's* daughter and he needed some way to impress her family in order to win her hand in marriage."

"I guess a purple pearl would work."

"Well, it probably would've, except King Philip's War interrupted things. Overwhelming numbers of English forced the Narragansetts inland. Are you familiar with The Great Swamp Massacre?"

"I've heard of it, yes."

"Well, massacre was right. The English succeeded in the bloody slaughter of some three thousand defenseless Narragansetts: mostly women, children, and elders. Those that weren't killed outright were hunted down and massacred, starved, or sold off as West Indies slaves."

"That's horrific," she said.

" . . . And combined with the diseases the English had brought, the Great Swamp Massacre just about wiped out the Narragansett people. They went from ten thousand strong in 1600 to about five hundred."

"Talk about genocide."

Tug nodded. "Just about, yeah. Mom said it was ironic that while the peace loving, civilized Narragansetts painted their faces, attempting to fool people into thinking they were *savages*—the English *savages* powdered their wigs, attempting to fool people into thinking they were civilized."

"Interesting, but what does all this have to do with the pearl?"

"I was just getting to that. So the legend goes, during the fighting, the brave saved his intended bride from being raped and killed by the English."

"How romantic. Did he give her family the pearl?"

"He probably would have, except for one thing."

"What's that?"

"He lost it."

"You're kidding."

"I kid you not," he said. "To this day, people still wander around in that swamp, hoping to find it. Can you believe that?"

"I suppose, sure. People are always looking to find treasures."

"Anyway, I always figured that pearl was buried under three hundred years worth of muck and no way anybody would ever find it. But now that I've seen your brooch—I'm having second thoughts."

She nibbled at a thumbnail. "What're the odds for two such rare quahog pearls? You think maybe the Colonists found it?"

"Could be."

"Did the brave and the girl ever get married?"

Tug raised his eyebrows, shrugged.

"Wow," Nikki said. "Wouldn't it be something if my pearl is the very same one?"

"You're reading my mind."

She stood up, tossed back the last of her coffee, and put both their cups in the sink, saying, "I really have to get going but thanks for the story. I knew the purple pearl was special but I had no idea it could be the stuff of legends."

He headed back toward his rig.

She straightened up the galley and was just slinging her purse over her shoulder when her cell phone rang. She dug it out and flipped it open. "Hello?"

It was Chief Anderson. "Where the hell are you?"

"I'm on my way," she said. "Give me five minutes."

NIKKI MET the chief in the marina parking lot. On the bay, graceful sailboats tacked back and forth. As usual, a few herring gulls were circling and complaining. She and Frank crossed over to the deli, got sandwiches and soft drinks, and settled at a table with an uninterrupted view.

"Sexy uniform," he said, eyes riveted to her chest.

"Standard Park Ranger," she snapped. "I'm not interested in your opinion of my clothes so you can skip the come on. Now, what do you have to tell me about Marion Hess that's so goddam important?"

He bit into his sandwich and a glob of mustard squirted out onto his chin. Chewing thoughtfully, he said, "We assumed right. The bastard's out."

"Shit. I figured."

"Yeah. Get this: Hess actually got himself a college degree and even got married while he was incarcerated. Played the system," Frank said. He polished off his sandwich, pulled out a cigar and started to light up.

Nikki pointed to the NO SMOKING sign and said, "Please don't."

He flaunted a gremlin-like grin and lit up anyway. That's when she snatched the vile thing out of his mouth and doused it in his soda.

He seethed. "Here's the deal," he said, spitting the words out, evenly spaced. "That pal of mine, that detective in Albuquerque? His name's Manny Garcia. Well, Manny knows Hess is from Rhode Island so, like I told you, he called and gave me the heads up about his parole and the connection to you."

"Me? What connection? What the hell are you talking about?"

"Yeah, you, babe. Way back, seems Hess carved your name in the wall of a holding cell in Albuquerque while he awaited trial. Not only that, but a prison snitch told a bull that word was spreading around the joint that Hess was out to get, and I quote: 'Jezebel Nikki'."

"Jezebel?"

"Yep. Christ, what'd you do to him? I mean, it's been how many years? Man, talk about your long-term obsessions, whoa."

Nikki's skin started to crawl. No wonder that feeling of impending doom had been dogging her.

Frank stood up. "Anyway, condition of parole, he's not supposed to leave New Mexico."

"Who're you trying to kid? You know how overloaded those parole officers are. If he wants to leave, he'll leave."

"Yeah. Well, then, I'd stay on my toes if I were you, babe."

"Dammit Frank, for the umpteenth time, don't call me 'babe'!"

Mystic Fear

"Whatever."
"And Frank?"
"Yeah?"
"You've got mustard on your chin."

CHAPTER 10

HESS REFUELED and bid *adios!* to Albuquerque. To avoid eastern New Mexico, he headed north on I-25, toward Denver. From Denver, he pointed the Winnie eastward on I-80, bound for Lincoln, Nebraska where just about every other car sported a bumper sticker saying: GO BIG RED! The stickers were referring, of course, to the University of Nebraska Cornhusker football team.

Football is everything in Nebraska. In fact, Hess had heard it said that—on any given Saturday in the fall—the football stadium in Lincoln would be the third most populous city in the state. On the other hand, it'd also been said that—on any given winter in Nebraska—life was so boring that the locals had to resort to kicking the tops off of cow pies and watching them steam for entertainment. No wonder they liked football.

But Hess didn't give a rat's ass about football or cow pies because he was in Nebraska for one thing and one thing only: to change identities. He changed highways in Lincoln and continued east to a little hamlet called Palmyra where he wheeled off the highway and drove a few miles over a dirt road out to a farmhouse. Around back loomed a gargantuan, corrugated metal heavy equipment shelter. Hess pulled up and tooted his horn. The mammoth garage door rolled up and he pulled in his RV.

A cadaverous, tattooed Hispanic man sauntered out of the shadows, a fellow Santa Fe prison alumnus and former friend of Snake Taggert. "*Hola,* Hess," said the man, his Latino accent heavy. "So jou finally got the fuck out."

Hess climbed down out of his coach. "Hey, Paco! *Como esta frijole,* how you bean?"

"*Chingase, cabron. Como esta la culebra?*"

"Whoa. I just used up my *espanol,* man. What'd you say?"

"The Snake. How ees Snake Taggert, *puto?*"

"Snake's an asshole. Listen, did you find out what I wanted?"

"Right here, *ese.*" Paco flipped out a notebook. "Nicole O'Connor. Mail address is a post office box in Benedict's Landing,

Rhode Island but she stays in a campground outside of town in a Pace Arrow motorhome on site *numero* feefty-two with her husband, a guy named Steve Marshall. I got her phone number, cell number, her winter address in town, got it all, *compadre*." He laughed and leered. "Jou gonna pork her?"

Hess smirked. "Among other things."

Paco's eyes became thin slits. "Jou got cash?"

Hess pulled an envelope out of his pocket, handed it over. "Courtesy of the former Mrs. Patricia Deeb-Hess."

Paco peered inside, and his lopsided smile returned. "*Bueno.*"

Hess's grin matched Paco's. "I'm assuming you got the other items I requested."

"*Si,* keek back while El Winnebago gets an 'extreme makeover'. I feenish all the paperwork. After you pick disguises, we'll make your new IDs."

Hess had also ordered a short barrel Remington 12-gauge pump, two Browning high-powered 9-mm pistols with a subsonic silencer threaded on one of them, and extra untraceable license plates with registrations.

"I have everythin', but I need details for the vehicle registrations," said Paco.

"Okay. Let's see . . . give me some truck plates for a panel van. Connecticut and Massachusetts will work. And I'll need a couple of car plates, Massachusetts and, say, Ohio, someplace like that. Can you do that?"

"Ees what I do, *ese*."

"I'll need some alternate identities, too."

Paco took him into a room filled with wigs, facial hair, glasses, and outfits.

"Whoa!" exclaimed Hess. He pointed, saying, "Give me that graying ponytail over there: it's perfect. A lot of older guys are wearing those these days. And a matching mustache and goatee, too. Van Dyke style, *amigo*."

"*No problemo, ese*. And for the other ID?"

"Let's try Eye-talian. How about that authentic-looking, curly black wig, over there? The one with distinguished white highlights on the combed-back sides, Paulie Walnuts style. Add a plain black moustache and some of those John Lennon style, wire-rimmed glasses. That should do it."

"Okay."

After Paco had Hess try on the disguises, he took photos for the IDs, and then showed Hess to his room.

"Terrific. Now, what about those other items we discussed?"

"Twenty kilos of marijuana and five kilos of cocaine, *que no*?"

"Correctimundo, Paco. It'll get me started."

"*Bueno.* I almos' forget. A package come here for jou, *ese.* UPS."

"Right. That'd be those magnetic signs I ordered from prison. Jerry's RV Repair."

"RV Repair? Jou going into RV beesness?"

"You might say that, yeah." Hess reached into his pocket, peeled two bills off a thick roll, saying, "You done good, Paco. Here's a little tip for you. Couple a Franklins."

THE FOLLOWING MORNING, Hess borrowed Paco's truck and drove back into Lincoln where he picked up some high tech video and audio equipment, then returned to Palmyra. He kicked back for a few days, while Paco finished up and secured all the requested items. His eye color had been altered from blue to brown, thanks to contacts. And with his quality hairpiece and beard? Why, the old Marion Hess was just about unrecognizable.

By noon, completely transformed into Mr. Karl Meyer, Hess directed his Winnebago onto the I-80 ramp. His RV, now a sleek, clearcoat beige and blue, displayed fresh Nebraska plates, registered to his new alter ego. In the back, he towed a new BMW, black as the Devil's soul and courtesy of Paco's chop shop—for a fee, of course. Good thing Trish had put away a decent nest egg.

Hess/Meyer started humming an old K.C. and The Sunshine Band tune that'd been festering in his mind ever since high school:

That's the way (uh-huh, uh-huh) I LIKE it (uh-huh, uh-huh).

He headed east, driving almost non-stop for the Atlantic coast, or, to be more specific: Rhode Island and the Seabreeze RV Resort and Campground where he was more than anxious to check in.

And complete his missions.

CHAPTER 11

JUNIOR FERGUSON DROVE, for what seemed like the gazillionth time, back to the campground, hoping to find Adrienne LeDoux, yet scared he might. She was wicked gorgeous, he was thinking, but mostly it was that awesome ass of hers, the stuff of wet dreams. Wet dreams? Shit, he hadn't had those in he didn't know how long, not since way back, back before he'd taught himself how to pinch his carrot.

This time, he was in luck and he spotted Adrienne's Camaro, parked near her tent. Embarrassed by his pink minivan, he parked out of sight, and hopped out. Before he could think too much about it, he hopped back in. After spending a couple of minutes screwing up his courage, he got back out and started strutting, peacock style in front of her tent.

He cleared his throat. Loudly.

He sure hoped he looked cool. Wasn't he wearing his baddest cargo pipes? And wasn't the waist slung way low so the pants bunched onto his unlaced Air Jordan high tops? His black *KoRn* (with that cool backwards "R") T-shirt stretched tight across his chest? No way could any healthy chick resist that, right? Besides, hadn't Petey Fottler's niece once tole everyone that Junior's bod looked 'zackly like a rock star's? Wicked macho. And he'd even taken the time to fill all his various piercings with his best zircon collection. How cool was that?

Adrienne crawled out of her tent, shading her eyes from the noontime sun.

Junior stared. *Her hair's spiked up all over the place, all wicked red and sexy.* He knew she couldn't help but see him, but it seemed like she was kind of acting like she didn't.

He turned and sort of swaggered back toward her, treating her to his baddest strut. He cut his eyes to her now and again, as he continued to parade, playing the same game of no-see and flipping his Kurt Cobain hair. The tiny bit of confidence he'd built up started to wither when he remembered how she'd been turned off by his moves in that park ranger's car. He figured she was just pretending, though, right? After all, chicks want it as bad as dudes do, right? Known fact, right? He lifted his chin and energized his strut.

She yawned, stretched, whipped out a compact and applied a thick, fresh coat of black lip gloss and turned her attention to a discarded pizza box lying on the grass.

"Oh, good," she said. "Breakfast." She nibbled at a stale crust of leftover pepperoni.

He leered at her luscious lips, her sexy lipstick, and the pepperoni slick. Working up more courage, he glided over and plopped down next to her.

"You again," she said, looking away.

He stared at the eight earrings in her left ear for a while, cleared his throat. "Like I tole you at the police station," he said. "I 'membered."

She eyeballed him with suspicion. "Remembered what?"

"Where I know you from. You were a bubble gummer. Back then, though, you had like brown hair. Not, uh . . . ."

"Magenta," she said, fluffing it up.

"I knew that," he said. "Anyway, we used to play doctor together."

"No we didn't!"

"Sure we did. When we were kids? I usta give you lotsa physicals. You know, exams?" He knew for sure she remembered when her face turned just about as red as her hair.

"I don't want to talk about it?" she said. "Like, just forget it."

"But—"

"I *said*, forget it. It never happened."

Stung, he reached inside and pulled up his gangsta persona, saying, "Yo, no need to diss me, know what I'm sayin'? Jus' be makin' some small talk here, dawg."

"Dog? Are you for real? Shut up."

"Say what?"

"The homeboy routine? It sucks."

"No way."

"Yeah, way. Big Time."

"Okay, okay. Uh, look, I'm sorry. I won't say nothin' more about the past, I promise."

She sniffed. "Well, that's more like it."

"Can I stay?"

"I guess so."

All right! He stretched out his legs, leaned back on his elbows. Thinking a little small talk might just hit a home run in the ballpark of appropriateness here, he said, "So. You like to camp."

"Duh. What gave you a clue?"

He squirmed. "I think you're awesome," he announced. *Where'd that come from?*

Another huge block of silence hung in the air during which Adrienne chewed at a black polished nail. But she was sort of smiling—a little.

Junior stared at his sneakers, squirmed some more.

She pointed to the greasy pizza box where a bold seagull was helping itself. "Want some?"

He shook his head; he'd really like some, but figured he was on a roll. Don't be a wuss, he thought. *Go for it!* "Wanna hang out at the pool some time?" he blurted. "With me?"

"Are you like . . . asking me out?"

"Yo, dawg. Jus' makin' conversation, hear what I'm sayin'?"

"You're doing it again."

"Doing what again?"

"That homeboy shit? You're starting to piss me off again."

"Sorry." *Oh, man, I'm blowing it here.*

They sat in silence again. "Would you go?" he forced himself to say. "With me? To the pool?"

She lifted her chin. "Maybe."

"Maybe?"

She laughed. "Say 'please'."

What? Fuck I will. "Uh . . . Please?"

"I don't know," she said. "I'll think about it."

It felt like a rock had dropped into his stomach. He looked away.

She giggled. "Just bustin' your chops, here, okay? Sure, I'll go."

"You'll go? You'll actually go?"

"I said I would." She went into the tent and came back out with a slip of paper. "Here's my cell number. Call me in a couple of days if the weather's nice."

Somethin's fishy here. A chick this hot'd never go out with me. He snatched the number and stared at it. "You rilly mean it?" he asked. "Why?"

She shrugged. "Why? Well, I don't know. I like that you're kind of shy, I guess. You seem a little needy but in a way, you're sort of cute."

Cute? "Well," he said, "Lotsa chicks *are* wild about my Kurt Cobain hair."

She laughed. "Kurt Cobain? I don't *think* so."

"What. I got the coolest hair around."

She laughed again, harder. "Yeah, almost as cool as your pink minivan."

He felt blood rushing into his cheeks.

She moved closer. "Would you like to kiss me?"

"Would I!"

She leaned in.

He cupped her face in his hands and pressed his lips to hers, trying to do it just like they did in the movies. He hoped his breath didn't stink, on account of the onions on that Italian grinder he'd snarfed earlier.

After a moment she drew back. "That was nice . . . . "

CHAPTER 12

NIKKI, ALTHOUGH SHAKEN by what Frank had told her about Marion Hess being free, obsessing about her, and vowing to get her, decided not to let the creep live rent-free in her head. She made up her mind to entertain only good thoughts—thoughts of say, gorgeous purple pearls, things like that.

Working outside, patrolling pristine salt marshes and a spectacular coastal view helped some, but eventually, insidious thoughts of Hess wormed their way back into her mind. She even remembered with disgust how Cheri Winkler had once admitted—cute as Marion Hess was—she was pretty sure she saw him eating his boogers in biology class.

Eeech.

Anyway, surely Hess wasn't somehow blaming Nikki for his mom's death, was he? After all, it was only a schoolgirl prank, for God's sake. His freaky mom was the one that had gone off on Nikki, not the other way around. Besides, his mom had passed away much later.

Nikki's cell phone trilled, rescuing her from her thoughts. It was Petey Fottler, wanting her to stop by the gatehouse. When she got there, Petey came to the door, mouth full, with a bowl and a spoon in his hand.

"What's in the bowl?" she asked, half-expecting Chinese food.

"Pfloonz."

"What?"

He swallowed, cleared his throat. "Prunes."

"Prunes?"

He nodded. "Man who eat prunes, get run for money."

She laughed. "Good one. So . . . what's up?"

"Only way to catch tiger is to go into tiger's den," he said.

"Translate, please."

"Got a park ranger job for ya."

"Okay."

"Turkey Kielbasa. He's at the pool and doing it again."

She rolled her eyes. "I'm on my way."

TURKEY KIELBASA was the nickname the campers had given to an aging hippie type who liked public attention. He drove a urine-colored '51 Nash Rambler. On the bumper, a sticker claimed he was a freelance gynecologist. The car was easy to find, prominent in the swimming pool parking lot.

One of the campers, a friend of Nikki's, was eyeballing the car when Nikki pulled alongside. Two toddlers were pulling at her friend's hands, anxious to get to the pool.

"Hi, Nikki," the woman said. She pointed. "You believe that bumper sticker?"

"I know, huh? It belongs to one Tommy Frederick, an infamous character from Benedict's Landing. He must've snuck in because he's been banned from here. Banned from the state beaches, too."

"What for?"

"Indecent exposure."

Her friend raised her eyebrows. "Oh, really. Why doesn't the man go find himself a nudist colony somewhere? Or go to Weenie Waggers Anonymous, something like that?"

Nikki laughed. "Well, he doesn't actually go the Full Monte."

"No? So what's the problem?"

"The problem is his swim suit. It's one of those thongs, you know? Basically, a flimsy little pouch where he stows most of his goodies."

"Most?"

"Well, yes, because part of him kind of, uh, *squeezes* out around the edges. You don't want details."

"I think you just gave me too many."

"And get this," Nikki added, "the pouch is more than full. Everybody's wondering what he's got in there. Couldn't be all Tommy. Nobody's *that* well endowed."

Her friend snickered. "You don't say."

Nikki nodded. "Some people are saying his package is augmented with a good-sized chunk of Polish sausage."

"Get out."

"Yep, hence the name: Turkey Kielbasa."

After bidding good-bye to her friend, Nikki marched straight into the pool area, rousted her miscreant, and escorted him out of the campground. With threats of calling the police next time.

And with all the excitement revolving around Mr. Turkey Kielbasa, Nikki hadn't given Marion Hess one thought.

Not for a whole fifteen minutes.

BY THE END of her shift, she was exhausted—physically and mentally. Steve must've divined this, because when she got home, he had a hot bubble bath ready for her. Andrea Bochelli was singing softly on the stereo.

Lights were dimmed; in fact, lighting was strictly by candlelight.

Oboy.

He presented her robe and a glass of wine, saying, "Hop into the tub and have a good soak. When you're relaxed and ready, I'll be waiting. After that, I'm sure we'll be famished so I'm treating for lobster at the Mariner's Bar and Grill."

Well, she certainly didn't need an engraved invitation but it wasn't too long before she relaxed enough to realize what she *really* needed wasn't a good soak. She got out, toweled off, misted a little strategic *Estee Lauder* on, ran a toothbrush over her teeth, bolted out the door and leaped into bed, *au natural.*

She snuggled close to Steve's warm body. He smelled wonderful. Reaching down, she found him ready, then moved slowly beneath the sheet, kissing her way downward.

"That's what I like about you," he said. "You're so subtle."

AN HOUR LATER, happily sated and starving, Steve and Nikki drove straight into Benedict's Landing to the Mariner's Bar and Grill for the house special: fantastic baked, stuffed lobster. She wore her new black Diamond-V sleeveless dress and the Via Spiga shoes—the ones she practically had to take out a small business loan for. Of course, she also wore her lovely new antique brooch.

As soon as they slid into their booth, she turned to him. "Thank you so much for this," she said, fingering the purple pearl. "Everyone's noticing."

He laughed.

"What's so funny?"

"Well, the women might be looking at the brooch, but not the guys. Trust me."

"Huh?"

"All the guys—including me—are all eyeballing your figure. In that sexy dress."

CHAPTER 13

AN OBLATE TANGERINE sun had just about cleared the treetops the following morning as Marion Hess eased his motorhome up to the gatehouse at the Seabreeze RV Resort and Campground.

"Help you?" asked the attendant

"Hello," said Hess, offering up a cordial smile. "I'd like a site for three days, if possible."

"Sure."

The gatehouse man grabbed a registration slip, clipped it to a clipboard and handed it over. Hess decided against writing down his new Karl Meyer alter ego. The name Phil Jackson popped into his head so he scribbled that down, along with phony details and handed it back.

The attendant studied it. "Thanks. Uh, Phil Jackson? You coach a little basketball?" he said dryly.

"Yeah, real funny," said Hess.

"Bet you get that all the time, huh? Sorry. Anyway, that'll be $120."

"Whoa! That's a bit steep isn't it?"

The gatehouse man shrugged. "Yeah, but hey, it's right on the bay."

"Could I see a map of what sites are available?"

"Sure." The attendant handed Hess a map with the open sites circled.

"How about number forty-eight, there?" asked Hess, selecting a site close to Nikki and her dipshit husband.

"Forty-eight it is."

Hess paid, in cash. "By the way," he said. "How's security in here?"

"Well, we got a park ranger. She lives over in site sixty-two. In fact, that'd be catty-corner to where you'll be staying."

"She?" asked Hess. "A woman ranger?"

"Yeah, but she's good at the job. Damn good looking, too. But newly married."

"Well, I feel safer already," said Hess. He headed into the campground where he trundled his motorhome around a curve and up a small hill to his spot. After he unhooked the BMW dolly, he backed in, leveled his coach, and hooked up to the water and electric. He looked over to site sixty-two and sure enough, there was a Pace-Arrow sitting there.

Once he finished setting up, he threw some of the items he'd gotten from Paco into the trunk of the BMW and headed back out of the campground and upstate, up Route 2 toward Warwick where there was supposed to be plenty of car lots on Bald Hill Road. On the way, he happened to pass by a grungy bar where there a white panel van stood out in the parking lot.

The van was for sale. *Outfuckingstanding!*

Hess slammed on his brakes. He U-turned, whipped into the parking lot, and crunched across the clamshell lot—trying not to run over any broken beer bottles. He parked, hopped out, and peered at the cardboard sign in the windshield of the van. In Magic Marker it read:

FOR SALE
'89 CHEVEY VAN. LO MILES. SEE BARTINDER IN TOADS.

Hess locked his car. With the for sale sign tucked under his arm, he headed for the bar. An impotent neon Narragansett Beer logo hung over the entrance and a hand-hewn sign rested just below it. Roughly scrawled in huge block letters, the sign said:

PEEP TOAD'S LOUNGE

The door, once painted electric red, was peeling and fading. Inside, a fog of air-conditioned cigarette smoke greeted Hess and even though it was now August, cheesy Christmas decorations still adorned the walls. The bar reeked of decades of spilled beer, lighting ranked somewhere between poor and non-existent, and recycled hubcaps served as ashtrays. A mangy Yellow Lab snoozed in front of the bar. Squadrons of flies busied themselves, investigating the dog's scabby hindquarters.

"What can I get ya?" asked the bartender, his Yankee accent raspy and palpable.

"Bottle of Michelob Dry," said Hess.

The only other bar patron chuckled. "Not in here, you won't," he said.

The bartender nodded. "We only serve draft, Rolling Rock, or somethin' like that," he said.

"Never mind," said Hess. He handed over the FOR SALE sign. "How much?"

"It's a good van. I'll need eight lodge."

"Eight large? Bullshit."

"Take seven."

"Four," said Hess.

"You shit, mistah. Six."

Hess smiled. "Five."

"No way, asshole. Five and a half."

Hess peeled off the bills, saying, "Done."

The bartender reached under the bar, pulled out a beer-stained legal pad, ripped off a fresh page, scratched out a hasty bill of sale, and signed it. He handed over the keys.

Hess examined the bill of sale and pocketed it. "You Peep Toad?"

The bartender guffawed until it mutated into a croupy bark. "No way, buddy. Hell, The Toad weighs about foah hundred pounds. Last time I looked, I tipped the scales at about one-eighty. Besides, some say The Toad might not even be a guy."

"Peep Toad is a woman?"

"Hod to tell."

Hess eased his way past the mangy lab. It rose, circled about itself three times before settling back down and chuffing out a sigh that made its serrated lips flutter.

Back in the parking lot, Hess popped the trunk of his BMW, pulled out his three "Jerry's RV Repair" logos, and affixed one on each side and the back door of his newly purchased van. After he screwed on his Massachusetts truck plates, he called and long-distanced the details to Paco.

"*Bueno, ese*," said Paco. "I weal put the registration in overnight mail."

Mystic Fear

With all those little details accomplished, Hess got into the van and headed back south to the campground. On the way, he temporarily removed his hairpiece and goatee and pulled a grimy John Deere ball cap low on his forehead. He donned dark glasses with huge lenses, popped a putrid-smelling cigar into his mouth, and figured no one could possibly recognize him. To top it off, Hess also had a clipboard with a phony invoice he'd prepared on a library computer.

At the gatehouse, the attendant ambled out.

This shitbird has *no* idea I'm the same guy that just checked in as Phil Jackson, thought Hess. There was a hum as the van window slid down, just enough for him to proffer the clipboard. "Repair job," he grunted, making his voice sound infused with gravel.

The gatehouse man peered at the clipboard. "Site eighty-eight? Do you know how to find it?"

Hess blew out a toxic cloud of cigar smoke. "No problem," he grunted.

The attendant backed away, fanned at the air. "G'head on in, then."

Smiling with satisfaction, Hess cruised forward, pitching out the cigar along the way. But instead of going to site eighty-eight, he drove straight for Nikki's Pace-Arrow motorhome. No one was home yet. *Outfuckingstanding!* He pulled in front, hopped out, and in no time, lock-picked his way inside. Once inside, he secreted tiny web-cams in strategic places.

Satisfied with his work, he boogied to his van, and sped out of the campground—headed back to Peep Toad's.

IN THE GRUNGY bar's parking lot, Hess got rid of the cap and transformed back into his Karl Meyer persona, snugging down his gray ponytail wig and pasting on his beard. He hopped out, removed the magnetic logos, locked up the van, crunched over the shells and strolled back into the bar. The mangy lab, still in the same position on the floor, eyeballed Hess, but this time didn't bother to raise its head.

"No refunds," said the bartender.

Hess smiled. "Not asking for one. I just wondered, think it'd be okay if I left the van parked in your lot for a few days?"

The bartender narrowed his eyes, pursed his fleshy mouth.

Hess broadened his smile. "Just while I take care of some business, man. A few days, that's all."

The bartender shrugged. "I guess. G'head."

"Thanks. I believe I'll have one of those Rolling Rocks now. By the way, you happen to know of any high school boys who're looking for work?"

"No."

"Just asking. I need some cheap manual labor."

A couple of beers later, Hess stood outside, relieved to be out of the air-conditioned smoke, sour beer stench, and canine flatulence. He slid behind the wheel of his BMW and drove back to the campground.

Mission one?

. . . accomplished.

CHAPTER 14

MOST OF NIKKI'S day had been spent checking to see if campers were sneaking gray water out of their holding tanks via secret hoses buried in the grass and warning them to cut it out. It was against campground rules but, so far, hadn't ever been enforced. She could see why, since gray water is non-septic and biodegradable, so no harm, no foul. Still, campground management wanted it done.

The problem with that, it gave her too much time to think. Hess had been commandeering a lot less of her head time but she knew she needed to tell her husband about him. She wondered why she'd been avoiding it. She supposed it was because she didn't want to upset Steve, burden him. He needed to know, though. He should be warned so he could be on guard, too.

The sun was setting, as if sliding into the bay when she got home. A full moon had just popped over the eastern horizon, looking both gigantic and romantic. The lighthouse across the bay winked and, in the distance, she could hear the ever-present clanging buoy. She was looking forward to a quiet evening with her lover and felt all fuzzy inside when she thought once again about how they'd made love last night and how much she adored the brooch he'd given her.

Something about that purple pearl was so . . . compelling.

Her reverie was short-circuited by that psycho, Marion Hess, once again intermittently diddling her thoughts. She decided she'd definitely have to tell Steve tonight. But inside the RV, her attention was diverted by dimmed lights, lit candles, and an iced bottle of champagne. Champaign? Steve didn't drink.

"Uh-oh," she said. "Is this *déjà vu*? Looks like yet another seduction in progress here."

Steve popped out of the galley, his smile expansive. "I've charcoaled some swordfish steaks and made a Caesar salad."

"I'm speechless."

"No you're not," he said. "No way, ever."

"Very funny. So what's the occasion? I thought we sort of celebrated last night."

He pulled the champagne from the ice, popped the cork, poured a glass, and handed it to her, saying, "I've got stupendous news."

"Won't this tempt you to drink?" she asked.

"No. I've got some grape juice here for me."

"Well? . . . What's the news?"

"Oh, nothing much . . . .." He looked smug.

She set the champagne on a table and punched him playfully, saying, "Out with it."

He laughed. "Okay, okay. No need for violence here. I won a little money in the Mass lottery, is all."

Her heartbeat quickened. "You did? How much?"

Steve's eyes danced. "Not much. Just $250 *thousand*."

She felt her eyes going wide. "Oh my God!"

Steve grabbed her up in a bear hug, swung her around, saying, "Yes, ma'am! And that's why we're celebrating. I wanted to wait until I had the actual check to tell you. I just deposited it in our joint account."

They started kissing and he carried her into the bedroom, luckily a very short distance in a motorhome. Sinbad, her gigantic feline, happened to be napping on the comforter. He scrambled for safety when they flopped on the bed.

Once they'd stripped off most of each other's clothing, she straddled Steve, reached back and unclasped her bra, saying, "Okay, Mr. Moneybags—I'm going to show you how to celebrate and do the job right."

He drew her toward him. "You talking about swordfish and salad?"

"I have something else in mind."

"Right. Let's get you out of those panties then and see what else is on the menu."

SOME TIME LATER, spent, showered, and ready to dive into the swordfish, they made it to the galley. Nikki showcased her new brooch on her bathrobe.

Steve laughed. "Goes well with that outfit."

"Doesn't it? Donna Karan, eat your heart out." She started dishing out the salad while he seared and reheated the swordfish in an iron skillet. Her first glass of champagne had gone flat so he poured her a new one.

"Dom Perignon?" she said. "I'm impressed."

"*Dom Perignon moet et Chandon a Epernay 1985,*" he said, managing to keep a straight face.

"Expensive?"

"Naw. Only $170 a bottle."

She took a sip, nodded in appreciation. "Big bucks, but what the hell, right?"

He reached for his grape juice. "Toast?"

"Toast," she said, holding her own up. "Here's to the Mass lottery."

They clinked glasses. He took a sip. "Life is good."

"I'll say. Here we are: happily together on the waterfront in a lovely new motorhome and now we're rich."

He looked at her brooch. "Let's just say we're more economically comfortable. But don't forget your purple pearl there. It might be worth some beans. Did you ever hear back from that antique jewelry expert in Newport?"

"No. I'll call her tomorrow and—"

Then, from out of nowhere, Hess crashed into her consciousness—unbidden and insidiously. She got a sinking feeling in her stomach and her heart started to pound. Her face must have given her away because Steve noticed.

"What's the matter?" he said.

Even though she'd definitely decided to tell him, she was hesitant to destroy his euphoria so she got out of her chair, sashayed over, and sat in his lap, saying, "Nothing. Nothing at all. Um, are you serving seconds?"

"There's no more swordfish," he said. "But I think there's a little Caesar left and plenty of champ—"

She interrupted him by untying her bathrobe and letting it fall open. "That's not the kind of seconds I had in mind."

"I guess not."

They headed back into the bedroom, discarding their robes on the way and, once again, Sinbad was forced to beat a hasty retreat.

Later, in the middle of the night she woke up, dreaming of Hess.

And glazed donuts—enough to make you throw up.

NIKKI WAS ALREADY sitting at the dinette, ready for work before Steve got up. Sinbad meowed, purred, and threaded a figure eight about her legs. She lingered over a mug of coffee and thought about her dream. It'd been a long time since she'd dreamed about making herself sick on donuts and that worried her.

Time was, she reacted to stress by craving sweets and obsessing about overeating and then purging but she thought she was over all that because it hadn't been an issue since she'd met Steve.

Maybe not anymore.

She shook her head, finished her coffee, fed her cat and got dressed. When she once again had trouble buttoning the top button of her uniform slacks, she decided on a penance breakfast of half an unbuttered English muffin and a tangerine.

Steve stumbled into the kitchen and poured himself a huge mug of coffee. "Woman," he said, "You wore me out last night."

She called him a wuss.

Still, he must have guessed right away that joking around wasn't what was on her mind. He sat down. A look of concern creased his brow.

"What," he said, his voice soft. "Something's wrong."

Again, she toyed with not burdening him but broke down and told him everything: what Hess had done, how he was out on parole, and how he'd been obsessing about her in prison; in fact, obsessing about her since high school.

"Jesus. Let me get this straight: this psycho murdered two women?"

"Only convicted of one. There was an evidence problem but everyone agrees he killed both. Maybe even more, who knows?"

Steve's voice started keening. "But even though he's paroled, he's still in New Mexico, right?"

She shrugged. "As far as I know, but I need to make some calls out there. And you be careful, too. Just in case."

"I'll be fine." He consulted his watch. "Shit, I gotta get going." He got up and rushed into the bedroom to get dressed. As he eased out the front door, he said, "Let me know what you find out." Then he looked her up and down, grinned.

"What," she said.

"Nothing. Just thinking that it's no wonder guys obsess about you."

Her mood lightened a bit. She posed seductively. "Why, because I'm such a bombshell?"

"No, because of that sexy park ranger uniform."

She laughed. "Go on, get out of here."

They shared a passionate kiss and he headed to his truck. She watched him drive away, thinking how much she loved him and how lucky she was to be married to him. She started tidying up. When she went to hang up her robe, she noticed the brooch and that reminded her to call the antique jewelry woman in Newport.

She admired it for a moment or so before unclasping it and storing it in her jewelry box.

Next, she logged onto the computer, thinking she'd e-mail her daughter and let her in on the good news about Steve winning the lotto. Not only that, but she hadn't told Erin about the purple pearl yet.

She mindfully ate her last slice of tangerine, typed Erin a windy message, sent it and clicked on new mail. After deleting a few ads, she read a couple of forwarded jokes before she came upon a message from someone called ETERNALHEART222.

Fearing viruses, she always deleted messages from unknown sources but the 222 sounded familiar and piqued her interest. She figured what the hell and clicked it.

"TRU LOVE NEVER DIES," read the text, in bold caps.

She frowned. True love never dies? And who the hell is ETERNALHEART222?

Probably some lonely-hearts miscue that ended up in her mailbox, she guessed—but Hess also came to mind. Couldn't be him, though, could it? She decided to find out so she picked up the phone and dialed information.

"What city, please?"

"Albuquerque. Could I have the number for the police?"

"One moment, please . . . . "

The desk sergeant answered. She told him who she was and that she needed to talk to a Detective Manny Garcia.

"What is this regarding, ma'am?"

"It's about a convict who was recently paroled from the state pen."

The sergeant put her through and a male voice answered: "Homicide. Detective Garcia."

Once more, she explained who she was and added that she was a friend of Chief Anderson, and what Frank had told her about Hess.

"Yeah," Garcia said. "Like I told Frank, that slimeball's out, alright. And now, it looks like he skipped."

"Don't tell me that."

"You should talk to Hess's P.O.; the man probably has more information than me. His name is Runyan. Once you talk to him, get back to me and I'll bring you up to speed on our end." He gave her Runyan's number.

She copied it down, thanked him, and dialed the parole officer.

"Rob Runyan," he answered. "How can I help you?"

She introduced herself and said Garcia suggested she call.

"Well, I'm afraid I have some bad news for you," said Runyan. "Hess checked in with me but I haven't seen him or heard from him since. I have to assume he flew the coop so I notified the police. He met a woman named Patricia Deeb while he was in prison. They sent letters back and forth. After just a couple of months, they got married."

"Really. I can't understand it but I've heard about such marriages. Wonder what makes a woman so desperate?"

"Who knows, but it happens more than you'd think."

"Go figure."

"Yeah, well, Hess *is* a master manipulator. Plus, he's real good looking and can be charming, part of his con."

"Like Ted Bundy."

"Right. Anyway, Deeb picked him up when he got out. He was supposed to live with her at her place in Rio Rancho. He told me he got a job at a gas station off Coors Boulevard here in Albuquerque. Hess was pretty convincing that he was turning the leaf, you know?"

"And that was it?"

"Yep. When he failed to show for his next appointment, I drove over to Rio Rancho. The house had been sold. Neighbors told me Deeb was one of those evangelical religious fanatics so I checked at her church, talked to her friends."

"Anything come of that?"

"Turns out, Deeb sold her house, cleaned out her bank account, and bought a motorhome. All that, some time before Hess's release. She got a pretty penny for the house, too. Big spread, good location."

Nikki's pulse quickened; she could feel it throbbing in her temples. "That means . . ."

"Well," said Runyan, "like I said, I notified the police. They've issued warrants but I don't think anything has turned up yet. Detective Garcia would know more about that."

She thanked him, hung up, and called Garcia back. "Detective? It's Nikki O'Connor again, Chief Anderson's friend? Hess's P.O. says Hess skipped. Says you guys got a warrant out?"

"We do. Listen, did Frank tell you how your name came up?"

"Yes. My maiden name: O'Connor. And believe me, I'm concerned."

"If you don't mind my asking, how come Hess is so obsessed with you, anyway?"

"Ah," she said. "It's along story but would you believe some girlfriends and I played a prank on him back in high school? His mother died right after that and, apparently, he's had a fixation on me ever since."

"Prank, huh? Well, you should know that the prick—pardon my French—carved your name on the wall in the holding cell before his trial."

"So Frank told me. Speaking of his trial, did Hess's lawyers present the insanity defense?"

"Naw. No doubt Hess is a pathological sociopath, though."

"Well," she said, "they could've used his mental history from Rhode Island, right? Beef up the defense? Hess probably should've been housed with the criminally insane."

"Couldn't agree more. But you know public defenders. Anyway, the reason I was able to remember your name so well is that when Hess chiseled it, it was surrounded by a bloody heart, there in the stucco plaster. Thing is, I'm talking *real* blood, his blood."

"My God, how gruesome."

"And," added the detective, "there was this dagger carved too, through the heart. With actual drops of blood coming off it, his blood."

Nikki's heart fluttered in her chest like a trapped bird. She struggled to sound calm. "Nice image."

"'Course, lots a skells scratch women's' names in the wall, you know?"

"In their own blood?"

"Well, uh, no . . . .."

"Yeah, and Frank also told me the word in prison was that Hess was out to get me."

"Yeah," Garcia said. "There's that, too."

"Anyway, what now?"

"Well, along with the warrant, we sent out both Hess's and Deeb's pictures. I've been trying to track down the plate number for Deeb's motorhome but it looks like she never registered it."

Nikki's pulse kicked into overdrive and a niggling sensation of panic plucked at her nervous system. "Shit, he's on the move, had this plan pre-packaged before he got out."

"Yeah, looks that way. Give me your phone number. I'll keep you posted on any developments. Do you have a fax? I'll make sure you get his picture."

She gave him all her numbers, thanked him, and hung up. She thought about calling Steve and updating him but decided it wasn't urgent just yet. She could tell him later.

And with Hess *really* diddling in her thoughts, she went to work.

CHAPTER 15

JUNIOR FERGUSON couldn't believe his good fortune. Here he was, at the swimming pool with the chick of his dreams! He and Adrienne scurried to their respective dressing rooms to change. Once he'd stowed his clothes in a locker, he scrambled into his makeshift swimsuit: a pair of cut off Levis. Back outside, he spotted his new magenta-haired squeeze, already poolside.

"Awesome," he said to himself, appreciating how *hot* she looked in her skimpy pink bikini.

She waved and glided over.

He gulped, figuring he'd better hurry into the pool because he was starting to get a woodie.

She must've noticed because she covered her mouth, giggled, and said, "Well, hello there!"

"Cannonballs?" She asked.

He nodded and, holding hands, they ran together and leaped into the pool, performing tandem splashes. They surfaced to the shrill blast of a lifeguard's whistle.

"No running!" the guard yelled. "And *no* cannonballs!"

Later, after they'd toweled off and were sunning themselves, Junior turned to Adrienne, saying, "I can't believe this."

"What?"

"Us. Here. You and me."

She laughed. "Well, it's true. Here we are."

"But you're this . . . this awesome *college* chick, you know?"

"And you? What are your plans?"

He tried to cook up a decent lie, but couldn't think of one. No way was he going to tell her he hadn't graduated yet and had to go to summer school. "Ah, I'm just, like, hanging out, you know? Enjoying the summer."

"Do you have a job?"

"Not rilly. Sometimes Freddie calls me up to deliver pizzas, is all."

She chuckled. "With your mom's minivan?"

He frowned. "Yeah. Shit."

Unexpectedly, she leaned over and kissed his cheek. "Well, Junior, I don't care. I think you're kind of cute and you don't seem as full of yourself as most of the guys I meet."

He beamed. "Yeah, well, I guess what you see is pretty much what you get."

"What're you doing tonight?" she asked. "Got any plans?"

"Not rilly."

"Good. You want to do a sleepover? You like to camp out?"

"Like, in your tent?"

"Duh. You got a sleeping bag?"

"Nunh-uh," he said.

"That's okay. You can share mine."

"What? . . . You? . . . Clam Doggies!"

"I thought you'd like that."

LATER THAT NIGHT, in her tent, they lay on her sleeping bag, kissing and undressing each other. Junior couldn't believe this was happening, wasn't a dream. He lunged at her, groped her breasts and started a little involuntary leg humping.

"Whoa," she said. "Slow down, take it easy."

"Sorry." He backed off and rolled onto his back. He was panting, couldn't help it.

"Do you have protection?" she asked. When he didn't answer, she snapped on a small flashlight and plucked a condom from her purse. Wide-eyed, he watched while she tore open the packet. Reaching over, she curled a hand around him and gave him a quick stroke.

Junior moaned, thinking: uh-oh. He gritted his teeth.

She started to roll the condom on.

He set his jaw and tried biting his tongue but it didn't work and he ejaculated, spurting in great, pulsing ropes.

"Whoa," she said. "You're a virgin, aren't you?"

In the dim light, he looked at the mess and watched, embarrassed, while his manhood deflated. "How can you tell?" he croaked.

She snuggled up. "Don't worry. In no time, you'll be ready to go again and we'll fix that."

And she was right . . . before long, he was hard again.

"Told you," she said.

DAYLIGHT FOUND Junior's woodie laminated against Adrienne's warm backside. But today, it wasn't your typical morning wood he sported, no sir. *This* boner was now your official, *non-virginal* hardwood! He pestered her with it until she stirred.

She turned to him. "Well," she said sleepily as her hand searched. "What have we here?"

CHAPTER 16

NIKKI DROVE AROUND the campground sometime about mid-day, doing her rounds. As she patrolled, she happened across Junior Ferguson's mom's pink minivan, parked by the salt marsh. Thinking he might be up to his usual antics of copping shellfish in a restricted area, she parked and went looking for him.

She found him, but he wasn't digging clams. That gothic girl with the wild hair was alongside him, what was her name? Adrienne? Yeah, Adrienne LeDoux. The two were holding hands and strolling along the nature path. Could this be budding puppy love? Junior lagged a shade behind, ogling the girl's petite rear end, which, Nikki supposed, was very ogleable. Ogleable. Was that even a word? Well, thought Nikki, maybe she'll keep Junior's mind off illegal fishing. At least, some of the time.

Nikki completed a circuit of the campground and then stopped by home to grab a bite, feed her cat and check her e-mail. Sinbad, World-Class Chowcat, started manipulating for food right away so she fed him first before fixing herself half of a ham sandwich on rye. While she munched, she logged on the computer and brought up her mail.

She stared at the old message from ETERNALHEART222. *What is it about that number?*

Wait, she thought. What's this? One new message.

Just as she feared: ETERNALHEART222.

She opened it:

DID YOU ENJOY THE DOM PERIGNON?
NAKED, YOU ARE A DELICIOUS LITTLE CUNNY

Her mind raced. Sweat broke out on her forehead, and her hands started to shake. *Dom Perignon? Naked?* Hess just had to be the e-mail ETERNALHEART222, just had to be. And he was right here in the campground. The bastard had been *spying* on her while she and Steve made love last night! She looked around. No way he could have seen in the windows, they were too high off the ground. Besides, the blinds had been drawn. What, then? A goddam video camera?

She started searching and when she unscrewed the bedroom air conditioner vent, she found one: a compact and ugly little thing—reminding her of a miniature robotic alien. She searched the remaining vents and discovered that the slimy pervert had also secreted web cams in the living room and even in the bathroom. How utterly sick and disgusting.

At first, she felt sick to her stomach at the violation, the rape of her privacy, but then, like a flash, the anger hit. She ripped all the cameras out with pliers, took them outside, and smashed them to smithereens with a hammer. Out of breath and still shaking, she grabbed the phone and jabbed in the number for the town police and demanded to be put through to the chief.

"Frank?" she shouted, when he came on the line. She realized her voice sounded hysterical but didn't care.

"Nikki? What's wrong?"

"That bastard Hess is here in Rhode Island! He bugged our RV with some goddam video cameras. At least, someone did, and I'm guessing it was him."

"I'll send a car right out. No, wait. Belay that. I'll come myself."

"I, um . . . I kind of lost it," Nikki admitted, once she'd calmed a little. "I ripped out the evidence and smashed it with a hammer."

"Whoa," he said.

"Anyway, I've got to get away from here. I'll leave the key with Clyde Haywood, my neighbor on the left."

"Okay, babe."

No sooner had she slammed the phone down when it rang again. She picked up, snarled a hello.

"Uh, could I please speak to Ms. Nicole O'Connor?"

"Who wants to know?"

"Detective Garcia here. From Albuquerque?"

"Oh, hi, Detective. This is Nikki. Sorry for the rude hello. Please tell me you've got some good news."

"Well, no, sorry. We haven't caught up with Hess yet but we found Patricia Deeb."

"Hess's jailhouse bride. She help you?"

"Unfortunately," he said, "she's not talking. A traveler walking his dog found her in an arroyo by a picnic area off I-40, just west of Santa Rosa. Hess and the desert animals did a number on Deeb but the M.E. said the initial cause of death was a stab wound to the abdomen."

Nikki sucked in her breath. "Oh my God."

"That's not all. Her female body parts were, uh . . . mutilated."

Nikki felt faint, her voice caught in her throat. "Mutilated?"

"Uh, gouged out, chopped up, bitten . . . you don't want to know. *Very* Sick."

"Bitten? You sure the desert animals didn't do it?"

"Not initially. Human animal did this and a blade was also used, a butcher knife."

Nikki was silent.

"Mrs. O'Connor? You still there?"

". . . Yes."

"Frank told me that you're a park ranger. You carry a weapon?"

"No."

"Any experience with one?"

"Well, when I attended the St. Louis Police Academy, I shot expert at the range. Been a while, though."

"Well," the detective said, "I suggest you arm yourself, keep it handy." *Click.*

ONCE SHE'D COMPOSED herself, Nikki grabbed her purse, locked up, and got the hell out of there. She dropped off her keys with Tugboat, told him what had happened, and that the police would be by soon. On the way out of the campground, she stopped at the gatehouse.

"Did anyone unusual come in while you were working the gate?" she asked the attendant.

"Unusual? What do you mean?"

"You know, non-campers. Deliveries, repair vans, plumbers, like that?"

"Not that I remember," he said. "But someone said an RV repair truck came in yesterday. You know, Dirty Ernie might've seen it. He was here pumping out the dump station and servicing a few campers. In fact, he's still up there today. Why don't you ask him?"

"I'll do that. Thanks."

She swung a U-turn and sped back into the campground where she soon spotted the infamous septic truck by the main bathhouse. She drove over to it, parked, and got out.

Signs proclaiming WHITTEMORE SEPTIC SERVICES, INC. decorated each potbellied side of the truck and a back bumper extolled the benefits of a pumpout by announcing that his flush beat your full house. On each of the cab's side doors, it read: ERNEST P. WHITTEMORE, PROPRIETOR

Ernie, affectionately called "Dirty Ernie" by the campers, was the official campground septic pumpout guy. Every week, he arrived with his smelly truck to service those campers who chose not to do their own dumping and also pump out the dump station.

As usual, Dirty Ernie's job dog, a white-muzzled black Labrador retriever named Mike, accompanied him. Mike and Ernie were inseparable. Ernie considered Mike a business consultant, owing to the fact that the lab had sniffed so much sewage in his twelve years on the job. Then again, so had Dirty Ernie.

They were pumping out the bathhouse septic tank when Nikki approached. Ernie manhandled the cumbersome hose while Mike supervised.

"Hey there," said Ernie. He beamed.

Mike barked. His tongue lolled while he happily sampled the air, in olfactory heaven.

Nikki went over, patted the dog's head. "Smells good, huh?"

Mike flagged his tail.

She turned to Ernie. "I see you're standing upwind. Good idea."

He snorted. "Yeah, huh? But it don't matter none. I've whiffed so much shit that someone could sit on my face an' fart an' it'd be a breath a fresh air."

She laughed and it felt cleansing after what she'd just gone through. "Dirty Ernie," she said. "Always a class act."

"That's me. What can I do for you? Your rig need a pumpout?"

"No. Just a question. Did you see an RV repair truck in here yesterday?"

"Sure did. White one. Jerry's RV Repair. Why, didn't he get the job done?"

She felt her eyes widen. "Excuse me?"

"Your rig's problem," said Ernie. "Didn't the guy fix it?"

She blinked. "The repair truck was at our motorhome?"

"Uh, yeah."

"We didn't call for any repairs. Did you get a look at the guy?"

"Not really. He was pretty far away and I wasn't paying much attention. Sorry."

"Yeah, why would you? Anyway, thanks."

She got back into her vehicle and as she started away, she glanced at Dirty Ernie's pot-bellied truck again, with that back bumper telling everyone that his flush beat your full house. On the way out, she stopped once more at the gatehouse, got Petey Fottler's phone number from the gatehouse guy, and called him at home.

Petey answered right away. "H'lo."

"Petey? It's Nikki. Sorry to bother you, but I need to know, did you—"

"Cheap things are of no value; valuable things are not cheap," he quipped, interrupting.

"What? Knock off the Fortunese, this is serious. Did you happen to see an RV repair guy in the campground yesterday?"

"Wise man say—"

"I *said* cut it out!"

"Okay, okay," he said. "Don't get your panties in a bunch. RV repair? Yeah, come to think of it, I did see a panel truck with Jerry's RV Repair on it. He was on his way out, though, so we din't talk. I think the Carlsons were having trouble with their fridge, weren't they?"

"No, they fixed it. They've been gone, up to The Cape for over a week."

"Journey of many miles start with single step."

She did a mental eye roll. "Don't start again. Did you get a look at the repair guy?"

"Looks may be deceiving," replied Petey.

"Ixnay on the damn fortunese! Would you remember him if you saw a picture of him?"

"Not sure. He had on big, dark shades and a ball cap. I couldn't see him too good. Come to think of it, though, one of the other campers asked me if you guys had RV problems. Said they saw that repair truck at your place, too."

"Thanks, Petey."

Wondering if Chief Anderson was still at her and Steve's motorhome, she sped over there. This time, Steve's truck was in the drive. He came out to meet her, give her a hug.

"I thought you were out on your boat," she said. "Listen, Hess—"

"I know all about it," he said, interrupting. "Tugboat called me. I was just finishing up so I steamed home. The police were still here; Tug had let our illustrious chief and his gorillas in to do their thing. I saw the wrecked video stuff, by the way. You did quite a number on it."

"I feel so violated," she said.

"If that bastard even comes near you, I'll kill him."

"What if he's armed?"

"You've got a point," said Steve. "Maybe we ought to get a gun."

"Maybe. Right now I have to go over to the campground office. I'm expecting a fax."

"Right," he said. "I'll clean up here. See you later."

At the office, her fax had come in. True to his word, that Albuquerque detective had sent head and shoulder shots of Marion Hess and Patricia Deeb. Actually, despite his evil nature, Hess looked even handsomer than she remembered, even with one of those awful prison haircuts. In fact, it wasn't hard to imagine how those innocent young women, his victims, had been taken in by his looks. And if his shoulders were any indication, he worked out a lot. His shoulders were more massive than ever.

But suddenly she envisioned him eating his boogers. *Ugh.*

Deeb looked morbidly obese. Poor thing had no idea she was signing her own death warrant by hooking up with Hess. Nikki put the pictures in her purse, wondering once again what could possibly attract a woman to a killer—whether she was obese or not.

When she got back home, Steve had the motorhome cleaned up and was sitting on the couch, petting Sinbad. "Orange furball's all shook up," he said, setting the huge cat aside. He got up and gave Nikki another one of his comforting hugs.

"Sinbad's not the only one who's upset," she said.

Steve stroked and smoothed her hair. "I know it's not a good time right now," he said, "but a visitor is coming over."

"Now? I don't really feel like—"

"I know, I know. But it's that lady from Newport. The one you called about the purple pearl?"

THE ANTIQUE JEWELRY expert arrived half an hour later. By that time Nikki'd had a couple of glasses of wine and managed to edge Hess and his creepy stalking out of her thoughts.

"Nice," the woman said, looking around the well-appointed interior of their motorhome. "I've never been in one of these before. It's roomier than I thought."

"Can I offer you something to drink?" Nikki asked. She hadn't eaten and her ears were buzzing from the wine. Her tongue felt a little thick.

"No thanks. Could you show me that brooch? I can't wait to see it."

Nikki went into the bedroom, retrieved it, and handed to the woman.

She pulled a loupe from her purse and examined the purple pearl, saying, "Oh, my."

"What?" asked Nikki.

The woman removed the loupe from her eye and her eyes were positively dancing. "This definitely came from *Mercenaria.*"

Nikki nodded, took another sip of wine. "A quahog."

"That's right," the woman confirmed, returning her attention to the brooch. "You'll be happy to hear that natural pearls of this color are extremely rare and one of this size, rarer still. In fact, if you put all the factors together: size, shape, color, and eye effect—each phenomenal in their own right—it's an exceedingly rare creation."

"Are you saying—"

"I'm saying it's extraordinary, plus the silverwork is exquisite," she interrupted. "It's colonial, dating back to the late 1600s."

"Uh, you said extremely rare," interjected Steve. "How rare?"

"Let me put it this way: I'm certain it's one of a kind."

"One of a kind? How much would it be worth?"

The woman shrugged. "I can't really put a price on it because there's nothing to compare it to."

"Please guess," Nikki said.

"Conservatively? I suppose a million dollars or more. And that's not taking into account the colonial silversmithing."

"Whoa!" cried Steve. "A million? *Dollars?*" His eyes were just about popping out of his head.

"You understand, of course, while pearls are quite common for bivalve mollusks such as oysters, mussels or even conchs—quahogs aren't expected to produce them."

"A million dollars?" Steve echoed again.

The woman nodded. "You see, the shell of the quahog is shut tighter than any other bivalve. That means it's much less likely that an irritant will get inside. Also, quahogs aren't as high in protein as oysters and mussels, which is what produces a nacreous lining. If a quahog does form a pearl, it's usually chalky and doesn't last."

"Well," Nikki said, finding she'd been holding her breath. "What should we do next?"

"If you plan on selling it, I'd think about auctioning it off in Hong Kong. Pearl collectors gather there each year to see what Sotheby's and Christie's have to offer."

"Hong Kong."

"Yes," the woman said, stowing the loupe back in her purse and getting up to leave. "I seem to remember a yellow conch pearl went for over half a million and it's nowhere near as rare as a purple quahog pearl."

"Thanks so much," Nikki said, once she'd found her voice. "We'll look into it. Just send me a bill for the appraisal."

"Oh, no charge," the woman said. "I'm not qualified to give you a full appraisal but I know what I'm talking about, believe me." A strange look crossed her face. She broke eye contact and looked down at the floor.

"What, something else?"

"Oh . . . nothing."

"C'mon, what? Sure you don't want any wine?"

"No, thank you. I . . ."

"What is it?" Nikki asked.

"Well, I hesitate to tell you this but it seems that every valuable gem has a story, usually a curse. You know, like the Hope Diamond?"

Nikki laughed. "Curse? I don't *think* so. Don't tell me a woman of your intelligence believes in curses."

"You never know," the woman said, letting herself out the door. "Anyway, keep me posted."

Once she'd driven away, Nikki turned to Steve. "Curse?"

He nodded. "It's started already. Name of Hess."

Her buzz evaporated.

CHAPTER 17

HESS CRAWLED OUT of bed, padded to the galley window, and peered out. Even through the light fog, he could see Nikki's motorhome, cattycorner to his. He turned and shuffled into the bathroom, where he pissed for what seemed like hours. He thought back on how he'd succumbed to The Temptation yesterday, after watching the goings on at the whore's RV and later, reviewing his precious new tapes:

Disgusting! That Jezebel Whore Nikki out of the shower. Doing her toilette. Slut. Fucking that Steve asshole, her goddam husband!

Truth be told, Hess almost wished she'd have been fucking *him*, instead. But then she'd probably worm her evil into his head and cause him to have a massive stroke.

Like she did to Mother.

And then, of course, there'd been The Purging.

He'd be fine.

Hess had been beside himself as he watched her smash the web cam. And after she'd gone, he got a kick out of how the stupid cops had milled around. Later, after her husband came back, Hess had watched him talk animatedly to the cops. A huge man from next door had joined them. Jesus, Hess had thought, that sure is one bigass nigger! Later on, he remembered that Nikki had come back home and then some lady had dropped by.

Grand Fucking Central.

Hess's reverie came to an end when he saw Nikki popping out of her rig. The morning sun highlighted her cinnamon hair, which was tucked back into a braid. In Hess's opinion, she didn't have nearly enough makeup on for the whore she was, though. She was wearing that ugly park ranger uniform, so he assumed she was heading for work.

Good, he thought. It was time for a little action. He rummaged in a drawer, pulled out one of his Browning 9-mm automatics and threaded the subsonic silencer onto the barrel. He

Mystic Fear

checked the load: jacketed hollow points. Guns weren't really his style, he thought, but best for what he had in mind.

"Later," he whispered to himself. "I'll have plenty of time to use my fine Henckels cutlery on Jezebel Nikki." *And once I'm through? Her evil will cease to exist, Mother will be avenged...*"

First things first: he stepped out of his rig, unhooked the water and electric, hitched up his dolly and drove the BMW up on it. After removing the wheel chocks, he went back into the RV and retracted the leveling—all set to pull out. He slipped the Browning into his belt and pulled his shirt down to cover it but just as he started to head out, across the way, a truck wheeled into his target's driveway. The truck had SEABREEZE CAMPGROUND STAFF stenciled on the sides.

It's that pizza-faced, chain-smoking, dick of a campground manager. But no sooner had *that* interruption gone away, when a leftover hippy type cruised by in an ugly old car. *What the hell? A goddam Nash Rambler?* Thankfully, the guy kept going. Hess was just thinking the coast was finally clear when a pink minivan pull up and a scraggly-looking kid popped out.

The kid went up to Steve's RV and they talked for a short while and then the kid left. Right after that, a van with CHANNEL –7 WSEA NEWS logos all over it raced up. Its antenna was as big as a sailboat mast. The van parked, all the doors flew open, and a passel of *paparazzi* piled out.

What the fuck?

Hess donned his oversized, extra dark sunglasses, jammed a Boston Bruins cap low on his forehead, and eased out to investigate.

Nikki's husband rushed out of his motorhome. "What's going on?" he asked the news crew.

A cute reporter with huge collagen lips, pert breasts, and lacquered hair poked a microphone in his face. "How does it feel to be the owner of a million dollar pearl, sir?" she asked.

Hess stopped in his tracks. *Million-dollar pearl?*

"Huh?" said Steve. "What'd you just say?"

The reporter moved closer. "Is it true it came from a quahog?"

"Get the hell out of here!" yelled Steve, retreating back into his RV.

Hess spun on a heel and ducked into his own rig, where he watched and fidgeted until the news people finally gave up. *Million-dollar pearl?* He smirked. "Might just get me a *bonus* here," he said to himself.

After making sure no one else was coming, he slipped out, hustled across the street and knocked at Steve's door.

Steve opened the screen. "It's beginning to feel like Grand Central here."

"That's my line," quipped Hess, grinning.

"What?"

"Never mind. I'm your neighbor. Over on site fifty-four?"

"Sure, I saw you come in. Welcome to the campground."

"Thanks. Uh, I haven't had time to go shopping yet, could you loan me a little cream for my coffee?"

"Come on in. I'll get it," said Steve. He turned his back, headed toward the galley.

Hess stepped up and into the motorhome and pulled out his silenced pistol. He started to aim but let his hand drop to his side, thinking: let's have a little fun first. "You live here by yourself?" he asked.

"My wife and I," said Steve. "Maybe you met her? She's the park ranger here at the campground."

"The park ranger is a chick? Wait . . . come to think of it, I did see a *cunt* in one of those olive drab uniforms. Tasty little number."

Steve whirled around. "*What* did you say?"

Hess raised the Browning. "I *said*, I'm aware of your cunt park ranger bitch. Now, get the fuck down on your knees."

"The hell I will."

"*Now!*"

Steve eased down, first on one knee, then the other. He looked around frantically.

Hess sneered. "Ain't no help, jerkwad. By the way, your sweet Nikki? I fucked her gash good and she loved it. Gonna fuck her again, too, fuck her brains out."

Steve's jaws tightened, his eyes narrowed. "You're Marion Hess, aren't you. Nikki told me about you. Can't we talk about this? She never did anything to you." He moved his knees slightly, inching his way toward the hallway.

"Never did anything? Bitch killed Mother with one of her evil spells, is all, you shit for brains asshole," said Hess. His voice had risen an octave. "Anyhoo, just wanted you to know I really, really enjoyed popping Nikki's cheerleader-slash-homecoming queen cherry, you know? She couldn't get enough of me."

His victim had eased his way closer to the bedroom entry now.

"You think I'm a complete numbnuts?" asked Hess, motioning with the barrel of his Browning. "Quit scrooching."

Steve stopped, threw a head fake to the left and lunged right, through the doorway. He rolled and scuttled behind the far side of the bed.

"Shit!" cried Hess. He held the Browning with both hands at arm's length. "Come out of there!"

Steve sprang up from behind the bed, swinging a baseball bat, but the swing was wild and barely clipped Hess' left elbow. Pain shot up his arm but he held onto his Browning. Steve hurled the bat at him, ducking low, bolted past, into the hallway, racing for the front door.

Hess sidestepped the bat; it whacked against a wall and clattered to the floor.

Steve was only a couple of steps from the front door now.

Hess leveled his pistol, sighted and fired twice. *Smock! Smock!*

Two crimson blossoms appeared in the center of Steve's back.

Hess grinned, feeling the power. He watched as his target grunted, fell face forward, twitched and convulsed, shuddered a few times, and lay still. For good measure, Hess popped another round into the back of Steve's head. *Smock!* He stuffed the gun into his belt and squeaked on latex gloves. He fully realized the cops and Nikki would know who did this, but by then he'd be long gone so he didn't care.

No sense leaving prints, though. Might get out of the habit of being professional.

Looking around, he spotted a wedding photo album, found scissors in a drawer, and started snipping and collecting. Seeing how much Nikki looked like Mother, he felt himself stiffening once again. Painfully.

What's happening? . . . Is she becoming Mother?

He reached into his pants and made an adjustment, wincing at the soreness.

Once he'd finished with the photos, he moved to the bedroom where he rummaged through drawers, looking for Nikki's intimates. When he found her panties, he sorted through and brought them, one by one, to his nose, looking for the evil stench of The Temptations.

Getting a better idea, he strode over to the laundry hamper where he picked out a few soiled ones, inhaled the fragrance, and found them with faint traces of whore musk. He was stuffing them into his pocket when something caught his eye on the dresser.

Her hairbrush!

He carefully combed out a decent clump of her gorgeous cinnamon hair and held it up to the light. Just as he remembered: it reflected the light like threads of heaven. *Exactly like Mother's!*

Outside, a car door slammed.

"Shit," said Hess, as he hurried back up front and peered out the galley window. Nobody was out there, must've been a neighbor. But this was taking too long. Feeling a little panicky, he stepped carefully over Steve's body, eased out the door, and hustled back to his own rig.

And forgot all about looking for the million-dollar pearl.

HAPPILY, HESS CLIMBED behind his steering wheel and in no time was barreling past the gatehouse, on his way to Benedict's Landing.

Across the bay, a foghorn moaned, but the fog seemed to be lifting. Gentle waves slapped at the shore, and a sulfurous, funky whiff of low tide overrode the salt air. Just past a small beach, he spotted a pink minivan, with Mary Kay logos plastered all over it. The minivan had a flat.

"Wait a minute," Hess whispered to himself. "It's that sorry-assed kid who was talking to Nikki's asshole husband."

The kid was leaning against a fender, scowling and smoking. And he had one of his hands down the front of his pants.

"Whoa," said Hess. "Is he giving in to The Temptations? Jesus, what a loser." He started to pass by but changed his mind. He jammed on the brakes, started backing up: *Beep! Beep! Beep!*

As he looked in his backup mirrors, Hess assessed the kid and smirked, thinking: Is this punk tailor-made or what? He stopped alongside, lowered his side window.

"What the fuck?" the kid asked, obviously trying to focus on Hess's face.

Hess opened the door, stepped down, sidled over, and grinned. "Playing a little pocket pool there?" he asked the kid.

The kid blinked, jerked his hand out of his pants. "What? Pool? *No!* Uh . . . they got a pool in the campground back there. You comin' from there?"

"I'm talking about pocket pool, son. Waxing the ol' dolphin?"

"Dolphins? Naw, they're way south."

"Forget it," said Hess. He stuck out his hand. "My name's Karl. Karl Meyer," he said, using his new alias. Pointing to the kid's flat tire, he added: "Looks like you have a problem."

The kid shook Hess's hand, saying, "I'm Junior Ferguson." He looked down at the flat and tossed back his long blond tresses. "I guess my spare's kinda flat, too."

Hess thumbed toward the motorhome. "Well, son, get your spare and put it in the starboard storage bin. I'm headed for town anyway; we can have it fixed at the garage."

"Forget that, man. I ain't got no cash."

"Don't worry about it, kid. I'll take care of it."

Junior frowned, narrowed his eyes. "How come you're helpin' me?"

Hess shrugged. "Good Samaritan, whatever. Besides, I want to talk to you. I think I could use a young guy like you in my business. You coming or not?"

"I guess so." Junior opened up the back of the minivan, jerked the useless spare tire out, and rolled it over to the motorhome.

Hess followed, opened a huge bin. "Like I said, put the tire in this starboard bin here and climb in."

"Starboard?"

"Right side."

"I knew that," said Junior. He stowed the tire and heaved himself up into the passenger's seat. "This here is one *righteous* ride," he said. "I could go for a motorhome like this."

Hess threw his head back and laughed. "Well, this isn't your ordinary motorhome, son—it's a Winnebago Chieftain. Brand-spanking-new. And, if you look in that little overhead TV there, you'll see that I tow a BMW, which is also new. Stick with me, kid, and I might just put enough casharooney in your jeans for toys like these."

"Sweet. Thanks for helping me out, Mister . . . um, what'd you say your name was?"

"Call me Karl. I have a feeling we're going to become good friends, Junior. *Real* good friends."

"Whatever," mumbled Junior.

CHAPTER 18

NIKKI'S ASSIGNMENT: to take the campground Boston Whaler skiff and check out a boat, which belonged to one of the campers. Someone had called in the boat illegally bullraking quahogs in the conservation area. This was really a job for the Environmental Police and she had called them, but while she waited for them to come, she was happy to get out on the water.

She cast off the dock and headed out into the bay. She loved it: the wind in her hair, the aroma of the ocean, and the throb of a powerful boat cutting the water. When she got to the quahogger, he was still raking. She eased up next to him, put out a fender, and tied off to his skiff.

"Sir," she said. "This is a restricted area. No quahogging."

"So? You ain't nothin' but a Yogi Bear park ranger," he said, laughing. "Cute, though."

She did a slow burn.

She heard a powerful outboard in the distance and pointed to a skiff that was steaming toward their position. "Oh, bad luck," she said. "Here comes the Environmental Police."

The offender shaded his eyes, looked out. "Shit. The goddam clam cops!"

The Environmental Police did their thing and by the time Nikki got back to the dock, tied off and made a last tour of the campground, it was well past dark. All she had to do was check in at the gatehouse and her day would be through. Physically and mentally exhausted, she headed there. What a long day.

Frenchie Funeer, Petey Fottler's cousin, was on duty at the gatehouse. In his seventies, Frenchie was a squat and porcine man. Beady, close-set eyes gave him the image of being a mental ward refugee and at best, he appeared homeless. He was wearing his moth-eaten U.S. Navy watch cap. A dead cigar stub poked forth from his fleshy lips.

"Evening, Frenchie," she said.

He saluted, saying, "Well, as I live and breathe, if it ain't the park ranger."

She sighed. "That's me."

"Say, what's this I hear about you and Steve findin' some purple pearl worth a million frogskins?"

"What're you talking about?"

"I caught it on the news. Hell, a Channel-7 van was at Steve's rig, earlier today, tryin' to interview him."

She nibbled at a cuticle. "The lady from Newport. She must've tipped them off."

"Huh? What?"

"Never mind."

Frenchie shrugged and shot back into his hut. Through the open door she could see him grabbing up a well-thumbed issue of *Hustler* magazine.

"Good to see that some senior citizens are still improving their minds," she observed.

He scowled.

"By the way," she added, " . . . how's your wife?"

"Better than nothin'," he said. "But these days, sex with her? It's like tryin' to stuff a marshmallow into a piggy bank."

Nikki was still reeling with the image *that* produced as she rounded the curve, drove to her campsite, and parked. She saw Steve's truck in the driveway and noted with relief that there were no news vans.

But when she opened the door to the motorhome, her smile mutated, into a rictus of horror. And when she saw her husband sprawled on the floor in all that blood, she screamed, and screamed, and screamed. She fell to her knees and must've gone on autopilot, because she found herself checking him for a pulse.

Nothing.

Two nasty, blackened holes pockmarked his back and a thick crimson puddle haloed his head, but she was in denial. It was only when she turned him over that she became convinced; it was his eyes: wide open, they'd clouded over, lifeless now—no longer Mel Gibson blue.

The eyes accused her.

Oh God, no, Oh God, no, she thought. "I should've been here to save him."

Her ears buzzed like a nest of angry hornets, blackness started closing in on the periphery. Her heart felt as if it might tear loose and burst out of her chest. Her hands were shaking and beads of cold sweat popped out on her forehead. Should've been here, she thought. Should've been here! Should've been here!

Then it was as if someone else was grabbing her cell phone out of her pocket, punching in 911, and screaming instructions. Blackness, closer now . . .

She knew she was going into shock!

And then: blessed nothingness.

THE PUNGENT STING of ammonia revived Nikki. She lay on the ground outside their motorhome, swaddled in blankets. It took a few moments for her to remember.

"No!" she cried out, bolting upright. "No, no, *nooo* . . .."

An EMT put a hand on her shoulder but she knocked it aside, got to her feet and wobbled. A police office tried to grab her but she pushed him away. She staggered toward the rig's open door, but never made it.

Chief Anderson blocked her path.

"Let me by, Frank!" she screamed. "Get the fuck out of the way . . .."

"Don't, Nikki. Don't."

She caught enough of a glimpse through the door to tell her it wasn't a nightmare. The crime scene people were hovering over Steve's body. She felt lightheaded again and she tasted bitter bile. Her whole body started to shake. Her knees wobbled.

"Ahhh, God . . ."

She collapsed like an abandoned marionette.

The medical examiner came over and offered her a sedative. She gratefully accepted. Frank knelt down, a concerned look etched into his face. On the other side of her, Clyde "Tugboat" Haywood, their good friend and neighboring camper, knelt. Worry twisted his face.

"When you feel up to it," said Frank, "I need to ask you some questions. I know it'll be difficult but once they're done in there, you'll need to see if anything's missing."

"She can rest in my rig until then," said Tugboat, scooping her up in his massive arms. "I'll put her on the couch and elevate her feet."

He carried her into his Avion fifth-wheel trailer. The sedative was starting to work and she had trouble focusing. Irrationally, she was thinking about how Tugboat's RV looked too damn neat to belong to a bachelor. With tender care, he deposited her on his couch and covered her with the blanket.

She closed her eyes and—like some grotesque Halloween billboard—the horrid vision of Steve's ruined body and bloody head reappeared.

Her eyes popped back open. So much for the sedative, she thought.

Tugboat tucked the blanket around her.

Her eyelids drooped, closing on their own. She revised her opinion of the sedative as it swept her into a dreamless void. The next thing she knew, Frank was standing over her. Disoriented for a few seconds, she shook her head and reality flooded back in.

She screamed, bolted upright and tried to get up off Tugboat's couch.

Strong arms held her down. "Easy, Nikki. Easy."

Tugboat handed her a cup of steaming tea. It burned her tongue but she gulped it down anyway.

"Oh, God," she said. "If I hadn't forgotten about the time and worked so late—I could've been there for Steve."

"It's not your fault, Nikki," said Tugboat. "You might have been killed, too."

"I'd rather be dead, than this. What time is it?"

"Going on midnight."

She turned to Frank. "How'd you know?"

"You called 911. Don't you remember?"

She shook her head.

She felt tears welling up again. Her nose started running. Tugboat handed her his handkerchief.

"Thank you," she said, after she'd wiped her nose. "I appreciate it."

"How are you feeling?" he asked, adding: "Dumb question."

"Empty, kind of numb. Guilty. I can't believe I'm not crying my eyes out. Maybe this is a nightmare . . . maybe I'm just dreaming. Maybe he's not really gone . . ."

"Sorry but it's no dream," said Frank. "If you're feeling up to it, maybe we could go back to Steve's rig. The crime scene team is done and Steve's been , uh . . . removed."

"Removed? I want to see him."

"You'll be able to see him later."

"Okay. I'm okay," said Nikki. She sat up. "Let's do it."

"You sure?" asked Tugboat. He helped her to her feet.

"I can do this," she said, pushing his hands away.

Back inside the motorhome, she made a point to avoid the spot where her husband's body had been lying. From the corner of her eye, she could see a tarp someone had been thoughtful enough to lay down, covering the gore. "I think I turned him over when I found him," she said.

"We figured," said Frank.

She had trouble concentrating and felt disoriented but checked the main area. Everything seemed to be there: electronics, computer. The file box with all their papers looked undisturbed.

"It just had to be that bastard Hess," she said. "I think he was here in disguise because there was an RV Repair truck here in the campground and people said they saw it here, at our rig."

"Yeah," said Frank. "Jerry's RV Repair. Petey Fottler told me about that and the television crew, in between a lot of Chinese fortune cookie bullshit. Surprise, surprise, we checked and there's no such company as Jerry's RV Repair. We lifted some prints, though."

"Did any of the other campers see anything?" Nikki asked.

"Well, one of your neighbors said she saw the campground manager's truck here. That, the news van, and Junior Ferguson. Wait a minute. Maybe whoever did this was after that valuable pearl, you think?"

"Forget that damn pearl, Frank. Read my lips: it was that goddam Hess! Your detective buddy in New Mexico faxed me a picture of the bastard," she said. "Did you get one?"

"Yeah. We're circulating copies statewide. Hess will be in all the papers and on TV. But that pearl? Why don't you check to see if it's missing, okay?"

"Fine," she snapped. She walked, zombie like, into the bedroom, jerked open her jewelry box.

The chief followed. He raised his eyebrows. "Well?"

"Shit, it's gone," she said. She stood there, mesmerized by the vacancy where the brooch used to be and became even more disoriented. She suddenly thought of Sinbad. "My cat! Where's my cat?"

"Cat? We didn't see any cat."

She groaned. "I'll bet the son of a bitch killed my cat, too."

From the main area, an officer called out, "Hey, chief," he said. "You should check this out."

They all hurried back up front. Nikki was still holding her jewelry box.

The officer had their wedding photo album in his hand. "Look here," he said.

Nikki flipped the pages and saw, with horror, that her image had been removed, with surgical precision, from all photographs. Once again, her knees gave way. Her jewelry box crashed on the floor and the contents went flying.

Just before she fainted, irrational thoughts of glazed donuts popped into her head—so many donuts, they make you throw up.

CHAPTER 19

EARLIER IN THE late afternoon, while Hess and Junior Winnebagoed toward Benedict's Landing, Hess mentally congratulated himself on his fantastic find. "None of my business, kid," he said, "but how come you're driving that cute pink minivan?"

Junior shuffled his feet, looked down. "Aw, it's my ma's. A temporary condition and stuff and everything."

Hess chuckled. "I'm sure."

"S'true, man. I'm sort of outta work so they're the only wheels I got right now, know what I'm sayin'?"

"Sure. Out of work? Are you even out of high school?"

"School sucks, man. I gotta go to summer school so I can graduate."

"I guess you go to Franklin High across the bay there, right?"

"Yeah. Franklin sucks."

Hess grinned and winked. "Know what you mean. I always hated school, too."

"No shit? You don't sound like it."

"No? Why is that?"

A shrug. "I don't know. You talk kinda all educated and stuff."

"Just a front, Junior. It's been my experience that school is a waste of time anyway, if you're an entrepreneur."

"See what I mean? Entre . . . what?"

"Businessman."

"Business. Right."

By that time, they'd reached town. Hess pulled over into the parking lot of a liquor store where he could maneuver the motorhome without having to back up. "Let's talk business," he said. "But first, I'll go get us a six-pack of cold ones. Having flats is thirsty work, right?"

Once he was back and they'd each twisted the tops off cold bottles of Michelob Dry, Hess turned to Junior. "I noticed you like to partake of the doobage."

The kid burped wheezily. "Doobage? What're you talkin' about, man?"

"Your pupils are the size of dinner plates, your eyes are bloodshot to the max, and I can smell the pot coming off your hair in waves."

"Hey, man—"

"It's okay."

Junior narrowed his eyes. "You a nark or somethin'?"

Hess shook his head, grinned slyly. "Not hardly," he said.

A smile started tugging at the corner of Junior's mouth. "You sure?" he asked.

"I told you, I'm a business man, an entrepreneur. And I'm looking for a partner. I could use a smart young man to sell weed, market the kids after school."

Junior's face lit up. "Rilly?"

"You interested?"

"I'm your man," said the kid. "For sure."

"Well, good enough."

Hess started the motorhome up, headed on down the street and pulled in at the town garage. He handed Junior a twenty saying, "Get them to plug your tire and then come on back. We can discuss business and polish off this handy six-pack while we wait."

"Awesome!"

FOUR BEERS LATER, the spare was ready. Junior climbed back in and they headed back to the pink minivan to replace the flat. Once that was done, Hess followed the kid back to his home in Benedict's Landing and they dumped the minivan off. Darkness had taken over the sky now, a fingernail moon and a scattering of the brightest stars had appeared. While the kid went in the house, Hess wondered if Junior's mother was anything like *Mother*.

His mind regressed . . .

. . . To filthy dishes in the sink, reeking of spoiled food, Mother's endless cigarettes, Mother's crucifix, Mother's Bible. Mother reading to him, over and over: "Thou shalt and thou shalt not".

Speaking in those scary tongues.

Another of those endless trips to the basement where he's strapped to the support pole with that extension cord, candles winking, Crucifix Jesus hanging on the wall, staring at him.

More Thou Shalt Nots, you little sinner. Release from Temptations, blacking out.

Waking in a bed with oh-so-fresh sheets.

Feeling the recent Purging. On his backside.

. . . Shaking his head to clear it, Hess pulled himself back from the abyss, grabbed his cell phone, and called information.

"Got a listing for a Raymond Nickerson?" he asked. Once he got it, he punched in the number.

A voice answered: "Hello?"

"Hi," said Hess. "I'm looking for Ray Nickerson."

"This is Ray."

"Ray! This is Marion Hess, your old pal from Franklin High. Remember me?"

"Franklin High? Go Swordfish! Yeah, I remember you. Kind of a loner, right? What've you been doing with yourself these past twenty or so years? Hey, wait a minute, didn't they send you away after your mother died? I heard some weird shit that—"

"Never mind," snapped Hess, cutting him off. "Let's just say I've been doing a bit of this, a bit of that, a bit of the other."

"Well, what's the haps?" asked Ray, his voice full of enthusiasm. "Wanna go grab a few beers an' catch up?"

"Sure, but later. Listen, buddy, do your folks still own that abandoned farm out in West Arcadia? I'm looking for a place to store my motorhome. It'd be great if I could rent the barn."

"Well," said Ray, "my mom and dad passed away a few years ago. I own the property now. It's totally run down and the weeds have pretty much taken over. It's tough just to get down the dirt road."

"How about the barn where you had that party one time. Is it still standing?"

"Yeah. But it's in poor shape, man. Leaks like a sieve and leans like a drunken sailor."

"No matter. Shit, I just want to keep my motorhome out of the weather this winter. Will it fit in the barn?"

"Sure. It's humongous."

"Great. Can you meet me out there in, say, two hours?"

"Sure. You need directions?"

"No, I'm pretty sure I remember how to get there."

"Okay, two hours it is, then. Be good to see you again, man."

"You, too. Bye."

That done, Hess hopped out of his rig, backed his BMW off the tow dolly and disconnected it.

Junior came sashaying out of the house, asking, "What's up?"

"Help me with this dolly," ordered Hess. "Think we could store it behind your mother's garage?"

"Uh, sure, I guess so. She's not here, works the night shift."

They dragged the dolly over. Once it was parked, Hess whipped a screwdriver out of his pocket and removed the Nebraska plates. He expected Junior to question him about it but the dumb kid wasn't even paying attention. They walked together back to the motorhome.

"Man," said the kid, pointing to his mother's minivan. "I am *so* sick a those wheels."

Hess nodded, winked. "Pink Mary Kay minivans aren't exactly status vehicles, that's for sure."

"Well, what now, sir?"

"Sir? Where'd *that* come from? Don't call me 'sir', son. Call me Marion."

"Marion? I thought your name was Karl."

"Uh . . . right. It is. Just keeping you on your toes, Junior. See if you've been listening."

The kid sniggered.

"What," growled Hess.

The kid shrugged, still grinning like the village idiot. "Oh, uh . . . nothin'. It's just that *Marion* sounds kinda faggy or—"

"You want me to rip your fucking heart out?"

"Nosir, I mean, uh, Karl, sir. Sorry, okay?"

"Okay. Now, let's head over the bridge all the way out to West Arcadia so I can store this motorhome. You follow in the BMW." Hess tossed Junior the keys.

"Me? Drive the Beemer?"

"Follow me. Can you do that?"

"Definitely."

ON THE WAY off Mystic Island, Hess noted flashing blue lights, sirens and cop cars racing back the other way in the direction of the campground and had to smile. He definitely knew what *that* was all about. *Outfuckingstanding!* Once over the bridge, they took a trio of highways westward and ended up then snaking down several miles of a narrow, rutted, and overgrown dirt road in the dark.

When they finally arrived at the abandoned Nickerson farm, Ray was already there, standing in the dooryard. The barn loomed in the background, wide open.

"Just pull on in," said Ray. "I cleared a space for you."

Hess eased the Winnebago inside, stepped down with a small gym bag in hand, locked the RV, and looked around. Although no farm animals had been in there for probably a couple of decades, the barn still smelled like hay and horseshit. Once they were outside, Ray shut the huge doors, and snapped a sturdy padlock on the hasp. He handed Hess two keys, saying, "All set."

Hess whipped a roll of bills out of his pocket, peeled off $400. "Good till spring, right?"

Ray pocketed the cash. "Yup."

Hess pointed, saying, "What's the deal with the farmhouse?"

"It's shot. Roof's even caved in on the backside and the floor's falling into the cellar. Power to both the house and the barn is long gone. You ain't stayin' here anyway, right?"

"Right," said Hess, thinking how happy he was that his Winnebago had a generator and full tank of gas.

Junior, apparently bored with waiting in the BMW, hopped out, and sauntered over. "What's happenin' dudes?" he asked.

"Who's the kid?" asked Ray.

"My ride back to civilization," said Hess. "We gotta go."

"But what about our reunion beers?" asked Ray.

"I'll call you," promised Hess. *When pigs fly.*

Hess let Junior drive again, going back. "Kid," he said, "you be sure to give me the phone number at your mom's. I'll be in touch in, say, about a week."

"Awesome."

Hess was ecstatic over his find—this perfectly malleable kid. He figured he'd use the lad up like one of those disposable toilet cleaners . . . and then take *particular* pleasure in flushing him down.

PART II

A SPIRAL INTO HELL

Happiness is the only sanction in life; where happiness fails, existence remains a mad and lamentable experiment.

—George Santyana

Jan Evan Whitford

CHAPTER 20

NIKKI REGAINED CONSCIOUSNESS in a panic, thinking she hadn't even called her daughter yet. She desperately needed Erin's comfort but was too damn depressed and doped up to call. Chief Anderson came over and let Nikki know he'd make sure Steve's body got to the local funeral home. Tugboat helped her up and escorted her back to his own trailer.

"I put fresh sheets on the bed," he said. "You can sleep there. I'll take the couch. Tomorrow, you can decide what you want to do."

"Thank you," she said. "You've been so wonderful . . . ."

"Just being a friend."

She nodded. "I suppose I could go to the apartment in town but I really don't know if I can handle being alone tonight. Are you sure you don't mind?"

"I'm sure."

"Um, could I get some more tea?"

"Coming right up," he said.

She was amazed at how a man his size could move around with such grace and ease. After putting on the tea water, he got out a bag of Earl Grey, handed her a glass of water and shook a pill out of a prescription bottle.

"What's this?" she asked.

"Another sedative. I called Doc Frazier and he wrote out a prescription for you. While you were out, I went into town and had it filled."

She popped it into her mouth and washed it down.

He nodded in approval. "I hate to bring anything else up but I want to tell you something before that pill takes effect."

"What is it?"

"It's about that brooch with the purple pearl."

She shook her head. "Not now."

"Just quickly. Then I'll shut up."

"I don't *care* about the damn thing, don't you get it? In fact, I doubt that I'll ever care about anything again."

"Someday, you might."

"Can't you see I just want to die?" She started crying again. Giant, ragged, gulping sobs.

He put a massive arm around her shoulder and gave her a gentle hug.

"All right, all right," she said, relenting. "Say what you've got to say."

"Someday, you'll feel better. Not soon, but someday. That's when we'll get it back."

"We?"

"Well, I mean—"

"I told you: I don't even want it. I'd like to be alone now, if you don't mind."

"Of course."

She wobbled into the bedroom and sandwiched herself between fresh, laundered sheets that smelled of bleach, salt air, and just a little bit like campfire smoke.

Once again, she thought of calling her daughter but that seemed monumental. How could she tell her? Nikki didn't have the words, not right now. And while she was thinking about it, the sedative knocked her out.

SHE WOKE UP the following morning, consumed with an intense feeling of pain and isolation—a slow erosion from within. It felt like her heart had been ripped out and a lead ball had replaced it. She found herself in sort of an emotional freefall, plummeting into a black, empty abyss yet grappling with rage, disbelief, and guilt. How could God let anything so cruel and so *wrong* happen? How could she let it happen? Did she warn Steve? Yes, but she didn't do anything to protect him.

She started crying again, sobbing and wailing into her pillow until she became too numb to feel. After a trip to the bathroom, she swallowed two more pills and passed out again. She didn't wake up until she'd slept the clock around. Vaguely, she remembered Tugboat looking in on her.

"Go away," she'd said.

He had.

By now, she'd learned that the pills would provide a dream-free respite so she washed down more of them and crashed again.

But the third day, she reached for them and found the bottle empty. Summoning a scrap of energy, she managed to get up and take a shower. When she went to get dressed, she spotted a neat stack of her clothes on the dresser and assumed the police had let Tugboat get her stuff. She dressed in jeans and a t-shirt, thankful she wouldn't have to wear her dirty uniform.

Her nose and ears told her that bacon sizzled in the kitchen but it didn't interest her in the least, even though she hadn't eaten in nearly seventy hours. She moped into the kitchen area.

"Good morning," said Tugboat. "How are you feeling?"

She plopped down at the dinette, cradled her face in her hands. "It's all so sudden, so damn *final*."

"Looks like you're pretty much cried out. Have some breakfast." He plopped a plate with an egg, two strips of bacon, and a piece of toast in front of her.

She stared at the food and felt nauseated. "Yes, I suppose I'm cried out for now anyway. Once I started, I thought I'd never stop and just drown in the sadness. And, I have to tell you, I'm almost as pissed at God as I am at myself."

"God?"

"Why'd He pick on Steve? Steve was such a good guy and—"

"Steve's being a good guy had nothing to do with it. And God didn't pick on him. Hess did."

"I should've—"

"Stop that kind of talk right now. Coffee?"

"Whatever."

He handed her a mug and she stirred in cream and sugar. Silence loomed. Her stomach roiled. She nibbled at a piece of bacon and managed to get it down. She poked her fork at an egg, moved it around. Usually, when she was under stress, she would eat more, not less. Maybe it was those meds.

"I guess I used up all my pills."

Tug got up, went to the cupboard, got out a different prescription bottle and handed it to her, saying, "Try these instead."

"What are they?" she said, looking at the label. "Are they for me?"

He nodded. "It's Valium, from the doc. He didn't want you addicted to that powerful sedative. Maybe it'll help you over the worst of it."

"Nothing can help," she said, but took one anyway, figuring what the hell. She forced down a bite of egg.

"What now?" he asked.

"I don't know. I know I can't keep popping pills and hide out in your trailer forever, even though it sounds like a plan."

"My trailer's all yours, if you need it."

"Thanks, but no. Once the funeral details have been attended to, I need to get out of here, far away from this island. I suppose I'll go to my daughter's, up near Boston. Maybe I can get my head together there and, oh, shit . . ."

"What?"

"She still doesn't know about Steve. I'm dreading telling her."

"Don't worry about it, she'll be a great comfort to you. Does she know about Hess?"

"No, and I don't want to saddle her with that, either."

"Don't blame you," said Tug.

"I'm scared shitless of Hess," Nikki admitted. "But you know what? I really don't care if he kills me. So what? It'd put me out of my misery."

Tugboat frowned. "That first night, you kept saying you wanted to die. You're not thinking about suicide or anything like that, are you?"

She forced a smile for his benefit. "Well, I admit I examined that K-Bar knife you keep in the nightstand by your bed. It's got the sharpest edge I ever felt, but, no, I'm not suicidal. Besides, I don't have the guts for it."

"That's good to hear."

She got up from the dinette. "Will you come with me to my motorhome? I need to get some personal things out of there and I don't want to go alone."

"Sure."

"And thanks for getting my clothes."

"No problem. And let me know if that Hess psycho comes looking for you. I'll shoot him."

"You have a gun?"

"Hey, I'm an injun, remember? Bow an' freakin' arrow!"

"Big as you are, you could just smush him."

He smiled. "Why didn't I think of that?"

"You really have a bow and arrow?"

"No."

After she'd gathered her stuff and was easing into her CR-V, Tugboat leaned on the window and looked her straight in the eyes. It felt like she was looking back into the ocean: vast, huge, welcoming, and, most of all—comforting.

"Remember," he said. "I'm your friend. If you ever need me, just call." He wrote down the number for his home in Westerly as well as his cell number.

"Thanks, Tug," she said. She felt a little better and guessed the Valium was kicking in. "You've been wonderful."

"Are you going straight to your daughter's?"

"Not right away. I'm going to my apartment in town and get a few things. I'll call her from there. Hopefully, she can come down."

"Well, I'm not a real religious type of guy, but I'll pray for you."

"Thanks." Her eyes started to fill again. "Shit, Tug. Steve and I were only married for three short months, you know? It's not fair."

"I know."

CHAPTER 21

"YOU DRIVE, sport," Hess told Junior, tossing him the keys.

"Clam doggies!" the kid cried. He slid behind the wheel. Hess could see Junior's mother watching their every move from the porch, making a sour face, hands on her hips. He got in on the passenger side, saying, "Okay, kid, here's the program. From now on? We need to meet somewhere out of town."

"Okay … sir."

"Call me Karl. Remember? Now, drive."

"Karl. Right. I knew that," said Junior, as he swung a U-turn and tromped the accelerator. "We could meet at Sal's Pizza Palace in Wickford. They got awesome pizza and—"

"Listen to me," interrupted Hess. "There's a grungy little bar off Highway 2 called 'Peep Toad's Lounge.' You know it?"

"No sir, um, I mean … Karl."

"I'll direct you. Just head over the bridge and then over to Route 2."

Junior looked worried. "But I can't do bars, man, on account of I ain't twenty-one. One time I snuck into the Mariner's Bar and Grill and got served, though."

"Don't sweat it. It's not like they give a rat's ass at Peep Toad's."

"Wicked cool."

"Here's the deal," said Hess. "We're gonna meet there every Friday at 3:30. Can you do that?"

"Sure. I'll be there. *If* I can get my ma's van."

"Don't worry about that. From now on, you'll be driving this BMW."

Junior's face lit up. "The Beemer? Fucking awesome! You're gonna let me keep it?"

"You can *use* it," Hess said. He pointed. "Pull over in that empty lot over there. I've got something to show you."

Junior did as he was told. He put the Beemer in park, and looked over. "What."

Hess thumbed toward the back seat and a gym bag. "Grab that bag, will you?"

Junior turned, snatched up the bag, unzipped it, and looked inside. "Whoa," he said. "Weed. And plenny of it, too."

"Labor Day is right around the corner," said Hess. "The kids'll be back to school, right? And even though you won't be going back, you can roll a few joints, make up some nickel and dime bags, and start building up some after school clientele. Okay?"

"Sure, but I hate all those assholes at that school."

Hess nodded. "I know, huh? Especially the popular crowd and the jocks, right?"

"Right."

"Believe me, kid, I know all about Franklin High assholes. Everyone treated me like shit there, too."

"That's right. You went to Franklin too."

"Yep. Class of '78. Anyway, don't let fear stop you."

"What? They don't scare me, man."

"Good. You know the places where all the kids hang out?"

"Well, duh."

Hess cut his eyes to Junior, giving the kid his shark stare. "Watch the smartass remarks, boy."

Junior's eyes widened. He gulped. "Sorry."

"Oh, you're sorry, all right. Anyway, you can make yourself rich off all those assholes and get even with them. Know what I'm saying?"

Junior's head bobbed. "Sure."

"And later, we'll get *proper* revenge, believe me."

"Revenge? You got somethin' in mind?"

"Later, I said. Now, listen up: you'll also find a small pipe and couple of vials of crack in the bag there. Call it a bonus for your own recreational use. Ever done crack?"

The kid looked shocked. "No way."

"Don't be a wuss, Junior. Give it a try. I think you'll enjoy it and there's plenty more where that came from."

"Well—"

"Don't sweat it for now. Just drive."

TWENTY MINUTES LATER, Junior whipped into the parking lot at Peep Toad's. A loud crunching of Michelins on clamshells provided the soundtrack. He put the BMW in park, asking, "Um, if I'm gonna be drivin' the Beemer, what're you gonna use?"

Hess pointed. "See that panel van? Over there in the back? One of the bartenders used to own it. I needed a van in my business so I made him an offer he couldn't refuse."

"Awesome! Like in the *Sopranos*?"

Hess snorted. "You're thinking of *The Godfather* and no, just a healthy wad of casherooni, that's all." He dipped into his pocket, peeled off some bills, adding, "Speaking of which, here's an advance."

Junior counted the bills. "Holy shit! . . . $400?"

"Like I said, an advance. Plus, you'll need some change for your transactions."

"Sweet."

"And Junior?"

"Yeah?"

"Don't tell *anyone* about this; not your mom, not your girlfriend, or your buddies—got it?"

"Sure."

AFTER DROPPING the kid off, Hess remembered Snake Taggert had said Central Falls was the place to buy drugs if you had the right connections and Hess certainly had The Right Connections. He cut and dealt off a portion of the stuff he'd bought from Paco for a nifty profit, and then went to Central Falls where he purchased more at wholesale—including all the crack he would need to control Junior.

Later, he drove back to the old farmhouse in West Arcadia. Inside, he shined a flashlight around the foundation and discovered the bulkhead going down into the cellar was intact. Dank, musty, and moldy, the cellar was in pretty good shape, except for a couple of caved-in floorboards from above. The earthen floor was packed down. That, he thought, would be just fine for his mission and maybe even a few *extracurricular* activities.

A little trip to Home Depot for a length of chain, a steel spike, some Quick-Mix concrete, and a couple of sturdy padlocks and he'd be all set. Oh yeah, and a kerosene heater and one of those Coleman lanterns. Maybe he ought to stop by Wal-Mart and stock up on adhesive tape, gauze, and Neosporin, too. Just in case.

He climbed the steps of the cellar, headed over to the barn, unlocked the huge doors, and went into his Winnebago. In the main living area, he'd composed a shrine to Nikki, made up of the treasures he'd copped from her motorhome. On the walls, he had taped copies he'd made of the article in the campground newsletter as well as a new article on that Whore Jezebel Nikki from the *Providence Journal*—clips about that purple pearl.

Now, he fashioned an altar on the coffee table, arranging her unlaundered panties just so, intermingling them with the photos he had sliced from her wedding album. Included, of course, was the lovely hair he combed out of her hairbrush.

Mother's hair? Was it Mother's or the whore's? He was confused.

And the centerpiece? He thought that goddam million dollar pearl would've been just fucking perfect if he hadn't been such a bozo to get spooked and forget it. In its place, he arranged a pair of what he considered to be her best panties, the slightly soiled lacy black ones. Running through his mind, inexorably and repeatedly: K.C. and the Sunshine Band:

That's the way (uh-huh, uh-huh) I LIKE it (uh-huh, uh-huh).

He completed the shrine by surrounding his precious altar area with votive candles, stood back, and admired his work. From the couch, he'd be able to worship at the shrine even as he reviewed his Jezebel tapes.

And anticipate The Sacrifice.

Feeling a familiar stirring in his loins, he moaned, thinking he'd better not let The Temptations win out. "When the time is ripe," he said to himself. "It'll be just me and you, Mother. Once the devil has the soul of The Jezebel Whore, we'll be together again. Like you said."

Content with that, he turned his thoughts to the more immediate future. Tomorrow, he needed to go somewhere in Connecticut and get an Earl Scheib paint job on his van.

Midnight blue sounded about right.

CHAPTER 22

FORTIFIED WITH VALIUM, Nikki finally dredged up enough courage to call her daughter.

Erin's gasp was audible. "Steve was *murdered*?"

Nikki's voice caught in her throat. "Yes."

"Are you all right? I mean . . . of course you're not. I can't believe . . . Mom, what can I do?" Erin started to cry.

That got Nikki crying again. "Just come and be with me, okay? Can you get some time off work?"

"Sure, no problem, I've got lots of vacation time saved and I'll come right away."

"I'm not at the motorhome. Can you meet me at the marina in town at noon? I need to make funeral arrangements and then I'd like to come up and stay with you for a while. Would that be all right?"

"Of course!"

After shoring herself up with another blessed Valium, Nikki called Chief Anderson.

"The autopsy's done," Frank said. "They released Steve's body."

"What did they find?" she asked.

"Sure you want to hear this?"

"I'm sure. Tell me."

"Okay. Steve died of three gunshot wounds: two in the back and one to the head, 9-mm, from about three feet away, but you knew that. Looks like the perp came in, they struggled and when Steve tried to run, he got it in the back. We're wondering if Steve knew the killer."

"Anything else?"

"Lab ran the prints. One set is unidentified."

"Unidentified? Did you check them against Hess's?"

"Yeah, no match. You know, that finishing shot to the head makes me think about a professional hit. Besides, we don't even know for sure that Hess is in Rhode Island."

"You can't be serious," she said.

"Well, there are other suspects besides Hess, too."

"Like who?"

"Like a whole campground full of 'em. Roger Starkweather's work truck was seen at Steve's that day. Junior Ferguson was there. Hell, even Tommy Frederick's old Nash Rambler was seen in the area."

"Turkey Kielbasa? What was he doing there?"

Frank chortled. "Probably hanging out."

"Not funny," she said. "All these so-called suspects, what would be their motive?"

"To steal your valuable purple pearl brooch, for one."

"I don't think so. Hess took it after he shot Steve."

"Or, maybe someone had a grudge against your husband, who knows? These things we gotta look into. I hate to say it, but we gotta look at you, too."

"Me?"

"You found the body. Your husband wasn't having an affair, was he?"

"No, Frank. Jesus. Read my lips: Hess did it, damn it!"

"Everything has to be checked out: alibis, timelines . . . .."

"At the time of Steve's death, I was at work. Check it out."

"Oh, we will, babe. We will."

From nowhere, an ugly vision of Steve's lifeless eyes—eyes that were once so full of love for her—slipped past Nikki's shield of Valium. She started sobbing, in hiccupping gulps. *Shit!*

"Um, ah, are you okay?" asked Frank.

"No, godammit, I'm not!" she screeched. "Now listen to me: you've got to find that murdering son of a bitch. And that unidentified set of prints you found? I'll bet they belong to the antique expert we had in to look at the brooch. Her shop is on Spring Street, over in Newport. I'll give you her number."

"You figure she might've stole it?"

"Oh, for Christ's sake, Frank. No way." Her eyes filled again so she hung up.

She cried hard but this time her tears were fueled by anger. She snatched the phone back up, called the antique dealer, and railed about how she wasn't any too happy that the woman had alerted the media.

The woman's silence on the other end confirmed Nikki's suspicions. The woman said how sorry she was to hear about Steve. "What a shock," she added.

Nikki still had time before she had to meet her daughter so she called the campground manager and told him she'd be unable to continue this year as park ranger. He understood completely, told her not to worry about it. Then she drove to the marina.

AT THE MARINA, Nikki and Erin shared a long, tearful hug and then headed to the funeral home. On the way, Nikki told Erin all about Hess, along with a few selected details about the murder. At the funeral home, she called Steve's son, living in Las Vegas and found he was ill and couldn't travel. She told his son that Steve wanted to be cremated so she would go ahead and make the arrangements.

But as heartsick and depressed as Nikki was, she completely lost it when the undertaker tried to coerce her into buying an expensive casket. "A $5000 casket?" she screeched, getting in his face. "He's being *cremated* for Pete's sake!" Erin had to pull her away but Nikki took some satisfaction in paying a much smaller sum for an urn.

"You may pick up the ashes of the deceased tomorrow," the undertaker said, with a sniff.

Nikki started to go after him but, again, Erin yanked her away.

He followed them out the door, saying, "May we help you arrange a service, ma'am?"

Nikki turned back, steeled her eyes, and that was enough to send him scurrying back inside.

Nikki and Erin walked across the parking lot to Nikki's Honda CR-V and then headed back south. Back on Mystic Island, as they neared Benedict's Landing, Erin turned to her. "What *do* you have in mind for the service?"

"Well, Steve always said he'd like for his ashes to be scattered in the ocean, across the bay, near the lighthouse. I'll call the friend of his who bought Steve's sailboat and see if he'll take us out. Maybe day after tomorrow? At sunrise."

"I can't believe you're doing all this, Mom. I mean, your composure and everything, um, you seem almost, well . . . almost calm about it. All except for that undertaker."

Nikki laughed, a harsh bark. "The miracle of Valium, sweetie. Like they say: 'Better living through chemistry'."

ON THE HORIZON, pale streaks of early light and a thin, vermilion smudge of sunlight heralded the day of Steve's burial at sea. The bay was placid, just starting to streak in reflected pastels as they powered out toward the lighthouse in *Honkycat,* a truly classic catboat that once belonged to Steve. Off the starboard bow, a green buoy clanged, directing them out of the harbor and into open waters.

Steve's friend manned the helm. Besides Erin, Tugboat, and Nikki, there were a couple of Steve's other friends onboard and a non-denominational minister from the Seaman's shelter in Newport where Steve sometimes volunteered his time.

As the lighthouse came into view, the wind picked up.

"Let's raise the sail," Nikki said. She was barely functioning, lacking any semblance of energy. There were no more Valiums available, which was a good thing because she craved the temporary illusion of peace they gave her.

That bothered her.

Not too much, though.

Tugboat grabbed the halyard and hoisted the voluminous gaff-rigged mainsail. It filled, they bore off on a beam reach and one of the guys cut the motor. With just the sound of seawater gurgling around the hull, they were now at one with the wind and sea. The breeze washed over their faces. The boat heeled over. They caught some light spray.

When they were abeam to the lighthouse, the helmsman brought them into the wind; the main luffed and they bobbed in the waves while Nikki ducked into the cabin and returned with Steve's ashes.

"Go ahead," she said. "Put us on a broad reach."

They came about, sailed back in the direction of the bay, and she made her way aft. She removed the lid of the urn. "Let's do this," she said.

The reverend offered a few kind words and quoted scripture.

Amen.

She started sobbing as she shook Steve's remains downwind into the ocean he'd loved so much. And with his remains, went the love and happiness that he'd brought into her life. How cruel that it should end after four short months. Yet, from somewhere deep within herself, she felt a tiny bit of warmth, sort of an ethereal embrace from Steve—as if to comfort her and thank her for leaving him where he wanted to be.

Erin put a protective arm around her.

Nikki glanced back over her shoulder. Everyone's eyes were wet, including the reverend. Returning her attention to stern, she watched swirling gusts of wind capture the ashes and feather them out over the surface of the water where they intermingled with the sea. An inquisitive gull swooped down, examined the ashes, and flapped away.

The reverend said a few more words but she was oblivious to them.

Amen.

Steve's remains were almost undetectable now. She reached into her purse, drew out a handful of rose petals, and tossed them out to where they chased the last few visible ashes.

Amen.

CHAPTER 23

FRIDAY AFTERNOON: Hess and Junior hunkered down, as usual, in a rear booth at Peep Toad's bar, engaging in earnest conversation. In a booth across the way, loomed the toad—sandwiched between the table and backrest.

Junior happily guzzled a beer for which he had not been carded and was thinking the bar stank like the Jolly Green Giant had drank about fifty kegs of beer and puked on the floor. An impotent smoke-dissipating machine hummed at the dense cloud of cigarette smoke.

"Take it easy," Hess advised. "You celebrating?"

"Not rilly," said Junior as his eyes roamed.

"Fuck're you looking at, boy?" asked Hess.

Junior pointed with his chin. "Peep Toad, there. I can't tell whether he's a dude or a chick. 'Zennybody know?"

Hess shrugged. "The jury's still out but I'm leaning toward guy."

Junior strained forward, slitted his eyes to focus better. "The moustache, huh? But I think I see boobs."

Hess snorted. "Listen, earlier, when I got here? I saw Toad out in a garden, out back of the parking lot, sitting on one of those plastic milk crates. *Not* a pretty sight."

"No, huh?"

"No. Get this: the toadster's gut was resting on another milk crate, probably so it wouldn't drag on the ground or cause back strain, you know? I have to say he's the most disgusting, pathetic schlub of blubbery shit since Jabba the Hut."

"For sure," said Junior. "But is he a dude or a chick?"

"I'm getting to that. See, Toad was displaying some serious butt crack cleavage. I'm talking the San Andreas Fault here."

"San . . . what?"

"San Andreas, boy. And here's why I'm leaning toward him being a guy: I'm pretty sure I saw his scrotum, drooping down from his shorts."

"Uh . . . *scrotum?*"

"Ball sack, you dimbulb."

"Whoa. TMI."

"TMI?"

"Too much information," said Junior, frowning. "For sure. More than I need to know."

"More than *anyone* needs to know," agreed Hess. "But maybe it was just an excess dollop of flab, something like that. Then again, I suppose it could've even been some droopy female genitalia or—"

Junior put that nasty image out of his mind and started swiveling his head, scanning the other side of the bar.

"What," said Hess.

"You ever see that Ray Nickerson guy anymore? The guy we met out in the boonies there in West Arcadia? Man, that was—"

"Shut the *fuck* up," hissed Hess. "Why're you bringing that up?"

Junior blanched. "No reason, man. Just makin' conversation."

Hess frowned, leaned in and lowered his voice. "Open your goddam shirt."

"What?"

"Open your shirt, you little dipshit douchebag. You're not wearing a wire, are you?"

"Wire?"

"Open it, goddamit."

Junior unbuttoned his shirt to reveal a pale, hairless chest and prominent rib cage.

"Okay," said Hess.

"You don't trust me?" asked Junior, his voice incredulous. "I may not be 'zackly always on the top of my game, but I ain't no rat."

Hess snorted. "Nothing personal. I don't trust anyone." He glanced around, kept his voice low. "How're things going at good ol' Franklin High?"

Junior beamed. He cupped his hand around his mouth, lowered his voice to a whisper. "I made up baggies. I put a couple joints in each one, sold 'em for ten bucks. I made a shitload of money, dude."

"How many times I gotta tell you?" hissed Hess. "I am *not* one of your dudes."

"Sorry."

"I'll say you are. How's your supply holding out?"

"I'm good."

"Okay. Keep what you earned, go buy your purple-haired girlfriend something nice."

"Her hair's magenta, man . . . hey wait a minute. How do you know about her?"

A shrug. "I've been keeping tabs on you, son."

"I don't think—"

"I don't give a flying fuck what you think," said Hess, interrupting. "I make it my business to know *all* about my employees."

Junior swallowed. He felt his Adam's apple bulge.

Hess narrowed his eyes. "You didn't tell her anything, did you?"

"No way."

"Okay. There's just one other thing. The popular kids give you any grief? The jocks?"

Junior laughed, a harsh cackle. "No way. I got somethin' they want, you know? Still, I'd love to kick their ass. Maybe if I learnt Karate or like that . . .."

"Forget Karate," said Hess. He lowered his voice. "Ever consider a gun?"

"A gun? Are you serious?"

"Think about it."

WHEN JUNIOR got home, his mom snatched up the nearest thing to her, a loaf of rye bread. She screamed and hurled it at him.

He ducked, saying, "Chill, Ma. Jesus."

"You're dealing drugs again, aren't you? That's why you're driving that fancy car."

"What? No. I—"

"Who is this man, anyway? Does he live in Benedict's Landing?"

"Karl's just a friend, that's all."

"Karl, huh. Well, he's too old. He's using you."

Junior shrugged. "Like I said, he loaned me the Beemer. For deliveries."

"Deliveries, my cellulite butt. Deliveries of drugs, unless I miss my guess. The police came by here, asking for you yesterday. You want to tell me about that?"

"Cops? I got nothin' to tell."

"Well, they want to ask you some questions."

"'Bout what?"

"How should I know? I hope to God you're not involved in that murder."

"Murder? . . . What murder?"

"You don't know? Someone got shot in the Seabreeze campground, right in his motorhome. I know you're always hanging out there, and that must be why the police want to question you. Were you involved?"

"No way!" With that, he banged out the screen door and marched straight for the BMW.

His mom came out on the porch. "Wait! Come back, Junior. We need to talk about this."

"I tole you, Ma. I don't know nothin'."

"I love you."

Junior cringed. "Yeah, yeah, yeah."

"And what about school? I got a letter in the mail saying you're still three credits shy, even with summer school. If you want to graduate, you'll have to go this fall and make them up."

"You know what? I am *so* not going back to that school. Fuck 'em."

"Please don't say those nasty words, honey. You don't mean it. It's those darned drugs talking."

He shot out the door, leaped into the BMW and burned rubber. He drove like a crazed commuter for a while, then started to chill, thinking how Adrienne, at least, would appreciate his new wheels. And besides, wasn't he a—what did Karl call it?—an enterpreener now? Something like that, anyway. He headed for the Seabreeze campground.

Petey Fottler was at the gatehouse, on duty. Sort of.

Junior stopped, thinking: it's that goofy old shit with all the weird Chinese hang-yang. But the dude's eyes were closed and Junior could hear snoring.

"Yo! Wake up, dude!"

"Szazz . . . er, ah , whup?" said Petey, jerking awake.

"You asleep?"

"Not all closed eye sleeping, nor open eye seeing," said Petey sagely.

"Hah?" said Junior. "Whazzup?"

"Up?" asked Petey. "Confucius say woman who fly upside down have nasty crack up."

"What the fuck? Hey . . . that's a good one."

"Fool who hold tongue, pass for sage."

"What? C'mon. You know I don't understand any a that shit."

"No?" said Petey. "Well, understand this: the cops're looking for you."

"Me? Shit. Why?"

Petey winked. "Better go see Chief Anderson."

"No way. Fuck 'em."

Petey narrowed his eyes, grinned. "Uh-huh. The wise does at once what the fool does at last."

Junior felt his bowels loosen and tightened his sphincter. "Uh, they say why they want me?"

"No. They're probably questioning everyone who knew Steve Marshall."

"Shit, man. I barely knew him."

Petey shrugged. "Truth serves to further," he said, and pumped his eyebrows.

"What the fuck does that *mean*?"

"Like I said, the cops're probably questioning everyone. Say, where'd you get the fancy car?"

Junior felt his stomach churn. "Fuck you, you old fart," he said as he eased away and drove into the campground. His hands were shaking. Like a mantra, he kept repeating: "Holy shit, holy shit, holy shit."

Adrienne was at her tent, just back from a swim in the bay. She was wearing her thong bikini and toweling herself off and it got Junior's complete attention. He parked and shuffled over.

"You hear anythin' about the park ranger's husband getting murdered?" he asked.

"Isn't it awful?"

He nodded, then: "Whoa. You look *hot*!"

"Thanks. I was just thinking about you."

He beamed. "You were? How come?"

"I don't know. Maybe I like the way you kiss or something."

He pumped his eyebrows up and down. "Yeah? Anythin' else you like? My body?"

"Maybe."

"How 'bout my cool hair?"

She rolled her eyes. "Don't push it." She pointed to the BMW. "Where'd you get the fancy car?"

"From this old guy dude. He gave me a job. Sweet, huh?"

"A job? Doing what?"

"Deliveries. Shit and stuff like that and everything."

"Deliveries."

"Right. And I get to use this awesome Beemer here. Is that too cool or what?"

She frowned, chewed at a knuckle. "Who's the guy?"

"I ain't 'sposta say."

"Why not?"

"Well," said Junior. "I guess I could tell you, but you gotta promise not to tell anyone."

"I don't like it," she said, and started toweling her hair.

"The dude's name is Karl, okay? Shit, nobody wants me to have that car! Not you, not my fuckin' ma, neither. Yo! All you beeotches be dissin' my ride, know what I'm sayin'? Well, you know what, Homes? Fuck you all!"

She dropped the towel, put her hands on her hips. "Listen to me: that homeboy shit is *so* not cool and don't you *ever* call me a bitch! You understand?"

He blinked, took a step backward.

She lifted her chin, narrowed her eyes. "Understand?"

He nodded.

"And don't go getting all huffy on me here? I'm just saying it doesn't make sense. You wouldn't happen to be delivering something illegal for him, would you? Like drugs?"

"Well, maybe. Kin you keep a secret?"

"I don't know. What is it?"

"A little pot, is all."

"You sure?"

"Yeah."

"Promise? 'Cause if you're like, into the heavier shit? Well, then . . . I'm history."

"I ain't. I promise."

She ducked into her tent, squirmed into hip-hugger cutoffs, discarded her bikini top, and pulled a cropped T-shirt over her head. It had a cute little cartoon dog on it, roasting a marshmallow over a campfire. The caption read: LIFE IS GOOD. Her braless, pert breasts poked out and plenty of bare midriff was exposed, all the way down to where there was a hint of the Promised Land below.

With his head installed just inside the tent flap, Junior missed none of the quick change. He lunged for her.

She held up a hand, saying, "Later."

"But I thought you liked my kisses and stuff," he whined.

She gave him a peck on the cheek. "I do, but I said later. Help me pack up my tent and everything. I'm moving into Benedict's Landing. I rented an apartment off Water Street, down by the marina? With the camping season coming to an end, I need a place to stay."

"Whatever. But I thought you were, like, going to Brown? Don'cha get a—whatdayacallit—like a dorm room and stuff?"

"I decided to skip this semester."

"No shit? So . . . where're you getting' the cash for an apartment?"

"My mom, Mr. Snoopy Snoop. I got this awesome trust fund, okay?"

"What about your dad?"

"Who knows? Who cares?" she said.

"So they're divorced. Mine, too."

"Big deal. Everyone's parents are divorced, you know?"

Junior nodded. "What about your clothes and stuff?"

"I got what I need and I'll buy what I don't have. Anyway, what's with all the questions? You Regis Philbin or someone? Help me pack."

After cramming her stuff into a duffel, she dragged all of her gear outside. They folded her tent, transferred the gear to her Camaro, and stowed it in the huge trunk. Junior helped her lug her cooler and Coleman stove to the car. They shoved it into the back seat.

"All packed up and ready to roll," she said, getting in the driver's seat. "Follow me."

He got the BMW and pulled up behind her. Forming a two-car convoy, they drove to the gatehouse and she checked out. Once that was done, they sped the few miles to Benedict's Landing. She headed straight for the apartment and parked. They got out of their cars and she handed him her duffel.

"Where you at?" he asked, looking up.

"In the back there, on the third floor? 3-C."

"Sweet."

As soon as they were in the apartment, she dropped her stuff and pulled the skimpy T-shirt over her head. She twirled it on her finger before flipping it aside.

"I'm horny," she said.

Junior was beside himself with lust. "Clam Doggies!" he cried, as he clawed at his belt. Once it came loose, he let go of his baggy drawers, which—already slung low like drapes—ended up pooled at his feet. An insistent woodie pulsed against his colorful boxer shorts.

She looked down, giggled. "Sponge Bob Squarepants? You got Sponge Bob undies?"

"Cool, huh? My ma got 'em for me." He reached for her breasts.

Giggling louder now, she skirted around him, headed for the bed, hopped up on it, and started jumping up and down. Eager to follow, he tripped over his voluminous pants and sprawled on the floor. Adrienne broke into peals of laughter.

He felt his face burning. Shit, he thought, embarrassing stuff like this didn't happen in James Bond movies! But his shame was short-lived once he saw how her breasts jiggled and bounced. He crawled over to the bed, reached up, grabbed her by the ankles, and yanked. She collapsed on the spread and he scrambled on top of her. They kissed greedily, young hormones racing. He unbuttoned her cutoffs.

She squirmed beneath him, making moaning sounds deep in her throat as she helped him pull her shorts and thong down. She kicked the pesky garments away, leaving Sponge Bob Squarepants as the only barrier between them.

And Sponge Bob didn't last long.

. . . Less than a minute later, they lay on their backs, sweating like marathon runners and gulping air in ragged breaths.

"That was quick," she said, rolling over and kissing him on the cheek.

He leaned up on an elbow, reached over, placed his index finger on a nipple, and stroked.

"Can I move in?" he blurted, before he lost the courage.

She laughed, grabbed his hand and moved it aside. "Are you for real?"

"Well, I just thought—"

"Like, I need to get to know you first?"

"Isn't that what we been doing?" he asked.

"We had sex. It's not the same."

"Whatever." He slid off the bed, tugged on his Sponge Bob underwear and padded over to the window where he looked out over the bay. A lobster boat was steaming toward some trap markers. On a nearby rooftop, a couple of seagulls argued.

The sky was cloudless, but he felt a slight hint of coolness in the warm summer day. Fall wasn't far away.

Adrienne got dressed, went to her purse, and pulled out her cell phone. "Awesome," she said. "I've got five bars here. I need to make a call." After punching in a long series of numbers on her phone, she said, "Hello? Can I have Ms. LeDoux's room?" A pause, then: "Hello, Mother."

Some talking on the other end: unintelligible sounds that Junior couldn't make out.

"I just wanted to let you know I rented an apartment in Benedict's Landing," said Adrienne. "I'm skipping this semester."

Nothing on the other end.

"Mother? Are you there?"

More unintelligible sounds.

Adrienne frowned. "A facial? Right now? Can't you, like, reschedule or something?"

Louder sounds, still unintelligible.

Adrienne rolled her eyes. "Whatever." She punched the "off" button on her phone so hard, it flew out of her hand and thumped on the carpet.

"Uh, everything cool?" asked Junior.

"Let's go get something to eat," she snapped. "I'm starved."

Junior beamed. "Well, awright. Pizza?"

CHAPTER 24

BEFORE LEAVING Rhode Island, Nikki went to the bank, took Steve's will out of their safe-deposit box, and turned it over to a lawyer. Being her husband's only heir and executrix and having her name on everything made it simple for Nikki. All that was left was to arrange for storage for their motorhome and Steve's boat.

And after an hours drive, in Hingham, Massachusetts, Nikki took great pleasure wallowing in self-pity for much too long at her daughter's apartment. She couldn't imagine ever being happy again. She marinated in her misery, figuring it was apt punishment for not being there for Steve.

On the kitchen table loomed a box of glazed donuts from Dunkin' Donuts. The clock showed nine o'clock A.M. and she'd already gobbled her fourth.

"Why don't you call Dana?" suggested Erin.

Nikki glared, licked glazing off her upper lip. "What, and subject my best friend to my miserableness?"

"That's not even a word, Mom. Did it ever occur to you that she might want to help?"

"No one can help me," Nikki snapped.

"Does she even know about Steve?"

Nikki shook her head.

"She'd want to know. Just call her, please? As a favor to me?" Erin looked her mom up and down, frowning. "And please give me that funky bathrobe so I can wash it. It's so . . . so *skanky.*"

Nikki heaved a great sigh. "All right, all right, I'll call her. But you're not getting this robe."

Dana Hart, Nikki's best friend since her days in St. Louis, now lived in Destin, Florida with David, her husband. Dana had married well: her husband was a first-rate thoracic surgeon. Their two daughters were grown and on their own.

Nikki dialed Dana's number.

She answered on the third ring and once the pleasantries were exchanged, must've sensed Nikki was distraught.

"Let's have it," Dana said. "What's wrong?"

Nikki burst into tears. Between sobs and blowing her nose, she blurted it all out.

There was a sharp intake of breath on Dana's end of the line. "My God, Nikki. He was *murdered*?"

"Yes." Barely a whisper.

"I'm coming right up."

"You don't have to—"

"Did you hear me? I'm taking the next plane up there."

"What about David?"

"He loves you, too. I'm sure he'll want me to be with you."

"Well, okay, if you're sure. But I'm not in Rhode Island. I'm at Erin's so you'll have to fly into Boston."

"Okay."

"Really, I don't want to be a bother to—"

"Will you put a sock in it? And no dramatic sighs, either. Nothing you can say or do will stop me. I'm catching the next plane to Logan."

"I love you," Nikki said, around a sob. "You're like a sister."

"Better than that. I'm your best friend."

After she blew her nose, Nikki told Dana how to take the water taxi from Logan and pick up the commuter ferry at Rowe's Wharf. From there, she could get to Hingham.

"Call when you get here. One of us will pick you up at the landing."

"Be there before you know it. And stock up on lots of that strong-assed Yankee coffee. We'll be needing *gallons* of it."

THE FOLLOWING EVENING, they stayed up all night, talking. By the time the sun came up, they were caffeinated to the point where every cell in their bodies was doing its own "River Dance".

"How did you manage to get off work?" Nikki asked Dana.

"Work? Hah! My husband makes as much money as Donald Trump, remember? My days as a nurse are over; in fact, I retired last week. You think I'm going to subject myself to bedpans and infections any longer than I have to?"

"So, what do you do with yourself now that you're the queen of leisure?"

"Shop, mostly. Get manicures, massages. 'Do' lunch. Stuff like that."

That elicited a small chuckle, but Nikki immediately settled back into her funk.

"I've about had it with those dramatic sighs," Dana said. "From my point of view, the best plan is for us to go to bed, sleep about forty-eight hours, and take that ferry back into Boston."

"Boston?"

Dana nodded. "Quincy Market, first: Bagels, pastries, Boston Baked Beans, pizza. Then over to the No Name Seafood for lunch. After that, a little shopping spree on Newbury Street. Get our priorities in order, you know?"

Nikki leaned on her elbows, rested her chin on folded hands, and stared at the floor. "No, thanks."

"Don't be a poop," Dana said. "I'll bet we can even find some glazed donuts."

Nikki shot her a nasty look, but an involuntary half-smile commandeered her lips. "How do you keep that figure?" she asked. "You eat like a piglet. Do you work out?"

"Victoria's Secret underwear," Dana said. "Enhances, even as it contains."

That brought on a real smile.

"That's the first smile I've seen since I got here. We're making progress."

"Hand me one of those donuts," Nikki said, straight-faced.

THE TRIP TO Boston and a refill of Nikki's Valium prescription helped a little but all too soon, she was feeling the overwhelming grief again.

Dana suggested they go to her place in Destin for a change of scene and Nikki accepted because she knew she was causing an undue strain on her daughter. Erin had enough stress from her job and didn't need Nikki mucking up her home life.

Erin protested, but her mom stood her ground.

"I'm going with Dana, and that's it," Nikki said. "You need your life back."

"But, Mom . . .. "

"No buts."

"Do you need any money?"

"No thanks, honey. Steve's lotto winnings will tide me over for quite some time."

"Lotto winnings?" asked Dana.

"Yeah, he got lucky," said Nikki. "I'll fill you in later."

"What about that pearl brooch?" asked Erin. "Did it end up being worth anything?"

Nikki barked out an excuse for a laugh. "Oh, that? Just a measly million dollars is all. It made the news in Rhode Island—"

"Pearl brooch?" interrupted Dana. "Million dollars?"

"More to tell you on the way to Florida," I said. "But it's moot, anyway."

Erin looked puzzled. "Moot?"

Nikki nodded. "That bastard Hess got it."

They packed up and loaded Nikki's little Honda SUV, but before they went, she had to make some calls. First, she called the detective in New Mexico asking if there had been any developments. There were none. Next, she dialed the Benedict's Landing Police Department and they put her through to Chief Anderson.

"The State Police are in on it now, " he told her. "Their geeks looked into those e-mails you got and it looks like the bastard sent them from a public library. A dead end."

"Anything else?"

"Yeah. A Statie detective wants to interview you."

"Give me his number, I'll call him."

Frank eventually found the detective's card, gave her the number.

"Okay. Listen, I'm going away for a while, to a friend's in Florida. I want to give you her address and phone number in case you hear anything."

He took down the details.

"Please, *please,* don't give my whereabouts to anybody, okay?"

"Sure."

"I guess this is goodbye, then," she said. "For now."

After they rang off, she called the detective, told him all she knew and gave him her cell number. The last call she made was to Tugboat Haywood, to tell him she was leaving.

"Good," he said. "Get the hell away from here."

"Thanks again, for being there for me when I needed a friend."

"Think nothing of it."

"Well, I can't do that. Anyway, I wanted to let you know how to reach me in Destin, Florida. But please keep it to yourself."

"Of course. Destin? I've been there. The beaches are the best."

She gave him Dana's address and phone number, they said their goodbyes, and she hung up.

Dana slid behind the wheel for the first leg of their 1500-mile journey. Nikki turned to Erin: they hugged fiercely and muttered tearful goodbyes. With great reluctance, Nikki broke the embrace and got into the car.

Erin shut the door for her, saying, "Mom, take better care of yourself."

"I will."

"Promise?"

"We have to get going . . ."

They were backing out of the driveway when Erin signaled them to stop. "Mom!"

Dana braked.

"What?" Nikki shouted, out the window.

"That skanky bathrobe of yours?" Erin yelled. " . . . Burn it!"

CHAPTER 25

DESTIN, FLORIDA: where a colorful sign welcomes you, proclaiming Destin to be "the world's luckiest fishing village". The Chamber of Commerce will tell you that their beach sand is as white as sugar and the waters of the Gulf are the color of Windex.

On the way down, Nikki had filled Dana in on the purple pearl and told her more about Marion Hess than she probably ever wanted to know.

Dana and her husband's lovely home perched on a dune, commanding breathtaking views of the Gulf. They also had a lanai, pool and boardwalk to the beach but none of those things dispelled the emptiness inside Nikki, or excised her feeling of desolation—neither did they remove her pain, nor bring Steve back.

Her world remained bleak, devoid of all joy.

"You sure David is okay with me being here?" she asked Dana.

"How many times are you going to ask me that? For Christ's sake, *yes!* The question is moot anyway. As you know, my husband is your typical, workaholic surgeon, so you'll never even see each other."

Not long after settling in, Nikki became a hermit. Her wardrobe consisted of either baggy shorts and oversized T-shirts or voluminous sweats. She was overeating, but also purging, making herself throw up about three times a day.

A wonderful side effect of such behavior was that she'd started getting toothaches because stomach acid was removing the enamel from her teeth. In spite of her grand efforts, she'd still put on fifteen pounds, so she naturally started taking laxatives.

Her hair disgusted her, so one day she assaulted it with scissors and ended up with the most horrendous haircut on the planet—a real chop job that left her smug and content. As fall arrived, her endless daily ritual consisted of getting up, eating, feeling sorry for herself, eating, bitching about her situation, eating, snarling at Dana, eating, and puking.

Wallowing on the beach was good. She had hopes of basting herself to death in cocoa butter. And on rainy days, she hid out in her darkened room, frying her brain with the idiot box. Not too much on TV though, except endless talking heads rehashing the rehashes of other talking heads and *ad nauseum* advertising. When Dana's satellite went on the fritz, it suited Nikki just fine.

Once in a while, she called those detectives in New Mexico and Rhode Island as well as Chief Anderson to see if there were any breaks on the case. There were none.

Today, she lolled on the beach in shorts and halter-top, eating glazed donuts and getting cooked way past that Onassis broiled-in-olive-oil kind of tan. She made a feeble attempt to read a trashy novel but couldn't concentrate enough to get past the first paragraph. She watched a squadron of brown pelicans patrol low over the water, gliding with almost no effort.

Dana plopped down next to her. "I'm going to Publix market for a few things," she said. "Want to come along? We could do lunch at Calahan's after."

Nikki noticed with envy that Dana sat cross-legged, still quite capable of the lotus position. With Nikki's new waistline and thighs? No way.

"No thanks," she said. "By the way, how old do you have to be?"

"Excuse me?"

Nikki picked at her face. "How old do you have to be before you quit getting zits? I mean, I thought they went away with adolescence."

"I'm guessing it's the Krispy Kremes."

"Hmpf."

Dana turned to her, grim-faced. "We need to talk. Seriously."

"Talk? No thanks. Look, I know you're sick of me and I don't blame you. I'll just pack up and get out of your hair . . .."

"Don't be silly. Look, I'm concerned."

"Well, don't be."

"I've been hearing you, you know."

Nikki didn't reply.

"When you throw up," Dana said.

Nikki waved her off. "Oh, that. I must have picked up a bug or something."

"It's no bug, Nikki. It's called bulimia."

"Why don't you mind your own goddam business?"

Dana looked hurt. "You *are* my business. You're my best friend. I thought you got over that binging and purging business a long time ago."

Nikki chewed at her lower lip. "Look, I'm in control of it, okay? It's not that bad. I mean, I just want to get rid of some of this bloat, okay?"

"I've read the pamphlets. They say it's a symptom of underlying angst."

"To hell with what the pamphlets say, okay? *Angst?*" Nikki let out an ugly little bark that tried to pass for a laugh. "Oh, I've got *angst*, all right."

"I'm worried. This needs to be addressed, you know? Before you become . . . I don't know, mentally ill or something."

"Not your problem."

"Well, I'm not backing off. Not only is your health literally going into the toilet, but you've got no motivation and what's worse, no hope."

"Hope? *Hope?* Steve's *dead,* goddamit! And it's *my* fault."

"No, it's not. We've been over this."

"I'm a pariah, don't you get it? All my relationships end up with the man dying."

"You didn't cause it."

Nikki shook her head; Dana didn't understand. "I should've been there for him."

"Shoulda, coulda, woulda. Means *didn't,* is all. You're no pariah," Dana said. "But you do look like shit."

Nikki turned away, stared down the beach. "Thanks for sharing."

Dana handed her a business card, saying, "Here. This is Dr. Janet West's card. She's an excellent therapist. Give her a call."

"No way. No shrinks, thank you very much."

"Why not? I went to her. She helped me."

"You? But you're so . . . so *together*!"

Dana laughed. "Not really. I never wanted to burden you with it, but my life here fell apart. With my husband working so much, I turned to vodka and ended up with not one, but two DWIs. After that, I was forced to check in at "The Gator Lodge", a tough 28-day addiction treatment program near Gainesville."

"Why didn't you tell me?"

Dana shrugged. "You had your new life. And I was ashamed."

"Still, I would've wanted to know."

"Well, now you know. Anyway, after treatment, I went into therapy with Janet. She did wonders for me."

"Do you still go?"

"Not anymore. I'm in Alcoholics Anonymous now. Those times I've been telling you that I'm going to a meeting? It's AA."

"Good for you. I guess."

Dana nodded.

Nikki sniffed, picked up another donut and bit into it. "Well, I'm happy for you but I'm *not* you. Thanks anyway, but meetings and shrinks can't help me."

"Your case is unique?"

"I believe so. No one could possibly know my pain."

Dana got up, brushed the sand off. "Well, Mz. Uniqueness, you'd better not stay in this Florida sun much longer. You're starting to look like a lobster."

"You see anyone here who cares?'

"At least put on some sun screen, will you?"

After Dana had gone, Nikki ignored her advice, closed her eyes. The sun felt like warm butter on her eyelids while squiggly lines and motes danced against the vermilion backdrop. Her sleep pattern ever since Steve had been murdered was hit and miss, more miss than hit. This time, though, she drifted off into a hard sleep, off into dreamland:

. . . Steve and her, lying on a blanket, on a beach. Steve is alive, assuring her that his murder was just a nightmare, a cruel nightmare. She's wearing a sexy bikini; Steve is leaning up on one

elbow and running his hand lightly across her flat tummy, playing with her navel. She's not fat!

Harsh laughing interrupting: a crude cackle from their right. It's an ex-boyfriend from just before she met Steve. A few weeks after she'd broken up with the lying jerk, he had died, drunk in a car crash. In her dream, he is saturated with blood, caked with beach sand—sand that was once white as sugar.

Next to the ex-boyfriend: her ex-husband, the father of her daughter, who she'd divorced long ago. She had heard he was killed in prison. A shank handle is sticking out of his throat.

He, too, laughs hysterically.

Nikki screams.

Steve is getting up, looking down at her; Steve with three enormous, ragged exit wounds, two in his chest and one in his forehead. Blood is coursing down his face and torso in rivulets, dripping in grotesque globs off his chin.

More screaming, coming from her.

Steve dusts the sand off himself, goes to join the other two bodies, all three of them walking away together.

Nikki is staring at two dark holes in the center of Steve's back. And one in the back of his head. She tries to scream again but her mouth only forms an "O" from which no sound comes out.

From a lifeguard stand a few yards away, her deceased father climbs down and lurches over to her. Daddy had died at sea, a fisherman. Seaweed still clings to him and dozens of little crabs are pinching off chunks of putrid and rotting flesh.

In his hand, a familiar bag: glazed donuts.

So many donuts, they make you throw up.

In his other hand, a fat purple pearl, about the size of a baseball.

Nikki gags, vomits up ropes of slimy, undigested donut.

Daddy nods approval, then joins Steve and the others. Steve is looking back at her as the men walk away, abreast—his Mel Gibson eyes, that impossible color of blue, like the waters of the Gulf.

Blue eyes accusing her.

"Why weren't you there?" he asks.

Her thoughts exactly.
She's screaming— screaming until she wakes herself up.

    . . . Shaking and fearful, she gathered her things and ran back up to the house, tortured by the fact that all the men in her life ended up dead. What was the common denominator? Her! Like a hermit crab, she scuttled into her room, closed the blinds, and headed for the bathroom. She looked into the mirror. A stranger with a scorched, pimply face and hollow, imbedded eyes stared back at her.

    Why me? she thought. Why did this have to happen to her? Hadn't she experienced enough death?

    She took a cold shower, coated her abused body and radiating face in aloe and cocooned herself in bed. She started sobbing again, blubbering into her pillow. Sugar sand and water the color of Windex just wasn't making it.

CHAPTER 26

IN RHODE ISLAND, after letting his thoughts tumble over and over in his mind, Junior finally decided he'd better go see what the police wanted so he drove to the police station, parked, and sauntered in to where an officer sat at a desk.

"Help you?" asked the officer.

Junior nodded. "Yeah. I heard youse wanted to ast me some questions."

Chief Anderson popped out of his office. "Junior? Where the hell have you been? Get your ass in here."

Junior gulped, followed the chief into his office.

"Take a seat," said the chief. "Just a few questions here."

Junior shrugged. "No big deal."

"You're a hard guy to catch up with. Your mom says you're hardly home anymore. Didn't she tell you we wanted to talk to you?"

"Yessir. But I guess I kinda forgot . . . ."

"You'd better lay off the pot, son. This is just routine, anyway. You were at Steve Marshall and Nikki O'Connor's motorhome the day of Steve's murder. Is that right?"

"I guess so."

"Doing what?"

"I dunno, I . . . wait, I remember now. I ast him for some cheap lobstahs, 'cause I wanted to impress my girlfriend, know what I'm sayin'?"

"Yeah. And?"

"He din't have any, said to check with him in a day or two."

"While you were there, did you see anyone else?"

"No."

"Where'd you go after that?"

"My girlfriend's tent."

"Will she vouch for you?"

"Sure," said Junior. "Her name is Adrienne Lee-doo."

"How do you spell that?"

Junior shrugged. "Beats me. But since the campground season is over, she's been living in town in one of those apartments on Water Street. Number 3-C."

"Anything else you can tell us?"

"Nope."

"Okay, you can go."

"I kin go?"

"Get out of here."

Junior didn't need an engraved invitation, no sir.

HE BEELINED THE Beemer and tooled straight to Hammune Park, where the kids hung out. After he finished conducting business, he took off, thinking: goddam jocks and popular kids weren't so quick to treat him like a fag with AIDS when he had something they wanted, now, were they? *Assholes!*

After that, he just cruised around awhile and thought about the vials of crack in his trunk. Shit man, didn't everybody say crack was wicked awesome, the best? One kid had called it The Big Bang. He'd also overheard a girl telling someone that it was like having a whole body orgasm. *Whoa!* . . . Scary shit, though. Heavy-duty shit, supposed to be super addictive. *Fuck!*

Deciding he was hungry, he headed for Freddie's diner where he ordered a large cheesesteak grinder with extra onions and hot peppers, to go. Next, he picked up a 16-oz. bottle of Pepsi and a bag of Wise's salt & vinegar potato chips at the convenience store. Then he drove down past the estuary, down a bumpy dirt road to the beach. He parked, grabbed his food, and he hopped out of the BMW. After locking up, he started hiking toward a secret place he'd found a couple of years ago—a secluded beach.

An insidious voice whispered in his ear, a siren's beckoning.

The crack. Why not?

He shook his head and started walking again but then stopped abruptly, turned, and trotted back to the car. He popped the trunk. Reaching behind the spare, he went right to the knapsack. Nervous fingers fumbled around until he came up with a vial but he couldn't find the pipe. Where the hell was it? No matter, he knew you could make a pipe out of the plastic soda bottle, he'd seen it done on TV. Let's see now . . . all he needed was a straw, which he found under the seat (McDonald's, the best). And some aluminum foil. One of Adrienne's stray gum wrappers would work just fine.

But what about Adrienne? he thought. What had she said? Any heavy-duty dope and he was history? *Shit, man, she'll never know.* Snagging his goodies, he hurried back toward the path.

Adrienne's warning continued to niggle at his brain but he managed to ignore it. Another, separate and teensy voice reminded him about how addictive crack is but he ignored that voice, too. What the fuck, he thought. *I'm bored!*

The path ended, forcing him to thread his way through huge bayberry bushes and thorny beach roses, down a steep draw. His secret place was surrounded by brush and hidden by rocks and you could only get there by crawling through a crevice behind one of the bayberry bushes. But it was worth it because the little cove inside joined a small patch of sandy beach, all but covered at high tide.

Right now, though, the tide was out. Perfect! Small wavelets tickled the sand. A green crab scuttled back into the water, disappeared.

Junior plopped down, unwrapped his sandwich and took a bite. He chewed, swallowed, and sipped at his Pepsi. He ripped open the chips, plucked a handful, and crammed them into his mouth. He chewed some more. Stopped.

Setting his food aside, he reached into his pocket, pulled out the vial, noticing how the rock looked all cool in there, awesome. It seemed almost like someone else was doing this, like he was in some kind of weird zone or something. He toyed with the vial, shook the rock a little. He checked to make sure he had his Bic lighter.

"Let's do it," cried the voice in his head. "Now!"

Junior guzzled the rest of his Pepsi, burped, and set to work on his makeshift pipe. First, he lit a cigarette, burned a hole in the side of the plastic bottle and crammed the McDonald's straw into it. After taking his penknife and spearing a few tiny holes in the gum wrapper, he fashioned the foil into a bowl and poked it into the neck of the bottle.

With nervous fingers, he dumped the rock into his palm and set it in the bowl. Holding the bottle in his right hand, he flicked his Bic with his left and took the straw into his mouth.

Once again, Adrienne came to mind, her pretty eyes and perky boobs and that other small voice in his head telling him not to do it. He groaned and it sounded like it came from someone else, a strangled sound of indecision.

He toyed with his Bic, flicking it a few times, took his mouth off the straw but put it right back.

And lit the rock!

It popped a few times and he started inhaling like there was no tomorrow. There *would,* in fact, be a tomorrow, but the teensy rational voice, faint in his buzzing head, told him it'd never be the same.

The rush was fucking *awesome*, he thought, like a gazillion times better than anything he'd ever felt before. How would his geeky-assed science teacher describe it? *An instantaneous reaction. Yeah!* His ears buzzed, a Mellow sound. His whole body felt a pleasant crush, like every goddam *cell* was being massaged!

Clam doggies!

But all too soon, the high evaporated, just like that! Already craving more, Junior scrambled through the brush and rocks, back up the path to his car. He returned with the other rock, popped it into his makeshift pipe and started to light up.

Thoughts of Adrienne and her warnings returned, stopping him. It took all the willpower he had, but he plucked the rock from the pipe, placed it back in its vial, and jammed it into his pocket before he could change his mind.

That's when he noticed a few crumbs that had chipped off and lay in his lap. He placed them into the pipe, lit up and inhaled down to his toes.

But this puny rush was just a teaser.

When could he meet Karl again? A week?

Shit!

JUNIOR SLEPT around the clock, and more—feeling more depressed and irritable than he'd ever felt and obsessing continuously about that other vial of crack. But it scared him, that intense craving. It wasn't like he was *addicted* or anything, though. No way. He just had this, what? . . . this desire to get high again and stay there?

Once his mother left the house, he took a shower and felt a little bit better. He got dressed and lit up a joint and even though he was still on a heavy downer, it seemed more bearable. Maybe Adrienne could elevate his mood, he thought. At least, maybe he could get laid, right?

He called her.
"Hello?"
"It's me," he said.
"Are you sick?"
He coughed. "No . . . why?"
"You sound awful."
"I'm *fine*. Okay?"
"Doesn't sound like it to me."
"Get over it," he snapped. "You my mother or what?"
"Whoa. Where'd that come from?"
He felt panicky. "Sorry. I guess maybe I'm in like a bad mood or something."
"*Duh.*"
"I said I'm sorry, okay?"
"I guess," she said.
"You wanna go to this, like, secret beach I know of?" he asked. "It's hidden."
"I suppose. If you promise to lose the rotten mood. Want me to pack a lunch?"
"Sure, that'd be awesome. Pick you up in an hour?"
"Just honk, I'll be ready."

JUNIOR DROVE STRAIGHT to Adrienne's apartment and when he picked her up he thought she looked good enough to eat. She'd poured herself into a pair of low-riding jeans and a bikini top, which you could see through her semi-transparent blouse. Her hair stood up in spikes and she'd put extra lip-gloss on her pouty lips. Her piercings gleamed with reflected sunlight.

"What a gorgeous day!" she said, as she put the picnic basket into the back seat and hopped in. She scooted over to the middle and gave him a peck on the cheek.

"Oops," she said. "Sorry."

"What."

"I left my mark."

He bent the rear-view mirror, checked his face out. "Same color as your hair," he said, taking a swipe at it. "What color is that again?"

"Magenta."

"I knew that. Y'know, I wouldn't mind havin' a few a those *magenta* lip-prints somewheres else, if you get my drift."

"Don't get crude. At least your mood is better, though. You were acting pretty sucky this morning, you know?"

"Whatever."

"Don't start again or you can just forget it."

They rode in an awkward silence down the dirt road toward the beach, parked, and got out. He slung his backpack over a shoulder and snagged a blanket. She grabbed the picnic basket.

Visibility was great and you could even see the lighthouse across the bay, not often the case. Crashing waves slapped at the boulders on the shore, sending spray into the breeze. A strong fragrance of beach roses and bayberry infused the air.

Spindrift swirled in the surf while seagulls floated on the wind, scouring the shoreline for lunch. They started down the path.

"What's to eat?" he asked.

"Egg salad sandwiches and—"

"Gross."

"Don't interrupt, Puss Face. I also have ham sammies, some fruit, and a couple of bottles of water."

"Ham'll do," he said.

"Well, don't force yourself." She balked when she saw the almost impenetrable tangle of underbrush. "Path ends?" she asked.

"Follow me." He started plowing through, warning her to stay close behind, lest she get whipped with any brushy backlash.

Soon, they made it to his secret little beach, crawled through the crevice, and spread their blanket on the sand.

"You were right," she said. "This place is way cool!" She gave him a hug, turned, stripped off her blouse, wiggled out of her cutoffs, and waded out into the water in her bikini.

Junior leered.

She dove in, swam underwater about a dozen yards, and surfaced, yelling, "C'mon in! The water's just right."

Figuring a swim might elevate his mood, he stripped to his suit and followed her. When he caught up, she was chest deep in the water. She put her arms around his neck and scissored his waist with her legs.

"This is more like it," he said, reaching around and fondling her.

She laughed. "Your mood keeps improving."

He pulled her close, ground his hardening groin against her.

"Let's eat first," she said. "I'm starved."

They waded back ashore, toweled each other off, and lowered themselves onto the blanket. From out of nowhere, a panicky feeling overcame Junior. He felt certain that he was losing her. "I love you," he blurted, unable to censor himself.

She laughed. "No, you don't. You love my body. There's a difference."

"Nunh-uh! I do! I love you."

"That's so sweet," she said, turning to him and cupping his face with her palms. "And I like you a lot, too but I don't know if I want a relationship right now? Let's just see where this goes, okay?"

He felt like he was about to fly apart or have a panic attack or something. His palms were greasy with sweat and his hands trembled. *She'll never love me.*

She frowned. "You look funny. Are you sure you're not getting sick?"

"I said no," he snapped. "How many times I gotta tell you?"

"Okay, okay. Pardon me all over the place for caring."

He got an idea: maybe he could win her over. "Sorry. Listen, uh, before we eat? I got somethin' I want you to try."

"If it involves sex," she said. "No way while you're in that mood. Anyway, like I said, I'm starved." She unwrapped a sandwich, took a healthy bite.

Junior had the idea if she just *tried* crack, she'd change her mind about it and maybe him, too. After all, the rush was *so* awesome, beyond what he'd ever imagined. He reached into his backpack, drew out the pipe Karl had given him, along with the other vial of crack.

She stopped chewing, swallowed hard. "Is that what I think it is?"

He held the amber vial up into the sunlight where the rock glittered like a 20-carat, yellow diamond.

"I told you," she said. "No hard stuff or I'm history. Or did you forget?" She crammed the remainder of her sandwich back in the basket and lowered the lid. "Take me home."

"I din't think you rilly meant it," he said.

"Oh, I meant it. Take me home. *Now!*"

"It's wicked awesome, I'm telling you straight. Once you try it, you—"

"Like, what part of 'no' don't you get?" she asked.

"Just *try* it, goddamit! It's like the most, uh, *intense,* feeling you ever felt. Like a giant cum!"

"You're disgusting."

"I'm tellin' you!" He whipped out his lighter, flicked it and started to light the rock but she slapped the lighter out of his hand and it flew into the water. He pulled the pipe back, protecting it with his body.

"I wish it was that fucking dope that went in the ocean," she said.

"You don't understand," he said. He knew he was whining but couldn't help it.

"Take me home! No . . . never mind, I'll walk." She dressed quickly and picked up her basket.

The tiny hold he had on his terrific new world was slipping away but Junior felt powerless, riveted to his spot in the sand. He remained frozen in place while she scooted out the crevice and hurried up the hill.

A stronger, more intense wave of panic hit him. *Go after her!* Still, he hesitated for a few moments before following and by the time he caught sight of her, she'd reached the car. She started walking faster, heading up the dirt road.

"Wait!" cried Junior. "Wait up! I'll take you."

She never turned, just picked up her pace and kept striding.

When she reached the pavement, a pickup truck rounded the curve and had to brake for her. She approached the driver, they talked for a while before she went around and climbed in the passenger side.

They drove away.

"Fuck me," said Junior. He went back down the hill to his beach.

And his precious crack.

CHAPTER 27

THAT FRIDAY, Hess and Junior met as usual at Peep Toad's bar. Junior sipped at his draft beer.

Hess was pleased to see the kid looking depressed, jittery, and paranoid. Good, he thought, the kid's finally hooked.

"I need some more, uh, you know, another hit of . . . you know," stammered Junior.

"Shut up, you idiot," whispered Hess, shaking his head and waggling a finger in the kid's face.

"But—"

"Not now. Tell me: what were you doing at the police station?"

The kid's eyes widened. "How'd you know?"

"Like I told you, I like to keep tabs on my employees."

"Ah, they called me in for questioning, is all. About that murder at the campground?"

"You didn't have anything to do with that, did you?"

"No way!" cried Junior. "They're questioning ever'one, man."

"Uh-huh. What'd you tell them?"

"Who, the cops?"

"No, the fucking passel of priests in the confessional, you moron. Of course the cops."

"I din't tell 'em nothin'," cried Junior. "Honest! That's 'cause I din't *do* nothin'."

"Well," said Hess, sitting back and crossing his arms. "They obviously didn't toss your car or you wouldn't be here."

"What. Oh, you mean the—"

"*Shh!* That's exactly what I mean."

Junior leaned forward. His face was strained, sweaty. "You gotta help me out, man."

"Take it easy, son," soothed Hess. "Didn't I tell you that I'd take care of you? Reach under the table." He slipped Junior a brown paper bag. The vials clinked together.

The kid looked relieved. "Awesome," he whispered.

"Now make this last, okay?"

"Sure."

They went to the parking lot. Junior left in the BMW and Hess drove straight to the Seabreeze campground, having decided it'd been long enough now for him to chance a drive through in his newly painted van. At the gatehouse, he asked Petey Fottler for a day pass.

"Ten bucks," Petey said.

"What? That's robbery!"

"Everything serve to further," quipped Petey.

"Pardon?"

"He who gives continually has continually."

Hess scowled. "What the hell's that supposed to mean? Spare me the bullshit. Here's your ten bucks."

Inside the campground, he cruised by Nikki's site where a gaping emptiness confronted him and he momentarily panicked. *Shit! She's gone!*

Keep cool, he thought. After all, no way would she stay in their motorhome after what happened, right? No way. Having previously investigated and discovered where her apartment was in Benedict's Landing, he sped there, parked across the street, and hustled to the manager's apartment. The landlady looked like a Norman Rockwellian schoolmarm, complete with hair bun and pinched expression.

"May I help you?" she asked, giving him a sour look.

Hess adopted his most charming smile, the same one he'd used for the parole board. And Patricia Deeb. "Yes, ma'am," he said. "Are any of these apartments available? I'm considering a winter rental."

"Not right now, but one might be available at the end of the month."

"Okay," he said. "I'll check back. By the way, I believe a friend of mine lives here, name of Nicole O'Connor?"

The landlady sniffed. "Nikki? She's gone."

"Gone?"

"Yes. Didn't you hear about the murder?"

"Murder? What murder?"

"It was just *ghastly,*" she confided, behind her hand. "Nikki's husband was murdered."

Hess tried to look sympathetic. "How awful."

She sniffed again. "She just locked up and left shortly after that. Said she was going away."

"And you're forwarding her mail?"

"I offered, but she said she'd put in a temporary change of address at the post office."

"Did she say where she was going?"

"No."

Shit.

Back in his van, Hess spat out obscenities and clenched his teeth as he sped down the highway toward the West Arcadia farmhouse. Once he got there, he hurried into his motorhome, lit the candles that illuminated his Shrine, and watched his videotape. But even the precious tape gave him no relief. He didn't even have The Temptations. Crying out in tortured angst, he dropped to the floor and curled into the fetal position where he drifted into a restless sleep. And dreamed:

. . . Of hunting, finding new prey, new meat: meat he recognizes.

Succulent young and tender meat with wild-ass hair.

Skinny, but do-able until he can find that Jezebel Whore Nikki.

Binding her. Gagging her. Tossing her in his van. Bringing her to the farmhouse basement. Getting his eight-inch Henckels Professional "S" chef's knife, testing the sharpness.

Going to work: lovely work, bloody and intimate . . .

. . . Hess woke up to discover he'd ejaculated in his trousers. He smiled. No harm, no foul—that doesn't count.

At least now, he had a diversion.

Until he could find Nikki.

True love never dies.

Mystic Fear

EXACTLY ONE WEEK later, Hess was again sitting on a bar stool at Peep Toad's, waiting for Junior. On TV, a weatherman droned on and on about a front moving in from the north. At least it would be a little cooler now. Through an open window, he noticed a few leaves turning color. A fresh breeze helped a little with the smoke and stink of the bar. Very little.

Junior finally schlepped in and they moved to their usual booth in the back. The kid looked extra jumpy and Hess assumed the crack was diddling with the kid's mind. Good, he thought—the addictive progression was right on track, moving exponentially.

"How's business?" he asked, once they were seated.

Junior fidgeted, wormed around in his seat. His leg bounced like a pogo stick and his eyes skittered all over the place, doing an obvious dance of paranoia. "I done a shitload," he said. "I sold it all."

"Outfuckingstanding," said Hess. "Hand over the cash."

Junior dug into his pocket and pulled out a fat wad of bills.

Hess counted it and gave some back, asking, "You wouldn't be foolish enough to skim, would you?"

The kid looked hurt. "Skim? No way!"

"Okay, okay, don't have a seizure. Finish your beer and we'll go out to my van. I've got something to show you."

"I hope it's what I think it is. It's like I'm dyin' here."

As their footsteps crunched across the parking lot, Junior looked around, "Where's your van?"

"Around back. Don't want any snoopy barflies prying into our business now, do we?"

"For sure, man."

Once they got to the van, Hess unlocked the back doors.

Junior blinked. He shook his head. "I thought your van was white."

Hess laughed. "Used to be." He rummaged in a bag and came up with an old sock, which he handed over. "You've been a good boy. Here."

"A sweat sock?" asked Junior. "What the fuck?"

"Look inside, Einstein."

Junior dumped the contents into his hand. "Ooh, awesome. Four eight balls."

"Make them last. If you chip it off, you can make one eight ball last the whole night."

"For sure."

"And remember," said Hess, "you get more only if I say so, understand? I'll give you more than you ever dreamed of but first, you've got to earn it."

The kid's head bobbed energetically. "Anythin', man. Anythin',"

"I want you to fulfill a fantasy I've had for a long, long time," said Hess. "One of my missions."

"Fantasy? Like *sex* fantasy? You ain't a fag or like that, are you? I don't go for that shit."

Hess laughed and winked. "No?"

"No fuckin' way."

"That's not what I heard."

"What'd you hear? Who said? . . . They were lyin'. I never done none a that shit, never."

"No?"

"Well, maybe once. In middle school me an' this kid sorta experimented, is all."

Hess snorted. "Chill out, boy. It's not that kind of fantasy, anyway."

The kid looked leery. "No? What, then?"

"I want you to do a *Columbine* on Franklin High."

"Columbine? I don't get it."

"Shoot up the school. Waste a few assholes."

"What? You mean? . . . What? No fuckin' way!"

Hess shrugged. "Your choice. No more eight balls or—"

"Okay, okay. Shit. Wait a minute, lemme think about this, right? . . . Uh, how come *you* don't just do it?"

"Because you're a student and can get right in."

"Nunh-uh," said Junior. "I ain't no student no more, remember? I quit and—"

"But they know you and will think you're still there," interrupted Hess. "Plus, you know the school layout and all. I'll bet a smart kid like you even knows a way to get out of there fast, too. You know you'd love to do it. Here's your chance to get even with all the assholes, right? You'll be famous. Your girlfriend will think you're a hero."

Junior barked out a short laugh, sounding strangled. "She dumped me."

"No shit. Well, forget her. After you do this? There'll be dozens of chicks after your bod. They'll be banging you like a screen door in a hurricane."

The kid chewed at his lower lip. "Hurrycane?"

Hess reached into the van, pulled out a short-barreled 12-gauge pump, and proffered it.

"Sweet!" cried Junior.

"It's a Remington 870. The plug is out so it holds four shells, plus one in the chamber. Three-inch magnum, double-ought buckshot. Do the job right."

"Awesome."

"Awesome is the word," agreed Hess, and handed over a cardboard box.

"What's this?"

"Plenty of shells for your pocket and a trench coat for cover. You'll be the man."

"Like *The Terminator* or someone, huh? The man? I like that kind of talk."

"And here's some heavy-duty backup," continued Hess, giving the kid a 9-mm handgun.

"Whoa," said Junior. On the floor of the van, he spotted another one and pointed. "Hey, that one's got a cool silencer. Can I have it?"

"I don't think so. The more noise, the better. Scares everyone."

"Uh, right. But how'll I get away? They'll catch me."

"You know a quick way out?" asked Hess.

"Maybe. I guess I could use that fire exit right past the principal's office."

"Perfect. Is the teacher's lounge still right there? You can waste the principal plus maybe a couple of teachers, off some students at their lockers in the hall. After that, you can screw through that fire exit."

Junior, obviously feeling the fantasy now, tried unsuccessfully to twirl the Browning by its trigger guard.

Hess laughed. "The Doc Holliday effect?"

"Yeah!" cried Junior. "Val Kilmer! You saw that movie, too?"

"I did."

"Seriously now, man. After I'm outside? What then?"

Hess shrugged. "Sprint like crazy. The BMW will be parked across the street in the back. Just jump the chain link fence. Can you handle that?"

"For sure, but—"

"It'll work," interrupted Hess. "Just before school starts, I'll drop you off at that circular drive right in front."

"Yeah, huh? In the morning, right? Like, when ever'one is getting' to school, plenny of targets."

"Now you're getting it," said Hess. "Walk fast but don't run, get in and do your thing and then quickly scoot out the back."

"But it'll be jammed with kids. Won't they be in my way?"

"Not once you start shooting. And once you're outside and over the fence? Drive like a motherfucker."

Junior nodded. "A NASCAR motherfucker. Where to?"

"Head for that farmhouse in West Arcadia. Can you remember how to get there?"

"Prolly."

"Probably?"

"No. Yeah. I 'member."

Hess grinned. "Okay then. I'll meet you at the barn and you can lay low."

"Fucking awesome. When?"

"I'll let you know."

CHAPTER 28

IN FLORIDA, NIKKI sat up in bed and rubbed her eyes; they were swollen, glued together with sunburn lotion and dried tears and she could smell Coppertone and Aloe. She felt disoriented for a few moments, but then it all came back to her.

Destin.

She heard the doorbell ring and shortly after that, Dana burst into her room, shooting straight to the window and raising the blinds, letting in the disgusting, cheerful sunlight.

"What time is it?" Nikki asked, making a face.

"Almost noon. You have a visitor. Actually, two visitors."

"I don't want to see anybody."

"Put something on and come downstairs, crabby. I think you'll be surprised."

Nikki scowled, dove back under the covers. "I *said*, I don't want any visitors. And I definitely don't want any damn surprises."

"Get up. They're not going away until they see you."

Groaning, and with great reluctance, Nikki crawled out of bed and dressed in her baggy sweats. In the bathroom, she peed. She looked in the mirror at her red, puffy face, pimples, and chopped hair—hair that she'd once taken such pride in. She dragged a brush through it a couple of times, slopped some more lotion on her scorched face and rubbed it in, thinking: Who the hell would want to see *me*?

In the hallway, she looked down the stairs, where she saw a young girl with brightly colored hair looking up at her. The girl looked familiar, but . . .

In the girl's arms, squirmed a cat—a gigantic *orange* tabby cat.

Sinbad!

In her headlong rush, Nikki almost catapulted down the stairs.

The girl handed the big cat over. Sinbad meowed, looked smug. Nikki showered his head with kisses—which he hated—hugged him fiercely, and then set him free. He shook his head, switched his tail, and trotted off to explore his new surroundings.

"I remember you," Nikki said. "You're that girl. The one from the Seabreeze campground."

"Adrienne LeDoux," she confirmed.

"That's right. Junior Ferguson's girlfriend."

"What happened to you?" the girl asked, giving Nikki the once over. "What happened to your beautiful hair? You used to be so pretty."

"Long story. Listen, Adrienne, how in the world did you find me? And end up with my cat? I have a million questions . . . ."

"Let's go into the kitchen," suggested Dana. "I'll put on a fresh pot of coffee. Are you hungry? I have some delicious crabmeat salad, made with real blue crabs, not the phony stuff."

Sinbad pranced back into the room, worked his way around and between Dana's legs. Did someone say crabmeat? He definitely looked interested.

With the nightmare featuring Steve and her crab-infested father still fresh in her mind, Nikki declined. "Coffee sounds good," she said. She gave serious consideration to a nearby box of day-old Krispy Kremes, though.

Following her eyes, Adrienne cut in front. "Can I have one?" she asked. "I drove here almost non-stop and I'm starved."

"Help yourself," Nikki said, backing off and sitting at the table. "I can't believe you're here. How did you ever find me?"

"A weird thing happened," the girl said, around a huge mouthful of glazed donut. "Your cat started like hangin' out at my apartment. Like some sort of *sign* or something? I wanted to bring him to you but knew you'd left the campground so I decided to go back out there to see if anyone knew where you'd gone."

"That's so thoughtful!"

Adrienne shrugged, munched some more donut. "Anyway, I ended up talking to that huge dude, the guy who was camped next to you?"

"Tugboat?" Nikki frowned. "I can't believe he revealed my whereabouts. He gave me his word."

"Oh, he didn't," interrupted Dana. "Blame me. He called here and asked for you. I told him the shape you were in and he told me about the girl and your cat so I had him put her on. She said she wanted to leave Rhode Island anyway so Tugboat and I agreed that it might be good for her to come down."

"Yeah," said Adrienne. "For sure. The big dude went: 'don't give *anyone* this address and phone number'. And I was like: 'no way'."

"I appreciate it," Nikki said. "Believe me. But you could've just shipped Sinbad."

"I needed to get out of there anyway. What happened the next day made it for sure."

"What happened?"

"That was when Junior shot up the school."
Nikki and Dana cried out in tandem: "*What?*"

Adrienne looked back and forth from one of us to the other, her face incredulous. "Yeah, didn't you hear about it? You don't watch the news?"

"The satellite dish is messed up," explained Dana. "They're coming to fix it this week."

"Well, you're totally not going to believe this: Junior took some guns to Franklin high school and started blasting people."

"Oh my God!" Nikki cried. "Was anybody killed?"

"No, but he wounded two students and a teacher. Some kid, a senior on the wrestling team, took Junior down. The kid and the school principal like held him there until the cops came?"

"Junior," Nikki said. "I can't see it. He's a burnout, sure, but definitely no killer."

Adrienne offered up a sickly half-smile, fingered the ring in her nostril. "Not the *old* Junior, maybe, but the *new* Junior was, like, totally wasted, into crack." She folded a stick of gum into her mouth, started chomping. *Snap! Pop!*

"Go on, go on," Nikki urged. "What else?"

"Well, Junior and I had been going out together and I was really getting into him," she continued. "Like, partying together and stuff and doing okay in our lives, you know? Then *he* came along."

Nikki raised her eyebrows. "He?"

"This older guy. It all started with him supplying Junior with pot to sell. It wasn't so bad at first. I mean, Junior had all this cash so he could feel all macho and everything?"

"A little self-pride," Nikki said.

"Something like that. And, we could party hardy and stuff, you know? I was *so* getting into Junior."

"Truthfully, I kind of wondered what you saw in him."

Adrienne nibbled at her thumbnail. "Well, he's cute and shy, not like a lot of guys, you know? Once you get to know him, he can be sweet and considerate and he's so, um, *fixable*, I guess. Plus, he's got this wicked cute butt and—"

"That's okay," Nikki said, interrupting. "We can skip Junior's anatomy,"

Adrienne shrugged. "Anyway, I decided not to enroll in college in the fall. I rented an apartment in Benedict's Landing."

"Did you and Junior move in together?"

"Almost. Junior wanted to. He wanted to get away from his smothering mom but then he started doing hard drugs. I don't go for that shit so I broke up with him."

"Good move," said Dana. "I don't blame you."

"Me, neither," Nikki said.

Adrienne offered up an anemic smile. "I really liked him? But I won't go out with a goddam druggie. No way."

"Good for you."

The girl's eyes flashed. "That old dude? Junior's . . .uh, mentor? Even though he looks like a movie star, he's such a creep."

Nikki leaned forward. "You saw him?"

Adrienne nodded. "It's like he had some kinda mind control over Junior or some shit like that. It sucked bigtime. Can you believe the asshole even loaned Junior his Beemer? Like, who loans a kid their BMW?"

Nikki moved even closer, got right in Adrienne's face. "A manipulating son of a bitch, that's who. You say this guy is really good looking. How old would you say he is?"

She shrugged. "I don't know. Old."

"Old. Like maybe my age?"

Another shrug. "I guess so."

"About six feet tall?"

"I don't know. Six feet sounds about right. He's got these really big muscles, you know?"

"Hair?"

"Gray. Actually, though, it looked like a stupid rug, know what I'm saying? All pulled back into a ponytail."

"Anything else you can remember?"

"Yeah. He's got like this stupid goatee. And dorky unlaced high-top basketball shoes. Like that's gonna make an old guy cool, you know?"

"Did Junior ever mention the guy's name?"

"He did, but I can't remember it."

"Was it Hess? Marion Hess?"

"I don't think so. I think it was, like, a 'K' name. Maybe Kurt or something like that? Listen, I gotta pee."

Dana pointed. "The bathroom is over there."

While Adrienne was in the restroom, Dana turned to Nikki. "That girl looks kind of freaky. Do you believe her?"

"Don't let her looks fool you," Nikki said. "Underneath all that goth and punk lies one extremely bright girl."

"Really."

"Bright enough to get into Brown University."

"Whoa."

They heard the toilet flush, water running, and Adrienne came back. They all sat with their own thoughts for a few moments. Adrienne started to nod off; the poor girl was exhausted.

"Let's get you to bed," said Dana, helping her up.

"No, wait," said Adrienne. "I need to finish."

They headed for the living room with their coffee but before they went, Nikki opened a can of tuna and fed Sinbad.

Adrienne settled back on the couch, tucked her legs up under her and frowned. "Before Junior shot up the school? He called and talked me in to meeting him at our secret beach. I decided to give him another chance, so I agreed."

"Secret beach?" Nikki asked. "Where?"

"Hard to describe. It's hidden; you couldn't find it if you didn't know where it was. There's lots of rocks there and it's like real private." Tears welled up in her eyes, started spilling over, leaving dark, mascara trails down her cheeks.

"Tell us," Nikki said, softly.

"When I got there?" said Adrienne. "I was in for the shock of my life."

Nikki and Dana looked at each other, then back at Adrienne. Nikki found she was holding her breath.

"I caught 'em in the act," Adrienne said, "caught Junior and that asshole doing the nasty. The old guy was on his knees. Get the picture? Gross!"

Nikki put a comforting hand on her shoulder. "How awful. What did you do?"

"The man saw me first. I can still see him taking his mouth away from Junior, wiping it off, and smiling this awful smile. I freaked and screamed."

Dana moved closer, took Adrienne's hand. "You poor thing."

Adrienne nodded. Rivulets of mascara-laden tears were streaming down her cheeks in a flood now. "When I screamed? Junior noticed me. He looked kind of embarrassed for a minute but then he just *shrugged*, you know? Like it was no big deal. Then he goes: 'fuck off, bitch' so I ran."

Nikki nodded. "Just wanting to get the hell away."

The girl shuddered. "I'll never forget that image, not ever. The old dude was naked from the waist down and all over his butt he had like these ugly little round scars? All over. It was so gross."

"Little round scars," Nikki said. "I saw those at the police academy on pictures of abused children. They're usually caused by cigarette burns."

"So, you ran, right?" asked Dana, handing Adrienne a Kleenex.

Adrienne nodded, blew her nose. "Yeah."

"Good for you," Nikki said. "Where did you go?"

"Back to my apartment. The next day I heard about the school shooting and Junior being in jail. I wanted to see what happened to him but then I just, like, *had* to get away, you know? I packed my shit, threw it in my car. I wanted to go anywhere— anywhere far away."

"Did you ever try to go visit Junior in jail? Talk to him?" asked Dana.

"No, but that evening, just before dark, I took a walk down by the marina. I wanted to think about everything and stuff, you know? It'd started to rain a little and Junior's asshole friend, the old bastard, cruised by in this van. He must have been following me? He pulled over and stopped."

Nikki thought about that. "Whoa, that same guy? Didn't you say he had a BMW?"

"Yeah, but Junior was always using it. The old guy was in a van."

"Was it a white work van? One that said Larry's RV Repair on the side?"

Adrienne frowned, looked at the ceiling. "I don't think so, not white, not that I can remember. Anyway, the asshole? He was like *apologizing* for that disgusting scene with Junior! Unbelievable! He offered to take me to see Junior in jail."

"Jesus," Nikki said, thinking: what a conniving shit. "What'd you do?"

"I'm like: 'No way, Jose.' He goes: 'Don't be like that, I know you're attracted to me.' And I'm like: 'In your dreams, you old fart. You creep me out!'"

"Wow," said Dana. "Bet that pissed him off."

"Big time. He grabbed my arm and tried to jerk me into his van."

"Obviously, he didn't get you," Nikki said.

Adrienne folded a fresh piece of gum into her mouth, started chewing and cracking it. *Pop!* Her eyes lit up. "Nope. I bit his hand really, really hard? And took off."

"You *go,* girl," said Dana.

"Totally," agreed Adrienne. "Then I went straight to the cops and told the chief the whole story but I don't think he believed me on account of that one time I was trashed and ended up in jail there. Remember?"

"I sure do," Nikki said.

"Well, what about your parents?" asked Dana. "Do they know any of this? Or that you left Rhode Island?"

Adrienne laughed, a tiny grunt. "Not an issue. My dad? He's like living with his latest bimbo somewhere. L.A., I think. And my mom? She's the one who *administers* the money from the trust fund my grandfather set up for me. Right now she's in like, Paris or Cannes or somewhere and couldn't care less about me."

"Can we get in touch with her?" Nikki asked.

Adrienne dug around in her purse, came up with her address book, and thumbed to a page. "Long distance to her five-star hotel," she said, handing Nikki the book. "Go for it."

Nikki dialed the multitude of numbers and asked for Ms. LeDoux's room.

Adrienne's mother came on the line: "Yes. Who is this?"

"Hi, my name is Nicole O'Connor, a friend of your daughter. She's here with me, in Florida. Would you care to speak to her?"

"What has she done now?"

"Done? Why, nothing. She's had a very traumatic experience."

"So why call me? I can't do anything about it."

"Are you serious? Look, I thought you might want to talk to her and maybe comfort her, that's all. But I guess I was mistaken."

Silence on the other end.

Nikki sighed. "Do you at least want my phone number here in case you need to get in touch with her?"

"I suppose," the woman said. "What is it?"

Nikki gave her Dana's number as well as her own cell number and the woman hung up without even so much as a perfunctory thank you. Nikki turned to Adrienne, saying, "Some piece of work, your mother."

Adrienne nodded, rolled her eyes. "I told you."

Sinbad, finished with his repast, came over and leaped up on the couch. He curled up in Nikki's lap, started purring, and made himself available for petting. His breath smelled like a fish market.

    Nikki watched Adrienne's eyelids start to droop again. She listed to port, her mouth sagged open, and the gum fell out. Slipping over onto her side, she curled up in the fetal position and immediately fell asleep.

CHAPTER 29

IN BENEDICT'S LANDING, on Mystic Island, Junior decompressed in the jail, awaiting interrogation and wondering how his life had gone from shitty to totally awesome and back to totally fucked in such a short time. Maybe he should've never done the crack. But what a rush . . .

Now that his head was pretty much detoxed, Junior closed his eyes and remembered:

. . . Calling Adrienne, hoping against hope for one more chance. Thinking: if she'll take me back, fuck Karl dude, fuck his missions, and fuck the goddam crack, I can quit.

Brrrrrrt. Brrrrrrt.

Adrienne answering: "Hello?"

"It's Junior? Don't hang up."

"Why shouldn't I?"

"Please. I've been an asshole but I can 'splain. It's the crack. I think . . . I think I'm hooked on that shit."

She laughs, real snotty like. "Oh, really. What gave you a clue?"

He's getting pissed, but pushes it aside. "Please? I'm not doing it anymore. I'll quit. I swear. Can we talk?"

Silence on her end.

He persists: "Can we? Will you meet me at the secret beach?"

"When?"

"Noon?"

More silence, then: "Alright. One more chance but you'd better be straight."

"I will."

Junior gets to the secret beach an hour early, sets up a blanket and is hoping for some great make-up sex but having way too much time to wait. The last vial of crack is calling to him, feels so hot in his pocket. He's thinking: Why did I even bring the shit?

Because, that's why. Just in case.

He fingers the vial, pulls the pipe out of one of his cargo pouches. Lights up, saying fuck it, thinking: I'll be okay, she'll never know.

The rush. The incredible, awesome fucking rush!

A sound. Things are fuzzing out, he's vaguely thinking: Oh shit, she's early. Wait, it's not her. Karl dude? What's he doing here?

It's Karl dude all right, grinning, reaching into his pocket, and coming up with another vial.

More is better. Too much is just right.

Karl dude, not such an asshole anymore but his awesome best friend, dropping a rock in the pipe, nodding, lighting it up for him while he inhales, inhales, inhales . . . .

Oh God . . . God . . . .

Karl dude: undoing Junior's pants.

What the fuck?

Karl dude: pulling them down.

Oh no. No. No. No. No.

Karl dude's hands moving. His mouth.

Oh God! I can't. Yes. Ungh. Oh. God.

He takes a last hit off the pipe, drops it, and closes his eyes to the wicked, forbidden pleasures.

Both of them.

Adrienne is suddenly poking her head into the crevice, saying, "Sorry I'm a little late."

Holy shit! Holy shit! . . . uh-oh, Junior is climaxing . . . the awesome spasms and fuck it, no hope now.

He hears her screaming.

He shrugs, saying, "Fuck off, bitch", wondering where that came from.

Karl dude: wiping his mouth. Grinning. Evil.

Thinking about going after Adrienne but then thinking: fuck it.

Fuck her.

Fuck me!

. . . All that remembering was giving Junior a nasty headache, so he flopped back on his bunk and tried to think of something else. He was snoozing peacefully on his bunk when the clanging of sliding bars startled him awake.

"Stand by, Ferguson," ordered the officer. "Your lawyer's here."

Junior sat up, rubbed his eyes. "Lawyer? Uh, I don't got no lawyer."

"You do now," said the lawyer, moving into view.

After the officer's footsteps echoed down the hall, the lawyer set his briefcase down on Junior's bunk and sat next to it. The man had a pinched expression, tiny head, tiny hands, and tiny feet—encased in tasseled loafers. His nose was ruddy and bulbous and his hair frizzed out. He offered his hand, saying, "Mr. Ferguson? I'm Gerald Pratt, Esquire. I'll be representing you."

"You like one a those weenie public defender dildos?" asked Junior. He chortled, adding, "You look like a fucking hobbit."

Pratt attempted a smile, a tight little lip curl that mostly failed. "Your benefactor, Mr. Karl Meyer, retained me. He said to tell you not to worry about a thing."

"Easy for him to say. He's not in here."

"And soon, son, you won't be either."

Junior leaped up. "Can you get me out? Get me out!"

"Shouldn't be a problem."

"Rilly? No shit?"

"I don't think so. We'll see at the arraignment. In the meantime, they're going to question you, but I'll be in the room with you. Let me make this perfectly clear: don't say *anything* unless I tell you to. Got that?"

"Yessir."

"And above all, don't mention Mr. Meyer."

"What, you think I'm a rat?"

The lawyer put his hand on Junior's shoulder and squeezed. "I'm not suggesting that, not at all, son."

"'Cause I ain't no rat."

"Sure." Pratt picked up his briefcase, opened it and tilted it toward Junior.

"What," said Junior.

Pratt gestured with his chin. "On the left side there's a roll of breath mints. No offense, but you could use a few."

Junior blew a puff of breath into his cupped hand and whiffed it. "Smells okay to me."

"Trust me, you need freshening."

Junior took the mints, popped a couple into his mouth. Pratt snapped his briefcase shut, stood up, and called for the guard. Before he left, he turned back to Junior, saying, "I'll see you in the interrogation room in a few minutes."

Junior crunched mints and nodded. "Okay."

When he was alone again, Junior flopped back onto his bunk, popped another mint and did some heavy-duty thinking about how that fucking lawyer had the nerve to think Junior could be a rat. No way, Jose. Sure, Karl dude was an asshole and he *did* get Junior hooked on crack but he also gave Junior *The Power*. The Power to get even for three years of abuse from those assholes at school; the power of *respect*; the power of *pure domination!*

He gobbled a few more mints, chewed. Thinking back, he relived his moment in the sun and relished the feeling:

. . .Franklin fuckin' High School: the bell ringing as he struts through the door; familiar smell of books, lockers and floor wax; kids and teachers eyeballing his trench coat but dismissing it as a student fashion statement or some shit like that. He's thinking: fucking fools got no clue.

Next he knows, he's busting into the office, shrugging off the trench, flicking the safety off the awesome shotgun.

Chunk-chunk, KA-BOOM! Chunk-chunk, KA-BOOM!

Then running, sneakers squeaking as he slams to a stop in front of the teacher's lounge. Several teachers wide-eyed, diving for the floor.

Chunk-chunk, KA-BOOM! Chunk-chunk, KA-BOOM! Chunk-chunk, KA-BOOM!

On the move again, just like Chuck Norris!

Uh-oh! An asshole jock in a letter jacket running at him, low and fast.

Chunk-Chunk . . . CLICK!

Shit! Jammed or out of ammo or something . . .

The jock closing in.

The 9-mm! He reaches for the Browning in his belt but gets knocked off his feet by the asshole jock taking him down low. The gun goes flying. Someone else crashes into his back, holds him down. From the side of his eye, he sees the fucker on top of him, even smells his oatmeal breath.

Fucking Ichabod, the principal.

Next comes a blur of cops, handcuffs, and faces of scared-shitless students watching as they load him into the cruiser and haul his ass away.

He is laughing, knowing he was, for once in his goddam miserable life, the man*!*

. . . The rattling cell bars opened again, bringing Junior's instant replay to an end. He gobbled the last mint while the guard ushered him down the hall. After all, he wouldn't want his breath to offend anyone, now, would he?

Junior thought the interrogation room looked just like on TV. Cool. He slouched in the metal Samsonite folding chair, leaned his elbows on the table, and studied the one-way mirror. There was a video camera on a tripod. Feeling a little nervous, he decided to cop an attitude.

First, his new lawyer bustled in, opening his briefcase, making a show of shuffling papers and taking out a legal pad. *Big fucking deal.* His mother followed the lawyer in with Chief Anderson close behind. A pair of state troopers stood in back, against the wall. The chief pulled out a chair for Junior's mother but remained standing.

"Remember, son," advised the lawyer. "Consult me before you give any answers."

Junior sneered. "Hey, Bilbo Baggins. I ain't your son."

His mother looked about ready to cry. "Please, honey," she pleaded. "Listen to your lawyer."

"Aw, Ma. Why you lookin' at me like that? Face all droopy and shit."

The chief had turned on the video and was saying, "Chief Anderson interviewing Junior Ferguson, a minor, in the presence of his lawyer and mother." He stepped closer to Junior, asking, "Ready to talk?" The chief had an unlit, half-smoked cigar butt in his mouth. Even from where Junior sat, the butt stank like a week-old dead skunk.

Junior was starting to feel sick to his stomach. "Yo, Chiefster. Is that, like, a turd in your mouth or what?"

"Shut up," snarled the chief.

The lawyer stood up. "Now there's no need—"

"I thought you wanted me to talk," interrupted Junior. He felt woozy, like he was kind of trashed or something. A small headache throbbed at his temples. He broke into a sweat.

"Nervous, Junior?" asked the chief. "Care to tell us why you did it?"

"You're the cop, you find out."

"Oh, we will, we will. Why don't you help yourself out here?"

"Fuck that." He was feeling *real* bad now and starting to sweat. *Shit!*

"We know you aren't smart enough to do this on your own. Where'd you get the guns?"

A shrug.

The chief came closer, frowned. "Are you all right? You don't look so good."

"I'm fine."

"Well, son, I've got good news and bad news. Want to know what they are?"

"No. But why do I think you're gonna tell me anyway?"

"The good news is: everyone survived."

Another shrug. "Whatever."

"The bad news? You're going away for a long, long time unless you talk to us. Know what else? Ballistics matched the bullets that killed Steve Marshall to that 9-mm we got from you."

"You see anyone here who gives a shit?" Junior was sweating like a WWF wrestler now. The room was starting to spin.

His mother, looking like she just ate worms, cried, "*Junior!*"

"Ma, you think I give a fuck in a rolling donut about any a this bullshit?" yelled Junior. "I'm the *man*!"

She opened her mouth like she was going to say something but then clamped her hand over it, shook her head, and started sobbing.

"Jesus, Ma," said Junior. He shot her a look of contempt. "Don't start." It felt like someone was twisting a goddam knife in his stomach now. His eyes wouldn't focus. *Shit!*

When he pitched forward, one of the troopers rushed to him, helped him out of his chair, and onto his feet.

"Call a doctor," yelled the chief. "*Now!*"

Junior slapped the trooper's helping hands aside. He felt his eyes roll back in his head and the next thing he knew, he was sprawled on the floor, flopping like a fish out of water. He kicked, foamed at the mouth, and realized he was dying.

The last thing Junior saw was the look of utter horror on his mother's face.

And that made him grin.

As he died, his exiting thoughts were of Adrienne: her magenta hair, and her fine, fine little ass.

And how he'd fucked that up.

CHAPTER 30

AFTER THE SHOOTING incident at the school, Hess got rid of the BMW at a used car lot in Stonington, Connecticut. Little did Junior know that Hess had made sure the car wouldn't be there for his escape should he have ever made it out of the school anyway. Nonetheless, someone could've noticed him dropping the kid off and maybe even taken down the plate number. Can't be too careful, right?

The car lot salesman happened to be sort of a miniature version of Peep Toad but decked out in a cheap suit, wide, flowery tie, and wingtip shoes. "Here you go, sir," he said, handing Hess a healthy check.

Hess pocketed it, saying, "Thanks. These Beemers sure hold their value."

The salesman rocked back on his heels, thumbs in his belt. "Sure I can't interest you in another vehicle? I can make you a sweet deal on a super clean, pre-owned Lexus."

"No thanks. If you could just call me a cab, I'll be all set."

The cab arrived a few minutes later and Hess told the driver to drop him off at a convenience store a mile or so away from the farmhouse. He walked the rest of the way, replaying in his mind—for the umpteenth time—how he'd screwed up the abduction of Junior's girlfriend:

. . . The sun going down but darkening clouds rolling in, obscuring it. Fat drops of rain starting to fall as he drives toward Prey's apartment.

Prey not there.
Driving around, cruising, looking.
Hunting.
Nothing.
But his unholy prayers are finally answered: he spots a lone shadow down at the marina, out on a dock. Drawing closer, he sees that wild hair that could only be hers. His prey.
How fortuitous!
Whipping a U-turn, he eases up, stalking.

Prey walks from the dock, head down.
His brakes squeak.
Prey looks up, and over.
He's getting out. Using his charming smile, getting ready to apply Silver Tongue 101.
The rain, steady now. Blinking the water out of his eyes, he's looking around. Nobody anywhere, must be the rain.
Outfuckingstanding!
That goddam K.C. and The Sunshine Band commandeer his thoughts again:
Uh-huh, uh-huh!
Stop it!
Prey, halts. Eyes wary, she's ready to bolt.
But to his surprise, Prey approaches! Unmitigated impertinence of Prey to glare at him! Call him an asshole!
Maintaining control, he smiles with pure charm, spreads his hands and serves up nice: apologizing for his' presumed insensitive indiscretion' with Junior.
Prey is telling him to go to hell. **Him!**
Seething, but still in control, he gestures to the open door of his van, offers her shelter from the elements and a promise to go see Junior, patch things up, or some such shit.
Prey declines. Pissed off.
He informs Prey that he is aware of her attraction to him.
Prey challenges him by denying him!
Why you little cunt! He's grabbing Prey by the forearm, thinking how tiny it is and how easy it would be to snap the bones. Thinking maybe he would, later. He pulls Prey along, jerking her toward the van.
Prey is dragging her feet, but he's just about home free when the little bitch bites him!
He is howling! Blood! The little whore drawing blood!
And in an instant: Prey vanishing, trailing into rain and darkness.
He howls again, leaps into his van, and speeds away.
Empty handed.

. . . By the time Hess hiked all the way to the farmhouse, his thoughts turned to Junior and he smiled, thinking how easily he had manipulated the stupid kid and gotten exactly what he'd wanted. And Hess had never really worried about Junior giving him up, mainly because of the powerful psychic hold he had on the boy.

But something was bothering Hess, a feeling quite alien to him. He analyzed the thought and decided—to his horror—that he might actually have started to *like* the dumbass kid.

What was up with that?

CHAPTER 31

IN FLORIDA, at Dana's house, Nikki placed a blanket over Adrienne and tucked her in, saying, "Poor girl's had it."

"She's been through one hell of a lot," agreed Dana.

They went into the kitchen and got fresh coffee. Dana turned to Nikki, asking, "What now?"

"First things first. Will you call your therapist for me? See if she can fit me in?"

"Really? I can't believe it. Dr. Jan? Sure, happy to do it."

"Meanwhile, I'm going to find a gym and start getting back into shape."

"I'm impressed," said Dana. "And after you're together mentally and physically?"

"I need to make an important phone call."

"To?"

"The Marines."

Sinbad meowed, went over to Adrienne, licked her nose and woke the exhausted girl up. She sat up, yawned, fingered her wild hair and started scratching the big cat's ears. Sinbad purred.

"The Marines?" asked Dana.

Nikki nodded. "Well, maybe just one."

"And this one marine?"

"Tugboat."

"That guy who called about Adrienne coming down."

"Right," Nikki said. "His real name is Clyde Haywood, he's huge, and a total badass."

"How huge?"

"I don't know, maybe six-five and about three-hundred. Anyway, I'm hoping Tugboat will help me deal with the monster. I got no doubt that the man Adrienne's been talking about is Marion Hess—the killer I told you about. I'll bet he used and abused Junior, sending the poor kid on a mission at Franklin High in order to satisfy some sick, twisted plan. I also believe this guy won't stop until he gets me. But you know what? I'm going to get him."

"I believe you will. Count me in," said Dana.

"No way," Nikki said. "David would never go for it. Besides, it's not your concern."

"Not his decision. And it *is* my concern. You're my best friend."

"Me, too," piped Adrienne. "I wanna come, too." She yawned once more, fell over, and crashed again, sound asleep.

"We'll see about that," Nikki said. Dana went into the laundry room and Nikki went upstairs to get dressed.

THAT NIGHT, Nikki heard Dana's husband come home. From their bedroom, Nikki could hear muffled sounds of arguing and knew only too well what it was about.

Even though she'd gotten a pauper's share of sleep after ruminating about their long talk with Adrienne, Nikki dragged herself out of bed early the following morning, determined to get herself in shape. She pulled on her baggy sweats, wrapped a red bandana around her head and headed for the kitchen where she feasted on half a grapefruit and a soft-boiled egg.

The sun was barely up, casting wonderful pastels onto the placid waters of the Gulf of Mexico but she knew the beach would soon be bright enough to cause snow blindness. She donned her oversized Panama Jack shades and shuffled away at a moderate jog, mentally complaining about the resistance from soft sand. A cluster of gulls scattered, milling about and setting up a raucous chatter. She just knew they were laughing at her, making fun of her.

Barely fifteen minutes later, she found herself hunkered over at the water's edge, bent at the hips and gasping like a terminal emphysema victim. Her chest was on fire. Her knees felt rubbery, her thighs: leaden. Her left calf cramped up. Hopping on one leg, she promptly threw up her meager breakfast—if you could call it that. How ironic, she thought. Here all those times she'd vomited on purpose and now that she wanted food to actually stay down, it had a mind of its own.

She scooped some sand and buried it.

After walking off the cramp and catching her breath, she felt better. She started jogging again, but slower. Twenty minutes later, she'd maintained sort of a rhythm but decided not to push it. She turned and headed back down the beach toward home. When she got back to those rude gulls, they scattered again but this time, they weren't laughing. Guess she showed them!

Back at the house, Dana and Adrienne were taking their coffee, fresh-cut pineapple, and Krispy Kreme donuts on the lanai, walled off by a screened-in Florida room. A blue heron watched intently from outside the screen.

Nikki slipped into the kitchen, got herself a cup, came back out and slumped into a chair.

"Well," said Dana. "Look at you!"

"I've been jogging," Nikki announced.

Adrienne giggled into her palm.

"What," Nikki said, scowling.

"Nothing . . . just that you look like some chick version of Rocky Balboa, is all. Only he had better hair."

"Yo, Adrienne," Nikki grunted out, in a poor Stallone imitation.

"So, champ," said Dana. "What's on tap for today?

"I've got a full day planned. First, I'm going to hit the gym. After that, I'm off to Sergio's to see if someone can perform a miracle on my chop-shop hair and then—"

"Like, Mission Impossible," interrupted Adrienne, giggling at her own joke.

Nikki turned to Dana and finished: "—and then I've got an appointment with that shrink you recommended."

Dana's eyebrows shot up. "Really. I'm surprised you got an appointment on such short notice."

"Well, when I mentioned your name, she squeezed me in. Guess it pays to know a VIP."

"Yeah, right. A VIP sicko."

Nikki laughed. "And what are you two up to today?"

Dana shrugged. "I don't know. Maybe I'll take Adrienne to Seaside."

"Seaside?" asked Adrienne. "Is it cool?"

"*Trés* cool," said Dana. "A village atmosphere, homes with pastel colors and West Indies designs . . ."

Adrienne looked bored.

" . . . and plenty of quaint shops and restaurants," concluded Dana.

"Whoa! Like, count me in."

"Sounds like fun," Nikki said, getting up. "Well, I'm going to shower, change, and be off." She started to walk away but Adrienne stopped her.

"Want to take my Camaro?" the girl asked, digging into her jeans. She pulled out her keys, and dangled them.

Nikki gave her a bear hug, saying, "Sure, why not? With your ultra-cool set of wheels, I'll be the talk of Destin."

"Yeah . . . until they see who's driving," said Adrienne, stifling a grin.

"Some old broad with a chop-shop hairdo," added Dana.

"Hopefully, not for long," Nikki retorted, over her shoulder. She showered, changed into jeans and a T-shirt and hurried out the door. But before she went to the gym, and in dire need of new clothes, she headed for the Destin Commons shopping area.

An hour later, laden with multiple bags filled with a new wardrobe, she jumped into Adrienne's classic car and took off for the gym where she put in half an hour on the Nautilus, fifteen ungodly minutes on the stair-stepper, and grunted out fifty stomach crunches. An extended period in the steam bath and her second shower of the day followed.

Exhausted but happy, she wriggled into one of her new outfits: a cute print skirt and scooped neck top from Chico's. She slid her feet into her new Birkenstocks and applied minimal makeup—the first her pathetic face had seen since Steve's murder. She pronounced herself good to go. Okay, maybe not good, but passable.

At Sergio's, her hairdresser wrung his hands and scowled. "Oh, sweetheart," he moaned. "What did you *do*?" Clucking his tongue, he started shampooing her woeful hair and then attacked it.

True to his reputation as a styling wizard, he wielded his magic and she ended up with a stylish, layered-cut bob that had her positively beaming. Mission Impossible made possible.

"What now?" he asked, eyeballing his handiwork.

"I'm off to get my head shrunk," she said.

"Whatever," he said, clucking his tongue. "Well, don't let him get you on the couch unless he's cute. It'll flatten your hair."

"He's a she."

"What-ever."

After paying and leaving a generous tip, she rushed away to complete her next mission. Dr. Janet West's office was in a cluster of medical office buildings not far from Sergio's. Nikki pulled into the parking lot, hustled into the lobby and found out from the directory that the suite was on the second floor. Even though her legs were already screaming and rubbery from physical abuse, she chose the stairs over the elevator. After a ten-minute wait in the reception area, Dr. West invited Nikki into her office.

Pastels of pelicans and dolphins adorned the walls, the carpet was plush, and the atmosphere felt soft, fragrant of what, vanilla? Krispy Kremes?

"Nice car," Dr. West said, once they'd introduced themselves to each other.

"Excuse me?"

"I heard the distinctive gurgle of the Hollywood mufflers when you drove up and looked out the window. I just *love* classic cars." She pointed to an overstuffed chair. "Please, take a seat. Let's get acquainted and see if I can help you."

The woman's infectious smile and offhanded manner captivated Nikki right away and, of course, she trusted Dana's judgment. Thinking, what the hell, she figured she might as well get right to it. "Well, I'm here because I'm a . . . um . . ."

"Yes?"

"Bulimic," she blurted. Once that was out, Nikki seemingly had diarrhea of the mouth, filling the woman in on all her disgusting habits and her peculiar compulsion for glazed donuts. Before she knew it, her hour was just about up.

"Well," Dr. West said, standing up. "It's apparent you realize that Bulimia is a disease of low self-esteem; recovery is a process of getting the knowledge from your head to your heart. Next time, I'd like to delve into your childhood, perhaps reveal something."

"The bulimia's not all."

Dr. West smiled. "Rarely is."

"Uh, my . . . my husband was recently murdered," Nikki said, softly.

"How horrible. Well, then, we'll certainly need to address your grief."

Nikki nodded and then turned toward the door. "By the way, that delicious scent I smell, is it Krispy Kremes?"

Dr. West smiled. "Not hardly. Sometimes, my patients need a little help to relax. I lit a scented candle earlier."

"Not Krispy Kremes. That's a relief," Nikki said.

The therapist ushered her out into the reception area, saying, "My schedule is pretty full but I'm willing to work you in after hours. I mean, you being a friend of Dana's and all." Again, that comforting smile.

"I appreciate it. I was hoping I could get a crash course therapy because I need to get back to New England as soon as possible. But to do what I have to do, I need to get into better shape, mentally as well as physically. I've got a couple of weeks."

"Crash course, then. I'll have to fit you in after my regular hours, though. Say, Monday, Wednesday, and Friday at 5:30?"

"Sounds good. I really appreciate this."

"You said New England? Where?"

"Rhode Island."

"Well, I can give you the name of some excellent therapists in Providence or Boston for follow-up therapy if you'd like. And a dietician."

"That'd be great, thanks."

"Okay. One more question if you don't mind my asking: why do you feel you need to get in shape so quickly?"

"Oh, no big deal. I'm going after a psychopathic killer, that's all."

CHAPTER 32

IN RHODE ISLAND, frustrated, Hess played, rewound, and replayed his tape of Nikki while he sulked. He concentrated on how, once he sacrificed The Jezebel Whore—Mother would return and life would be complete. The tapes salved some of his angst but they could only go so far. He had no trouble resisting The Temptations. Well, almost none.

Needing *blood* involvement, he got into his van and started driving around. He was consumed once again by rage, wondering how he had botched the job with that bitch with the freaky hair. He was thinking how he'd love to give the wily little cunt one more try when another, better idea popped into his head:

Hunt for meat in some other state.

Yeah, he thought. That way, the cops would think he took off. Excited, he headed west, out to I-84, through Connecticut, New York, and into Pennsylvania where he cut south, down through the Delaware River Gap and into the heart of the Poconos. Now that fall had arrived, most of the tourists were gone. The leaves had started to turn and the old euphemism of "rolling up the sidewalks" held true in the small town of Pinekill.

Pinekill, what an appropriate name.

And it was good nobody was about; that meant less prying eyes, but also fewer abduction prospects. After about an hour of fruitless hunting along the back streets, Hess was just about to give up when he happened across what looked to be a college-aged girl.

All alone. Walking her dog.

Prey!

The girl's mutt was one of those goddam yappy lap dogs he despised. He pulled over to the curb, down the street, just ahead of her. He shut off the headlamps but left the engine running.

The only light was a weak offering by a World War II-era vintage streetlight, the kind with a reflector of corrugated tin and a solitary light bulb underneath. A remaining chunk of the Big Mac he'd had for supper sat in a crumpled wrapper on the passenger seat of his van. Sometimes, when you get the super-sized fries, you just can't finish your Mac—Big Mac Attack or not.

He unwrapped it, thinking that he knew of no dog, yappy or otherwise, that could resist a Big Mac. No Siree Bob. He checked the opposite side mirror. The girl was within a dozen yards now and he could see that she was in thin, but curvy.

She looked pretty. With maybe red hair even! And so skinny, she'd be easy to overpower . . .

Delicious.

When she was alongside, he flipped the passenger door handle and the door swung open.

The dog barked: *Yark! Yark! Yark!*

Obviously, it sniffed the Big Mac because it strained at its leash, pulling the girl forward. She dug in her heels but the stubborn mutt wouldn't be stayed from its succulent quest.

"Excuse me, miss," Hess said, in his most charming tone. "What kind of dog is that?"

The little beast: snuffling, snuffling, salivating.

Hess fed it a bite of Mac.

Snarf.

The girl was definitely leery but he could almost read her mind. She was probably thinking: he *looks* nice, and besides, anyone who'd give his hamburger to a dog must be okay.

Yark! Yark!

He treated the dog to another morsel.

Snarf.

"She's a Bichon Frise," said the girl, looking proud of the fact.

"I thought so. That's why I couldn't resist stopping and sharing my dinner. She is *so* cute! What's her name?"

"Princess."

The girl edged closer. He could smell her, a delectable scent of whatever fragrance the college girls were wearing these days. Kinda like vanilla.

Yummy.

"Princess? How adorable. Here Princess, c'mon, sweetie, have another little snack."

Sniff. Sniff. Snarf!

And even as Princess glommed the snack, Hess latched onto the girl's arm, clutching it in a vise grip. This one would *not* get away. He yanked both girl and dog into the van, whipped the door closed, and thumbed the lock. He pulled out his chef's knife from under the seat. The weak beam from the obsolete street lamp, though dim, glinted off the blade.

The girl screamed.

Yark-Yark! Yark, Yark, Yark! went Princess. She bared her teeth.

Without hesitation, Hess plunged the knife into Princess's body: *chork!*

Princess yelped and collapsed between the seats. Blood pulsed out. The dog whimpered, panted, and fell silent.

The girl screamed again.

"Shut the fuck up, you little cunt," Hess growled. "Or I'll do you right here, right now."

He reached down, stroked Princess's bloody fur, saying, "Poor baby. Did I interrupt little Princess's din-dins?"

Turning to the petrified girl, he smiled, saying, "Just do as I say, and you won't get hurt."

In a pig's eye.

PART III

RECKONING

Much of pain is the bitter potion by which the physician in you heals your sick self.

—Kahlil Gibran

The female of the species is more deadly than the male.

—Rudyard Kipling

Jan Evan Whitford

CHAPTER 33

BACK IN FLORIDA, a squadron of pelicans patrolled the Destin beach while the sun peeked over the Gulf, infusing the eastern sky in a multitude of pastels. Nikki, Dana, and Adrienne just finished cramming all their stuff into Nikki's Honda CR-V, getting ready to head back to New England. The little SUV barely held all their bags and boxes of girlie stuff, plus a few gifts for Nikki's daughter, Erin. Adrienne had stored her Camaro in Dana's garage. Dana and Nikki still weren't sure if bringing along an eighteen year old girl was the wise thing to do, but given her situation, they had little choice but to let her tag along—for now.

"We need a bigger vehicle," said Dana.

"This'll work, " said Adrienne.

Dana shook her head. "No, we need something huge, like a Lincoln Navigator or a Hummer, like that. Something that chug-a-lugs gas and pumps out vile emissions."

Nikki laughed. "Yeah, right. Join the legions of eco-terrorists, right?"

David followed them out to the driveway, wearing only pajama bottoms. He fumed and gesticulated. "You're not going!" he shouted at Dana. "I don't want you anywhere near some psycho killer."

Hands on hips, she stared him down. "Who's going to stop me?"

"I am."

"How? Tie me up?"

"If I have to. Listen, Honey, I—"

"No, you listen. Nikki is my best friend and she needs my help. Case closed."

"David's right," Nikki interjected, eyeballing Dana. "You ought to listen to him."

Dana spun on her. "You stay out of this." Turning back to David, Dana said, "I thought we settled this last night. Can we put it to rest?"

"I can't let you do this," he said flatly.

Dana raised her eyebrows. "You see the irony in this? In the movies, these scenes are usually reversed: the white-hat hero is going to a gunfight somewhere and the "little woman" begs him not to."

David snorted. "If you go ahead? I just might not be here when you get back—*if* you get back."

"Look," she said, softening and putting a hand to his face. "I know you're upset and I pretty much understand, but the fact is: I'm going."

Apparently unable to respond, he stormed back into the house.

Silent, Nikki, Dana and Adrienne piled into the overstuffed vehicle and took off; Dana drove and Adrienne curled up with Sinbad the cat in the back seat. Within a few blocks, both girl and feline were sound asleep

"You should've listened to your husband," Nikki finally said.

Dana sniffed, raised her chin. "My mind is made up."

"I'm serious. What if he really leaves you?"

"It's all bark. He won't leave. We love each other too much."

"Well," Nikki said. "I don't want to jeopardize your marriage but I'm so thankful you're here for me."

Dana softened. "Since Steve—"

At the sound of his name, Nikki felt the dark sadness jab once again, at her heart. It probably showed on her face, although she tried to hide it.

"I'm sorry," Dana said. "I didn't mean . . .."

"I know. Things are much better but I'm still pretty vulnerable, I guess. And I'm still bitter about the fact that I only got to be with him for a few short months."

Dana nodded. "It's so sad. I guess it's some sort of lesson, though. They say some lessons must be learned by adversity."

"Who is this famous 'they'? It's always 'they say'. I'd like to know who the hell 'they' are."

"Me, too. Anyway, *they* say difficult situations are opportunities for growth."

"I don't want to hear it. Opportunities for misery, if you ask me."

"You'll heal . . . eventually."

"*They* always say that, too. I do feel a little better, though, even with just a few sessions with Dr. West. Two weeks at the gym didn't hurt, either. I've already lost ten pounds."

"Well," said Dana. "You definitely look thinner."

"Maybe. Anyway, last night, I called Erin. We talked for over two hours, cried together, and even laughed at the pitiful condition I'd gotten myself into."

"Pitiful is right. Granted, grieving is necessary, but it's definitely unacceptable behavior to kill yourself, especially by vomiting. It must be so awful to have bulimia."

"I just hate being this way."

They marinated in their own thoughts for a bit.

"On the plus side," Nikki said after a few minutes. "Erin was delighted to find out I finally trashed my skanky bathrobe."

Dana laughed but when she looked over, her eyes were misting up. "I didn't tell you this, but Erin and I talked on the phone a lot when you were so sick. We felt helpless, not being able to fix you."

Nikki reached over, patted her shoulder. "I'm sorry I put you both through that."

Dana pulled some tissues from the dash dispenser and they dabbed their eyes.

"Sometimes," Nikki said. "I still do the 'why me?' thing."

"I told you the answer to that."

"I know, I know. Why *not* me, right? What makes me so special that I should be spared from bad things."

"You're beginning to get it."

"But why does God do this to us?"

"I believe God doesn't 'do' anything to us," Dana explained. "God created nature. Life and death are subject to the laws of nature, you know? And, nature is indiscriminate."

Nikki raised her eyebrows. "You're saying Mother Nature is a bitch?"

"She can be, but I don't think nature has anything to do with what people do or don't deserve. Enough of this heavy talk, though. You're back, and I'm declaring that we've learned whatever lesson we were supposed to learn from all this."

"So declared and so decreed!" Nikki shouted, with a laugh.

That woke Adrienne. She stretched and yawned. "Declared and decreed what?"

"That we've learned all the lessons we need to learn," said Dana. "I guess."

"Like, I'll go along with that and stuff and everything else."

Dana and Nikki burst into laughter.

"What," said Adrienne. "What?"

THEY HEADED UP through Atlanta, angled over to I-95 and had just crossed into Virginia when Nikki's cell phone rang. She picked up: "Hello?"

"Nikki? It's Frank."

"Oh, hi, Chief. Guess what? I'm on my way back home. What's up?"

"Babe! That's great. I got news about your boy, Hess. Looks like he left Rhode Island. They found the body of a college girl in Pennsylvania, his M.O. Probably had DNA over it. She was only nineteen."

"Oh my God. But how do you know he did it?"

"They discovered the body near a closed tourist attraction in the Poconos, you couldn't miss it. Like I say, the murder was Hess's M.O.: mutilations, biting. You get the picture."

"Gruesome. Can you match the bites? Do you have Hess's dental records?"

"They're on the way, but everyone knows he did it."

"How can you be so sure?"

"There was a note attached to the body, and I quote: 'Tru love never dies', in caps, with 'true' spelled T-R-U. Then the note said to 'look in the classified ads'. Sound familiar?"

"T-R-U. Oh my God. That message was meant for me."

Frank was silent, then: "I don't know. Maybe that's his calling card now, has become part of his M.O.—aimed at any female he can attract by using the classifieds."

"No, he's directing *me* to the classifieds."

"But in Pennsylvania? Anyway, the Staties are all over it. Not only that, but after Junior's school shooting? The goddam FBI just sent us a Special Agent profiler geek to wet his beak. I guess it's on account of the interstate serial killer aspect and also the rise in school violence lately. Anyway, it's a real circus, all the suits running around here. I'm sure it's just a matter of time before Hess is caught."

Nikki brought the chief up to date on what Adrienne had told them and said she'd answer any inquiries as soon as she got home. "The school shooting was unbelievable," she said.

"Yeah. No proof, but Hess definitely put Junior up to it. Junior's mom said the kid had been hanging around with an older guy and the kids at Franklin High said Junior was dealing."

"Poor Junior," Nikki said. "So needy. Probably fall for anything that'll raise his self esteem."

"Yeah, well, that's no longer a problem, huh?"

"What do you mean?"

"You didn't hear? He died in the County jail."

"What? How?"

"Hell's bells, Nikki. I thought you knew. You didn't know? Well, the autopsy showed he was poisoned."

"I'll bet Hess is behind it somehow."

"Probably. One other thing: we found a tow dolly from Hess's motorhome that he stored at Junior's mother's house."

"Interesting. I'll make a note to talk to her."

"What? Now, just a minute. You're not police, Nikki. Stay out of this, we'll handle it. Besides, she's already been interviewed and nothing came of it."

"But maybe woman to woman . . . ."

"I *said* . . . oh, what the hell, maybe you're right. G'head, see what she says. Anyway, about that valuable brooch of yours? The one with the purple pearl? The F.B.I. Feebies are checking the international markets to see if Hess fenced it."

"Well, please let me know if you hear anything else, okay?"

"I will, babe. And, I'd be only too happy to watch your back if you get my drift."

"Oh, I'm sure you would," Nikki said, her tone going frosty. "But I'll manage, thanks. I'm grateful for the update, though." After she punched the phone off, she slumped in the seat.

Dana looked over. Nikki relayed what the chief had told her.

"Junior's *dead*?" cried Adrienne, looking incredulous. Her eyes filled. "How?"

"I'm sorry," Nikki said, and gently told her how.

"I just can't believe Junior's dead!"

"I'm afraid that's not all," Nikki said, and told them about the mutilated body the police found in Pennsylvania.

"Oh my God, that could've been me," cried Adrienne.

"Yeah," said Dana. She tossed Nikki a serious look. "And guess who's next on the monster's wish list."

Nikki nodded. "So it seems, even though he's in another state. Look, if you girls want to bail, now's the time—"

"No way," Dana interrupted.

"No *fucking* way!" piped Adrienne.

Sinbad meowed.

Nikki slumped further in her seat but had to smile at their grit. "So it's like that, huh?"

"We'll kick his ass," said Adrienne. "We're like an all-chick version of Dog, the Bounty Hunter or something."

While they shared uneasy chuckles at that, Dana's cell phone rang. Nikki picked it up out of the console. The caller I.D. read: "home".

"It's David," she said, offering Dana the phone.

"He just wants to control me some more. I don't want to talk."

"Hi, David," Nikki said, into the phone. "It's Nikki."

"Could I speak to Dana, please?"

"Sorry, she doesn't want to talk right now."

He asked where they were. Nikki told him and brought him up to speed on Hess, adding, "He's resourceful, so he may end up in Destin looking for me."

"Jesus."

"Do you have a pencil? I've got something for you to tell him if he calls, okay?"

"I don't like this," growled David. "But go ahead."

"I think Hess wants to communicate through newspaper classifieds so I called one in. Tell him that I said to keep his eye on the personals in *The Providence Journal*. Tell him to look for a message from 'Tru Love'. Spell that t-r-u, got it? If he's in Destin, he can go online for it."

"If I hear from him or he comes by, I'll give him the message," said David. "But I'll also notify the police, count on it. Can I talk to Dana now?"

Nikki held the phone out to her.

She sighed, took it and said: "I'm through talking," then listening, softening, and, "I love you, too." More listening, a frown, and emphatic, "Absolutely not!" She hung up.

"Well?" Nikki asked.

"He won't give up. First, he said he wanted me to drop you off and come home. When I didn't respond to that, he said he'd join us and you heard my reaction. Anyway, I believe he finally realizes I won't cave on this."

"I think you—"

"Never mind what you think," said Dana, interrupting. "You'd do this for me."

"I can't argue with that."

Dana looked over at Nikki again. "Listen, I've been thinking. We probably shouldn't stay at your apartment in case Hess comes looking for you. Why don't we get a bed and breakfast in Newport?"

"I don't know if—"

"Hey, I'm loaded, remember? I say: if we're going to be snuffed? Let's go out in style."

"Like, with shopping along Thames Street?" asked Adrienne, now leaning up between the bucket seats. Streaks of mascara trailed down her cheeks and her eyes were bloodshot.

"Of course," Nikki said, with lightness she didn't truly feel.

Adrienne looked hopeful. "Does that mean I'm in?"

Nikki snorted. "The jury's still out on that."

Adrienne sulked. "Look, I know I'm young? But I'm a self-sufficient woman and I've already faced the bastard down once. Like, what else do I have to do to prove myself?"

"She's got a point," said Dana. "And her parents? Forget them."

"If you don't let me be part of this, I'll just follow you anyway," insisted Adrienne.

"And she *is* the only one of us who's actually seen the monster," Dana argued.

Adrienne started bouncing in her seat. "So I'm in?"

Nikki turned, looked her straight in the eye. "I guess. For now. Until I say no."

CHAPTER 34

DOING THE GIRL had relieved some of Hess's sexual frustration, allowing his bloodlust to simmer. The Temptations had returned and he had capitulated but then came The Purging so he was all set on *that* score. But now, he was back at his hideaway and thoughts of Nikki were no longer on the back burner; in fact, they were boiling away on the front. He paced until an idea occurred to him with such intensity, he felt like one of those cartoon characters with a light bulb over their head. He scrambled for his cell phone and dialed Paco's unlisted number in Nebraska.

"Yeah?"

"Hey, Paco? It's Hess again."

"Hola, cabron. Qué pasa?"

"I got a little problem, buddy. Maybe you can help."

"What kind of proglen?"

"A little one. I need some information."

"Información? No problemo."

"Great. I need to find the new address of someone who left town and put in a temporary change of address at the post office. *Comprende, amigo?* Whatever it costs, you know I'm good for it."

"$500, *ese*."

"$500? That's outrageous, you little chimichanga fuck."

"What can I say? I am just a humble beaner, *qué no*? Jou wan' it or no?"

"Alright, okay. How's it work?"

"Easy, *puto*. I have a phony utility company and paid up service for "return address requested for delinquent customers". That way, I geet access to the post office files, *no problemo, mang*."

After giving Paco Nikki's full name and old apartment address, Hess hung up, rubbed his hands together and grinned.

Less than twenty-four hours later, Paco called back, saying, "She ees in Florida, *ese*. A town called Destin. Staying with somebody name of . . . lemme see here . . . ah, Hart. H-A-R-T."

"Destin? No shit. Got an address?"

Paco gave him the information and Hess scribbled it on a pad, saying, "Got it. Thanks, *amigo*." He hung up.

Destin, Florida, huh? He wondered if he should take his RV but figured it'd be too much of a logistical problem and decided against it. He snagged a suitcase out of a closet, tossed it on the bed, and started packing but stopped abruptly. *Wait a minute. Why don't I try calling information first?*

He got out the phone book, looked up the area code and called.

"What city, please?"

"Destin, ma'am. Do you have a number for Hart, H-A-R-T? On Beachside street?"

She gave him the number and he hung up. Deciding not to place himself by using his cell phone, he boogied to his van and tooled down the road to a Quik-Mart. He was in luck, they had a pay phone—not many left these days. He dropped some coins in, punched the numbers.

While he waited, he turned up his collar against the early November chill, chewed on a ragged fingernail, and shifted from leg to leg. The first snow flurries of the season were mixing with a brisk nor'easter wind.

A male voice answered: "Hello?"

"Sir, this is uh . . . Chief Anderson of the Benedict's Landing police," said Hess. "Could I speak to Nikki O'Connor, please?"

"She's not here any longer."

"No? Do you have any idea where she went, sir?"

"Back to Rhode Island. But if you were really the chief, you'd know that by now. You're that Marion Hess prick, aren't you? Well, listen up, asshole. Nikki just phoned from on the road. She told me if you called, to tell you she got your message. She's on her way to get you."

"She's—"

"Keep your eye on *The Providence Journal* personal ads. Look for a message from 'Tru Love'. Spell that T-R-U."

Mystic Fear

Hess slammed the phone against the cinder block wall of the Quik-Mart until the plastic shattered. "What the fuck?" he cried. "Gonna get me? *Me?* You don't get me, bitch, I get *you!*"

He dropped the ruined receiver and sprinted to his van, flung open the door, jumped in, and squealed away. Once he was back home, he screeched to a stop outside the barn, stumbled out, and headed for the Winnebago.

He jerked open the door, scrabbled in, and started lighting all the votive candles on his precious shrine. But before he could get the last one lit, a gust of wind followed him in.

Blowing them all out. *Snuff!*

THE FOLLOWING DAY, Hess decided it was time for an ID change so he retired Karl Meyer and employed the new persona of Joe Falciano. He shaved his beard, trimmed his moustache, and applied some jet-black "Just for Men" to get rid of the gray. Satisfied, he tried on his authentic-looking, curly black wig, the one with distinguished white highlights on the combed-back sides and then the John Lennon specs. That done, he drove his van to Massachusetts and traded it in for a sensible Ford Taurus. Once the transaction was complete, he called Paco in Nebraska and relayed all the details.

"*No problemo, ese,*" said Paco. "I'll put your registration in overnight mail."

"*Gracias*, Paco. You are one hell of a resourceful beaner." *Click.* That done, Hess drove back to Providence where he pulled in at a Starbuck's for a regular, plain-ass coffee. No yuppie double-latte cappuccino macchiato bullshit for him, no sir. To his way of thinking? The more ingredients in a coffee, the bigger the asshole. He snatched up a stray newspaper, sat down, and unfolded it to the classifieds, in particular, the personals.

And there it was:

SINGLE WHITE FEMALE SEEKS MEANINGFUL RELATIONSHIP WITH HIGH SCHOOL BRAVEHEART. IF YOU KNOW MY OLD LOCKER NUMBER, CALL ME. WE'LL TALK.

TRU LOVE NEVER DIES.

The ad listed a local phone number.

He sipped his coffee, frowned, wondering if it was a setup. No big deal because he figured he could call her from a public phone and keep it short. He smiled. *Braveheart? I like that. And her old locker number? Easy.*

HESS SOON FOUND that public phones in the city were either non-existent or vandalized beyond use and covered in graffiti. Then it occurred to him to try the airport where there was anonymity as well as plenty of people so he drove straight to T.F. Green airport, parked in the short-term lot, and headed into the terminal.

On the lower level, a large bank of vacant pay phones stood against the wall. He picked one on the far end, lifted the receiver, dropped in his coins and punched in the number that Nikki had listed in her ad.

His hands were shaking.

Tiny beads of sweat popped out on his forehead.

CHAPTER 35

NIKKI, Dana, and Adrienne had just crossed the border into Rhode Island. Dying to see her daughter, Nikki called Erin and she picked up on the second ring.

"Hello?"

"Hi, sweetie, it's me. I'm on I-95, in Rhode Island. We're going to be staying at a B&B in Newport but I really want to see you first. Is it okay if we come up?"

"Sure! I can't wait to see you. I've missed you so bad. Did David talk Dana out of coming?"

"Nope. So plan on three of us, and, of course, Sinbad."

"Hurry, but drive safe."

"We will. Um, I have a couple of favors to ask . . . ."

"Anything, Mom. You know that."

"It's Sinbad. Could you board him for a while? The B&B doesn't allow pets."

"Sure, no problem. Brewski, our new Rottweiler, will love him."

"You got a *Rottweiler*? Why didn't you tell me?"

Erin laughed. "I'm telling you now. He's a puppy and a real cream puff. I'm not even sure if he's as big as that giant fur ball you call a cat."

"Yeah, I'm not worried. Sinbad can hold his own."

"No doubt."

AT ERIN'S, after giving Brewski a few wary looks, Sinbad ignored the puppy and trotted off to explore. The baby Rottweiler pranced after him, looking to play but when Sinbad turned, arched his back, and hissed—Brewski wisely scrambled back to his mistress and lay at her feet.

Nikki, Dana, Adrienne sat at the kitchen table until after midnight, drinking gallons of lethally strong Beantown Blend coffee, eating ice cream, and bringing Erin up to date on everything that had happened.

"I'm worried about you, Mom," she said. "That monster is a *serial killer!* Hello?"

Nikki tried to appear nonchalant. "With my bodyguards here, we can kick anyone's ass, even a serial killer. Right girls?"

"Right," said Adrienne. "We're an all-chick version of Dog the Bounty Hunter."

"Would that be the Dogettes?" joked Dana.

"Yes!" cried Adrienne. She pumped a fist in the air.

Erin scowled and waved her arms. "Cut the cutsey crap! Have you forgotten what he did to those young women? And Steve?"

"I haven't forgotten," Nikki said. "Not for a moment, believe me."

"Mom, *please* let the police handle it."

"Well, *if* they handle it, good. But if not, I will. Besides, I also have Tugboat—my three-hundred pound trump card."

"Three-hundred?"

Nikki nodded. "With a forty inch waist."

"How is it you know his waist size?" asked Dana.

"I saw his Levis, okay?"

Adrienne grinned. "Whoa. Like, on or off?"

Nikki steeled her eyes. "None of your business, missy, but 'on'. I've known him for over a year. As a *friend.*"

Adrienne grinned wider. "If you say so."

"I'm ready to turn in," said Dana, standing up and yawning. "I'm beat."

Erin started clearing up. "You gals can joke all you want," she said. "This is deadly serious. But if you have to do this, I want in."

"Absolutely not," Nikki said.

"Why not?" Erin gestured toward Adrienne. "You let her come along and she's just a kid."

"I am not a kid!" cried Adrienne.

Nikki stood up and slapped a palm against the table. "Look, Adrienne has some ugly family issues and the jury's still out on whether she even stays with us or not. At the most, her involvement will be limited. But you? You're my daughter and are most definitely *not* getting involved."

"But, Mom—"

"And that's final!"

In the end, Nikki talked Erin out of it. They stayed at her place a couple more days but, anxious to get on with their quest, they headed back to Newport.

CHAPTER 36

NIKKI OPENED HER window as she and her sidekicks approached Narragansett Bay. She took in a lungful of that incomparable salt air, her favorite fragrance. Scattered whitecaps punctuated a Prussian blue sea while mighty waves crashed against the rocky shores. She allowed that the Gulf coast was spectacular and the beaches were some of the most beautiful she'd ever seen, but the New England coast held a special charm for her that she'd yet to find in any other place.

"First things first," she said, whipping out her cell phone.

"Where have I heard *that* before?" asked Dana, smirking. She was lounging in the back seat, reclined all the way.

Adrienne drove and simultaneously slurped the last of her Beantown Blend. "It's like I'm totally addicted to this shit," she said happily. "Um . . . who're you calling?"

"First, the state detective and FBI man, then Tugboat," Nikki said.

"I forgot," said Adrienne. "What's Tugboat's real name?"

"Clyde. Clyde Haywood."

Having no luck with her first two calls, Nikki tried Tugboat.

The phone rang three times. He picked up. Nikki recognized his voice right away and it gave her an instant feeling of security. Who could be afraid with a guy that size in their corner?

"It's Nikki," she said.

"So good to hear from you! Where are you?"

"Just getting to Newport."

"You're in Rhode Island? I've been wondering if you were okay."

"Well, I had a . . . um . . . rough go of it for a while, but I think I'm better. For now, anyway. You said that I could call on you anytime if I needed help. Does that offer still hold?"

No hesitation on his end: "Sure. Whatever you need."

She breathed a sigh of relief and began filling him in on Marion Hess's grisly activities.

"And the police?" he asked.

"I've kept in touch with all the authorities, including the FBI. Nobody has made any headway and I guess Junior died before anyone could get any information out of him." She looked over at Adrienne and felt bad bringing Junior up again in front of the poor girl. Holding her hand over the phone, she mouthed, "Sorry."

Adrienne nodded and gave her a weak, vulnerable smile that looked completely out of place with her black lipstick.

Back to Tugboat, Nikki said, "Anyway, I'm going after Hess. I'm going to get him, too. Take it to the bank."

"Well, they say the best defense is a good offense. Or is it the other way around?"

"And you were a football player? Anyway, I've got a couple of tough-as-nails women with me but we could use a little more muscle. An ex-marine would do."

"That'd be me. What's the plan?"

"Well, I don't know, just yet. But basically I'm thinking I'll put myself out there as bait."

"Bad idea. What's plan B?"

"If plan A fails, I won't need a plan B."

"That's why you need a good plan B to replace plan A," he said.

"What is this, Abbott and Costello? Who's on first?"

"Not you. You can't—"

"Look, Tug. If we do this thing—if you come in on it—it's got to be my way. My keester is on the line here, so I have to have the final say. Okay?"

"Aren't all our asses on the line?"

"Of course I'll welcome suggestions," she said. "But in the end? It's got to be my way."

"If you say so."

"Okay. Let's meet and brainstorm. Are you free right now?"

"Sure."

"Great," she said. "How about the Mariner's Bar and Grill in Benedict's Landing? They have terrific fish n' chips and chowder. We're all suffering from a serious New England seafood deficiency."

"I want twin lobsters," piped Dana. "Fishermen's style."

"And, like, plenty of stuffed quahogs," added Adrienne.

Tugboat chuckled. "Seafood," he said. "Lucky for me I'm on a seafood diet."

"Heard that before," Nikki said. "You *see* food, and you eat it, right?"

"You got it. I'm on my way."

ENTERING THE MARINER'S bar and grill hit Nikki like a punch in the gut and her ebullience evaporated. She and Steve had had their first date here and it'd been their favorite hangout. Had it only been a few months now since he'd been murdered? It seemed like a lifetime.

Tugboat wasn't there yet, so the women picked a booth in the back.

Dana laid her hand on Nikki's. "Are you sure you're okay with this?" She asked, most likely intuiting what the Mariner's Bar and Grill meant to her best friend. "We can find some other place, someplace less, um, painful."

Nikki started to talk but her voice hitched, so she just shook her head. Tears spilled down her cheeks and she couldn't do a damn thing about them. She pulled a compact out of her purse, grabbed a Kleenex and dabbed at her eyes, saying, "Ah, shit."

"You gonna be okay?" asked Adrienne.

"Order me a double vodka," Nikki said to Dana. "I'm going to the restroom. I'll be right back."

After a quick, repressed cry and reapplication of makeup, Nikki gave her hair a few perfunctory swipes with a brush, and forced herself to pretend everything was just fine. She came back and scooted into the booth.

Dana tried to lighten the mood. She pointed at Nikki's double vodka, saying, "You trusted an alcoholic alone with your double vodka? Are you crazy?"

The waitress came back over. "Ready, hons? What can I get you?"

"I'd like one of those?" said Adrienne, pointing to my drink.

The waitress snorted. "And I'd like to lock my legs around Brad Pitt, Honey . . . but it ain't gonna happen. You don't look like you're old enough to drive, let alone get served."

Adrienne pouted, reached into her purse, whipped out a cigarette and lit up. When Nikki and Dana glared at her, she snubbed it out, saying, "Christ on a crutch."

Nikki tossed back her drink.

The waitress raised her eyebrows. "Whoa, sister! You want another?"

"No thanks," she said. "That's my limit."

"One drink limit," said Dana. "What a lush."

Nikki smiled. "It was a double."

While they were waiting for Tug, Dana's cell phone rang. "Hello?" she said. After a pause: "What part of 'no' don't you understand?" Another pause, then: "Okay, I'll tell her . . . and I love you, too." She hung up.

"David?" Nikki asked.

Dana nodded. "Would you believe he's still trying to talk me out of this? Anyway, he said to tell you that you were right: Hess called, pretending to be a cop. David delivered your message."

"Well," Nikki said, "The bait's out there now. Think we can reel him in?"

"As long as we stick together," said Adrienne. "We're like—"

She was interrupted when three guys, obviously local, sauntered over from the bar, probably thinking the women were fair game. All the guys wore filthy flannel shirts coated in fish scales, stained Levis, and rubber fisherman's boots. As they got closer, Nikki smelled bait, spilled beer, and tequila shooters. She looked at her watch, wondering what was keeping Tugboat.

Dana served up a "don't come any closer" look.

The guys eased up anyway. One of them had his shirt unbuttoned and his grubby undershirt read: SHIT HAPPENS.

He stared at Nikki, tried to focus, and let out a beery burp.

"Hey-yyy," he said, slurring. "You're that park ranger."

Nikki stood and eased her way out from behind the table. "I was, once upon a time. Now go away, please."

He sneered, looked her up and down. "Not all park rangers are as *hot* as you."

She could smell his fetid breath. "I like your T-shirt," she said.

He looked down at it. "What, shit happens?"

"Yes. It's true. It's happening right now."

"Back to the bar, boys," said Dana, stepping between them. "Here's a clue: we're not interested."

"Bitches think their shit don't stink," said the guy in the middle. "Let's go." They reclaimed their barstools and ordered another round.

"Losers," said Dana, once they'd gone. She and Nikki sat back down.

"I don't know," said Adrienne. "The one on the left? He's kind of cute."

The guy must have heard her, because he turned his head. Adrienne tossed him an encouraging smile. He smiled back and it, too, reeked of encouragement. All three of the fishermen conferred, after which they slid off their stools again and sauntered back.

Dana frowned. "Way to go, girl," she told Adrienne. "Here they come again."

"Cool," said Adrienne, preening.

That's when Tugboat showed up. He strolled over to the table and when the fishermen saw him, they boogied back to their barstools. The waitress came over and after she took the dinner orders, Nikki made all the introductions.

"Tugboat, huh," said Dana, looking him over. "Easy to see how you got your nickname."

He grinned and his teeth were even whiter than Nikki remembered.

Mystic Fear

Tugboat turned his attention to Adrienne.

"What," she said, averting her eyes.

"I remember you," he said. "From the campground. Junior Ferguson's girl?"

She picked at one of her ebony fingernails. "I was. For a while."

Nikki shook her head. "Let's not talk about Junior, please."

Tugboat realized his *faux pas*. "Oh, yeah. I'm . . . sorry. I didn't think."

Nikki jumped in, suggesting an investigative tack. "Might be a good idea if we talked to the kids at Franklin High," she added.

"Before or after the 'you being bait' plan?" said Tug.

"Well, in the meantime."

"What've the police got?"

"Zip," Nikki said.

The guy at the bar whom Adrienne had encouraged came back over. The other two stayed put. "'Scuze me," he said, taking his ball cap off and throwing Adrienne another one of those encouraging smiles. His New England accent was heavy. "I apologize for my buddies, they're a little shitfaced."

"So we noticed," Nikki said. "What's on your mind?"

"Well, I couldn't help but overheah you talkin' 'bout Juniah Ferguson and that other guy. I used to know Juniah and I saw 'em togethah. Lotsa times."

Nikki felt her heartbeat quicken. "Yes? Where?"

"Peep Toad's bah. When I ain't out on the salt? I like to play pool there."

"Peep Toad's bar?"

"I know where it is," said Tugboat. "It's a grungy little place over on Route 2."

"Right," agreed the fisherman. "Pretty grungy."

Nikki turned to him. "Anything else you can tell us?"

He shrugged. "All I know is that guy with Juniah was weird, with his faggy ponytail and all. The dude's eyes looked dead, man. Like a shark's."

"Anything else?" asked Dana.

237

The guy shrugged again, turned his cap around in his hand. "Peep Toad knows ever'thin' what goes on in his place. You should ask him. Or her. I can never figure out 'zackly which the toad is."

"Androgynous?" Nikki asked.

"Hah?"

"Never mind. Anyway, thanks," she said. "We'll do that."

The guy went back to his buddies, but not before he and Adrienne exchanged more flirty grins.

Well, thought Nikki, at least the girl had picked the best of the three, so her radar wasn't completely whacked. "Okay, it looks like we'll need to check out Peep Toad's. How about Wednesday?"

"How about we meet at the marina park over in Wickford?" asked Tugboat. "Know where it is?"

Nikki nodded. "One o'clock?"

"Awesome," piped Adrienne. "We can sleep in."

"So we're all set," said Tug.

"Yep," Nikki said. "In the meantime, maybe Hess will respond to the ad I put in the classifieds of *The Providence Journal.*"

Tug groaned. "Bait," he said.

Nikki just grinned ruefully.

CHAPTER 37

THE ELIJAH BRAY Inn was a lovely, historic building in the Point District of Newport, Rhode Island, not quite on the waterfront, but only a few blocks from Thames Street and a veritable plethora of shops. Nikki had shoehorned herself into a new pair of jeans and was tossing a critical eye over herself in the mirror.

"These jeans look horrible with the top I selected," she told Dana.

"Yeah?"

"Okay," admitted Nikki, turning this way and that. "Maybe the problem isn't the top. It's my disgusting thighs and ass. These jeans seem pushed to their stress limits."

Dana laughed, saying. "You need glasses, girl. You're ass, thighs and jeans are just fine."

Nikki was alternating between arranging her hair in a French braid and slurping coffee when she got a call.

Ring! . . . Ring! . . . Ring!

"Hello?"

"Nikki?"

"Yes. Who is this?"

"Braveheart."

Silence, then: "Mr. Hess." Her eyes cut to Dana and Dana nodded, raised her eyebrows.

"I want to be sure," continued Nikki. "What was my locker number?"

"222."

"It's you then."

"Oh yes, it's me," he said, with a chuckle.

"Where are you?"

"Forget the games, Whore."

"Whoa. What happened to 'True love never dies'? True spelled with no 'e'?"

"Are you in your apartment?"

She forced a laugh. It sounded sort of strangled. "What do you think?"

"No. You wouldn't be that stupid or brazen."

"Brazen? Big word for a convict. Oh yeah, I forgot. You got *educated* in prison. I'll bet you even learned what your anus is for."

A protracted silence, then: "You'll be learning what *yours* is for soon enough."

"Listen, are you still pissed because I kissed you and ran from you and your freako mom?"

"Don't call her names," he snarled. "Mother is becoming you and vice-versa. She is the true love that never dies."

"What? Look, let's forget the verbal foreplay here. Let's meet somewhere."

"So you can trap me? No thanks."

"No trap," she said. "Just you and me."

"Aren't you scared?"

"What, of a dipshit loser like you? I don't *think* so. Tell me, do you still eat your boogers?"

"Don't talk like that; it's not nice," he hissed. "Anyway, we'll see what I eat soon enough."

"You know what I wonder? Why they ever let you out of Butler hospital. You're insane."

"That pit was hell, worse than jail, but that goddam Socanosset Boy's Home was worse. I didn't belong in either place and I'm *not* fucking insane, bitch. I'd rather die than be in one of those places."

"Ah," she said. "So that's why there was never any insanity defense."

"You're pretty smart for a dumbass whore bitch Jezebel.'

"I'm curious, too," she said. "Once you were out, why'd you move to New Mexico?"

"I heard you got married and moved there, so I followed. But I couldn't find you."

"Well, true. My first husband and I were headed there a long, long time ago. Never made it."

"Why not?"

"Not that you need to know, but on the way, we stopped overnight in St. Louis at my husband's sister's. He called his cousin in Albuquerque and found out the job had fallen through so we were kind of forced to stay in St, Louis, set up there."

Hess snorted. "Hunh. Well, I had fun in The Land of Enchantment anyway."

"Two horribly murdered young women, maybe more."

"Ah-ah, now. Law says only one. But you're correct. It could be more, many more. Bitches with hair the color of uh . . . yours. And Mother's. Silky."

"Screw you, Hess."

He laughed. "That *will* happen. Hey, you wouldn't be trying to keep me on the line long enough for a trace, would you? Is someone with you? Perhaps the police?"

"Nobody is here."

"No? . . . I thought I heard something."

"You're mistaken. So . . . what's next?"

"I'll think about it, slut," he said. "Keep checking the classifieds." *Click.*

Nikki's hands were shaking like a wino's now and she'd forgotten all about excess body fat, imagined or otherwise.

"Well?" asked Dana.

"Bastard," said Nikki. "I think I got to him, though." She tried to smile but it failed; instead, she found herself gnawing at her lower lip.

"Good for you."

"I guess. Listen, Hess said he heard someone in the background. Did you say anything while I was on the phone?"

Dana thought about that. "No, I was concentrating on your end of the conversation. I . . . wait a minute, Adrienne just went out. I think she might've called out something from the door."

"Called out something. Do you remember what it was?"

"I wasn't really listening. Sorry."

Nikki looked at her watch. "Shit, I'd better get going. I'll see you this afternoon."

"What's up?"

"I'm going over to Mystic Island. I need to talk to Chief Anderson."

THE RIDE OVER the bridge was, as always, breathtaking: small islands, sailboats under sail, and uncountable moored boats dotted the bay. Once she hit Mystic Island, Nikki drove straight to Benedict's Landing. It felt familiar, yet strange. Almost like a different lifetime.

Perhaps it was.

At the police station, Frank rushed out and greeted her effusively. She kept the reunion talk short and asked if they could go to his office.

"Sure," he said, placing his hand on the small of her back and ushering her forward. Once he'd shut his office door, he said, "How're you holding up?"

"Well enough, I suppose."

"I'm not so sure you should be back in Rhode Island."

"Well, it doesn't matter. I'm here and I'm staying."

"Suit yourself," he said. "Listen, that little Adrienne gal told me about a secret beach where she saw Junior and Hess met up. I happen to know were it is, babe. It's right next to Pickle Park." A bemused look spread across his face.

"Pickle Park?" Nikki asked, raising an eyebrow.

He laughed and nodded. "Fags congregate there. It's sort of a homo nudist scene. That's why my guys nicknamed the area 'Pickle Park'. Anyway, it's an unusually warm Indian Summer day so they might just be at it again. This afternoon, we're gonna go and try to make some arrests. Wanna come along?"

"I'll pass, thanks."

He grinned. "You should go. Hess might be there, too. Who knows? After all, Adrienne told me Hess treated Junior to a little white owl smoking right near there. Maybe the perv isn't capable of resisting the variety of young bare asses there."

"You're disgusting, Frank."

"Why thank you, babe," he said. "I consider that a compliment. I'm telling you, though, seriously: you oughta ride along."

"No way."

"Well, if you change your mind, come back about fourteen-hundred. That's cop talk for two o'clock."

"I know military time," Nikki said. She left the station, but before pulling out, she gave Tugboat a call.

"Hello?"

"Hi. It's Nikki."

"How's it going?"

She told him how she'd placed the ad in the paper and how it had resulted in the call from Hess.

"Gutsy work," said Tug. "You still want to go to Peep Toad's bar?"

"Let's put that off for a bit. I didn't find out where Hess actually *is* or anything so we'll have to draw him out, somehow. I asked the bastard to think of a plan where he'd feel safe."

"Be interesting to see what he comes up with," mused Tug.

"Very."

"I still don't like you being the damn bait. We should let the FBI in on the plan.'"

"No way. We've been over this. Anyway, I've got you for backup, right. You think I should get a firearm?"

"Definitely. Dana and Adrienne should have protection, too," he said.

"Got something in mind?"

"Oh, some light firepower. Something they can handle."

"I don't know," Nikki said. "I'm thinking Adrienne is too young."

"Well, she *is* eighteen and on her own, you know. Kids her age have fought in wars."

"That's different. I feel kind of responsible for her right now and I'm going to make her stay in the background on this."

He snorted. "From what I've seen, that won't be so easy. Anyway, we need to get her some protection, just in case."

"She'd probably end up shooting her boobs off or something."

He laughed. "Don't need that."

"Certainly not."

"What about Dana?"

"No problem. She was an operating room nurse; she can handle anything."

"Okay. We can get some light, easy to handle handguns and practice at my gun club."

"It'll take too long to get the paperwork on the handguns," Nikki pointed out. "You know how that is."

"You let me worry about that," he said. "I know a guy who can help us out."

"Legally?"

"Don't ask. You remember Ernie Whittemore, right? From the Seabreeze campground?"

"'Dirty Ernie', the septic pumpout guy. Sure."

"Okay, I'll set it up. Let's all meet Friday at five for dinner at Marinosci's in Narragansett Pier. Are you familiar with it?"

"Of course. Best Italian food in South County."

"And dinner's on me," he said. "After that, we can go over to Dirty Ernie's. He doesn't live that far from the restaurant."

"You got it. And thanks, Tug. I feel so much better having you in on this."

"My pleasure."

CHAPTER 38

HESS WAS ABOUT to have a brain cramp from thinking so hard. What had he heard in the background of The Whore's phone? It'd sounded like a female voice and some unintelligible words, then: "shopping", and some more words sounding like "uppity dames".

Dames?

But the last word he was definitely sure of: "Starbuck's." He was thinking someone probably liked double latte cappuccino macchiatos or some yuppy shit like that, but uppity dames? The women of today wouldn't even use a word like "dames", would they? He decided to worry about that later because right now he needed to think of a way to draw Nikki out, *sans* risk to himself.

From I-95 south, he headed back to his West Arcadia hideaway. His mind was churning, trying to formulate a plan. Sometimes, if you quit trying so hard—it'd come to you later. He flicked on the radio and listened to some mindless talk show, figuring if that didn't make him brain-dead, nothing would.

Once he was back to the barn and secure in his motorhome, he lit all the shrine candles and compulsively touched each and every photograph of The Jezebel Whore. Closing his eyes, he imagined working on her body and he smiled.

I actually talked to her today!

First time since high school.

He clicked on the VCR, replayed his precious tape, and was surprised that The Temptations returned—creating a substantial tent in his trousers. Freeing himself, he gave in to them, stroking furiously. As the spasms shook him, he ground his teeth together in a grimace and cried out.

Mother!

Afterward, in a ritualistic trance, he lit a cigarette from one of the candles, clamped his teeth down on a belt and submitted to the horror of The Purging. Once he was cleaned up and properly bandaged, he realized he was exhausted so he laid back, closed his eyes, and drifted off.

DARKNESS RULED when Hess woke up; the days were getting much shorter in New England now. The candles had burned out, producing an acrid odor that made him sneeze. The heater kicked on and roasted dust, leftover from all summer, made him sneeze again.

He was groggy, hungry, and had a headache so he took several aspirin, started a pot of coffee, and whipped up some bacon and eggs. The aroma of frying bacon had him salivating and he felt much better once he ate. His mind felt clear, sharp. When he checked his watch, he saw that it was time for the news so he grabbed the remote and clicked on the TV.

There was a loud, annoying Toyota commercial on, so he switched channels and found that an imbecilic ad ruled that channel, too. He was just thumbing the mute when he heard something that stopped him. An announcer, a vivacious brunette wearing a stupid-looking captain's hat was jabbering in a loud, nasal twang: "And remember," she was saying, "the Nautical Nook is right across the street from Starbuck's right here . . ."

Starbuck's?

" . . . in historical Newport, on upper Thames Street."

Upper Thames? Why did that ring a bell? He muted the TV, closed his eyes, and racked his brain.

Upper Thames. Upper Thames.

Nothing.

Upper Thames, upper Thames, upper Thames.

. . . Uppity dames!

"Bingo," he said, out loud.

BY MID-MORNING, Hess was in Newport, the city by the sea. In summer, Newport was a tourist Mecca but now the streets were almost deserted, with just a few scattered shoppers and post-season tourists straggling. Good, thought Hess, he liked it that way. Since he'd figured out Nikki was probably staying somewhere near the Starbuck's in Newport, he'd be spending a lot of time hanging out.

Right now, he was wearing his wool Greek fisherman's cap and amber sunglasses like the ones Bono of U2 wears, but with a heavier tint. He'd also dyed his goatee, making sure it stayed as black as Darth Vader's helmet. He kept a newspaper handy, of course, in case he needed to duck behind it. And a Meerschaum pipe. For the local effect.

Around dusk, his patience paid off.

The little bitch with the magenta-fucking-hair and another whore entered the coffee shop and got their beverages. If this freaky little twat was around, Nikki couldn't be far. No doubt the sluts were ordering fucking double latte cappuccino macchiatos with a hint of fucking nutmeg or some such pussyness.

They headed for the opposite side of room and settled in overstuffed chairs.

Outfuckingstanding, thought Hess, they couldn't see him from where they sat. He waited patiently while they talked, about an hour or so but when they finally got up to leave, Hess thought it was about fucking time.

He followed, at a safe distance. They left turned at the second corner and went down toward the historic Point District where they turned right, onto a narrow side street.

Hess hung back. *Careful.*

They disappeared into the front lobby of a place called The Elijah Bray Inn.

"Who the fuck is Elijah Bray?" Hess whispered to himself. He paced back and forth and waited for a light to come on in one of the upstairs rooms. When none did, he hurried around to the rear of the inn. One light was on.

Was that their room? Sure. It had to be, since all the rest were dark. He nodded with satisfaction, smiled as he noticed the convenient fire escape rising to that lit window.

Now that he knew where the Jezebel Whore Nikki was staying?

His mission was back on track.

CHAPTER 39

FRIDAY FOUND NIKKI, Tugboat, Adrienne, and Dana sardined into a tiny booth in Marinosci's restaurant in Narragansett Pier. The air was redolent of Marinara sauce and garlic. A chubby bottle of Chianti, swaddled in wicker, squatted between two flickering candles on a traditional red-and-white checkered tablecloth. Believe it or not, Dean Martin was actually crooning on the sound system. A curly-haired, olive-skinned waitress with both the largest hoop earrings and largest bosom Nikki had ever seen dealt out their menus and delivered her spiel on the specials of the day.

"Healthy girl," muttered Tug, with a grin.

"I'm starved," said Adrienne. She ordered the calamari appetizer, linguini in white clam sauce, and a Caesar salad.

Nikki and Dana each chose *Pescado Fra Diablo* and decided to share a Caesar.

Tugboat asked for the Eggplant Parmesan dinner. Two orders of it.

"Whoa," said Dana.

Tugboat shrugged. "What can I tell you? I'm a growing boy."

"And yet you maintain that forty inch waist," quipped Dana. "How do you do it?"

Tugboat frowned. "How is it you know my waist size?"

Dana and Adrienne shot Nikki an amused look and she felt the color seep into her face.

"Drinks?" asked the waitress, saving her.

"No alcohol, ladies," advised Tug. "Remember that firearms will be involved later. We wouldn't want to impair our judgment."

The waitress looked shocked. "Firearms? You gonna, like, rob a bank or something?"

Tug laughed. "Nothing quite so adventurous. Just going to the shooting range, that's all. Coffee okay by everyone?"

They all nodded, the waitress scribbled on her pad, and bustled away. While they waited for their food, Nikki related Chief

Anderson's description of Pickle Park and had everyone laughing and rolling their eyes, maybe a little too exuberantly.

Other restaurant patrons looked at their booth as if they'd escaped from a mental ward.

Adrienne glared at them and said, "What're you looking at?" Turning to Tugboat, she added, "See, we not only love a good hoot, but we're tough-as-nails chicks, too!"

That elicited more chuckles but when the food arrived on huge oval platters, the size of the portions generated silence. The foursome dug in and all you could hear was tableware clinking on plates. Once they'd finished, they lingered over coffee.

Nikki turned to Tug. "What now?" she asked.

He wiped his mouth on his napkin, suppressed a burp, and excused himself. "Let's get on over to Dirty Ernie's house. I called him and he'll be waiting for us."

While Tug was talking, Nikki studied his face and realized she'd never really paid attention to his eyes before. They were unusual: sort of hazel, or, no . . . kind of green. And they flashed with his enthusiasm. Here the man was half-black, half-Native American, and had those amazing green eyes. Unreal.

Dana was saying something.

"What?" Nikki asked.

"I *said*, go ahead and ride with Tugboat. Adrienne and I will follow you."

"Okay by me," said Tug as he signed for the check and walleted his credit card. "Let's go."

On the ride to Dirty Ernie's, Tug turned to Nikki. "So, what's your experience with firearms?"

"Well, let's see. At the police academy, I shot a .38 Special, a .357 revolver, 9-mm SIG, and a 12-gauge Remington. Been a while, though."

"How'd you do with the 9mm?"

"Good. Plenty of firepower and not totally overpowering. I liked it."

"We'll go with that, then. How are you feeling?"

"Okay," she said.

"I mean emotionally."

"Honestly? Well, I didn't think I'd ever climb out of the pits there for a while but now I feel as if I'm getting on the other side of it."

"Grieving: it goes on and on. I lost my wife over ten years ago and it still gets to me sometimes, the overwhelming sadness."

Nikki's brow knitted. "I remember you mentioning you were a widower. How did it happen?"

"Well, like I said, that was over ten years ago. Nobody's fault—just snow, ice, and drivers who couldn't handle it."

"You never said, but I assumed you didn't have kids."

"No kids," he confirmed.

"My God, ten years. And it still hurts, huh?"

"Once in a while, but less and less. But life goes on. It's true what they say about time healing all wounds."

She nodded. "Time does help. I feel a little guilty because I'm not thinking about Steve as much as I used to. It's only been a few months since he's been gone, yet his face is starting to blur in my memory. That pisses me off because it makes me feel guilty."

"Give yourself a break," said Tug. "You knew him for such a short time."

"Yes, but still . . .."

"Well, like they say, time heals. Maybe you're healing."

By that time, they'd arrived at Dirty Ernie's. They parked, Dana pulled in behind them, and they all trooped up the walk.

Dirty Ernie's black Labrador retriever, Mike, bounded out of the house and ran up to them. Mike's tongue lolled and his tail flagged while he made himself available for petting.

Adrienne dropped to her knees and started scratching the happy dog's ears. "I'm in love," she said.

Dirty Ernie followed the dog out. His hair was wet and slicked back. He was obviously fresh out of the shower, but a few septic tank odors still lingered beneath the Irish Spring.

"Hey, there," he said, hailing us. "My favorite park ranger, the Tugboat, and two gorgeous specimens of the female persuasion, right here on my doorstep!"

Nikki made the introductions.

Mystic Fear

"Always a pleasure to meet good-looking ladies," Ernie said, winking and motioning them to the back of his house. They stopped at the bulkhead to his basement where he unlocked a thick chain and swung the doors open. At the bottom of the stairs a thick steel door with three more locks confronted them. He keyed them open.

"Pretty secure," Nikki noted.

"Can't be too safe," he said, smiling.

Ernie eased the heavy door partway open and she noticed it was no less than three inches thick. He reached inside and fiddled with something.

"Trip wire," he explained. "It'll set off a tear gas booby trap in the unlikely event the wrong person manages to get past the locks."

"Whoa," said Dana. "A little paranoid?"

Ernie looked at her and winked. "Like I say, can't be too safe."

The basement housed an arsenal.

"My God," Nikki said. "How many guns do you own?"

He shrugged. "I don't know, maybe five-hundred. I got handguns, rifles, shotguns, automatic weapons, grenades, a 30-calibre machine gun, a bazooka, an elephant gun, RPG's, and even access to a 20-mm cannon. Plus, plenty of ammo for everything. I load my own. And I got knives, too. All kinds. And martial arts stuff, too."

"Holy shit," said Adrienne, still petting the dog.

"Holy shit is right," agreed Dana.

Tugboat laughed. "If you want ordinance, Dirty Ernie's your man."

Ernie bowed, gave a magnanimous sweep of his hand. "So. What'll you have?"

"Nikki wants a 9mm SIG," said Tug. "The other ladies will need something a little lighter, I think. Something they can handle, but with enough kick to do the job."

Ernie looked at Adrienne. "Even the kid here?"

She scowled. "I'm not a kid." She cut her eyes to Nikki, pleading.

Nikki chewed at her lower lip. "Yes. Her, too, I suppose."

Ernie shrugged. "Okay, I got just the thing for you gals: Beretta .32's."

"Cool," said Adrienne.

Nikki smiled. *Yeah, like she has a clue.*

Ernie produced the Berettas and distributed boxes of ammunition, saying, "The wad-cutters are for practice, save the hollow-points for real."

"What do we owe you?" Nikki asked, reaching for her checkbook.

"Forget about it," said Ernie. He slapped Tugboat on the back. "This guy keeps a running tab."

"Really," she said.

"From my days as a mercenary," explained Tug. "Those days are over."

After locking up, Ernie led them to the back door of his house and invited them in, saying he'd get them some holsters. They followed him in and met his wife—a pretty, dark-haired woman with a rosy complexion and thick ankles.

"Pleased to meet you," she said, with a shy smile. The way she looked at Ernie, you could tell she was head over heels in love with him so Nikki guessed the woman had grown used to the ambient septic odors.

Not to mention the arsenal looming beneath her cozy home.

FROM ERNIE'S, they drove straight to Tug's gun club, someplace in the boonies, off Route 138. Inside the handgun range, Tug morphed into a different person as he fell into his instructor mode: all business, no fooling around. Of course, since Nikki had her firearm training at the St. Louis Police Academy, she knew that the range master ruled with an iron fist.

"In here, my word is law," Tug said. "You *will* wear proper eye and ear protection and you *will not* touch your weapon until I say so. Is that clear?"

"Yes, sir," the women chimed, in unison.

"All muzzles will be pointed down range at all times."

"They will be," Nikki said, adding: "Sir."

He started by showing Adrienne the proper grip, stance, and how to squeeze off the rounds, making them dry fire their weapons several times. He demonstrated how to insert clips, move the slides, and work the safety. They repeated that procedure until everyone was comfortable and fairly proficient.

"All set, ladies," he said, at last. He ran some paper silhouette targets down the line for them to shoot at. "Lock and load."

They shoved clips into their weapons, ratcheted the slides and took aim.

"All ready on the firing line?" he barked.

They said they were.

"Unlock and commence firing!"

Once their clips were empty, Tug ordered them to cease firing, and lay down their weapons, muzzles downrange. They complied and he reeled in the targets. Nikki's target had a decent, four-inch grouping radius, in the head and neck.

"Nice shooting," said Tug. "If you were a guy, I'd call you Dirty Harry. But you're not, so I guess that'd make you Dirty Harriett."

She laughed. "As long as it isn't Dirty Ernie. I guess it's because I've got good vision and a fairly steady hand."

"You sure do."

To Nikki and Tug's surprise, Adrienne was a natural; her shots were scattered but most were on target. Dana's were about the same, with a little better grouping. An hour later, both of them were hitting the silhouette every time. Confident and ready to go, they all climbed into Nikki's CR-V.

"Okay," said Tugboat, in parting. "Carry your weapons with you at all times. They're for protection. They won't do you any good if you don't have them."

"Of course, that's illegal," Nikki said. "What about carry permits?"

Tug blinked. With those unbelievable green eyes. "Would you rather be illegal or would you rather be dead?"

"He's got a point," said Dana.

"Especially at the hands of that psycho," said Adrienne.

"A fine and even a little jail time would be preferable," Nikki admitted.

"Kiss, kiss," said Dana, and the three markswomen blew Tug kisses of goodbye.

"Thanks for everything," Nikki said.

"Sure. You've got my number, so stay in touch. And keep me posted when and if you hear anymore," said Tug.

"We will."

He shot them an expectant look.

"What," Nikki said.

"Uh . . . maybe you ladies would feel safer if I moved in with you?"

"Sure," piped Adrienne.

"Sorry," said Nikki. "No men allowed."

He projected a hound dog look. "Don't trust me?"

"Oh, we trust you," Nikki said. "Maybe we don't trust ourselves."

Dana threw her a weird look and Nikki dropped the gearshift into drive. She mashed the accelerator. As they drove away, she looked at the rearview mirror and saw Tug waving.

THE FOLLOWING DAY they were entrenched in their favorite chairs at Starbuck's in Newport, sipping Grande bold brew coffees and jabbering like proverbial magpies. Yeah, diamonds are wonderful, thought Nikki. But in her opinion? Strong coffee and meaningful conversations were a girl's best friends.

She hadn't heard anything more from Hess and they were in idle mode.

"I love you guys," announced Adrienne. "It's like you're my *aunts* or something."

"We've pretty much adopted you, that's for sure," said Dana, nodding her head.

Adrienne sneezed, shivered, and hugged herself.

"Bless you," Nikki said. "Coming down with something?"

She shrugged. "I think I might be getting a cold. But what I was saying? I mean it. You guys have, like, made a real difference in my life. Have you noticed I quit smoking?"

Dana snorted.

"What," said Adrienne. She scowled and coughed.

"True, you quit smoking *around us* but we can still smell it on you. And then there's that cough."

"The cough? It's 'cause my throat's all scratchy."

"Hey," Nikki said, "At least you're giving *our* lungs a break by not smoking around us. You'll quit. It'll happen."

Adrienne beamed. "See? You're like the best influence, I swear. I wanna hang out, pack heat, and chase bad guys. Forever."

"Not forever," said Dana. "I happen to have a life, you know."

"And a husband who loves you and misses you terribly," Nikki said. "I think you should go back to him."

"I can't right now," she asked, looking wistful. "What about—"

"Tugboat can cover me."

Adrienne chortled. "I'll bet."

Nikki turned scarlet. "Not what I meant. And as for you, young lady . . . ."

The girl's eyes got huge. "Young lady? You sound like my . . . my *mother*."

"I've made up my mind. We need to get you out of harm's way. What if Hess tries to abduct you again?"

"You mean I have to go?" Adrienne asked in a small, quavering voice. She looked panicky.

Nikki stared directly into her wide, mascara-laden eyes. "Until Hess is caught."

"Is it the smoking? I'll quit, I swear!"

Nikki shook her head. "That'd be good but that's not it. Listen, after this is over? You can live with me if you want. While you go to college."

Adrienne sneezed and coughed. This time, the cough sounded bronchial. "Where'll I go in the meantime? This sucks!"

"We'll figure something out tomorrow."

Dana's cell phone rang and she plucked it from her purse. "Hello? . . . Oh, hi, honey, just a second." To Nikki, she said, "It's

David. We must have telegraphed our thoughts, huh? I'm going outside where there's a better signal."

While she was out front, Adrienne and Nikki, uncomfortable, chatted neutrally about the university.

"What courses do you think you'd like to take?" Nikki asked.

"I don't know. I want to be with you."

"You will. Later. Now . . . your courses?"

Adrienne shrugged, frowned. "Maybe oceanography? Sea life is pretty awesome."

"Well, if you don't have your heart set on Ivy-League, they've got an excellent oceanography school at URI."

Adrienne sneezed again, wiped her reddening nose, and nodded. It looked to Nikki like the girl's cold was taking some of the fight out of her.

Dana returned and plopped down.

"What's up?" said Nikki.

"What can I say? The poor man misses me."

"Tell me something I don't know. He's been calling you at least three times a day."

Dana nodded. "He even apologized, actually said he had no right to be so demeaning and controlling, can you believe that?" She tossed out an anemic smile and raised her eyebrows.

"Well, then, don't be such a stubborn idiot. Go to him," Nikki said.

"I . . . are you sure?"

"I'm sure. Like I said, we've got Tugboat now. We'll be okay."

"Okay, then. I really do miss him; it's on my mind all the time and I don't know how much help I'd be. Uh, could you run me to the airport?"

"Right now?"

"Yeah, now that I've made up my mind, I really want to get going."

"Well, sure. But what about your clothes and things?"

"We'll deal with that later."

They gathered their purses and jackets but Adrienne hung back, saying, "I'm feeling worse. Would it be okay if I head back to the B&B? I want to take a hot bath and guzzle some Nyquil."

Nikki frowned, saying, "I don't like the idea of you being alone."

Adrienne sniffled and waved her off. "I'll be okay. Just come back as soon as you let Dana off, okay?"

"I will," Nikki said. "Right away, I promise."

CHAPTER 40

KNOWING THE JEZEBEL Whore and her friends were back at Starbuck's, Hess cased the lobby of The Elijah Bray Inn and discovered that the bozo on the front desk was oblivious of just about everything except his tittie magazines. *Outfuckingstanding!* He slipped back outside and waited, turning up his collar and shivered against the chill. A pleasant odor of smoke from woodstoves and fireplaces wafted in the air. Brittle leaves whispered as they tumbled by, bustled along by the wind.

In the distance, he spotted a familiar shape. *Aha, it's that ditzy-assed little twat with the punk hair, coming back!* And she was alone. Not Nikki, but quite useful for leverage. How did those southern crackers in the joint say it? A little *in-shurnce*? Of course, Hess hadn't forgotten he had a score to settle with her; there was that, too. He stepped back, pressed himself into the shadows.

She had weaseled away from him before.

Not this time.

Once the light went out in the bedroom, Hess slung a book bag with break-in tools over a shoulder and squeaked on latex gloves. By standing on the trash can bin, he could easily reach the bottom rung of the fire escape. Like a seasoned fireman, he scaled the ladder.

At the window, he was prepared to cut a hole in the pane and unlatch the lock but, happily, the window was cracked. Just a bit, but enough.

He eased it open and slipped inside.

Nobody in the bedroom. Hess figured Jezebel Nikki and her bitch friend must've commandeered it and delegated the waif to the sitting room. Age before beauty, right? He moved down the hallway to the sitting room, where—just as he had assumed—a bed was made up on the couch. There was a puddle of clothes beside it. He investigated, finding a pink thong. He also discovered a nifty little Beretta .32 in an ankle holster, next to the jeans.

Smiling, he slipped the pistol into his jacket pocket.

Back in the hallway, flickering light seeped from underneath a closed bathroom door. He sniffed at the air, thinking: bayberry candles. And what was that other scent? . . . Just a touch of lavender.

How inviting.

With stealth, he moved to the side of the bathroom door and tried the knob. It rotated and he felt a familiar stirring in his loins. Reaching into the back of his belt, he drew out his Henckels chef's knife—thinking he didn't want to do her now, but would if necessary.

The latch released. *Snick!*

There was a sound of water sloshing, a sneeze, and a very scared, nasal voice: "Nikki? Is that you?"

Hess barged into the tiny bathroom, grinned, and flashed his cutlery. "Oops," he said. "Sorry. Guess it's not Nikki."

The girl's mouth gaped but no sound comes out.

"If you scream," he snapped. "I'll kill you right here, right now. Understand?"

She clapped a hand over her mouth, nodded, and coughed.

He focused on her pert, soapy breasts and smiled. "Nice titties," he said. "Small, but nice. The nipple ring is particularly enchanting. Do you suppose I could chew it off?"

She cringed, covered herself with her palms and sunk lower into the water. The suds were all but gone. Nothing was left to Hess's imagination.

"What's this?" he asked, leaning forward. "Why, your rug doesn't match your curtains. Didn't you have enough *magenta* dye for your bush? I think black would be a better color for all your hair, anyway, don't you? Death black?"

She was squirming in the tub now, whimpering: a mewling sound that aroused him further. He grabbed a towel off the rack and handed it to her, saying, "As much as I'd like to continue this, I'm afraid we must go. Dry yourself off and get dressed, you're coming with me."

They moved to the sitting room and Hess watched with lust while she fumbled her way into a midnight turtleneck, jeans, and black Nike hi-tops. Little twat was so scared, she was actually quivering.

Nodding his approval, he moved closer, pulled the turtleneck down, and clutched her by the throat. He squeezed until her face turned crimson and her eyes bulged owlishly.

Then he let her go and patted her cheek, saying, "Don't worry, my delicious little cunny, I'm not going to kill you. In fact, I'm going to give you some nice medication."

Choking, gasping, and coughing, she held her hands at her reddened throat and then collapsed into the nearest chair. She cut her eyes to him while he got a bottle of Poland Spring out of the mini-fridge, uncapped it.

He took a small vial out of his pocket, dumped three tablets into his palm. "Ever hear of 'roofies'?" he asked. "The so-called date rape drug?"

She nodded, eyes growing wide again.

"Actually," he continued, "It's Rohypnol, known generically as Flunitrazepan. A form of Benzodiazepine. Impressed?"

"You're going to rape me?" she asked, her voice a shallow croak. She glanced at the pool of dirty clothes she'd cast off earlier, over by the couch.

"Rape? Perish the thought my pert little snatch. I just want you a little more—shall we say—manageable?"

She shook her head, glowered at him, and looked once again at the clothes.

"Why do you keep looking over there?" he asked.

"Looking? I'm not looking anywhere."

He pulled the Beretta out of his pocket and grinned. "Hoping to get this?" he asked. Ambling over, he tapped the barrel on the tip of her nose before pocketing the pistol again, adding, "You lose."

She leaped up and tried to run but he snagged her skinny forearm in a bone-crushing grip and forced her back into the chair. She yelped.

"Open up," he said, digging into her jaws with his thumb and middle finger and forcing her mouth open. With his other hand, he jammed the pills far back in her throat, making her gag. He handed her the water, saying, "Drink."

Before long, her head was lolling and her eyes were glazed. Hess knew she could hear and, with aid, walk. She wouldn't be able to speak, though.

He smiled. "Just enough Rohypnol, Sweet Cheeks. We're all set." He lifted her out of the chair and held her up. He started to usher her toward the door but pulled up. "I've got an idea," he said. "A *good* idea."

A drizzle of drool escaped the girl's lips. He eased her back into the chair and snatched her purse from the sideboard. He fumbled around until he came up with her black lipgloss.

Grinning, he strode back into the bathroom. On the mirror, in lipstick, he scribbled a message:

TRU LOVE NEVER DIES

Standing back, he admired his work, then grabbed two of the fat, flickering candles and returned to the living area where he placed them under each section of curtain. He watched with glee as the curtains ignited and a nasty stench of burned polyester filled the room. He hauled the girl to her feet again and herded her out, pulling the door shut behind them.

Opting for the brazen route down the front stairs, he was pleased to note that the dipshit on the desk didn't even bother to look up. Once they were on the street, it wasn't far to his Taurus, but a problem loomed: a man and woman had turned the corner and were headed straight for Hess and his captive.

Hess smiled, thinking: unsuspecting fools. He loaded his captive's limp body into the passenger side. "My daughter," he explained to the couple. "She's had a little too much to drink."

The man and woman nodded knowingly.

Hess rolled his eyes. *Dumb fucks. I ought to cut these simpleton's throats and rid the earth of two more genetically inferior creatures. Whatever happened to survival of the fittest?*

ONCE OVER THE bridges and on the way to his hideaway, Hess glanced around his Taurus with contempt, vowing to get a more prestigious vehicle in the near future.

In the back, the girl moaned. Spittle, still seeping from her lips had formed a pool in her lap.

Hess whipped into a McDonald's drive-up for some takeout, hit the road again, and forty-five minutes later, they were in the cellar of the farmhouse.

Still under the effects of the Rohypnol, his prisoner was powerless to resist while he stripped her and noted with pleasure how her taut nipples popped out like plump, ripe grapes in the cold air. He brought a forefinger to his lips, wet it, and traced it over the nipple with the ring before twisting and pinching—hard.

Her eyes showed pain and fear, the only response she was capable of.

He threw his head back and laughed. He needed to get back to The Elijah Bray House and gloat over his handiwork but had a few moments to enjoy, securing his tasty little prisoner.

Locks and chains were involved. And a steel spike, set in concrete. These things made him hard but he really needed to go. After reluctantly going up the stairs and locking the bulkhead, he headed for his car.

Hesitated. Turned back. Stopped again. Held his face in his hands. Twin extreme forces were tearing his tortured soul apart: the *need* to see the results of the fire versus the compulsion of The Temptations. His phallus still taut and needy.

In the end, he managed to put his sexual urges on hold; after all, he'd soon be back.

Quickly, before he changed his mind, he jumped in his car and sped back toward Newport, thinking: Who knows? Maybe I'll get even *luckier*.

Maybe I'll have a shot at capturing the Jezebel Whore . . .

CHAPTER 41

NIKKI PULLED OVER in front of the departing flights entrance of the Bruce Sundlun Terminal at T.F. Greene airport. She and Dana got out and held each other's hands. Tears brimmed in their eyes.

"I'm already missing you," Nikki said.

"Me, too, you."

"You know what? I think you'd better give me your gun. I'm pretty sure they frown upon them here in the airport."

"Oh, right," said Dana. "Christ, I almost forgot." She unstrapped the gun, handed it over.

Nikki opened the car door, slid it under the seat, saying, "I'll miss you but I'm happy that you're going. Give David a big hug for me."

"Okay. Will you be all right?"

"Don't worry. I feel safe as long as I'm with Tug."

Dana cocked her head. "What's that look in your eye? Am I missing something?"

"No."

"Uh-huh, sure. How long did you say you've known him?"

Nikki shrugged. "A while. He was Steve's best friend. Didn't I tell you?"

"You two wouldn't be—"

"Don't even go there. We're just friends, okay? Now hurry, before you miss your plane."

"Was that a coy smile I just saw?" said Dana. "I'll bet you—"

Nikki grabbed her and they wrapped each other up in a tight, heart-felt embrace.

"Those outfits I left at the B&B?" said Dana. "Feel free to wear any of them you like."

"Yeah," said Nikki, choking up. "Like I'm going to fit in them."

Dana's eyes filled, she broke the embrace, turned, and hurried into the terminal. With that, she was gone, mixing in with a teeming clot of travelers who were jostling for position at the ticket counters.

Teary-eyed herself, Nikki got behind the wheel, pulled away. On the ride back to Newport, a great sadness enveloped her now that her best friend was no longer by her side. Nikki had plenty of time to think and that wasn't a good thing because she started feeling sorry for herself.

How could her life turn so sucky, so fast? How could she go from being so happy to losing the love of her life and then—as if that wasn't enough—end up being stalked by a serial killer? The secret to healing lies in my attitude, she told herself, repeating it in her mind like a mantra. She knew she had to change it but it wouldn't be an easy task—especially without her best friend at her side, keeping her on track.

Okay, she thought. Focus. What next? How come she hadn't heard from Hess? Didn't he say he was going to put another ad in the paper? Maybe not, since he had her cell phone number now. She knew the evil bastard was up to something, but what?

She picked up her phone and punched in Tugboat's number, but he wasn't home. Wanting to check on Adrienne, she tried calling The Elijah Bray Inn.

No answer there, either.

She hung up, figuring the doofus at the lobby desk was probably in the restroom with his porn magazines, developing carpal tunnel.

What now? Well, she could go talk to Junior's mom, see if the woman could tell her anything. Or not. In the end, Nikki decided to drive to the B&B, check on Adrienne and catch a bite to eat. By that time, maybe Tug would be home.

I-95 was smooth sailing and once she'd crossed the bridges and arrived in Newport, she turned into the Point District. She hadn't gone far when she heard the wail of a siren and noticed a thin trail of black smoke rising into the air. As she turned onto their street, she saw with horror what had caused the smoke.

A fire at the Elijah Bray House!

Nobody stopped her as she sprinted past a cluster of firemen, through the lobby, and scrambled upstairs to their room because the fire had been doused. The door stood open and inside, she could see that the sitting room curtains and surrounding wall

Mystic Fear

had been scorched. The last fireman was just leaving. She grabbed his arm.

"Did you find a girl in here?" she implored.

"No one was in here when we busted in."

"What happened?"

"Fire started over there," he said, pointing. "Candles did it. They were right under the curtains."

The fireman moved to go downstairs and moments later, a heavy man came clomping up, a plainclothes cop if she ever saw one.

"Newport Police?" she asked.

He gave her a weary nod. "Yeah. Fire guys said it's probably arson so I gotta take a look. And you are?"

"My name is Nikki O'Connor. I've been staying in this room with a couple of girlfriends. One of them was supposed to be here, but apparently she escaped. Wait a minute . . . arson?"

"Could your friend have set the fire?"

"No way."

He moved to the window, knelt, and examined the charred remains of the curtains. "Yeah," he said, picking at the Melted wax on the hardwood. "This was on purpose. Think your friend might be in the lobby? I need to question her."

"I didn't see her when I came in but I blew by there pretty fast."

"Well, maybe the desk clerk knows something. I'll talk to him. First, let's have a look around, shall we? Maybe you can tell me if anything looks fishy."

They headed into the bedroom. There was quite a bit of water damage from overhead safety sprinklers. All of the women's stuff was intact, but smoke damaged. Nikki smiled ruefully, anticipating a new wardrobe.

In the bathroom, they came across what had been written on the mirror, in black lipstick:

TRU LOVE NEVER DIES

Hess! Nikki's knees threatened to buckle and her hands started shaking but then a sudden rush of fury erupted, breaking through her fear. "You goddam *bastard!*" she screamed. "If you harm even one magenta hair, I'll kill you!"

"Whoa," said the cop, coming closer. "What bastard you gonna kill?"

She gave him a nutshell summary of the ongoing nightmare with Hess and told him she knew now without a doubt that Hess set the fire and kidnapped Adrienne. "Call Chief Anderson over in Benedict's Landing," she said. "He can verify my story and fill you in on all the details."

"I will. In the meantime? Keep me posted, will you?" He handed her his card.

She pocketed it, saying, "Sure thing." She gave him her own card, adding, "And please let me know if *you* find out anything, okay?"

"Absolutely."

They did a quick walk through of the area before going downstairs and questioning the kid on the desk. As expected, the doofus knew zip. She settled the bill, telling him she'd be back to collect their belongings.

"Where will you be staying, in case we need to contact you?" asked the cop, as they stepped outside.

The crisp, autumn air soothed Nikki's smoke-irritated nostrils and lungs. "I have no idea," she said. "Some place far away from here, though. I'll let you know."

After the cop left, she headed for her vehicle. She desperately needed to consult with Tugboat, so she reached into her purse for her phone.

And that's when she received the incoming call.

CHAPTER 42

HESS WATCHED all the activity at the Elijah Bray house at a distance from the driver's seat of his Taurus. He consulted his watch. Fidgeted, thinking: better get back to the farmhouse. He was just about to key his ignition when a little SUV pulled up to the scene.

Hello? What's this? The Jezebel Whore and she's alone!

After she ran into the inn, he smiled and settled back to wait and mull this over. Brilliant gold and tangerine-colored leaves parachuted down from the gigantic maple tree above his car, deploying across the hood. By that time, the fire trucks were pulling out and a crime scene van arrived.

A few minutes later, Nikki reappeared, walking out of the building with a cop. And while the two of them talked, Hess mentally reviewed the precious few moments he had already spent with his tasty, magenta-haired prize in the cellar of the farmhouse:

. . . The cellar: dank and cold and perfect—just fucking perfect. Mother would love it.

Shining his 6-volt camping lantern and watching his prey's pale, lithe body finally begin to stir, jerking and convulsing. The little cunt moaning, coming around, the Rohypnol wearing off.

He's getting aroused, wanting to tarry but oh-so-anxious to get back to Newport, compelled, obsessed by his true mission.

He secures Prey: wrapping an end of chain around one pale ankle and snapping the padlock, chain is tethered and locked to a steel spike, buried and set in concrete—allowing Prey an eight-foot radius circle of movement.

He's double-checking all locks, tossing an unzipped sleeping bag over her, saying, "I'd light the kerosene heater and lantern for you, Sweetcheeks, but we wouldn't want another fire, now, would we?"

Her: moaning again.

He makes sure the heater and lantern are far out of her reach and shuts off his flashlight, creating absolute darkness. He places the flashlight near the entry. Hurrying up the stairs and out, he slams the heavy bulkhead doors, locks them. Just about tripping over himself, he's scrambling back and forth between the car and cellar, undecided . . .

. . . Hess's mind slithered back to the present when he saw the cop drive away. His Mission Object was now alone again, by her whoring self. A plan had been fermenting in his head for days. He decided to phone her, right here, right now! He entertained no worries about using his cell phone because this one was wisely prepaid; he'd simply toss it and get another one.

His hands shook as he dialed. Once the call was over, he planned to follow her and maybe get an opportunity to catch her alone. If it didn't take too long. Worst case scenario? He'd at least find out where she was going to be staying.

He watched and even from this distance, he could see her reach into her purse and pull out her phone.

CHAPTER 43

NIKKI'S PHONE WARBLED.

"Hello?"

Silence.

"Hello?" she repeated.

"True love never dies."

She felt the color drain from her face. Her insides turned to jelly. "You insufferable bastard," she spat out, but her voice shook. "What've you done with her? If you—"

"Now, now," Hess said, his voice sounding carefully moderated. "You're in no position to make threats. Why don't we meet and discuss the matter? No cops and you come alone, understand?"

"And?"

"Why, we ride off into the sunset together, of course."

"I'd rather die."

He laughed, a snitty sound. "That might be arranged, too. I know you feel bad about Mother but she understands. You will become."

Become?

"Anyway," he continued, "You'll meet me because of your little bitch friend. And, if we're not followed, I'll call my associate and he'll let her go. I promise. Of course, if anyone tries anything or if my associate doesn't hear from me every five minutes, he'll simply slice her throat."

Nikki snorted. "What's to keep you from killing us both?"

"Well, now, there, then. You'll just have to take that chance, won't you? Thanksgiving's right around the corner, right? Let me think about that. If you don't honor my invitation . . . well, I'll just have to start carving the bird without you, won't I?"

"Don't you—"

"*Magenta-haired* bird," he said, interrupting. "You like white meat? Breast meat? Huh? I'll be sure to carve around the nipple ring so you don't break a tooth."

As angry as she was, Nikki cringed, realizing she had no idea of the depths of this sociopath's sickness. "Okay, okay," she said. "I'll come. Where?"

"I'll let you know." *Click.*

She dialed Tugboat. This time, she caught him at home and quickly told him everything that'd happened. They decided to meet at the Mariner's Bar and Grill bar and formulate a plan.

She fired up her vehicle and sped across the bridge to Mystic Island and into Benedict's Landing, beelining for the Mariner's where she parked and hurried inside. Once her eyes had adjusted to the dim lighting, she spotted Tug, already waiting at a booth in the back. He stood, and she slid in across from him.

"Weren't you girls supposed to stick together?" he asked.

"Don't start."

"Right. Maybe you should try to eat something. Think you can?"

"Yeah, about a dozen glazed donuts."

"Huh?"

She sighed. "I'm sorry. It's just that when I'm really stressed, I crave sweets, in particular—glazed donuts. It's a little defect in my character, which I don't feel like going into right now."

"So . . . you want to go to Dunkin' Donuts?"

"Tempting. But not today, thanks."

"You want a menu?"

She shook her head. "You go ahead."

"Well, if you don't mind, I will get a little snack." He ordered a fish sandwich, fries, and a side of pasta.

She ordered coffee. "Some snack. If I 'snacked' like you, my butt would be the size of a Hyundai."

"I don't *think* so. Now, about Adrienne. How come she didn't shoot the psycho bastard?"

Nikki shrugged. "It looked like he caught her in the bathtub."

"I thought we agreed nobody goes anywhere without their gun," he said. "Anywhere includes bathtubs."

"Well," she snapped. "She didn't have the gun and nothing can change that. Can we move on?"

He held his hands up defensively. "Okay, okay. So you got a plan? I mean, other than using yourself for baitfish."

"I don't see any way around it. If we do nothing, Hess will get frustrated and kill her."

"Maybe we could find out where he is and get to him before that."

"Even if we could," she said, "I can't stand the thought of him playing his demented games with her between now and then."

"What about the cops?"

"No police. Hess said and I promised. Absolutely not."

"State? FBI?"

"No. If Hess even gets a hint of police, he'll kill her, Tug. You know that."

"You're right, no cops. But if you go for the exchange, he'll kill you both."

"I've thought about that, believe me."

"Not to mention what you call his 'demented games'."

She shuddered.

"What if I got there way ahead of you?" Tug suggested.

"What, do your recon Marine thing? Hide out somewhere?"

"Something like that. Maybe I could get the drop on him while you distract him, before he can get on the phone to his partner."

"Distract. How?"

"I don't know. You could wear a low-cut blouse. That ought to do it," he said, grinning.

She shook her head. "Won't work. For one thing, I'm not exactly Pamela Anderson. For another: we still won't know where Adrienne is. Besides, he said his buddy would know if he was captured."

"Yeah. There's that, too."

She nibbled at a thumbnail, thought awhile, and said, "Couldn't you just beat the information out of him right there? Maybe you could convince him to phone his partner and call it off?"

Tug shook his head. "Torture wouldn't work. I've known guys like him."

"Like Hess?"

"Yeah, I mean, just as dedicated to their obsessions. Believe me, those kind of nutcases would rather die than get caught, or even compromise."

"Shit."

He leaned forward. "Know what, though? I don't believe he has an accomplice. I think he's making that up."

"Even if you're right, we can't take that chance."

He sat back, looking frustrated, then finished his sandwich and signaled the waitress for more coffee. "Let's think on it," he said, patting her hand. "By the way, where's Dana?"

"She went back to Florida."

"That's a surprise, I thought she said—"

"With my blessing, okay?"

"Sure. Just wondering."

They sipped coffee for a while, alone with their own thoughts.

"Well," Nikki said, finally. "Goddamit. We've got to do *something*."

"It appears that all we can do right now is wait for him to call you again."

"No, we can't just sit. Let's at least go talk to Junior's mom and see what she has to say."

Tug's eyes lit up. "Good idea," he said.

"And," she continued, "We need to follow up with Peep Toad's bar."

"I'm free. You?"

"Yeah . . . um, Tug? I need to ask you something. This is so awkward but I need a big favor."

"For you? Anything."

"Well, um . . . ."

"C'mon. Out with it."

"Well, with Dana gone, I'm alone. Could I, uh, sort of stay with you for a while? I mean, until we nail the bastard?"

"Of course!"

"I mean, I don't want to intrude. If someone's living with you or something, I'll find someplace else."

He laughed. "You're not intruding. I live by myself."

"This is embarrassing," she said.

"Why? We're friends, aren't we? And it makes sense. If he comes after you, he'll have to deal with me."

"That's what I was thinking, but I didn't want to impose."

"No imposition, okay?"

"Okay."

"All set, then." He looked at his watch. "It's getting kind of late. Let's go to my house and you can get settled in. Where's your stuff?"

"I don't have any. Everything is fire damaged."

"We could go by Wal-Mart," he suggested.

"Or not," she said, making a face.

"Well, pardon me all over the place. The mall? Macy's?"

She laughed. "That's more like it. But I guess Wal-Mart will do for now. All I need is a change of clothes, a toothbrush, and toothpaste."

"Toothpaste I got. We can share."

"We're not sharing your toothbrush, though."

"Perish the thought."

"Okay," she said. "And first thing tomorrow, we interview Junior's mom and the Peep Toad."

"Right."

CHAPTER 44

HESS HAD FOLLOWED, discreetly. He hung back a safe distance back while the Jezebel Whore parked and hurried inside the bar and grill. She stayed in there for well over an hour and he was getting nervous, dying to get back to the farmhouse. But, he was quite used to doing time, thank you very much. Piece of cake, right?

When she eventually came out, she was with some huge guy. Hess racked his brain. He was sure he knew the guy but couldn't quite place him. They went to different vehicles, though. She climbed into her Honda and the guy heaved himself into a Ford pickup. But then the guy drove away and the bitch followed him.

Hess was smoldering at the thought of yet another asshole sniffing around her, another horn dog to contend with. He started his car and followed them at a discreet distance. It looked like they weren't in any hurry, though, so it was simple to stay back. He trailed them up across the west bridge and to the highway. They eventually exited and turned into a Wal-Mart. Once more, he parked, waited, and fidgeted.

After they came out, they headed south and he followed them all the way south to Westerly where they turned off into a residential area and swung into a driveway that led behind an old clapboard Victorian.

Hess slowed, cruised by. The mailbox read: HAYWOOD.

"Now I remember this big-ass mulatto fuck," Hess said to himself. "Asshole was camped right next to the whore at that campground. I saw the turd talking to that dick of a husband of hers."

Smiling a malevolent grin, he drove slowly away, saying, "Later."

BACK AT THE farmhouse cellar, Hess watched Adrienne squirm and strain at her chain tether. He yanked the sleeping bag off her, causing her nubile body to break out instantly in goosebumps.

Behind her black lipgloss, her teeth started to chatter. The tips of her taut little breasts stood out from the cold and that aroused him—again.

K.C. and the Sunshine Band started up in his head: *uh-huh, uh-huh.*

The girl glared at him. "I have to use the bathroom," she said. She sneezed.

"*Gezundheit!,* my yummy little twat," said Hess. "Have we taken a chill? I suppose we'll have to get you some Nyquil, won't we?"

She coughed again. Deeper. "I *said,* I have to pee."

Hess laughed. "Well, dear, what's stopping you? G'head."

She scowled. "What, like, right here? What kind of filthy perv—"

"Now, now," he interrupted. "Sticks and stones, Sweetnips. Sticks and stones."

"Fuck you."

"Oh, all in due time, my tidbit. And if you're a good little girl, I'll introduce you to Mr. Henckels."

She looked wary. "Mr. Henckels?"

"Yes indeedy. Rumor has it, he's an eight-incher. Bet you never had one *that* big, did you? Who knows, maybe I'll even get The Temptations."

"Temptations? That singing group from the oldies station?"

"You stupid cunt, you don't know nothing, get back." Hess tossed the sleeping bag back to her, went back up the stairs and out. But before long, he returned with a pillow and a bottle of Nyquil.

"Can't have you getting pneumonia on me," he said. "Not before my plan jells, anyway."

She pulled the bag up tight around her shivering body, took a deep pull of the medicine, fluffed up the pillow, and lay down with a deep sigh. She coughed again.

Hess went away once more and came back with a bag of leftover McDonald's, which he placed next to her.

"I realize the fries taste like shit when they're cold," he said with a chuckle. "But the Big Mac won't be too bad. Better than nothing, anyway."

She eyeballed him warily, snatched up the food.

"I have to go now," he said, his voice going singsong. "You behave yourself, hear?" He snapped the flashlight off and headed for the stairs.

She sneezed.

On the way out, he hesitated. Before shutting the bulkhead, he listened while Adrienne shed the sleeping bag and crawled to the end of her chain. Once he heard the liquid, splashing sound, he snapped his light back on, shined it directly on her, and started cackling like a schoolboy. "Nice," he said. "Very nice."

"Asshole pervert," she said. She finished up and crawled back to her sleeping bag.

He licked his lips and rubbed himself through his trousers.

What's this? Why, The Temptations are returning.

"Later," he hissed, as he closed the bulkhead, locked it and headed for the motorhome in the barn. Still tumescent, he just *had* to replay his tape of the Jezebel Whore Nikki, the one where she was in the shower.

And succumb to The Temptations.

Sorry, Mother.

CHAPTER 45

AN EARLY NOR'EASTER rattled the windowpanes, but Nikki was cozy in Tugboat's guest bedroom, swaddled in fresh sheets and a toasty down comforter.

Alone.

Like untuned woodwinds, the wind howled through the eaves, an eerie sound. Rain pelted the window.

Tick-tack. Tick-tack.

Outside, a giant Norway Spruce groaned and whistled as it swayed. She was just drifting off when she heard a clunk and muffled crash, coming from downstairs.

Hess! She reached under the pillow for her weapon, eased out of bed. Since she'd forgotten to buy nightclothes at *chez* Wal-Mart, Tug had loaned her one of his size-19 XXL white dress shirts. And a bathrobe the size of Baltimore. After she rolled the sleeves up about eighty-five times, the shirt kind of made a makeshift nightgown but the bathrobe was more like a terrycloth tent. The sleeves hung a foot below her hands and the hem dragged the floor so she tossed it aside.

She had to assume Tug was still asleep in his own bedroom, down the hall. Gripping her 9-mm equalizer in her right hand, she eased the slide back with her left, chambered a round, and flicked off the safety. She eased the door open and checked the hallway.

No one.

Exhaling and blinking to adjust her eyes, she padded barefoot toward the staircase. On the way, she noticed Tug's door was open, so she eased inside, whispering, "*Psst!* Tug? You there?"

No answer.

She went to the staircase and started down and that's when she saw the dark shadow coming up. Tugboat? What if it wasn't? Pressing herself against the wall to make less of a target, she aimed her weapon and steadied it with her left palm. She took a breath, and said, "Stop right there! One more step and I shoot."

"Don't shoot!" cried Tugboat. "It's me."

She exhaled and lowered her gun, saying, "Jesus, Tug. You scared the crap out of me."

"Sorry. I was getting a snack, ran into an end table, knocked over a lamp."

"I thought you marine types were supposed to be stealthy."

"Not getting a snack."

"Anyway, why didn't you put a light on?"

"I did. But I'd turned it off and was coming back."

She frowned. "If this is your best at sneaking around in the dark, then we're in trouble."

He laughed. "You've got a point," he said. "But I wasn't trying to be quiet. It wasn't my best, trust me."

He stepped to the top of the stairs and flipped on the hall light. That's when Nikki noticed he was shirtless, wearing only cotton pajama bottoms around his trim forty-inch waist and well-defined abs.

"Where's your handgun," she said, joking. "Aren't you the one who said, '*always* carry it, even in the bathtub'?"

He reached behind him and pulled a Walter PPK from his waistband, one just like James Bond used in the movies.

"I'm impressed," she said. She noticed him looking down and realized that she'd neglected to fasten the top few buttons of her makeshift nightgown. Not only that, but a lot of thigh was showing through the wide split in the shirttail. She felt a blush seep into her cheeks.

He averted his eyes and cleared his throat. "Well," he said, "It's late. We'd better get to bed."

"Yes."

"I mean . . . well, you know what I mean."

"Our own beds."

"Right. I don't want you to think . . .."

"I know."

As she crawled back in bed and pulled the covers up, she noticed that the wind had died down somewhat but the rain was still pelting the windowpanes. She looked over at the clock on the nightstand. Three o'clock and here she was, still awake, her mind restless.

I need to be held, she thought.

She turned over, squeezed her eyes shut, and cocooned herself in the fresh sheets and toasty down comforter—hoping she'd sleep.

She did not.

AROUND DAWN, sleep finally found Nikki. The next thing she knew, she woke to the sound of a knock at her door.

"Time to get up, sleepyhead," said Tug.

"What time is it?" she asked, sitting up and stretching.

"Close to noon. Can I come in?"

She propped herself up on the pillows and pulled the covers up around her. "Sure."

He opened the door and she saw that he was dressed in Levis and a flannel shirt. "Looks like you're all set to go," she said.

"I thought I'd let you sleep in but if we're going to get anything done, we'd better get hopping. I made you some breakfast. Hungry?"

"Starved. I'll be right down."

He turned to go but before he left, she said, "Tug?"

"Yeah?"

"Um, about last night . . . . "

"Forget it," he said. "I already have."

"Really?"

"Well, no. I'm lying." He went out and pulled the door shut behind him, adding, "Get dressed, let's eat."

She wriggled into her new jeans and pulled on the thick, Boston Red Sox sweatshirt she'd picked out the previous day. After applying minimal makeup, she scrunched her hair into a ponytail and joined Tug at the breakfast nook next to his kitchen. She couldn't say she loved his choice of curtains, but otherwise the nook was well lit and cheery. While they ate eggs and toast, they talked.

"Given any more thought to Hess?" she asked.

A shrug, and a slight smile. "Among other things."

She avoided eye contact. "I'm worried about Adrienne. I shudder to think about what that monster might be doing to her."

"Don't go there," he said. "But I'm pretty sure he won't kill her. She's his Ace in the Hole."

"Being alive with him might just be worse."

Tug forked some egg into his mouth, chewed, and swallowed. He shook his head. "Don't go there, I told you. You'll drive yourself nuts."

"I'm trying not to, believe me."

After polishing off his third egg, he said, "I've been going over that 'meeting' scenario in my mind, and can't see any way we can get him. It's just too risky."

"I agree," she said. "But if he sets it up, I'm going to meet with him. I have to. I'll bring my gun and tell him I'm not going anywhere with him unless I feel absolutely safe."

Tug frowned. "Then what? He can't give you an ironclad guarantee without risking himself, so it'll be a stalemate."

"I suppose you're right. And if he gets frustrated, he might up the ante by torturing Adrienne."

"Well, no matter what, I'm not letting you meet the bastard alone."

She raised her eyebrows. "Letting me?"

"I just meant . . . ."

She reached across the table, took his hand, and looked him straight in the eye. "I know what you meant. Look . . . this is getting us nowhere."

"You're right. But, man, what I wouldn't give to throttle that psycho."

"It'd solve a lot of problems," she admitted, standing up. She threw her purse over her shoulder. "C'mon. Let's go talk to Junior's mom. And then I want to check out that grungy bar."

He stood, polished off his coffee. "Peep Toad's."

"Yeah."

Her CR-V needed servicing, so she decided to drop it off. Tug followed in his truck. On the way, she decided to give Dana a call.

"Hello?"

"Hi. It's me."

"I hope you're calling to tell me they caught Hess," Dana said.

"Sorry. He's still out there." Nikki brought her up to date on all that had happened.

"Oh my God. That poor girl must—"

"We're trying our best to locate her," Nikki said quickly, interrupting.

"Anything else you want to tell me?"

"No, not really."

"Not really? That means you're not telling me everything."

"I've got nothing else to tell," said Nikki. "Honest."

"C'mon, girl. Out with it."

"Um . . . well, it's sort of embarrassing."

"So? Has that ever stopped our sharing before?"

I guess not."

"So?" demanded Dana.

Nikki let out a sigh. "It's Tug. I . . . I think I might be falling for him."

Dana laughed. "Tell me something I don't know."

"Am I that transparent?"

"Duh. So . . . have you slept with him yet?"

"No, but we came close last night."

"You're at his house? Hell, girl. What stopped you?"

"Me. And my guilt. I feel like I'm betraying Steve."

"Get off it. Steve would want you to be happy."

"I don't know—"

"Well, I know," said Dana, interrupting. "Put the shoe on the other foot. If you were gone and it was Steve falling in love, wouldn't you want that for him?"

"Well, yeah. But if it wasn't for me, Steve would still be alive."

"Stop it! If it wasn't for *Hess,* Steve would still be alive. Look. I've heard that broken record too many times now. I can't stop you from your imaginary demons or from beating yourself up but I think you should follow through with Tug. He's a good man. Besides, it's time you got laid."

Nikki had to laugh. "You're so subtle."

"Use protection. That's all I've got to say."

"Hmpf. You *never* say all you've got to say."

"Well, keep me posted. I want all the juicy details."

"Sick," Nikki said.

"You bet. Now, go forth and fornicate, with my blessing."

Nikki laughed. "You're impossible. How're you and David doing?"

"Fabulous, better than ever."

"That's wonderful, so glad to hear it. But listen, I better go."

"Okay. Thanks for calling. You be careful. Stay in touch."

"I will. Bye." Nikki clicked off.

Once she dropped her vehicle off, she jumped into Tug's truck and they took off for Benedict's Landing. He cleared his throat. "You see the newspaper on the kitchen table this morning?"

"I saw it but didn't read it. What section?"

"Front page. That referendum passed, allowing the tribe to build a casino."

"Really," she said. "How do you feel about it?"

He shrugged. "I don't know. Good for us Narragansetts, I guess, but then again there's the moral issue of the destruction gambling can cause to families. And I don't feel any too great about the Las Vegas sleazeballs having their sticky mitts in it."

She nodded. "And I'm sure the Rhode Island politicians are already rubbing their hands together, greedily planning how to skim some of the big bucks that'll come in."

"They claim the funds will go for education."

She snorted. "Yeah, right. And I'm going to be a model in the Victoria's Secret catalog."

Tug grinned. "Now *that's* an intriguing possibility," he said.

By that time, they'd reached Mystic Island and drove directly to Junior's mom's house. They were in luck, she was home. She agreed to talk to them and she was adamant.

"I'm convinced that man caused the ruination of Junior," his mom said. Huge tears welled up in her eyes and spilled down her cheeks.

"And you told this to the police?" Nikki asked.

Junior's mom took out a Kleenex, dabbed at her eyes, and blew her nose. "Yes, for all the good it did. Although they *did* take the tow dolly away, the one that evil man stored here."

"I'm sure they went over it thoroughly and checked out the serial numbers," Nikki said. "But Hess most certainly made sure none of it was traceable or he wouldn't have left it here."

"I feel faint. I need to sit down."

Nikki and Tug helped her to the couch where she lost it and broke down, sobbing and shaking. They sat on either side of her, patting her back and comforting her as best they could. It took several minutes before the distraught woman could regain her composure.

"Like I said, I already told the police all I knew," she said, "but at the time, my mind was a mess. My brain was mushy, like termites had invaded and turned it all to powder. I couldn't concentrate."

"I know what it's like to lose a loved one," Nikki confided.

"You do?" Junior's mom asked.

"Yes. That same guy who was messing with Junior's head murdered a man I loved very much."

The woman's eyes went wide. "Oh my God . . . ."

"It's true," Nikki said.

"Well, the FBI man was mostly interested in Junior's upbringing. I think he thinks I was a bad mother but it's so hard raising a son when there's no man around, you know? I tried to give him everything he wanted. You think I was a bad mother?" She wrung her hands.

"I'm sure you weren't," Nikki assured her. "I knew Junior from the campground and found him to be basically a good kid. And I know his girlfriend; she thought the world of him."

Junior's mother made a weak attempt at a smile. Her bottom lip quivered. "My boy fell prey to drugs. And he drank a lot of beer."

"We know, " said Tug. "Can you tell us anything else, now that you're thinking is clearer?" he prompted. "No matter how trivial it seems?"

She thought about that. "I don't think so. Wait a minute, there was that one time Junior came back from being with that man and mentioned West Arcadia, going out in the 'boonies' he said."

"West Arcadia?"

She nodded, blew her nose for the umpteenth time. "But I don't know just where. Does that help you?"

"It's a start," said Tug, getting to his feet. "Thank you very much, ma'am."

"My," said Junior's mom, a slight smile toying with her thin, quavering lips. "You're a big one, aren't you?"

Nikki leaned in, hugged her and handed her one of her cards, saying, "Feel free to call anytime, anytime you need to talk."

"Or if you think of anything else," added Tug.

Junior's mom sniffled, dabbed Kleenex at her nose. "I hope you get that evil, evil man." She walked them out to Tug's pickup.

Nikki hugged her again, and then Nikki and Tug hopped into Tug's truck.

"Nice lady," he said, as they drove away.

"Very."

"Peep Toad's?"

"Let's do it."

ON THE WAY to Peep Toad's bar, Nikki turned to Tug, saying, "You know, like in Junior's life, there was no male figure in Hess's life, either."

Tug nodded.

"That might make him feel entitled by way of compensation," she added. "Probably got everything he wanted or just took it."

"And?"

She started ticking things off on her fingers. "Okay, Hess had no male influence, and a feeling of entitlement: that's two characteristics. Toss in alcohol and drug abuse, criminal behavior, and abuse at the hands of his own *mother*, no less. Three, four, and five, right? And he sets fires."

Tug nodded. "Right."

"Well that pretty much goes along with the criteria I've heard that makes a sociopath. But why? Is it nature or nurture? Anyway, I've read that most experts agree that the condition is exacerbated by horrid parenting, that's for sure. But some say there's a biological component, traced to the limbic system of the brain, which houses the *amaygdala*, an almond-shaped structure in the front of the temporal lobe. And that leads to antisocial behavior."

"Amy . . . what?"

"Amaygdala," she said, with a smile. "Anyway, that alternate theory suggests the sociopath shapes the parent, not the other way around. But given what I know about Hess's mother? I have to side with the lack of nurture team on this one."

"Whatever," said Tug. "All I know is he's an evil scumbag screwball. That's all I gotta know."

CHAPTER 46

AFTER CAREFULLY re-applying fresh Neosporin and bandaging to his backside, Hess fed his sickly prisoner a bowl of gluey oatmeal. He then locked the cellar bulkhead, jumped into his Taurus and headed back toward Westerly.

And that Jezebel Whore Nikki.

He gripped the wheel so tight, his knuckles turned bone white. His mind seethed with resentment, aimed at the big guy: yet *another* asshole who'd touched her, yet *another* asshole that needed to die! Impatient, he threaded his way between slowpoke motorists, laying on his horn and cursing until he glanced at the speedometer and realized he was blasting along at 85-mph in a 50-mph zone. "Holy shit!" he cried out, thinking if he didn't slow down and happened to get caught in a radar trap, that'd be it.

He checked the rearview mirror, slowed to the speed limit, and diverted this sudden eruption of rage by chewing at a cuticle until he made it bleed. He relished the coppery taste.

Outfuckingstanding!

Finally in Westerly, he drove straight to Haywood's house and parked down the block. He got his lock picks out of the glove box, fit the silencer to his Browning high-powered 9mm, slid it into his waistband, and walked back toward the house. Noticing that both the truck and Navigator were gone, he worried that Nikki might have moved elsewhere but he figured odds were, she'd be back, no doubt thinking the giant mulatto turd could protect her.

Yeah, when pigs fly.

To make sure nobody was home, he rang the bell and then ducked around the corner of the house, behind a huge bush. No answer. Shielded by a tall privet hedge, he stole around back where he found the back door to be a cinch for his picks. Once he slipped inside, he took a deep breath and listened.

The only sound was the ticking of a grandfather clock, coming from the living room.

Outfuckingstanding!

After a quick trip around, Hess selected a bottle of spring water from the fridge, made a sandwich and carefully cleaned up the minor mess. He went into the bathroom, peed, flushed, and prepared a place to hide in a louvered closet—just behind the hall, across from the couch in the living room. The louvers would afford a view of the front door and the closet was large enough for him to squat down.

For now, though, he plopped on the couch and looked out the front window.

He would wait, no matter how long it took.

CHAPTER 47

NIKKI HAD EXPECTED Peep Toad's to be grungy but she had no idea.

"Not exactly what you'd call a happening place," said Tug. On the floor, multi-layered filth coagulated in spilled beer and precipitated nicotine. Ambient cigarette smoke restricted visibility to a few feet.

Squinting, she waved her hand in front of her, saying, "Do they issue foghorns in here?"

He chuckled.

A few scruffy characters at the bar leered at her. They probably hadn't seen a woman in this armpit of an establishment—ever.

"I believe that might just be Peep Toad over there in the corner," said Tug, indicating with a nod of his head. "Either him or Mount Washington."

They approached. Nikki got Peep Toad's attention, asking, "Okay if we sit down?"

"Free country," he said, his voice almost falsetto.

To her, he sounded a little like Mike Tyson or someone she couldn't quite place—someone she'd seen a while back on Turner Classic Movies.

The Toad burped flatulently, asked if they wanted a drink.

"No thanks," she said.

"You cops?"

She shook her head. "No. We're looking for a young man named Junior Ferguson."

"Never heard of him."

"Long, scraggly blond hair. Kind of a good-looking kid in a rock star sort of way," said Tug.

Peep's eyebrows went up. "Might've seen him."

Nikki leaned in closer. "The kid was probably in the company of a guy in his early forties, a guy with a gray ponytail."

"Might've seen that asshole, too."

"Asshole?" asked Tug.

"Oh, excuse me. I meant *phony* asshole. So full a shit his breath smelt like it. One a my bartenders sold him a van."

"Is that bartender here?" Nikki asked, excited.

"Nope."

"Well, is he working today? Tomorrow?"

"Nope and nope."

"When?"

"Never. Not here anyway. I fired his ass. All bartenders steal but this dickhead was unbelievable."

"Do you know where he lives?" she asked.

"Nope."

"Shit," said Tug. "Dead end. Could you at least give us the bartender's name?

"Nope."

"Nope?"

"Nope. Won't need it. What you need is to talk to a man named Ray Nickerson."

"Nickerson."

"Yep. Friend of the ponytailed asshole. I overheard the kid mention it before the asshole could hush him up. Said they'd met this Nickerson guy in the West Arcadia boonies somewhere. Sounded like they were up to no good or sum'pin."

"Holy shit," said Tug. "You hear anything else?"

"Sure. I hear plenny, but nothin' that'll help you any. Anyway, that's all I heard from those two, 'cept for a few Jabba the Hut insults they paid me and like that."

"Hey, wait a minute," Nikki said. "I think I might remember a Ray Nickerson. From high school."

Tug looked hopeful. "Think he's the same one?"

"We'll see," she said. "Let's go find him."

After thanking Peep Toad, they headed for the parking lot.

"What's your verdict?" asked Tug. "The Toad? Male or female?"

"I have to go with male," she said. "Even with that high-pitched voice of his. Sounds like someone I've heard before, someone in the movies but I can't place him."

"I don't know," said Tug, thoughtfully. "I think I detected breasts. Or a couple of lumps that might be, anyway. And The Toad's eyelashes are pretty long. For a guy."

"True."

Tug winced. "Did you check out the cockroach that ran out from one of the creases in Toad's neck?"

"I did," said Nikki. "Gross. And his skin? The consistency of a dumpling."

Their conversation ended when a familiar, rusty pickup pulled in. A troll-like guy whom she recognized right away was driving. "I'll be damned," she said. "Looks like Petey Fottler."

Tug squinted. "From the Seabreeze campground gatehouse? The Elucidator of Fortunese?"

She laughed. "The very one."

Petey popped out of his truck, started schlepping along, spanking the clamshells in the parking lot with his huge Converse All Stars. When he saw Tugboat and Nikki, he broke out in a toothy grin.

"Petey!" Nikki cried. "How's it going?"

His brow knitted. "Architect of one's destiny is one's self," he said.

"I heard *that*," said Tug, laughing.

"Cleverness is serviceable for everything, sufficient for nothing," quipped Petey.

"Uh-huh," Nikki said. "Listen, we're looking for someone. Do you come here often?"

"The only certainty is that nothing is certain."

"Enough," she said. "Cut it out."

"Never does nature say one thing and wisdom—"

Tug interrupted by thrusting his ham-sized hands under Petey's armpits and hoisting the tiny man up to where they were eye to eye. "Didn't she just tell you to cut the Fortunese?" he growled. "We're in kind of a hurry here."

Petey gulped. Tug set him back down.

"Okay, okay," said Petey. "Yeah, I come here once in a while. Jesus."

"You remember Junior Ferguson?" Nikki asked. "Ever see him here?"

Petey looked at Nikki, at Tug, and back at her. "Sometimes even love shows a rerun," he said. Cowering and cringing, he cut his fearful eyes back to Tug.

Tug turned crimson, smoldering. He reached for Petey, saying, "Why, you little—"

Petey scrambled around behind Nikki, saying, "Out of the abundance of the heart, the mouth speaks."

"Can't hide there forever," she said, looking back at him over her shoulder.

Petey peeked out. "Because of your melodic nature, the moon never misses an appointment," he observed.

Tug scowled, brandished his fist.

Petey gulped. "Okay, okay. Sorry," he said. It's just that you two have the *look*. I couldn't resist." He came out from behind Nikki adding, "Don't kill me, okay?"

"Look?" said Tug. "What look?"

"You know," said Petey. "The look of—"

"Answer our question," Nikki said, interrupting. "Did you ever see Junior here?"

"Junior? Naw, never saw him in here."

"How about a guy with a gray ponytail. Ever see him in here?"

Petey shook his head, no.

"You know a guy named Ray Nickerson?"

Another head shake. "Nunh-uh."

"See how easy that was?" she said. "Why didn't you just cooperate in the first place?"

He flashed his toothy grin. "What, and skip all this meaningful dialogue?"

"How about if I do a little 'meaningful dialogue' on your head?" offered Tug.

"Pardon is the choicest flower of victory," quoted Petey. And before Tug could grab him, he bolted—fairly flying into Peep Toad's Lounge.

"Well, that was fruitful," said Nikki, as they headed for Tug's truck.

"What the hell was that 'look' he was talking about?"

"I, um . . . I was hoping it didn't show."

"Huh?"

"Never mind," she said.

Once they were back on the road, she got on her cell and called information. They were in luck. Ray Nickerson's had a listed phone. She called the number but got the answering machine:

" . . . This is Ray. I can't come to the phone right now because I'm in Maine, whupping up on some Moose ass. Leave a message."

"This is Nikki O'Connor," she told the machine. "I don't know if you remember me but I'm an old classmate of yours from Franklin High. It's urgent that I talk to you so call me when—"

She was interrupted by a female voice cutting in, overriding the machine:

"Ray's not here," the unfriendly voice said. "He's in Maine."

"So I heard. Whom am I speaking to, please?"

"Whom? Ray's wife, that's *whom.*"

"Hi, I'm Nikki—"

"I know who you are: that pretty cheerleader and homecoming queenie. I went to Franklin, too, only I wasn't 'zackly no cheerleader. Or goddam queen."

"What's your name?"

"Used to be Rachel Pepoon." A pause, then: "What you want with Ray?"

"I remember you, Rachel. Listen, I'm a cop now. I think Ray met a very dangerous man out in the West Arcadia woods somewhere. You remember Marion Hess from high school?"

"Yeah, sure. His mug's been in all the papers and on the news. In school, he was that real good lookin' kid what kept to hisself an' ate his boogers. We used to call him 'Booger King: Have it Your Way'."

"That's him," Nikki said. "He's holding a friend of mine hostage, maybe out there in West Arcadia. It's a matter of life and death."

"If it concerns Ray, it'd be at the old farmhouse. Be my guess."

"Farmhouse?"

"What, you cheerleader types all end up *hearing impaired* from all the crowd noise?"

Nikki gritted her teeth. "Where's this farmhouse?"

"It belonged to Ray's parents. I ain't never been there, Sweetie."

Nikki lost it. "Look Rachel, I'm sorry for any imagined threat you think I am to you but I don't have time for your shitty attitude, you understand me? If you don't want to cooperate, we can call the local police. They might just haul you in for obstruction."

A long pause, then: "I got no idea where that old place is, okay? Like I said, I ain't never been there. You'll have to ask Ray."

"Can I get in touch with him in Maine? Does he have a cell phone?"

Rachel snorted. "Yeah, like a cell phone's gonna work way out there."

"When will he be back?"

"Tomorrow. In the afternoon."

After giving Rachel her number and pleading with her to have Ray call as soon as he got back, Nikki hung up.

"Yet another fruitful conversation?" asked Tug.

"This time it actually was. Sort of. She—" Nikki snapped her fingers.

"What," said Tug.

"I just remembered who Peep Toad sounds like!"

Tug looked over at her. "Yeah? Who?"

"Aldo Ray," she said. "An old character actor. Never mind that, though. Nickerson's wife told me about an old farmhouse his parents own in West Arcadia but she doesn't know exactly where it is."

"West Arcadia. Junior's mom mentioned something about West Arcadia, didn't she? How can we find out where the farmhouse is?"

"Public records, maybe." Nikki looked at her watch. "But it's too late now. We can look into it tomorrow but we definitely need to show up over at Ray's house in the afternoon."

"Sounds like a plan. I'm hungry, wanna eat?"

She laughed. "You're *always* hungry."

"Name a place."

She thought about that. "How about if we just go to the grocery store, pick up a couple of T-bone steaks and go back to your place?"

"I can do steak."

"And I'll toss a salad."

"Big salad?"

"Enormous."

THE SUN CUT a much lower arc on the horizon that time of the year and set much earlier. By the time they'd finished at the store, it was dark. Tug flipped on the headlights and they headed toward his house.

"You remember telling me the legend of the purple pearl?" she asked.

"Sure."

"Well, after that, I got on the Internet and did a little research. Me being twelve and a half percent Narragansett and all."

"Research, huh," he said. "You've been studying your ass off lately."

"Really," she said. "Anyway, I found out 'Narragansett' is an English corruption of the word *Nanhigeanuck*. Did I say it right?"

He chuckled. "No, but close enough. What else did you find?"

"Well, you probably know all this but in 1621, Massasoit, the leader of the Wampanoags, willingly entered into a peace treaty with the Pilgrims. He believed that King James wanted their friendship and alliance. They co-existed during the early period.

Massasoit's son, Metacom, was even given the nickname of King Philip by the English colonists."

"I knew the general story, not the actual date. But tell me more, O Fountain of Native American History."

She stuck her tongue out at him. "What's your tribal name? 'Smarts Off A Lot'?"

"Actually, it's Grey Shoes. But go on."

"Well, by 1675, relations between the Wampanoag Indian Federation and the colonists were stressed to the breaking point and Metacom warned the whites that he was determined 'not to live until he had no country'."

"And?"

"And that was to become a prophetic pronouncement which ultimately drew the neutral Narragansett tribe into a bloody conflict that would change the landscape forever."

"Now who's 'Smarts Off A Lot'?"

She grinned. "Guilty. Anyway, not too much more, I promise. By early December of 1675, a dusting of snow covered the ground, north winds brought more than an occasional chill to the air, and King Phillip's War was raging between the Wampanoag allied force and the English. Our people, the uh, *Nanhigeanuck*, retreated to their fortified winter village in a swamp on the mainland."

"The Great Swamp."

"Yes, but they weren't safe. Fearing the powerful Narragansetts would soon enter the war, the English made a pre-emptive strike on the village. With overwhelming numbers and firepower, they slaughtered the Native Americans indiscriminately. And you know the rest."

"Only too well."

By that time, they'd reached Tug's house. They parked in the drive and headed for the front door. Brittle leaves crunched underfoot and Nikki could smell the fall decomposition as they strolled up the walkway. The air felt crisp, with a slight bite to it.

She took the bag of groceries from Tug as he keyed the lock and let them into the darkened interior.

CHAPTER 48

HESS HEARD A truck pull into the driveway and looked out to see the Jezebel Whore and her ginormous escort coming up the walkway. He leaped up, smoothed the couch, and looked around to make sure he wasn't leaving signs of his presence. Ducking into his place in the closet, he eased the door almost shut, barely cracked. By moving his head up and down and peering out the louvers, he could see pretty good—good enough, anyway. He reached behind him, into the back of his belt, and pulled out his high-powered, silenced Beretta.

He chambered a round: *snick-snack!* Once he'd flicked off the safety, he fingered the trigger for reassurance. Not that he needed any.

Hess heard the key in the lock and the front door swung open. The big guy came in first, brandishing a gun that looked to Hess like a peashooter. Hess gave serious thought to doing the asshole right now but then Nikki might escape. *Better to wait.*

"Stay here while I look around," the big guy told her.

How gallant, thought Hess. He smirked. *Think you can protect her, you fuck?*

When pigs fly.

The big guy checked all the rooms downstairs, then clomped upstairs and it sounded to Hess like a goddam rhinoceros was walking around up there. Moments later, the man thumped downstairs again. Hess figured this shitbird weighed a ton if he weighed a pound.

Jesus H. Christ.

The man checked the hall bathroom before going into the kitchen. Hess steeled himself, thinking: if this asshole decides to look in this particular closet, it'll have to be his dirt-nap time.

Across the room, the Jezebel Whore, still holding the bag of groceries, had a strange look on her face and Hess wondered if she heard something. Had he made any noise? He didn't think so.

She followed the big guy into the kitchen.

Hess heard murmuring and the sound of groceries hitting the floor: a muffled splut of broken glass, canned goods, and soft foods.
What the hell?

CHAPTER 49

WHILE TUG SEARCHED the house, Nikki thought about the previous night, how much trouble she'd had getting to sleep, and how her body had responded to his physical attraction. But even as her knees started weakening again and the delicious warmth started spreading, guilt jabbed at her because her mind just wouldn't let go. She was still in mourning for Steve, despite her body—which seemed to have a mind of its own. She was emotionally confused and scared shitless. What a combination. She craved a comforting touch and definitely needed to feel protected.

Tug came back downstairs. As she watched him, moving about like a wary animal, she couldn't help but cave in to her fantasies. Deciding that she couldn't concentrate on anything else until she pursued this, she followed him into the kitchen, saying, "All clear?"

"Yeah." He stowed the Walther PPK into the back of his belt, stared at her. "Are you okay?"

"Me? Sure. Why?"

He came up close, put a hand on her cheek. "Your face."

"What about it?"

"It looks kind of, I don't know . . . flushed."

"I . . . I'm . . .," she stammered. Unable to form a sentence, she turned away, moved over by the sink, intent on setting the groceries on the countertop.

Tug came up behind her. He put his hands on her shoulders and she could feel his breath, warm on the backside of her ear. She wasn't sure if her legs would support her much longer.

Moaning, she turned to him, and when she did the groceries fell to the floor with a muffled crash. They kissed as if possessed, their hunger evident. On tiptoes, she pressed her body tight against him and felt his instantaneous response.

He grabbed her hand, led her into the living room, over by the couch. Leaning down, he held his enormous hands on either side of her face and kissed her; kisses that were soft, tender at first, but soon turned urgent.

A sudden invasion of guilt—always lurking just below the surface of her consciousness—wormed its way into her head, interfering with the passion and giving her second thoughts, even though her body was on fire. And if Tug had fumbled for a breast, she might've had the will to stop him. Instead, in one smooth motion, his deft fingers unbuttoned her jeans, worked their insistent way into her panties, and she knew stopping was no longer an option.

Experienced fingers busied themselves while his other hand stripped her jeans and panties down, and off. She stepped out of them.

"Won't need this," he said, as he set her gun on the coffee table. He hoisted her up, lifting her high, just like he'd lifted Petey at Peep Toad's bar. Somehow, he'd managed to unbuckle his belt and his trousers had dropped. He lowered her, easing her down onto him.

She worried for an instant about his size but needn't have; she was already sodden, more than ready. She wrapped her legs around his torso, her arms around his shoulders, and buried her face in his neck. Involuntary sounds of pleasure erupted from deep in her throat.

They'd just begun to move against each other when she gasped, feeling the waves of pleasure, on the verge of orgasm. But instead of picking up the tempo, Tug stopped and stutter-stepped them to the couch where he lowered her down and off him.

"Hurry," she said, feeling the incredible void. "I'm—"

"Not yet," he said, lifting her sweatshirt. He reached behind her, unfastened her bra and freed her breasts, lavished them with kisses.

She squirmed, consumed by unfulfilled desire.

He moved lower, lower, and she felt his tongue, his lips at her core and her orgasm arrived with a vengeance—the crush rocketing through her like a runaway freight train.

Just as she was feeling the last pulses of pleasure and her senses had started to return, she heard an odd, nasty sound, right next to her ear.

Smock! Thud!

CHAPTER 50

MOMENTS AFTER HEARING the crash in the kitchen, Hess had watched while The Jezebel Whore and Haywood waltzed into the living room. He'd watched with rage and disgust while they embraced and kissed, thinking: *doesn't she realize she's sucking face with a goddam nigger?*

Straining to see better, he'd bobbed his head up and down behind the louvers. The next thing he knew, the big guy had Nikki's pants down. *Filthy bastard!* Hess had been dying to burst out of the closet and start blasting, wanting desperately to ventilate Haywood and turn him into a bloody mass of 9-mm holes. But before Hess had been able to move, Haywood had pulled her jeans all the way off and set her gun on the coffee table, well within reach. *Fuck!*

Hess'd been mesmerized. As much as he'd hated to, he'd decided to wait—wait until they were totally distracted by their obscene carnality. *Their Temptations.*

He'd continued to watch, mesmerized. And, despite his rage and disgust, he'd found himself painfully aroused with his own case of The Temptations, pulsing sorely from too much self abuse. And when Haywood lifted Nikki up, Hess had gotten an unobstructed view of her naked, magnificent backside.

He closed his eyes. *Don't get distracted here. Keep your mind on your goddam mission.*

Unbelievably, Haywood had been able to hold Nikki up with one hand while he dropped his jeans with the other. Hess had felt a throbbing pressure in his temples; he'd bitten down hard on his lower lip and had tasted blood. And that's when he'd heard a solid thump.

So engrossed with his passion, Haywood had forgotten about his own gun and had let it fall onto the floor, into the pool of his Levis. Hess had assumed the big man was going to do the whore standing up but to his relief, they had moved to the couch. Haywood had lowered her off him, laid her down.

Now's my chance!

With great care, Hess had eased the closet door open. Crouching like a feral cat, he'd crept toward the lovers. He'd steadied his Beretta in a shooter's stance, aiming on the passionate couple. He hadn't wanted to shoot Haywood just then, but he would have, if necessary.

Oh, shit! He'd thought. Haywood was going down on her. *Mother-FUCK!*

Nikki's thigh had blocked Haywood's view and that had allowed Hess to move right up. Her eyes had been closed and it had looked like she was in the throes of orgasm.

Hess had pointed his Beretta just above her head.

He'd fired a silenced round into the couch: *Smock! Thud!*

CHAPTER 51

THE NASTY SOUND Nikki had heard next to her ear was the spit of a silencer, followed by a bullet slamming into the couch, scant inches from her head.

Her eyes flew open. *Hess!* "What—"

Tug jerked, raised his head.

Hess pointed his weapon at her head but his eyes were on Tug. "Don't even think about it, motherfucker." He booted Tug's gun out of reach, picked hers up off the coffee table, and flung it against the far wall.

Tug shook his head. His shoulders slumped.

"Sorry about the *cunnilingus interruptus*," said Hess. He glanced at Tug's deflating erection, adding, "Still aroused? Let's see if I can take your mind off that." He quickly swung his pistol over and down and fired a round into one of Tug's kneecaps: *Smock!*

Tug cried out, doubled over in pain.

Nikki screamed.

Hess smirked. "That should take your mind off your dick for a while," he told Tug.

Tug winced. He grunted something and held his knee.

"Nice guy that I am, I'm going to do the humane thing," said Hess. "I'm going to put you out of your misery by slamming a round into your big nigger head."

"Please," Nikki pleaded. "Please . . ."

"But, not just yet," continued Hess. "Not before you suffer bigtime for violating the temple of She Who is Becoming."

Nikki screamed again; this time, much louder—a scream created of anger and frustration rather than fear. That distraction provided just enough of an opportunity for Tug to straighten up, swing one of his massive arms and slap the gun out of the monster's hand. It spun across the floor, thumping against the far baseboard. Springing from his good leg, Tug tackled Hess and brought him down.

She heard Hess's head hit the floor with a satisfying thump and watched Tug apply a death grip to the bastard's throat. Hess's eyes bulged, a strangled gurgle escaped his lips, and his heels pummeled the hardwood, beating out a terrifying tattoo.

Just as she was scrambling for one of the guns on the floor, the roar of a shot froze her. She turned and brought her hands to her face in horror as she saw Tug, lying on his side, hands on his own neck where a massive amount of blood spurted out, pulsing from his carotid artery.

On his knees, Hess leveled a gun at her. "Stay where you are," he croaked, his larynx obviously damaged. He glanced at Tug, who had rolled over and now lay motionless. Tug appeared to be dying; his hand still clutched his neck where the geyser of blood had slowed, but not stopped.

She cried out, fell to her knees. Expecting the worst, she felt her senses go numb.

"Lucky for me," Hess rasped, "I just happened to have your little friend's Beretta in my jacket pocket."

Nikki slumped.

Hess got to his feet and staggered over. "Get up," he ordered.

She rose, tugging at the bottom of her oversized sweatshirt, stretching it to mid-thigh.

Hess scooped up her jeans and tossed them to her. "Hurry up and get dressed," he said, still hoarse but getting better. "We need to get the hell out of here." He hawked up a glob of blood and spit it on the floor, saying, "Mmm . . . tasty."

In a daze, she reached for her panties.

"Un-uh," he said, snatching them up and pocketing them. "You won't be needing those. I'll just add them to my collection."

Under his lecherous eyes, she reached behind and refastened her bra. As she stepped into her jeans, she thought about making a run for it once they were outside. Maybe she could zigzag out of his line of fire.

As if reading her mind, he said, "Forget about it. No way you'd make it."

And then there was the problem of Adrienne. If Nikki willingly went with this bastard, at least she might get a chance to save the poor girl. As for herself? All this loss was too, too much. She didn't really give a shit whether she lived or died. And maybe, just maybe, she might find a way to kill the evil scumbag.

He secured her hands behind her back with a thick nylon zip tie before picking his ugly, silenced handgun off the floor. After he dropped Adrienne's .32 back into his jacket pocket, he looked around. "Let's go," he rasped, pushing Nikki ahead and ushering her out the front door. He pulled it shut behind them, looked both ways.

A light, cold drizzle had begun to fall and no one was in sight. Only a few porch lights shown and the dim streetlights, a joke. It didn't matter, though; if anyone showed the least bit of interest in them, she had no doubt Hess would kill the person on the spot.

They headed up the block, Hess slightly behind and to the side of her, hand clamped to her upper arm. Denuded tree limbs swayed in the cold wind and chilled rain spattered in her face. "You can ease off the grip," she said. "I'm not going anywhere."

"Bet your whoring ass you're not going anywhere," he hissed, and tightened his hold, making her wince. At his car, he shuffled her into the passenger side, hustled around, and got behind the wheel. He jammed the barrel of the Browning into her ear.

She cried out.

"Don't make me use this," he said, laying the pistol in his lap.

Her ear was throbbing and ringing at the same time but she still heard the thump as he auto-locked the doors. He started the car, put it in gear, and eased away from the curb. He flipped on the wipers and they sluiced away the mist. As they drove, the wipers lulled and almost hypnotized her.

Thump-thump. Thump-thump.

They drove for about twenty minutes and once they were off the main highway, she leaned forward and squinted through the windshield at a caution sign:

DETOUR – YOUR RIDOT HIGHWAY DOLLARS AT WORK

Orange barrels with their flickering caution lights did little to affect the black hole darkness. Rows of red and white striped sawhorses funneled them along until they veered off onto a two-lane blacktop.

Hess looked over, ran a lizard tongue over his lips, saying, "You are *so* beautiful. You look just like Mother."

Nikki closed her eyes, didn't respond.

"You ignoring me? Didn't you hear me tell you that you're beautiful?"

Her eyes flew open and she looked down at gnarled, ugly fingers moving in slow motion, fondling the inside of her thigh. Filthy nails, bitten to the quick, tipped his fingers. His hand felt like a diseased vermin paw, even through her jeans. Recoiling, she closed her eyes again.

He put his hand back on the wheel and pulled off the blacktop, onto the shoulder. He left the ignition on. The wipers continued: *Thump-thump.*

She opened her eyes, expected the worst but Hess sat in silence, looking at her for a few moments before putting the car back in gear.

He drove back onto the highway, saying, "Later."

"Where are we going?"

"I'll give you a clue," he said, his voice still like sandpaper. "'Eee-I, Eee-I, Oh'."

"Old McDonald's Farm?"

He laughed. "Brilliant deduction."

"Or maybe it's Ray Nickerson's Farm," she said, forcing a smirk. She thought she saw a shadow of worry flit across his face.

His eyes narrowed to slits. "How'd you find out?"

She forced a laugh. "Easy," she said. Then she remembered how misogynistic Hess was and decided to rattle his cage by adding, "Especially for a *woman*."

He slammed a palm against the steering wheel, glared at her. His eyes went back to the road and he sped up. His hand, shaking, went to the Beretta.

Uh-oh! "I didn't—"

"Shut the fuck up!" he cried, and pistol-whipped the side of her head.

Her lights went out.

SOME TIME LATER, she regained consciousness and heard branches and bushes clawing at the side of Hess's weaving car. They were bumping along a rutted dirt road, presumably in the forested area of West Arcadia. She could feel a trickle of blood spilling down the side of her face. A dull throb pounded at her temple and her ear was still ringing. Keeping her eyes slitted, she pretended she was still out.

Hess looked over. "You shouldn't make me do things like that," he said, his voice a gravelly whisper. "I love you. You are Becoming."

That 'becoming' bullshit again, she thought. *You love me? Some way of showing it.*

At the end of the road, they lurched into a clearing and the headlights illuminated a large, dilapidated barn. Hess was mumbling something to himself and rubbing a bulging penis through his trousers. *Disgusting!* He hit the brakes and a cloud of dust swirled in the beam of the headlights. He flicked them off, twisted the key. Darkness and silence flooded in, except for the ticking of the cooling engine.

"I know you're awake," he said, his voice almost a whisper. "Who else knows? Who'd you tell?"

"Knows what? Tell what?" she asked.

He raised the gun, waved it around. "Don't play that shit with me. Want another love tap?"

"No, please, please. You talking about the farm? I haven't told anybody, I wasn't sure."

He sneered. "Like you'd tell me the truth anyway." He got out, went around the car, and opened her door. He yanked her out, saying, "Lose the jeans."

"No."

"No?" He raised the pistol and tapped her on the nose with the silencer. "Need an incentive?"

The drizzle had stopped and the sky was clearing but it was colder—much colder. She felt her shoulders slump.

"Do it now," he ordered. "That way, you won't be so apt to run. Besides, I like watching your sweet ass."

She wriggled out of the jeans, left them in a pool at her feet and stepped away. She tugged her sweatshirt down, but not before he'd gotten an eyeful.

He leered. "Nice beaver," he said. "It'll be the jewel of my collection, never mind that goddam million dollar pearl."

"The brooch?" she cried. "You've got the purple pearl? . . . I *knew* it."

"Actually, no," he said. "I didn't get it because I had to get out of your motorhome before I could find it. But I have to say that I truly enjoyed snuffing your fucking husband's lights out. Yessireebob."

She glared at him. "I will kill you for that."

He snorted. "Sure you will. When pigs fly."

She didn't reply.

"What, no smartass comment on that?" Then, inexplicably, he clamped his palms over his ears, screaming, "Shut up! Shut the fuck up!"

"What," she said. "I didn't say anything."

"Not you. It's that fucking K.C. and The Sunshine Fucking Band."

"Huh?"

"In my head," he explained. " 'That's the way, uh-huh, uh-huh, I liiiike it!' . . . Over and fucking over!" Placing a hand behind her back he shoved her ahead, adding, "Never mind, let's go."

At the barn, he unlocked the padlock to a pair of massive doors, swung them open. A big Winnebago motorhome loomed in the darkness and he shoved her toward it.

She stumbled, and slammed up against the door. He unlocked it. She started to step in but he grabbed her elbow, stopping her.

"We're not going inside, not just yet," he said. Reaching inside, he snatched a camping flashlight, and shut the door.

Turning her around, he marched her back outside, away from the barn. He shined the light on the remains of the decaying farmhouse, saying, "Over there."

The woods were silent, except for the wind. The sky had cleared and she could see their breath in the dim moonlight. In the distance, a screech owl cried out.

"Supposed to be a hard freeze tonight," Hess said. "Are your tootsies cold?"

She didn't answer.

"Nipples stiff?"

She narrowed her eyes, glared at him.

He laughed. "We'll see." After directing her around back, he stopped at a cellar bulkhead, took out a set of keys, and unlocked a padlock. With a flair, he flung open the doors. "Ta-da! Wake up, my tasty tidbit!" he shouted into the dark cellar. "Good news! You've got company." He shoved Nikki down the steps where she lost her footing, collapsed on the earthen floor, and cried out.

Hess followed Nikki into the cellar. He played his flashlight all around and ended up resting it on Adrienne. She was sitting up, the sleeping bag wrapped tightly around her. Cringing and looking as vulnerable as a cornered rabbit, she blinked against the harsh light. Her breath plumed out in rapid puffs.

"Glad to see me?" Hess asked.

Adrienne glared at him. "I'd sooner see the devil, you fucking rat bastard asshole pervert!"

He cackled. "Nice mouth, you little slut. How about if we get a little more light on the subject?"

After setting down his flashlight, he picked up a Coleman lantern. He pumped the plunger a few times, removed the glass, and lit the mantles with his Bic. The lantern hissed into life, bathing the cellar in a harsh glare. Next, he fired up a heater and a pungent odor of kerosene filled the air.

"Much better," he said, holding the lantern over his head.

By this time, Nikki had gotten to her feet. "Try not to worry," she told Adrienne.

Hess laughed. "Oh, by all means, don't worry. We're gonna have a little party here, that's all."

"Where's your so-called *accomplice*?" Nikki asked him.

His brow furrowed. "Accomplice? Huh? What accomplice? Oh . . . you mean . . . uh, yeah, well, I guess I lied. Sorry. "

He set down his lantern, and picked up a length of chain. Grabbing her roughly by the arm, he forced her over by the opposite wall, where he padlocked her ankle to a separate tether, set in concrete. Her wrists were still secured with the nylon zip tie.

Now, she and Adrienne were out of reach of each other yet at the monster's disposal. Digging into his pocket, he whipped out another nylon zip tie for Adrienne. As he approached the poor, trembling girl, she shrank back, cowered, and whimpered.

"Leave her alone," Nikki said. "You've got me, let her go."

"When pigs fly," he said, with a chuckle. He snatched the sleeping bag off Adrienne, flung it aside, and groaned with lust. "Get up," he growled.

She slowly got up, looking at him timidly. Her legs were squeezed together and her arms were crossed, hands in tiny fists, protecting her breasts. Hess reached for an arm, but she twisted away, flicked her wrist.

Hess cried out in pain.

It all happened so fast. Nikki heard Hess howl and grab at his face and Adrienne twisted away. Somehow free of her shackle, the girl dropped to all fours.

Hess screamed, whipped out his gun and fired a blind shot: *smock!*

Powerless to help, Nikki watched Adrienne snatch up the Coleman lantern, swing it in a great arc, and slam it into the side of the bastard's face. The sound of shattering glass against his cheek sounded promising and Nikki thought she heard a sizzle just before the cellar went dark.

"Fucking *bitch!*" Hess yelled.

Nikki saw muted muzzle flashes as he fired more blind shots: *smock, smock-smock!* She dropped onto her stomach on the floor and hugged the damp earth. She could hear him scrabbling around and moments later, the beam of his flashlight cut the darkness as he searched the cellar corners.

Adrienne had disappeared.

"Fuck!" he screamed. "You fucking little *cunt!* . . . I'm going to cut your heart out!"

Nikki wondered how the girl had slipped her shackles.

Hess trained his flashlight on the open bulkhead. "Fucking bitch won't get far," he said. "No clothes, and we're miles from anyone. She'll probably freeze to death, right?"

Nikki didn't answer.

He shined the light on her, moved over and kicked her in the side. "I asked you a question!"

She cried out, jackknifed, and gasped for air. It felt like he broke a damn rib.

"The little cunt put out my fucking *eye!*" he cried. "Just look at my fucking face!"

Like a kid at Halloween, he shined the light under his chin, exposing the carnage where a thick rivulet of blood mixed with vitreous fluid. The gore glistened on his cheek and oozed from the darkened socket of his pierced eye. A mass of small, bleeding cuts and charred skin from the lantern covered the other side of his face. A pungent odor of white gas and kerosene mingled with the mildewy stink of the cellar. Underneath all that, Hess's body odor reeked—the kind of stench that's born from nerves and stress.

"Get up," he ordered.

She rose on wobbly legs, tucked an elbow close to her side, and took a few shallow breaths. But now, anger was starting to override the pain and fear. She knew she had to find a way out of this, but how?

He gestured toward the bulkhead with his light, saying, "Go."

"Where to?"

"Out. To the Winnebago," he said, his voice keening. A crazed laugh and, "I think you'll like my tribute to you."

"Tribute?"

"Shrine, actually. You know, I've waited for this moment for so long. Now you will Become."

Mystic Fear

Outside—in the woods and away from town lights—the stars shone as if God had turned up the wattage tenfold and she wished she were in a position to appreciate it. She decided to play up to the monster, see what she could stir up.

"You know," she said, "All you had to do was say something back when we were in high school. We could've skipped all this."

A sneer accented his ruined face. "Yeah, sure. You blew me off and went out with some jock asshole, got pregnant, and got your whoring ass married."

"But you were gone. They took you to a . . . hospital."

He stopped, turned to her, looking like something out of a Stephen King novel. "Don't mention that place, ever again, you Whore Jezebel!" He slapped her on her injured ear. It started ringing again.

Tears filled her eyes. She clenched her teeth.

"You think you're gonna play games with me?" he cried. "I don't *think* so."

She twisted away. "No games," she said.

"Why do you keep making me hit you? I told you . . . I love you."

"I believe you," she said, trying her damnest to sound sincere. "Anyway, about that shrine, what—"

"It's my primary mission to make sure you Become. For Mother. For me," he said, interrupting. He halted, shined his light around. "And then I'm gonna find that little goth freak and carve her up."

In the short time it took to reach the barn and the motorhome, the nude lower half of Nikki's body had become numb and she shivered uncontrollably. Hess opened the door of the coach and shoved her up the three steps.

She realized that—instead of descending into hell—she was climbing into it. The actual culmination of their little 'Marion Hess Fact-finding Commission" from a long, long time ago.

CHAPTER 52

THE MOTORHOME REEKED of sickly-sweet, rose-scented candles infused with the faint stench of body odor, stale semen, and something rotten—maybe dead. Nikki half-turned and watched Hess press the heel of a hand to his damaged eye socket, obviously trying to stop the pain. When he removed his hand, she could see a caked mass of gore but the bleeding had stopped. He scrunched his bad eye shut and glared with the good one. With a snarl, he turned her forward again, hooked a foot in front of her shin, and shoved her—sending her sprawling to the floor.

With her hands bound behind her back, she couldn't break her fall and landed directly on her face. Leveraging with her chin against the floor, she got to her knees. She felt blood running over her upper lip and tongued it. It tasted like bitter pennies. She clenched her eyes, grit her teeth, and took shallower breaths.

Hess looked grotesquely orgasmic. Pink fluid still oozed from his ruined eye, but he seemed to be ignoring it. He whipped out his Bic, and went around lighting what looked to be a couple dozen candles. In the eerie, flickering candlelight, Nikki could see all the taped up clippings and pictures of her and felt the hair on the back of her neck prickle. Her eyes came to rest on the centerpiece on the coffee table.

"Like that?" he asked, with a wide grin. "It's a pair of your sexiest panties and a lock of your gorgeous hair."

She thought about calling him the sick, perverted bastard he was when a movement from the shadows in the hallway caught her eye—movement, and a glimpse of spiky hair.

Adrienne!

"You look like you're in a lot of pain," Nikki told Hess, stalling.

"No shit," he said.

"Why don't you let me tend to your face?"

He snorted.

Adrienne had moved out a little further in the hallway and Nikki could see the girl was wearing an oversized flannel shirt,

Mystic Fear

obviously one of Hess's. She gripped something in her right hand, but Nikki couldn't tell what it was.

Hess turned. He headed toward the back of the motorhome. *No!*

Adrienne vanished, back into the shadows and maybe into the bedroom.

"Don't go," Nikki pleaded with Hess. "Oh, please don't go."

He looked over his shoulder at her and sneered. "Like you care. Don't make me laugh."

"I thought you loved me."

"Not yet, but I will. Once you Become," he hissed. He moved a step closer to the back.

"Where are you going?" she asked.

He chuckled, his voice still harsh and raspy from the choking Tug had given him. "I'm gonna get a couple of Percocets, is all. I'll be right back." He slipped into the tiny bathroom on the side of the hallway, leaving the door open.

As she got to her feet, Nikki could hear a cabinet snap open and water running. Suddenly it came to her: in the evil bastard's sick mind—by sacrificing her—she'd *become,* and his dead mother would return to him.

She was searching frantically for a way to create a diversion when she heard him scream out, an agonized cry from the depths of Hell. Moments later, he appeared in the bathroom doorway, stark naked—a glass of water in hand.

And a raging erection.

"Now look what you've done," he said, snarling. "You've given me The Temptations. Again."

Nikki dashed around, blowing out candles. She hipped a lamp and sent it crashing to the floor. Things turned semi-dark.

"What the *fuck* are you doing*?"* cried Hess. He rushed forward and hurled his water glass at her. It whizzed by her ear and shattered against the wall.

He screamed in frustration, leaped and began scuttling on all fours toward her.

She tried kicking him but he was too fast and grabbed her foot. Holding her leg high, he twisted her ankle. She heard something pop, felt white-hot pain, and went down hard. Her head bounced off the floor, the wind whooshed out of her, and another sharp pain shot from her tailbone to the base of her neck. She saw stars and all but blacked out.

He straddled her, started moaning and slobbering and blubbering and choking her, crying, "Become! Become!"

She felt his urgency pulsing against her thigh. His fetid breath caused the bile to rise into her throat. She tried to knee him in the crotch, but he moved to the side and punched her with a closed fist, just below her left eye. She saw stars again. She continued to struggle but she was spent, used up.

Then, like an ivory-faced apparition, Adrienne appeared, over the bastard's shoulder. The fury in the girl's eyes equaled that in his one good eye. Adrienne raised her arms, both tiny fists around the handle of an enormous knife.

And plunged it down, deep into the monster's back, screaming, "SAY HELLO TO MR. HENCKELS YOU ASSHOLE BASTARD!"

His good eye owlish with surprise, Hess stood straight up, yelping in outrage and pain. With a backhand, he slapped Adrienne aside.

She flew against the wall and slid down it, crying out.

Hess fell forward beside Nikki, prostrate on his belly. His body shuddered, and then lay still.

Good, she thought, eyeing the knife protruding from his back. *The bastard's dead.*

She crawled over to Adrienne. The poor girl sat up and Nikki put an arm around her. Adrienne's eyes widened in horror and Nikki heard a gurgling sound coming from behind them.

Hess was getting to his knees. Incredible! The bastard was still alive! Without thinking, Nikki spun around, screamed, sidestepped him and leaped on his back. With both hands, she tugged on the handle of the knife.

It let go with a sucking sound not unlike a boot coming out of mud.

Hess flailed, trying to throw her off, but she threw an arm around his forehead and jammed a thumb in his good eye. She pushed hard and was rewarded by the satisfying sound of his eyeball popping like a squished grape. With the knife in her other hand, she reached around and drew the razor sharp blade across his throat.

Blood pulsed out in great spurts. He gurgled and collapsed under her. This time, he was in the certain throes of death.

"Mother," he whispered. "Was I bad?" His eyes glazed over, fixated, while he expunged the last fetid breath he would ever exhale.

Adrienne was screaming. Wailing like some lost animal, she scuttled to a far corner of the motorhome, slumped to the floor, and started sobbing.

. As Nikki backed away from Hess, she noticed the flow of blood was a trickle now and she thought grimly that this was just desserts—exactly as he had killed Tugboat. Just to be sure, she checked for a pulse and found none. She managed to stand but her ankle wouldn't support her so she held on to the wall and hobbled over to Adrienne. Kneeling down, she rubbed the trembling girl's back.

"Hey, you saved our lives, you know," said Nikki, soothingly.

Adrienne started to say something but a sound in the distance caught Nikki's attention. She put a finger to her lips, saying, "Shh! . . . Listen."

Sirens.

Help on the way.

EVERYTHING FUZZED OUT after that, but Nikki remembered an EMT checking her vital signs and asking her about her injuries, whether she was allergic to anything. She remembered him shining a small flashlight in her eyes, checking for a concussion. She recalled being wrapped in a scratchy, but wonderfully toasty wool blanket and carried on a wheeled stretcher outside the barn to an ambulance.

"A Henckel's eight-inch, Professional 'S' chef's knife," a familiar voice was saying, off to the side, talking to one of the State troopers. "That's Hess's signature, for sure."

She swiveled her head around so she could see with her good eye, the one that wasn't swollen shut. "Frank?"

"At your service, babe," Chief Anderson said, coming over.

"How did you . . . how did you find us?"

"That big guy. Clyde Haywood? He called 911."

Her heart fluttered like a trapped bird, felt like it was up in her throat. "Tugboat? . . . but he's . . . he's …"

"Dead?" said Frank. "No. Almost, though."

The EMTs heaved her into the ambulance and started to shut the doors but she told them to wait.

"Please do me a favor, will you Frank?"

"Sure. Anything for you. You know that."

She asked for his pad and wrote down her daughter's phone number in Hingham. "Call Erin, please. Let her know what happened, that I'm okay, and to meet me at the hospital."

"You got it."

Nikki closed her eyes, took a deep breath and opened them. "And Frank? Please tell her to bring some clothes. Both for me and Adrienne, okay?"

"Right."

The EMTs slammed the doors. Through the back windows, Nikki watched the red and blue flashing lights reflecting off the barn and farmhouse walls as the ambulance whisked her away. She closed her eyes, but a flashback of rose-scented candles, body odor, stale semen and something dead made her nauseous again.

Nonetheless, she felt a tiny smile tugging at the corners of her mouth.

Tug was alive!

CHAPTER 53

OUTSIDE THE HOSPITAL, snowflakes the size of quarters drifted down like inaugural confetti while the EMTs wheeled Nikki into the ER. A doctor and several nurses had met them at the door.

"Forty year old female," reported the EMT. "Temp 98.4, elevated blood pressure 150/88, pulse 100, respirations 20. Multiple lacerations, contusions and abrasions, possible fractured rib, and ankle sprain. No known allergies."

In the examination room, the doctor checked her eyes with a penlight. "No concussion," he said, and felt her head. "Nasty contusions, though."

"Ouch," she said.

He gave her a shot of local anesthetic and once it took effect, he stitched the cut below her eye. "No scar," he said, finishing up. "I promise."

"My nose?"

"Not broken. It'll be sore, but fine. On the other hand, we need to X-ray your ankle and ribs."

They wheeled her away and by the time X-ray released her, Erin had arrived.

"Oh, Mom!" she cried. "Are you okay?" A look of horror crossed her face as she looked at Nikki's angry red nose and the bandage below her eye.

Nikki nodded. "A little beat up, but yeah, I'm okay." They hugged for a long time before Erin stood back. Nikki gestured to her fashionable hospital gown. "I hope you brought me some clothes."

Erin handed her a bag. "These will have to do," she said. "I didn't exactly have time to go to Neiman-Marcus."

Nikki pulled out cotton underwear, baggy fleece pants, wool socks, tennies, and a thick, hooded sweat. With NEW ENGLAND PATRIOTS in raised letters across the front.

"This'll be fine," she said.

"I got Adrienne the same ensemble," said Erin. "She's out in the waiting room."

"How is she? That girl saved my life."

Erin's eyes widened. "Get out! That little bit of a thing? Well, she seems okay. Physically, anyway. The cops were interviewing her."

The doctor came in. "Good news," he said, as he held Nikki's X-rays up to a backlit box on the wall. "Your ankle isn't broken, just a bad sprain. And no broken ribs either, but one is cracked."

"So I can go?"

"Soon as I tape you up. You want pain meds?"

She shook her head. "No thanks. Ibuprofen's good."

Once she'd been taped and ace-wrapped, she grabbed her crutches and hobbled with Erin to join Adrienne, whom Chief Anderson had just finished questioning.

"Ah, Nikki," Frank said, heaving himself to his feet and whipping out his notepad. "I've got a few questions for you, too."

She sighed. "Later, okay? We're beat and need some rest."

He shrugged. "Okay, sure. You might want to know, we searched Hess's hideaway thoroughly but never found that valuable purple pearl brooch of yours. Sorry."

She waved a hand dismissively, saying, "I don't care about that. What I want are the details about how you found us?"

"Simple, babe. Haywood told the 911 dispatcher you'd been taken to Ray Nickerson's old place. Hell, me and ol' Ray used to drink beer out there, back in high school. Knew right where to go."

"Talk about serendipity . . . ."

"Yeah, huh?" He pocketed his pad and started to go, but turned back. "By the way," he said. "Haywood's upstairs."

She dropped her crutches and just about toppled over.

Erin grabbed her. "Mom?"

"Tug's here?" Nikki cried. "In this hospital?"

Frank nodded and walked away.

She thumbed toward the closing door as it hissed shut behind him. "The man has the compassion of a grapefruit; I can't believe he told me that."

"Uh, mom?" asked Erin.

"What."

AFTER AIRING OUT the kitchen, Nikki got on the phone and called a local Asian restaurant. "You open today?" she asked, unconsciously adopting the singsong voice of the restaurant owner.

"I didn't know you spoke fluent Chinese," quipped Tug.

She stuck her tongue out at him, ordered, and hung up. "I'm surprised they're open. I guess maybe more than one Christmas meal got messed up."

After the food arrived, they ate Moo Shi Pork, Pot Stickers and Kung Po chicken until they could hold no more, then joked and laughed until they heard a car horn outside, announcing Adrienne's cab. Everyone shared tearful goodbyes and then watched her go.

"That little girl saved my life," Nikki told David.

"So I heard."

"Courageous little thing," said Tug.

"Nice hair, too," added Dana.

ONCE THE LAST of their guests departed, it was just Tugboat, Nikki, and her fat cat. Nikki plopped down in front of the fireplace. As she petted Sinbad, she looked over at the tree and watched pockets of colorful bubbles chasing each other up the fluted stems of Tug's traditional tree lights. The room exuded an aroma of spruce, burnt cookies, and Kung Po chicken.

Tug had his nose stuck in the newspaper. "I see here where the Narragansett casino is almost done," he said. "Hey, wait a minute . . . wow!"

"What?"

"They put it up near Garden City, using those scary old buildings where the Socanosset School for Boys used to be. Bet I guessed right, somebody in the tribe has Vegas connections. They managed to buy the land from the developers. Those old buildings will be part of the Grand Hotel."

"When are they going to open, does it say?"

"This month."

She shooed Sinbad off her lap, went over to Tug, knelt down, and took the paper out of his hands. "How's the knee?" she asked.

"Did I hear right? That cop, did he just call you babe?"

Nikki took a deep breath. "Yes, the man's a jerk. It's *very* ancient history. Not worth repeating."

"Oh," Erin said. "I see . . . I guess."

Nikki eventually made her way to Intensive Care and a nurse led her to Tug's bed where he slept, sedated to the gills. They had swaddled his thick neck wound in gauze and elevated his wounded leg. It lay outside the sheet, his knee braced and bandaged. Tubes snaked everywhere while an ominous heart monitor beeped. As Nikki looked down on him, her eyes filled with tears.

A nurse tended to his IV. "He's improving," she said. "Luckily, the bullet didn't damage the femoral artery but he'll need some surgery on that knee. We've immobilized it until the orthopedic surgeon can assess the damage and recommend treatment."

"His neck?" Nikki asked.

"Mr. Haywood was very fortunate his carotid artery wasn't severed; the doctor was able to repair it with mesh and skilled suturing. He'll probably be transferred to a regular room tomorrow. Why don't you come back then?"

Nikki went back downstairs where Erin and Adrienne were waiting and the three of them trooped out of the hospital, Nikki hobbling and bringing up the rear. Erin had had the foresight to reserve a motel near the hospital and once they'd checked in, they immediately crashed into bed, sleeping until noon the following day.

During a late breakfast, they answered each other's questions and Nikki explained to Erin how Hess had abducted Adrienne, set the fire, and how he must've followed Nikki to Tugboat's house.

Once the women were caught up on everything, they headed straight back to the hospital. They stopped at information, got Tug's new room number, and rode the elevator.

"I hate hospitals," said Adrienne, eyes following the blinking floor numbers as the elevator ascended. "They all smell bad."

"You don't like the yummy antiseptic odors?" Nikki asked.

Adrienne rolled her eyes. "*No!*"

At the fifth floor, they got off and easily found Tug's room. A nurse saw them hesitating outside his door and approached, shoes squeaking on the glossy floor. "Go ahead," she said. "A visit from three gorgeous women will be excellent therapy." But then she did a double take at Nikki's face. "Okay, maybe *two* gorgeous women and what—a prize fighter?"

They eased their way in to where Tug was propped up in front of enough pillows to supply a department store. An IV dripped, gauze bandaging still swaddled his neck, and his leg remained braced from mid-thigh to ankle, preventing it from bending. But he was awake and looked halfway alert. Nikki gestured for Erin and Adrienne to sit in the two available chairs and then she hobbled over, propped her crutches against the wall, and perched on the edge of his bed.

"Hi, there," she said, adopting a perky voice to camouflage her emotions.

His brow furrowed. "You look like you tangled with a grizzly bear."

"Worse," she said. "I tangled with Hess."

"Yeah, I heard all about it. Our illustrious police chief was already here. Bright and early."

"Mr. Compassion, that's Frank."

"Right. So . . . tell me, what happened?"

She reached out, touched his cheek. "After Hess shot you, I thought you were dead. I mean, there was so much blood . . ."

"I thought I was a goner, too," Tug said. "When he shot me, I knew the artery was hit, so I fell face down and pinched it off with my thumb and forefinger. I figured the only way to survive was to play dead."

"Well, you should get an academy award or something. You fooled both of us."

Tug grinned. "Good thing you left quickly, though. I almost blacked out before I could get to the phone and call for help."

She pointed to his brace. "How's the knee?"

"I'm floating on Demerol so I don't really give a shit."

Everyone laughed.

"Seriously," Nikki said. "How's the knee?"

"Okay, I guess. They tell me it'll be fine but I'll need a couple of surgeries and a long time healing. So . . . what happened out there at the farmhouse? Or would you rather not talk about it."

"No, I don't mind." She told him all about how the monster chained her and Adrienne.

"It was like a living nightmare," piped Adrienne. "For sure."

Nikki looked at her. Blinked. "Wait a minute. You never told us how you got loose from that chain."

Adrienne frowned. "While Hess was out looking for you? I felt all around the dirt floor of the cellar, far as my chain would let me. I found a piece of really sturdy wire, like about six inches long?"

"Ah," Nikki said, thinking about the damage she'd done with that wire.

"The wire was strong but, like, skinny enough to poke into the padlock on the chain," the girl continued. "I didn't have a clue about picking locks, but I had plenty of time to fiddle with it and it finally popped open."

"Why didn't you just run?" asked Erin. "Get the hell out of there?"

Adrienne fluffed her magenta hair. "Two things. One: I was bareass, okay? And two: the bulkhead was locked from the outside."

"Oh."

"Anyway," Adrienne said, "I turned the padlock on my chain back to where it looked like it was still locked? And then I just waited."

"It was beautiful," Nikki said, jumping in. "She jumped up and poked the bastard's eye out."

"The wire. It worked perfectly."

"Then, get this," Nikki added. "This little wildcat grabbed up the Coleman lantern and slammed it into Hess's face."

Tug and Erin looked at Adrienne in admiration. She blushed.

321

"Wow," said Tug. "What'd he do? What happened next?"

"He went totally bug shit. I bolted," said Adrienne, with a shrug.

"She sure did," Nikki said, jumping in. "And that *really* pissed Hess off, too. That, and losing his eye and all."

"And because of that," said Tug, his eyes misting. "He took it out on you."

She nodded. "In spades."

"I knew I'd freeze my skinny buns off fast out there," said Adrienne, jumping back into the conversation. "And I didn't know how far out in the woods I was, so I like doubled back to the barn, saw the motorhome inside. It was unlocked so I climbed in, hoping to find some clothes or a gun or something. When I heard Hess dragging Nikki over, I hid and—"

"Hess forced me into the motorhome," Nikki interjected. She then told Tug all about the candles, pictures, and shrine, omitting, of course, the part about her hair and panties. "I saw Adrienne and when Hess headed for the back, I thought he'd catch her so I decided to create a diversion, wreck the place. My hands were still bound but I managed to do some damage."

"That set Hess off again," said Adrienne. "And Nikki got another beating for it. But in the end, it gave me the chance to get the bastard."

"Get him?" said Tug. "How?"

"I found this gym bag in the bedroom with some stuff in it, including this huge knife. Like one of those kind you see on *Emeril*?"

"She rushed him and stabbed him in the back," Nikki said.

"Yeah, but it didn't kill him," added Adrienne. "He knocked me away and Nikki tangled with him again. Pulled the knife right out of his back and cut his damn throat, the perv son of a bitch. Like, right after that? The cops came."

"I've had a lot of time since to think about the whole deal," Nikki said. "Hess kept saying I would 'become'. I think he wanted to kill me; that way, he thought I'd become his mother and it'd be okay to have sex with me. Otherwise, I was just another example of what he called 'Jezebel Whores'."

Tug nodded. "Just one more of the many temptresses he needed to butcher and then move on."

"Something like that," Nikki said.

"Well," said Tug. "You gals are so courageous and amazing. "It's an honor to be part of your team."

Everyone was silent for a few moments, alone with their thoughts.

Tug broke the silence: "You know, the chief told me the purple pearl wasn't in Hess's motor home."

Nikki waved a dismissive hand. "I don't care."

"Okay, but I was positive Hess had it," interrupted Tug.

"Well, me, too," she admitted. "But I'm sure he told me he didn't get it, didn't have enough time to look."

More silence. Adrienne said, "Maybe he lied. Maybe he, like, hid it somewhere in the farmhouse?"

"Maybe," said Tug.

Nikki pinched the bridge of her nose gingerly, saying, "I don't think so."

"Well, shit. If Hess didn't take it, who did?" asked Tug.

"Who else had the opportunity?" asked Erin.

Tug and Nikki looked at each other.

Tug's eyebrows went up.

"Chief Anderson," they said, together.

CHAPTER 54

NIKKI SHARED HER suspicions with the State Police and they asked her to wear a wire. She figured since the chief wasn't exactly Mensa material, weaseling incriminating evidence out of him ought to be a cinch.

A week later, on an overcast and gloomy December day, she phoned Frank at his office and asked him to meet her at the Benedict's Landing deli, down by the marina on Mystic Island.

They met up just inside the door, waited in a short line for their food and chose a table with a view of the bay. They settled in with their coffee and blueberry muffins and looked out. Waves the color of steel spanked at abandoned docks, a few seagulls hunkered against a bulkhead, and flags snapped in the wind. Lonely moorings bobbed in the whitecaps, longing for their boats.

"You'll never guess what I found out," said Frank, snoffling his muffin and slurping his coffee loudly.

"Enlighten me," Nikki said.

"'Member how Junior croaked in the interview room?" he asked, mouth full, bits of muffin shotgunning out.

"Yes."

Frank chuckled. "Poisoned."

"So I heard."

"Well, guess what? Turns out, the little shit's *lawyer* poisoned his ass."

"His lawyer?"

"Yeah, huh? Sneaked him some vile shit in a roll of breath mints. Wolfsbane, I think the ME called it. Turns out, Hess hired the lawyer and set it all up." Frank scratched under an armpit, stretched and yawned. "Y'know, babe, anybody kin get them poisoned mints off the freakin' internet, you b'lieve that?"

"I believe it."

Frank slurped more coffee, spilled a little on his tie. "Shit," he said, dabbing at it with his thumb. "Anyway, what'd you want to see me about?"

"I *know*," she said simply, getting right to it.

"Know? Know what?"

"That you stole my brooch. The one with that valuable purple pearl."

He swallowed hard, blinked, and averted his eyes.

He's got it, all right. She took the lid off her coffee, sipped at it, then stared him down, saying, "Don't insult my intelligence by denying it."

He said nothing, took another bite of muffin.

"Look," she said, softening her tone and touching his hand. "You busted your hump getting out to that farmhouse to save me from Hess and I really appreciate it."

Frank looked hopeful, yet wary.

"So," she said. "I'm willing to repay the favor. Give the brooch back to me now and I won't press charges."

"I got no freakin' idea what you're talking about."

"You've got to trust me. Otherwise, I'll tell the State Police and let them handle it."

He sneered. "You got no proof, babe."

"Suit yourself," she said, shrugging and standing up. She started for the door.

"Wait a minute," he hissed. "Sit back down."

She stopped, turned, and eased back into her chair.

"You win," he said, still seething.

"Okay. Go get the brooch for me and there'll be no problem."

"It's at home. Stay here and I'll be right back."

Bingo!

He hustled off to his cruiser. Knowing Frank, Nikki figured he was lying and would never make it back, so she simply called the State Police barracks and they collared Frank at home.

Like she'd said, he wasn't exactly Mensa material.

THAT AFTERNOON, Nikki visited Tugboat in his hospital room. The orthopedic surgeon had operated on his knee and delivered a positive prognosis. In fact, Tug was slated for discharge.

"Tell me again about the chief," he said. "And go slow, I want to savor it."

She laughed. "What, you two aren't best buds?"

"Not hardly."

"I suppose you saw right through him," she said.

He snorted. "I saw how he leered at you, is what I saw."

"Well, it was so cool how they caught Frank half-in and half-out, shimmying out a bedroom window in back of his house. And his wife actually fainted."

"With the disgrace of it all."

"Yes."

"But he didn't have the brooch on him?"

"No," she said. "Apparently, he was going for his safe-deposit key. After a court-ordered search of his box, the Staties found the brooch. I got it back, but . . . .."

"But what?"

"I'm wondering if that damned purple pearl really *is* cursed and—"

A soft knock at the door interrupted her. It was followed by a red-haired, jug-eared head poking into the doorway, saying, "Physicians heal, nature makes well."

"Petey!" Nikki cried. "Good to see you."

"Out of the abundance of the heart, the mouth speaks," he replied.

Tug laughed. "C'mon in here, Fottler. I could use a good fortune about now."

Petey apparently thought about that, chewed at his lower lip. "You will conquer obstacles to achieve success," he said happily.

Nikki laughed. "Okay, enough with the fortune cookie talk, how are you?"

"Fine," he said. "I heard 'boat was in the hospital so I thought I'd drop by. I didn't figure on his room being infested with park rangers, though."

That brought another round of laughs.

He dropped a couple of paperbacks on Tug's nightstand. "Here's some reading material, big guy. You gonna be back at the campground next season?"

"I sure hope so," said Tug.

Petey turned to Nikki. "How about you? You coming back?"

"Sure," she said. "I love it there; being a park ranger is fun and . . . interesting. Mostly."

A plump, effervescent nurse materialized in the doorway pushing a wheel chair. She bumped into Petey. "Oh! Pardon me," she said.

"Pardon is the choicest form of flower," quoted Petey.

"Choicest what?" she asked, clearly puzzled. "Are you some kinda nut?"

Petey frowned, saying, "To be wronged is nothing unless one continues to remember it."

The nurse started to retort, stopped, then cocked an eyebrow. "Really," she said. "Y'know, that's kinda heavy."

"Yeah," said Nikki. "It actually makes sense. Profound even."

By that time, Petey had eased out the door and they could hear the fading sound of his big sneakers squeaking down the hall, headed out.

The nurse said, "Cute little fella. What's his story, anyway?"

"Don't ask," Nikki said.

"Right," the nurse said. She waved some papers. "Okay, Mr. Haywood. Get dressed and we'll go over your discharge orders. Then we're going home."

"What's this 'we' stuff?" asked Tug. "You going with me?"

"In a heartbeat," the nurse said. "Problem is, I'm married. Besides, I have to finish my shift."

"Darn the luck," he said, before turning to Nikki. "How about you? Will *you* go with me?"

"In a heartbeat," she said.

EPILOGUE

CHRISTMAS DAY FOUND Nikki and her friends together (complete with animals) at Tugboat's house in Westerly. His operation, although successful, had left him pretty much immobile, delegated to the couch. His leg was encased in a thick cast, propped up. He wore gym shorts, a size XXL Red Sox sweatshirt, and Nikki had laid a blanket over him. As for herself, she'd healed up, for the most part. She was off crutches, breathing normally, and her bruises had faded to the color of Gulden's mustard. No more stitches, either.

Dana and David had driven up from Florida, David taking great pleasure in driving Adrienne's classic Camaro and Dana in a new, snazzy red convertible—a Viper. Erin had come down from Massachusetts, with Brewski, her Rottweiller, and Sinbad, Nikki's huge orange tabby cat in tow. By this time, Brewski was the size of a T-Rex. Cat and dog had become inseparable.

Adrienne had been staying with Tug and Nikki ever since he got out of the hospital. Today, as usual, she wore her trademark basic black—including fingernails, toenails, and lip-gloss. But her hair was no longer magenta; it now resembled something like chartreuse.

Sinbad and Brewski trotted around the house, sniffing out their new surroundings.

Adrienne's cell phone rang. She answered it, put her hand over the receiver and mouthed, "My mom." She took the call into a bedroom. Several minutes later, she returned, smiling as if she'd won the lottery.

"Guess what?" she announced. "Since it's heading for Christmas, I got an urge and called my mom a couple of days ago? Anyway, she actually called back. And she's had, like, some kind of *epiphany* or something? She actually wants me to come to *Paris*, actually live with her, and, like, go to school there."

"Really?" Nikki said. "That's . . . uh . . . wonderful."

Adrienne's eyes were enormous and it looked like she could barely contain herself. "Can you believe it?"

"Well," Nikki said. "Given your mother's past record, it seems too good to be—"

"I know, I know," Adrienne interrupted. "But wouldn't it be a hoot to go to college in Paris? I just gotta take the chance, see if she's, like, for *real*."

"Cautiously optimistic," said Dana.

Nikki's smile was tentative. "Sure. Go for it . . . I guess."

Adrienne beamed. "You think so? Good, 'cause I already called the airport. There's a plane leaving in like four hours."

"What about your Camaro?" asked David.

Adrienne shrugged. "Could you guys take care of it for me?"

"I have a buddy who's in a classic car club," offered Tug. "He'd be only too happy to store it for you."

"Awesome."

"I'll run you to the airport in it," volunteered David.

"Thanks," said Adrienne. "But actually, I called a cab and—"

"Something's burning!" Nikki yelled, interrupting.

The cookies!

She rushed into the kitchen, grabbed a pair of potholders and yanked the charred mess out of the oven. Smoke billowed. The fire alarm started shrieking.

Shit! She opened a window and fanned the alarm with a dishcloth until it stopped. She was just heading back into the living room to deliver the bad news, when she saw Brewski's blocky head rise up on the other side of the kitchen table, then Sinbad's.

Licking their chops.

"No . . . not the *ham!*" she cried, noticing a vacant platter on the table where it *used* to be.

She rushed around the table and beheld the chewed remains of what had been a mouth-watering, smoked Virginian. Brewski and Sinbad looked up at her for the briefest of seconds before going back to devouring the meal of a lifetime. She turned and found her guests all standing in the doorway, laughing.

"Anybody for Chinese?" she asked.

"It's good. How're you feeling? Emotionally, I mean."

"I'm not sure," she admitted. "Of course, I still think about Steve quite often but I think I've finally realized and accepted that I need to move on. I don't know if I'm ready for a serious relationship or not, though. All I know is that right now, I need plenty of closeness and tons of healing."

He nodded. "You've been through the mill."

"We all have." Inching closer, she pulled his blanket back and traced a finger along the upper part of his cast, up by the edge of his gym shorts. "You say your knee is good?"

He raised his eyebrows, pumped them up and down. "Very good. In fact, excellent."

"Speaking of good," she purred. "I've been a really, really good girl because of your, um, *condition.*" She traced some more, slid a nail under his shorts.

"I know," he said, his voice thick.

Her fingers moved further up. "Know why I've been such a good girl?"

He swallowed hard. "So Santa will bring you what you want?"

She stroked, teased. "Yes. And guess what I want?"

He groaned, closed his eyes, and mumbled something unintelligible.

"Um, are you sure this is okay?" she asked.

"I . . . ungh. Oh God yeah."

"No pain?"

"No pain."

She slipped out of her clothes, and as she straddled him, she leaned in close to his ear, whispering: "I have something *very* important to tell you."

"Important?" he gasped. "What is it?"

She started moving and he never did get his answer.

ONE MORNING, a couple of weeks later, NIKKI brought Tug breakfast in bed. It wasn't even noon yet and here she was, quite elegant in her clinging Traveler's Diamond V Sleeveless dress from Chico's, the sexy black one. Sinbad leaped onto the bed, circled a few times, and settled near the foot. Nikki placed the tray on Tug's lap, sat on the mattress next to him, and crossed her legs.

"Wow," he said. "To quote Billy Crystal: 'you rook mahvelous!' What's the occasion?"

"I'm making a point. Like your breakfast?

"Three eggs, bacon, sausage, and leftover Chinese dumplings. What's not to like?"

She leaned in, kissed his cheek. "Nurse Ratchet: ministering to the sick, lame, and lazy."

His eyes cut to the V area of her dress. "Just how far does that 'ministering' go? Do you do massages?"

"Full body."

"Huh. Hey, I got an observation," he said, and popped a piece of bacon into his mouth.

"Shoot."

"You know how you're always going on and on about how fat your thighs and ass are?"

She narrowed her eyes. "Yes?"

He shrugged. "Well, not to worry. Everything looks just *fine* to me, especially in that dress."

"Well, maybe you're blinded by lust."

"Could be. But seriously, now: how much do you weigh?"

She widened her eyes. "You know the rules: *never* ask a woman how old she is or how much she weighs."

"I'm guessing one-twenty, give or take," he said.

"I avoid all scales."

"If you say so. Now . . . will you please tell me why you're all dressed up?"

"Like I said, I'm making a point, a transition if you will. I bought this dress for a special occasion, but after Steve was killed, I stored it away, thinking I'd . . . I'd never be able to wear it again."

Tug looked thoughtful, intense.

She had to break eye contact.

He touched her chin, turned her face gently so she would look at him. "I understand. So why are you wearing it now?"

332

"Because," she said, "I want to move on. I'll always have a place in my heart for Steve and I'll always miss him, but I know it's better to cherish the brief time we had together rather than dwell on his passing. He would want that—want me to get on with my life and be happy. And I'm going to get serious about therapy. I've actually made an appointment."

Tug looked deep into her eyes and nodded.

She dabbed at a tear that had escaped and was rolling down his cheek. "Anyway," she said, "a very significant accessory is missing from this dress. Last night, before we got, um, distracted? Do you remember me saying I had something important to tell you?"

"Vaguely."

"Well, I'm telling you now. I'm no longer a prospective millionaire. So, if you're after me for more than my body . . .."

"You are one mysterious woman, you know that? What the hell are you talking about?"

"That brooch? The one with the purple pearl? I gave it away."

"Excuse me?"

"You heard right," she said. "I gave it back to its rightful owners, the Narragansetts. For their new casino. They assured me it'll be properly showcased in the lobby of the Grand Hotel at Socanosset. And guess what? The hotel is finished and I'm all dressed up to go see it."

Tug groaned. "You *gave* them the purple pearl? Tell me you're joking."

"No joke," she said. "I believe unless it's in the right hands, it'll remain cursed."

"That's bullshit."

She kissed him tenderly on the forehead. "Bullshit? No, it's not. Haven't you heard? . . . It's the stuff of legends."

* * *

Jan Evan Whitford

JAN EVAN WHITFORD originally hails from Albuquerque, NM. After active duty in the Marine Corps Reserve and graduation from the University of New Mexico, he moved to St. Louis, MO where he and his wife raised five sons and he spent 20 years as a cartographer at the Defense Mapping Agency. Retired now, he splits his time between New England and Florida where he writes fiction and pitches it as equal parts mystery, romance and humor. *Mystic Fear* is his second novel, second in the Nikki O'Connor series and sequel to ***Mystic Island.***

Check out his website at: www.janwhitford.com